A strange heroic figure—

KIOGA OF THE WILDERNESS!

A strange heroic land—Nato'wa, wild newfound region beyond the Arctic north of Siberia, warmed by uncharted ocean currents and by great volcanic fissures and hot springs; a land thickly wooded with evergreens, and supporting many and varied wild animals.

Stranger still its human population: a people so like the North American Indians that Kioga's father, who had discovered that land and people, had decided that here was the original birthplace of the Amerind race.

Strangest of all—the story of that medical missionary's son, raised by the natives after the death of his parents, known as Kioga or the Snow Hawk, who rose to manhood to become the war-chieftain of his tribe.

KIOGA OF THE WILDERNESS is the story of Kioga the man. It is a strange and unparalleled adventure in the great tradition of heroic fiction.

KIOGA
of the
Wilderness

William L. Chester

DAW BOOKS, INC.
DONALD A. WOLLHEIM, PUBLISHER

1301 Avenue of the Americas
New York, N. Y. 10019

Copyright, 1936, by The McCall Company, for Blue Book Magazine; copyright renewed, 1964, by The McCall Company and assigned to Irene L. Chester as The Estate of William L. Chester.

All Rights Reserved.

Cover art by John Hamberger.

FIRST PRINTING, SEPTEMBER 1976

1 2 3 4 5 6 7 8 9

PRINTED IN U.S.A.

I

The dawning of that day is unforgettable in my memory. The Arctic breeze was chill, and sharp as the ice-cakes scraping and tearing along the steel sides of the whaler *Bearcat*, bulling her path steadily through the floes off the north Alaskan coast.

Breath poured from my nostrils thick as cigarette smoke, condensing to hoarfrost on the collar of my greatcoat. The southern sky was warmly aglow, crossed by alternating fanlike rays of red and bluish gray, reaching and broadening high into the vault. When the slim rim of the solar disk appeared, it was a brilliant green, blending into blue—the curious optical phenomenon known as the "green flash." Even the sun was strange on that memorable morning.

At my side, elbows on rail and shaggy iron-gray head a little bent, stood Captain Phineas Scott, thoughtful and silent. Since apparently he had not heard my earlier question, I put it to him again.

"Three years is a long time for the *Narwhal* to be missing. Do you think she could have survived, or—"

"Aye—ye asked me that before," he answered to my prompting. "I heard ye, sir. But faith," he continued, pursuing anew a line of thought that evidently fascinated him more than did the missing *Narwhal*, "I was thinkin' more of him ye call Kioga the Snow Hawk. There, bedad, is one who led a strange life if ever man did!" Holding up an immense red paw, he told off on his fingers some of the dates relating to the story I had recounted to him. " 'Bout nineteen-two 'twas, when Lincoln Rand and his wife set sail in the ship *Cherokee*, accompanied by an Injin named Mokuyi. They get wrecked on an unknown inhabited land in the north, which is overrun by red-skinned men like our American Injins. Sometime later they have a little one, which the natives give the name Kioga. When his parents are killed, he's adopted into the tribe, an' grows up to be a high chief among them. So far am I right?"

Scott undeniably has a retentive memory. I nodded, irritated a little by his continued failure to answer my question regarding the missing schooner *Narwhal*.

"Yet," continued Scott, as if unaware of this, "nobody civilized knows anything about Kioga until the yacht *Alberta* sinks in the Arctic. Me an' my ship take on the survivors, abandoning Kioga to save the rest, who rave about new inhabited land in the Arctic until we think them mad. Later on Dr. James Munro, skipper of the science-ship *Narwhal*, picks Kioga up. Dr. Munro takes him to the States, where he lives a while. Then, sick o' civ'lization, Kioga starts back for his native land. That brings us to the late twenties. Then the *Narwhal* goes out to search for Kioga and gets lost. And here are we, now on the *Bearcat*, lookin' for the *Narwhal*!"

Having thus briefly chronicled the events leading up to our presence together on his ship, he sucked noisily at his cold pipe. Then: "Ye've been the whole night tellin' me Kioga's story—me who should have been in my bunk hours ago! But what I want to know is, what happened to Kioga after he left civilization!"

"Find the schooner *Narwhal*," I reminded him, triumphant at being able to pin him down at last, "and you may get an answer."

The brow of Captain Scott clouded.

"I'm a whalin' skipper, sir," he answered. "Not a fortune-teller. But knowin' what I do of the Arctic Ocean, I'd say ye've seen the last any man ever will see of the good ship *Narwhal*," Puffing reflectively at his pipe, he continued: " 'Tis three years and more since she went away, in search of that strange new land you call Nato'wa. That's how ye calc'late, is't not?"

"To the day, almost," I answered, with the accuracy of one who had weighed every factor of time, risk, and possibility in this peculiar case of the Arctic against the schooner *Narwhal*.

"Then give it up, sir," answered the burly skipper, laying a great hand on my shoulder. "I'll not delude ye with false hopes. Ye seek only a ship's ghost. The *Narwhal* herself has gone to Davy Jones's locker long ago, so she has, sir."

I knew what the assertion meant to that honest, foursquare old tar. The whaling industry is not what it once was; profitable chartering by well-to-do Americans in search of lost ships doesn't await a master in every harbor. Yet though by his words he had sacrificed a small fortune, Phineas Scott calmly turned his attention back to the sunrise, blurred not by a bank of mist moving across the waters.

The *Bearcat* steamed silently through a stretch of open sea. A seaman's cough sounded distinctly from eighty feet up in the crow's nest. The air itself grew somewhat warmer as the mists thickened round about the moving ship, and for a little time silence reigned supreme. And then—

With startling suddenness, loud as thunder, the voice of the lookout roared down:

"Schoo-o-ner! Schooner aho-o-y! Two points off the starboard bow!"

Scott jumped as if stung. Together we both wheeled, facing forward. What I then saw I should scarce have believed if recounted to me by another.

Bearing down on us was the hugest ship my gaze had ever fallen on, coming slowly on, like some overpowering colossus, beneath which we must surely go under to destruction.

A stentorian roar at my ear was Scott's voice, raised in command.

"Port your helm!"

Came the helmsman's instant response: "Helm over, sir!"

"Half-speed ahead!"

"Half-speed—aye, sir!"

Came then the muffled clangor of the engine-room bell, and a sensible diminution of the ship's way. Excited shouts and the pound of running feet echoed aboard as the men off watch came awake and rushed on deck.

Only vaguely conscious of these sounds, instinctively I leaped behind the deckhouse, there to brace myself against the shock of collision when that looming vessel should crash into us. And then I heard Scott's reassuring voice.

"All right, sir—all's well."

I turned at the words, not a little astonished by his calm, and moved to where I could again look upon that terrifying image. It was gone as if it had never existed, though the fog still hung thick on the water, tinted by sunrise colors!

"Talk of a phantom, and 'twill surely appear," laughed the skipper. "But 'tisn't often a body comes along with the ghost!"

"You mean to say that what we saw was a phantom?" I demanded, with all the incredulity of the tenderfoot in the North.

"Mist-magic, sir," he assured me in all seriousness. "Though some call it 'looming,' when fog magnifies a ship like that."

"But it *was* a ship?"

"Aye!" And now the captain's voice quivered with excite-

7

ment. "Look across the sea, there, through that scatterin' fog-bank. What d'ye see?"

For a moment I saw nothing but ocean vapors. Most all the hands had gathered forward with an excitement akin to mine, having long watched for just such a meeting. Then from aloft came the lookout's cry, taking the words fairly out of my mouth.

"Schooner aho-oy! Dead ahead! It's the *Narwhal!*"

Vague and dim through the rosy mists that overhung the sea, came a ship—a schooner under shortened sail, making slow headway toward the *Bearcat*. My heart leaped with exultation. It was a long-overdue *Narwhal*, Munro's adventure-ship.

Never do I think again to see a sight so rare and wonderful.

She was a thing of pastel beauty, a fairy creation of snow and frost, the ice-coat on her all afire, her hull agleam like plated gold, her yards and spars all glittering with reddish sunlight, her hanging anchor a silver double-crook, carved with ice-designs in high relief and hung on clearest crystal rope. And in the mirror of the sea the splendor of her image floated.

Yet what about her chilled me deep, made me expect the worst that could befall? This: She seemed the very soul of solitude, lone and inexpressibly forlorn—but why I could not quickly understand.

No less excited than myself, who searched the fog-obscured decks of the *Narwhal* keenly with binoculars, the crew crowded forward, waiting for her to come within hailing distance. The foghorn bellow of Captain Scott rolled across the water:

"Aho-o-y! *Narwhal*! Welcome home!"

Ensued a pause. The thunderous echo of Scott's mighty voice beat back from the *Narwhal's* flank, now little more than half a cable's-length broadside of us. But from the *Narwhal* no sign, no sound, no slightest evidence of having heard our hail. No movement on her icy decks—a silent ship, moving slowly astern on a silent sea.

A steamy *whoooooom*! from the *Bearcat's* whistle brought no more response. I found Scott's narrowed eyes boring into mine beneath his rime-rimmed brows.

"There's your *Narwhal*, sure enough," he said. "But somethin' must be wrong aboard." Then, without awaiting my answer, he gave the order to go about. In answering the helm, the *Bearcat* took the little wind from the *Narwhal's* sail, which slatted noisily as she yawed to port, drifting under our lee. From astern a rope leaped from a seaman's hands, to fall upon the *Narwhal*'s after bitts. A moment later she was bound to our side, fore and aft. Scott turned to me.

"Come along!" he snapped. Down the ladder he went, to tread the *Narwhal*'s icy decks. Close upon his heels came I.

None save Munro, her owner, knew better than I the physical equipment of this modern ship when she left for the Arctic. What changes I saw aboard of her are burned indelibly into my memory. As for Scott:

"Christ save us!" he exclaimed after a quick glance about the gleaming decks. " 'Tis the *Narwhal*, sure enough. But what in God's name did they do to her!"

For the *Narwhal*'s remaining sail was not canvas, but some coarse woven stuff defying description, and punctured with ragged holes torn through as by a blast of grape-shot.

Her foremast was split and scored beneath a rude binding of hand-twisted rope; and imbedded in its base beneath the fracture at the deck-line was a round sphere of pitted rusty iron—an old-style cannonball of medium caliber.

Forward of her deckhouse, mounted upon a wooden block and built to swivel, was a small weapon of cast iron, shaped much like a medieval saker. The strange cannon had been fired, and contained neither shot nor powder, though nearby were several six-pound balls, imbedded in ice, which also coated the gun-carriage.

From one side of the deckhouse, a little aft, protruded a thin piece of reddish metal, a hard-thrown knife-blade whose handle, broken off, lay in the scuppers. Farther astern, on the same side, piercing deep the deckhouse wall, was a scattered group of long arrows, the feathers scarcely ruffled. A spear, bladed with copper, was wedged between the after mast and a rope coil which was also a crude hand-manufacture. Far astern a heavier battery, of the size known as demi-cannon, was mounted in oak, bolted to the deck. The wheel was lashed, the lashings ice-sheathed.

All this I saw as I moved toward where Captain Scott battered at the deckhouse hatch, which presently came open before his heavy exertions. A moment he vanished within, while I struggled across the slippery deck. When I reached the deckhouse, he was emerging, his face noticeably pale. Our eyes met, mine questioning his.

"There's death down there," he answered solemnly. "I'll let ye go in first—they may be your dead, sir. But if ye want me, sing out."

"Better come with me now," I replied, oddly reluctant to go below alone.

God alone knows with what dread I passed through the narrow hatch into that funeral ship, followed by Scott. As my eyes became accustomed to the interior darkness I started, feeling the hairs on my neck rise. A man faced me stiffly, staring unwaveringly. Beneath his hand lay a few sheets of paper, covered with writing, and also a chart of some kind. In the breeze from the open door a lock of hair blew up and fell before the staring eyes. I was grateful for that breeze. Otherwise the thing did not move.

"Dead," muttered Scott softly; and indeed this was a man of ice, frozen stiff with open eyes, perfectly preserved in this natural refrigerator, the ice-clad *Narwhal*.

I knew every man of Munro's crew. This man, however, I had never seen before. Nor had I laid eyes upon him who lay dead with crossed hands upon a bunk nearby. Forward was the forecastle, empty of humanity. Aft was the main cabin through which I passed to Munro's own quarters, via the engineroom. Therein it was darker still. The porthole blinds were drawn.

On the floor two more forms met my gaze. With feelings of utmost relief I ascertained that neither was Munro nor anyone else known to me. Nor were there any other bodies on the death-ship. But I subjected those we had found to the minutest scrutiny and proceeded from surprise to surprise.

When death overtook them, these men had worn apparel not of woven or loomed cloth, but of deerskin, fringed on arm and trousers leg. The boots on the feet were crudely made, and soled with leather twice the thickness of cowhide.

"Starved, or froze to death," guessed Scott; and I all but agreed when I made a startling discovery. In all cases save him who sat erect, external violence had preceded death. The body nearest the door bore an arrow in its breast. The second was twice pierced through the vitals low down, and transversely from arm to arm through the thorax; and both arrows were intact. The man in the bunk—a round clean bullet-hole, blue-circled in the brow, and running through the back of the head, told its grim tale.

Other strange facts aboard the *Narwhal* brought an exclamation of mixed bewilderment and incredulity from Captain Scott.

"Am I daft," he exclaimed fiercely, "or had I one nip too many from the brandy-jug!"

My eyes followed his glance. Beneath the ports in the

owner's quarters was a rack laden with old-fashioned flintlock pistols, no two exactly alike. Just above them hung several old-style muzzle-loading rifles, between which were horns filled with black grains—gunpowder. In one corner hung a small melting-pot, half-filled with cold solid lead—source of the bullets for these antiquated arms. Beneath it was a small oil-stove. In every available place were curved knives, cutlasses, and swords, exactly like none of which one finds among old museum collections. The modern owner's quarters of this modern ship were thus a veritable armory, containing not one up-to-date rifle or pistol in its entire fighting equipment.

Dr. Munro's most valued possession, his photographic equipment, was scattered, and a small motion-picture camera, dented by gunshot, lay on a shelf just under a porthole. To one side was the scientist's workroom. Here was ample evidence of his activities in the new land.

In a great chest I found dozens of bows, arrows, knives, feather headdresses, and works of native art. Two of these were most extraordinary. One was the body of a stuffed bird, resembling a great hawk, its curved beak engraved with beautiful miniature Indian heads. The other was a pair of walrus tusks, attached to a dry skull, similarly carved with effigies and crests. These were labeled in conservative scientific language: *Very unusual. Source unknown.*

Deep in one chest was a masterpiece of feather-robe making, in many harmonizing colors. But most amazing of all, an immense curving ivory tusk, waist-thick in diameter (and measuring, we found later, almost fourteen feet in length), hung crosswise from corner to corner from the ceil-beams. A tag hung from it. It read, again in Munro's hand: *Elph. primigenius. Habitat unknown.*

There were other chests and lockers, all filled with primitive articles which amply evidenced Munro's successful contact with the natives of Nato'wa. And in one I found a piece of brass, lettered *Cherokee*. The scientist had come upon fragments of his friends' lost ship!

Going through Munro's personal closet, I found what I most eagerly sought, his diary, the record of his accomplishment, wrapped in layers of deerskin and tied with a leather thong.

Camera, diary, and chests were removed to a place of greater safety on board the whaler alongside. From under the hand of him who sat erect forward, I removed scribbled notes and chart. All day the crew labored, and nothing was left that might be damaged during the long salvage-tow back to the coast. By now it was nearly dark, and bitterly cold, the short day waning. We worked by lantern-light. The men were hoisting the last chest from the *Narwhal* to the *Bearcat* when I returned to the cabin for my own lantern and to arrange suitable burial for the *Narwhal*'s unknown dead.

As I opened the door, there was a muffled explosion. The ship was afire, already blazing fiercely.

My lantern—gunpowder in the horns, and perhaps on the floor! I had little time to reproach myself for my carelessness, for on the whaler there was wild activity. The after line, cut with a hatchet, slipped into the sea, and the *Narwhal*'s stern drifted free. Scott was bawling down at me from the rail.

"Grab the ladder and we'll haul ye aboard! Jump, man! She has gunpowder forward!"

A last look back, and I knew it was too late to stop the blaze. I leaped, seized the rope ladder, and was hauled up. The *Bearcat* drew away out of the danger zone. The schooner behind was afire from stem to stern, blazing and crackling, the ice upon her melting fast. ... A moment later the deck-house seemed to rise in midair. As the sound of the explosion reached us, the entire ship erupted like a volcano. There was another silence; then the terrific detonation of gunpowder. Ten seconds later the *Narwhal* started for the bottom, quenching her death-agony in the Arctic Sea.

A shot from the bow rang out sharply—salute to the dead from the *Bearcat*'s whaling harpoon-gun.

Above the swirling waters a column of smoke lingered. Prosaic Captain Scott was not without an imaginative spark. It was he who said:

"There sinks a mystery-ship, boys, God rest her! With one sail set, and all hands dead aboard, she had a strange tale to tell, whatever 'twas. And look ye now!"—to me, at the rail beside him. "D'ye not see a gi'nt question mark over her grave?"

I nodded agreement, for though the smoke-formation had little resemblance to a "question mark," I knew what Scott meant. Here was another riddle, of which the sea propounds so many.

But it was a riddle to which I had the key. Alone in my cabin, to refresh my memory, I reread an unfinished paper, written by my friend Dr. James Munro, famous polar scientist and authority on the American Indian, before he sailed away. It ran, in part, as follows:

THE AMERICAN INDIAN
AND HIS ORIGIN

At the beginning of this century my colleague, Dr. Lincoln Rand of California, his wife Helena, and his intimate friend and aide, the full-blooded Indian Mokuyi, sailed from San Francisco in the hospital-ship *Cherokee*. They intended to bestow free medicine and treatment upon certain primitive Indians of the Pacific Coast. Fate, however, decreed otherwise.

There came to be written in the *Cherokee*'s log two of the most remarkable discoveries of modern times. One was a hitherto unknown land called Nato'wa—somewhere north of Siberia—upon which storms hurled the *Cherokee*. The other was a race inhabiting it, unmistakably cousins of the American Indian.

Twenty years after the discovery, the outer world still knew nothing of this land and its peoples, for the *Cherokee* never brought her passengers home. Seeking vainly for traces of my missing friends, one of whom was particularly dear to me, I finally conceded their deaths.

Then came a tragedy which gripped the world—the sinking of the missing American yacht *Alberta* in the Arctic, and the dramatic rescue of her survivors by the whaler *Bearcat*. Two deserting sailors had to be abandoned, however—as was a third man. This third man, according to the radio broadcast of names by the *Bearcat*, was Lincoln Rand!

Hastening to the scene in my schooner *Narwhal*, I located and took aboard this Lincoln Rand—not the friend I had long sought, but his surviving son! This young man, born and raised in the new wilderness of Nato'wa, bore the Indian name Kioga, meaning the *Snow Hawk*. He had preserved the *Cherokee*'s logbook and kept a curious record of his own life in pictograph, hieroglyph, and mnemonic signs—all drawn upon a buffalo-hide.

From the logbook and the buffalo-skin, and from photographs which sustained these records, came a strange and amazing biography, which it is my intention to publish in the near future.

I submit these statements by way of introducing this new evidence to disprove two accepted scientific theories. In my opinion the Indian is not of Asiatic descent. The Arctic was his original home, whence he moved southward in antiquity, over both North America and Asia, to inhabit both continents. In the light of these new records, the Arctic, long believed landless or almost so, contains the land of Nato'wa, warmed to a habitable climate by volcanic outlets or some uncharted warm ocean current, and the ancient home-land of the Indian. There the Red Man still dwells as hunter and warrior like those the first white men found in America. . . .

Proof of Lincoln Rand's discoveries will be adduced in the person of his son Kioga who is now in New York, and willing to tell what he knows. This man is literally the link which connects modern science with this remarkable discovery. . . .

Here the paper ends, obviously unfinished. The reason, as I later learned, was that Kioga, the human link to which Munro referred, had dropped suddenly from view. But as you shall learn, James Munro was not one who could leave such matters long under the shadow of uncertainty. After an unsuccessful search for his young friend, he moved swiftly, refitting his *Narwhal*. Fired by the *Cherokee*'s epic record of discovery, forth then went the scientist in his modern *Narwhal*, eager to verify the existence of the new wilderness and its copper-skinned peoples, explore it, and if possible find his friend Kioga the Snow Hawk. . . .

Now, like Captain Scott, I too pondered on many things. What amazing facts lay behind the manifold physical changes in the *Narwhal*? Why had she been fitted and armed as if for siege, transformed into a ship of a century ago? What dangerous run had Munro contemplated in so equipping her? What perilous gauntlet *had* she run, to be thus bristling with the discharged bolts of the enemy? Where were Munro and those who sailed with him?

Above all, the Snow Hawk, whose story this is—what befell him from the hour when he left civilization behind and turned back to Nato'wa, savage land of his birth?

These thoughts plagued me during our return to the States, where I sent the films found aboard the *Narwhal* to an expert in developing.

Safely back in the private museum which bears Munro's name, I carefully unwrapped the scientist's diary. Soon came answers, not regularly but completely nonetheless. I established a certain continuity of events from the time Kioga, known as the Snow Hawk, wrote farewell to his friend James Munro, and vanished in the very midst of civilization. And this is what I read or deduced from these records found aboard the schooner *Narwhal*.

II

Once in an aeon you see such a man as Kioga, the product of generations of fine heredity, a man slowly developed by time. Two inches over six feet he stood, bearing a magnificent spread of shoulders with stately ease. He walked as tigers walk, with an easy loose-muscled swing, treading light as the well-trained athlete.

Such was the quiet personage who walked along an unpaved street, on which hungry dogs skulked between rows of squalid and dreary shacks. To one hut, more pretentious than the others, clung a crude porch, hung with mattress and unwashed bedding. A black-haired little girl-child, thin and scrawny, played with an old rag doll, and coughed harshly.

Down the street came an obese middle-aged woman, kerchief about head and many folds of colored cloth forming a voluminous dress. She bore muddy water in an unsanitary tin pail. Her skin was dark—indeed almost black. She disappeared inside a cabin.

Along the road hobbled an old man. He wore ragged overalls, shoes almost without soles, no hat. His hair hung about his neck. He walked stooped over and with effort. His face, too, was almost black.

Slouching on a corner, a sullen-faced youth of about sixteen proffered to the visitor a basket containing trinkets, of which he bought a few. The hands which delivered the purchase were covered with sores—impetigo.

Enough, you will say. Why recall sordid ugly pictures of poverty-stricken China, India, or whatever this is!

But this scene was none of these. The stranger walked in an American village—an American Indian settlement, gift of the generous white man to his red brother. Each day, for many days, Kioga had walked among these surviving red men. Each day he had witnessed this tragedy of a great race in slow decay. He had seen Indian children—child peons, shipped in gangs, toiling in the beet-fields beneath a blazing sun on hands and knees for sixty days—to earn fifteen cents a day. Some were tubercular, coughing as they grubbed in the earth—innocent victims of what Abraham Lincoln called an accursed system.

The aged woman who had entered the hut was cooking something at the stove when there came a knock at the door. A shadow fell athwart the earthen floor. The tall stranger stood in the doorway.

He spoke to her without sound, in sign-talk, that means of communication invented by the First Americans and understood almost universally by Indians, whose local languages differ.

"I am hungry, Mother."

The old woman muttered in her own tongue, and answered, in sign-talk: "I have only horse-meat. That is why my skin is black. Good 'nough for red man; not good for white man."

"I will eat horse-meat, Mother," answered the tall visitor.

"Then be welcome," came the gestured answer, with the instant hospitality of her Indian race. In silence the unbidden guest ate of the unpalatable meat, set before him on the earthen floor on a tawdry cracked plate. Of that muddy water he drank.

Finished, he did not at once rise, but looked down upon his wrinkled, stoic hostess, weaving a vision about her grizzled old head.

In the vision she was garbed in clean new buckskin skirt, beautified with dyed porcupine quills. Upon her gnarled feet were fresh-made moccasins of deerskin, worked in geometrical designs. About her head there was a buckskin band, and from her neck a string of elks' teeth depended. She sat within a translucent skin tepee, one of a hundred clean skin lodges nestling against the breast of the verdant plain. Nourishing buffalo meat roasted before the fire and hung in plenty on the racks outside, curing in the sun. From the distance came the cries of the hunters, pursuing on swift ponies the wild buffalo. . . .

The child across the street coughed. The visitor rose, his vision broken.

In the sign-language he gave his thanks, and as quietly as he had come, departed.

That night to the old woman's cheerless lodge came a great

gift: a freshly slaughtered steer. When she had called in her neighbors, and shared with them in the Indian manner, they asked:

"Where did you get all this fine meat?"

"A white man came. He was tall, strong, made like a warrior! He tasted the meat we eat. He must have sent the steer. May he see many winters!"

Everyone clapped hand to mouth in wonder. A miracle had happened: a white man had given something to an Indian! But the generous stranger was seen no more, though they talk of him to this day.

Hot midafternoon of a day in roundup time found the visitor in a western American grain-center. The streets were filled with cowboys, ranchmen, and Indians. The steely ring of horses' hooves mingled with the noise of automobile horns and the distant lowing of steers. Smells of wood-smoke hung on the air along with gasoline fumes. Down near the roundup ground there was a touch of olden times—clustering scores of Indian tepees, among which Indian women and children moved, dressed in gala attire for the gala event. All day there had been hard riding of fierce mustangs, the bulldogging of active sharp-horned steers; horse races, parades, and pageantry.

But that was over, and the excitement had died down somewhat. Fires sprang up, preparatory to the sunset meal, and magnified black shadows moved upon the inner tepee walls. Somewhere a drum beat softly and was silent. An old chief sang half-forgotten snatches of a war-song. Horses whinnied nearby and stamped the ground.

But most of the old Indians did not sing. They thought of the old days before the white man came, when buffalo fell to their swift arrows. They recalled swift dashes on bare horseback, with the wind talking in their ears—days when there was no check to the proud-spirited brave, when there was no reservation and all were free to roam, hunt, do battle. There was much discussion of a Texas-raised horse, Firebrand, an unbroken bucker whom no man had ridden; and of Maniac, the steer whose curving hooks had done murder this day, and who now dodged about the arena, pursued by two yelling daredevil cowhands. At the rail a group of Indians laughed as they played a gambling game.

Amid boisterous laughter the two mounted range-men headed the steer between them, when of a sudden, pivoting on all fours, the enraged animal wheeled, charged for the rail, and leaped catlike. An instant it hung in midair. A cry went up.

"Gangway! Hi! Hi! Maniac's loose!"

Destruction personified fell among the Indian gamblers. A single swing of that horn-armed head, and a bleeding brave hurtled full twenty feet, while another, gashed and torn, quivered beneath the pounding hooves.

A moment's pause, with lashing tail, before the goaded steer swung its head, wicked red-shot eyes fixing upon a gaudy dash of color in its path. An Indian mother, wrapped in a blue and red blanket, stood there paralyzed with fear. A child, strapped to her back in a cradle-board, slept in blissful oblivion. All too quickly the snorting animal pounded toward the screaming woman.

Gripped first by the instinct to escape, the bystanders had leaped away in every direction. Now, stirred by the promptings of chivalry, they turned to offer aid. But their efforts had come late. A scant twenty paces separated the bellowing steer and the innocents in its path, when as from nowhere, came a lightning interference.

One there was among the milling crowd to whom instant reaction had ever been the price of his survival: this dark-haired stranger bounded at an angle across Maniac's mad charge. There was a moment's hush, in which the clatter of the steer's split hooves rose clear and distinct. In that instant men's hearts stood still, as the witnesses thought to see the stranger hooked and tossed, a bloody corpse, into air.

But straight at the sweating shoulders he leaped, clinging as the panther clings to the deer. One iron hand, passing beneath the drooling jaw, sought the killer's outer horn, gripped it and wrenched the head savagely round, bringing the animal crashing to its side in a cloud of dust, scarce five feet from the frightened squaw and child.

Twice did Maniac struggle, half rising. Each time its attacker threw the great animal flat, as if it were a yearling calf, holding it down until the ropes of the cowhands, straining on head and hoof, held the steer at full stretch. Only then did the stranger rise, dust himself off, and move back toward the obscurity whence he sprang.

But he who had laid low a thousand pounds of horn and bone was no match for the excited admiring throng which now surrounded him, shouting, cheering in their enthusiasm. Of these none were more vociferous than the Indians, who love a brave feat above all things, and him in particular whose daughter and grandson had been endangered by

Maniac. Old Big Shield thumped him on the back and shook his hand.

And Kioga the Snow Hawk, thinking of a day when twenty prime buffalo bulls had fallen beneath his sharp steel, could not but smile inwardly.

That night, at a place of honor in Big Shield's tent, the tall stranger sat. Though bronzed, this man was unmistakably a white; yet in some indefinable way he resembled these Indians. Mayhap this was due to the apparent fierceness of expression, relieved only by the finely chiseled lips, which now seemed somewhat softened.

Big Shield, resplendent in a buckskin shirt studded with elks' teeth, introduced the stranger thus:

"One there is among us tonight who is called the Snow Hawk—Kioga, in the language of his own people. He will speak to you with the hands. Open your eyes. Watch his words, for his tongue is not ours, although he speaks the English which some of you know not."

And in the language of the hands Kioga began to speak in the graceful deliberate sign-talk, as "spoken" by a master. He gestured without haste. This is what he said:

"Oh my brothers! You ask me whence I come, and many other questions. Thus I answer: I have come a long way from my own land, which lies many marches in the north. We call it Nato'wa. We think it is the first land of the red man. For there he lives as of old. No law exists save that made by the red man, for the red man. Men never say: 'Do not kill the buffalo. Do not kill the deer.' There is meat enough for all."

Some there were, at the beginning, who smiled incredulously. But there were others who grew tense as Kioga continued, and in whose eyes appeared the glitter of hope and excitement. And before an hour was past, incredulity was forgotten in a deep fascination. For several hours the Snow Hawk spoke, almost without interruption; and in the telling he mentioned the name Mokuyi, of beloved memory.

Among those present was an old chief, Bull Calf by name, dignified as a Roman senator in his simple attire of plain war shirt and a feather hanging under one ear. Of them all Bull Calf was most stirred beneath his outer cloak of calm. His dark old eyes, still keen, searched the face of Kioga long and intently. He spoke with his hands.

"Him you speak of—Mokuyi," he said slowly. "Was he not learned in the white man's path? Did he not have many tongues to speak many Indian dialects? Did he not have a long scar—thus?" drawing a forefinger from shoulder to breast.

"Even so," answered Kioga, wondering at the old man's description. "It was Mokuyi who taught me to read and speak white man's language."

"Was he not as tall as I, with a small birthmark on left cheekbone?" pursued the agitated old man.

"Wait," said Kioga, drawing from his pocket an envelope. It contained some of the photographs which had been developed from old negatives exposed in Nato'wa twenty-odd years earlier. He selected one, a portrait of a family group, consisting of a broad-shouldered man and a beautiful young woman—his father and mother. Beside them, in civilized dress, stood Mokuyi as he had been then. Kioga handed the photograph over. Bull Calf studied it a moment.

Electrified, he leaped to his feet, waving the picture in air, all his Indian's stoicism falling away as he addressed the others.

"*Ai-yah*! Kioga speaks with honest hands! This is Mokuyi, my son. Stands beside him one we called Linnikun. *Ai-i*, I remember well." The chief's eyes held a faraway look. "They were like brothers, those two, always together. When Linnikun went away with his woman, Mokuyi said: 'Father, my friend goes away. Where he goes, I go.'" Bull Calf's trembling hand fell upon Kioga's arm. "You son Linnikun?" he asked in broken English.

"I am his son," answered Snow Hawk.

Bull Calf's next question came as with great effort, scarce audible in the crowded tepee.

"Where is Mokuyi?"

The old man stiffened, relaxed, sat suddenly down, staring

"Mokuyi hunts with his ancestors," said Kioga quietly.

long into the fire. No one spoke. At last he turned to Kioga, his cheeks wet.

"Tell me what happened to my son."

While his audience watched, in silence unbroken, Kioga began at the beginning, sketching briefly the history of the *Cherokee*'s landing in Nato'wa, and telling them substantially what his father had recorded in the ship's logbook:

Almost immediately on landing they were attacked and captured by a band of savages and taken to a village called Hopeka. This, to their amazement, was thronged with redskinned men whom, later, Rand came to believe were cousins of the American Indian.

Their land was called Nato'wa, or Sun's Land, a place of

dark enchantment whose savage grandeur had not been gazed on by the eye of modern civilized man until Rand came. But with pencil and camera he corrected that, leaving behind him a record surpassing anything ever recorded by the first explorers of the New World.

Nato'wa is not another Greenland of today, bleak and cold, but an Arctic oasis, a northern Yosemite—such as Greenland doubtless was in distant aeons, before cold and glaciation made it all but sterile. The mountains of Nato'wa are robed in primeval forests and turbaned with everlasting snow. The land's stark geographic features have kept it a place apart all down the centuries. It is girt by fogs and eternal ice, hemmed in almost completely by impassable seacombed reefs; warmed volcanically and by unknown mild ocean currents. No map pictures it. Its history had never been written, excepting what little appears in Rand's notes. ...

In a night raid by enemy tribesmen Rand and his wife were slain. But Mokuyi escaped to carry on the logbook record and adopt their little white son as his own. And in Mokuyi's handwriting it is told how Mokuyi himself had risen among his captors, the Shoni tribe, to high place.

Alone Mokuyi had sought to put down treachery by the Long Knife secret society. In dead of night the shaman Yellow Weasel, acting in behalf of all the society, murdered Mokuyi and his native wife Awena, and deliberately implicated the child Kioga in the deed. Two days later with his own knife Kioga slew the shaman beneath the yellow waters of the river, in the presence of twenty of the shaman's braves.

Thereafter Kioga was exiled, hunted down by the medicine man's henchmen like a wounded beast, until beast he became, turning, rending, and tearing his foes whenever he came upon them—and that was often. In the end he kept his vow of vengeance, sworn beside the smoking bier of his loved ones. Man by man he killed many of Yellow Weasel's secret society, until the name and fame of Kioga the Snow Hawk spread far and wide among the Shoni.

This Kioga told the attentive Indians about the lodge-fire. And he told how the fame of his outlaw years had grown, how he broke the power of the Long Knives single-handed, how his prestige thus grew, resulting in nomination to the war-chieftainship, which honor he accepted, leading his tribes to victory against their hereditary foes, the ever-raiding plains Wa-Kanek.

And having told these things exactly as they happened,

without false modesty, he was about to conclude, when there was an unexpected interruption. The Snow Hawk had just completed a particularly exciting account of an Indian raid, with its attendant trophy-taking. Suddenly one of the younger braves let out a cry of surprise.

A thin little boy of ten, overcome by excitement, had absentmindedly seized the man by the hair, as if to take his scalp. Much confused by his sudden entry into the limelight, he now sat crestfallen and embarrassed amid the laughter of his elders, then sought to escape the public eye by hiding behind his laughing victim, before dashing from the tent in confusion.

"Who was he?" asked Kioga of Bull Calf.

"Tokala the Fox," answered the old chief. "Nephew of Smiling Woman. He is sick. He will not live long. We never punish him."

Interrupted by this event, the meeting came to an end, postponed until the morrow. When Kioga would have bidden the Indians farewell, it was Bull Calf who insisted that he remain the night. After some hesitation he consented.

And so it was that while James Munro searched for Kioga in the great seaboard city of New York, Kioga slept in the tepee of Bull Calf, far to the westward.

But the words of the Snow Hawk had penetrated deep into the minds of his hearers. News of his talk spread among the lodges. And next day, to the lodge of Bull Calf came several visitors for Kioga. First was Two Coups, whom the Snow Hawk made welcome with the deference due to great age. His woman Sits-in-Sun was with him. The pipe was lit and passed around. Then Two Coups addressed Kioga.

"I have watched the hands of Kioga," said the old man. "Eighty summers have grayed my head. It is long since those days. But I have not forgotten the buffalo. With these hands I killed many when I was young. I will go back to Nato'wa with you, to kill another bull before I am wrapped in my blanket."

Startled, Kioga gave no sign. Refusal was on his lips, but the sight of that ancient face seamed with countless wrinkles and marked with a strange deep longing struck him with pity. He laid down the pipe.

"It is good. Together we will go."

Sits-in-Sun, who had sat beside Two Coups in silence, came back from some far place of memory.

"Ai-i-ha!" she cackled suddenly, turning to Two Coups. "I remember when you killed the Crow brave who was stealing your horses. A white man's village sits on that place now. Those were good days." Her eyes, black as shoe-buttons and all but lost in wrinkles, snapped as she turned to Kioga. "I have not forgotten how to tan a skin. My fingers have remained cunning with the needle. I can make moccasins—see this pair I have brought you, my son. No white man's beads, no white man's thread, but quills of the porcupine, thread of sinew, the skin of a deer. I will go along also, and bring my needle."

Expressionless was the face of Kioga, as his downcast eyes examined the old woman's gift, poor pitiful produce of hands that never more would possess aught of their youthful skill. Silently the old crone waited on his answer. Finally:

"My heart stretches," said the Snow Hawk softly. "There will be a place for Sits-in-Sun."

"Eh," exclaimed the old woman delightedly. "Then I shall see my man strike the enemy yet once more before I cross the slippery log."

As the hours passed, many other visitors came to talk with Kioga. First a delegation of several young men, in company with their elders. Of these, Kills-Bear, of warrior's age, spoke in good English.

"I went to white man's schools and college. I studied law. But I cannot practice—because my skin is red, the clients do not come. Therefore I am a laborer. I dig ditches, swing a pick. Dollar a day. I too wish to go to Nato'wa."

Eats-Running, of middle years, rose.

"My race dies of white man's disease. I do not wish to die thus. I would go with Kioga."

Bets-His-Shirt, an old man, then spoke laconically:

"Buffalo gone. Hunting-ground gone. Children all dead, only I am left of a family of eleven. What the hell! I will go."

A woman, White Calf, spoke softly:

"My children—three of them—sickened in the white man's school far away, and came home to die. I will cook and bear heavy burdens. Let me go."

Many more spoke, one by one.

"We are sick of eating horse-meat. Better to die than live like dogs forever. We will go.... We were rich. Oil on our reservation. White men cheated. Pigs are better fed than we. Let us come.... I cannot live long, anyway. My time is almost up. I would go."

And of all who came, wishing to make the journey, none was refused save one. A boy of ten, thin and stoop-shouldered, sidled up to the Snow Hawk. It was he of the volatile spirit, who had disrupted the meeting of the night before. He spoke in a whisper.

"I wish to go to Nato'wa, please," quoth Tokala. "I wish to rise high in Shoni councils. I hate school. I hate the whites. They were cruel to my people. They make us wound Earth Mother with the plows. They made me cut my long hair." Supplication filled the child's trembling voice. "Please—please let me go too."

"Little warrior," said the Snow Hawk gently, placing a hand upon the slim shoulders of Tokala, "it may not be. The journey will be long and far. The Great White Father would not approve." There was finality in the words, at which the boy wilted perceptibly. Kioga knew a pang of sympathy. To soften the refusal, he slipped something into Tokala's hand. It was a small knife, in a leather sheath. At another time the boy's eyes would have glistened. But though he clasped the gift tightly as he left the lodge, there was misery in his heart, and in his thoughts. He bit his fist till the blood came. Great tears hung in his dark eyes and splashed on his hand. But Tokala did not give way: he was an Indian.

Back in the lodge, before the councilors, Smiling Woman pleaded for Tokala.

"You saw him. You saw how his ribs stick out. He was the white man's cough. The doctors say he will die. Let him come with us!"

"He is but a child," answered one of the chief's inflexibly. "The march would surely kill him."

Smiling Woman turned to Kioga. The Snow Hawk said nothing. Little had he thought, two days since, to be burdened on his return with a band of Indians, some of them old and almost feeble. He had consented to their company out of a desire to lighten their hardships. But it would be no journey for a child. His silence confirmed the chiefs. Smiling Woman went away, saying no more.

So it came about that strange activity animated the neighborhood which was once the hunting-ground of these Indians. One by one articles for the trip were assembled. The tent-poles were taken down, the canvas folded. *Parfleche* bags and leather boxes long unused made their appearance, filled with personal possessions long treasured.

There were painted shields, bows, arrows and quivers, brittle with age. Old spears tipped with flint or iron came forth along with war-hammers and tomahawks, rusty and broken. Conspicuous among the other items were trusted objects of veneration, valued for their potency as "strong medicine." Many of the old chiefs had these, and even Smiling Woman had a large square box, of which she said:

"It belonged to my brother. It was very *wakan* to him. I promised never to leave it behind. It is heavy, but it is sacred."

Such objects were very carefully handled, and their contents considered inviolate, for every Indian respects the "medicine" bundle of his fellows.

Some few there were who produced old rifles, even heavy buffalo-guns, rusted and pitted, relics of another day, when the Indian power was being broken by the advance of white civilization.

One old chief fell ill, and lay dying in his lodge. But he sent a benediction and the welcome gift of a dozen horses, with all their Indian equipment. Not many hours later, well-mounted and eager to be away, a strange cavalcade melted into the gloom of a starless night, and passed into the hills on the first stage of a long journey.

Thus the silent cavalcade began its long northward trek, as from time beyond recall, oppressed peoples have emigrated in search of better worlds in which to dwell. The Jew returned to Palestine; the Negro went back to his native Africa; the Pilgrim fled oppression and sought freedom in the New World of America—and then oppressed the people he found there.

Greater movements have begun on this earth than the Snow Hawk's little caravan, but none went forth more inspired. With eyes facing toward mysterious Nato'wa, these Indians sought their particular promised land—land of that liberty denied them by white civilization.

All changed now was Kioga's original plan to embark on a ship bound for Alaska, whence he had had vague ideas of proceeding farther north by crossing ice and sea by whatever means seemed likeliest to bring him home to Nato'wa.

For such an itinerary he had ample money on his person. But he had not enough to pay the passage of his entire present band. Even possessing enough, he could not have equipped a ship for Arctic sailing in a week. Moreover, in ships he had no great confidence. He recalled what the ice had done to the yacht *Alberta* and others of which he had read—many of them sunken wrecks today, though designed to survive in the Arctic.

These obstacles were now temporarily overcome by their use of the gift horses to bear them on the first part of their journey. But his thoughts turned again and again to the future. A ship was not required—as yet. Better go over the polar ice than attempt to break through it. But arrived at the warm currents which give Nato'wa its maritime climate, they would need some kind of craft in which to navigate open water and later the dread reefs surrounding that little known land. Of what materials could this craft be made? This was a major and vital concern.

He thought of the driftwood whereof the Eskimo fashions frames for his skin boats; of whalebone, which can be used in case of need for ribbing and thwarts. He thought, too, of all those water-logged hulks, which float about a certain ship's graveyard in the unknown north, near Nato'wa. Of them all, assuredly some materials could be found of which to create, on the spot, the craft they would need. So he worried no more about materials, but applied himself to design, sketching out mentally the plans for his proposed craft, and calculating how in the past he had constructed his many own canoes.

III

Thus for several days the band maintained a steady northward pace, resting frequently on the hilly plain and throwing up a circle of tents by night, then away again before the dawn.

With the railheads of civilization in the south, sunrise of a day that dawned red and sharp with early morning chill, found a strange metamorphosis worked upon the mounted party—a change which rolled back the scroll of time two hundred years, to a day when the wild red men roved the grassy plains, and like the prairie wolves, roamed in the wake of the long-vanished buffalo herds.

Gone were the rude castoffs, the white man's clothing. In its place had returned the picturesque raiment of the Indian. As the sun rose higher, the scouts rode naked to the waist. The ancient rifles had been brought forth, and were carried athwart the saddles, which rested upon woolen fringe-hung blankets striped with designs in red, black, and orange. The white man's pack and diamond hitch were abandoned. In their place the Indian travois returned—two poles fastened at the horses' shoulders and dragged around behind, with a woven net across, in which were carried *parfleche* bags, boxes, and tents. Upon the travois-horses rode the women in old buckskin garb brought along for the purpose, fringed and embroidered with beadwork. At their belts were their thin skinning-knives. Many bore proudly atop their saddle-horns the shields of their lords, who rode nearby—some wearing warshirts ablaze across the back with stained quillwork, and carrying *coup*-sticks adorned with feathers tipped with weaseltails.

Thus, like their ancestors of the dead centuries, a band of Indians moved northward, armed as for battle—such a band as must have sworn allegiance to Sitting Bull in the sunset of his power. The old men chanted war-songs and cavorted like youths on their eager mounts; and the young men listened, expanding to a new life; and the women chattered continually. For this was a proud and happy day!

Well on their journey's way, the caravan paused one night in a sheltered hollow far beyond the last large outposts of civilization—so far, indeed, that forage for the horses had become a serious concern. Over the fires this night the band was deciding upon its future itinerary.

Of a sudden Smiling Woman came running into camp, pale and frightened. Before she could give voice to her fears, one of the horseherds came galloping behind, leading two animals. He hung low over the neck of his horse, and slipped fainting from its back, ghastly and bloodless of face. Kioga was at his side in an instant, to catch him before he fell to the ground.

"Black Kettle! You bleed!" ejaculated Two Coups suddenly.

"Yes!" answered the injured man heavily. "We sought pasture for the horses. Two Tongue knocked me from my horse, and did this thing!"—indicating an ugly bleeding gash in the neck. "He has turned back, stolen the other other horses—all of them but these. Four Bear lies also dead, tomahawked from behind." The wounded man coughed thickly. "Ah-i-i, I think I am going away. Bury me where the sun will strike my face. I shall never see Nato'wa."

While the others ranged about, Kioga dropped to one knee, supporting Black Kettle's head on his forearm.

"You shall not die, warrior—" he began—to be interrupted by the faint voice of the Indian.

"Our ancestors killed horses—over dead man's grave. Do not do this—when I die. Take my good roan. Treat him well. You will need good horses. I—"

"Yes, brother?" prompted Kioga gently. Then he stopped, felt of the man's breast, gently lowered the head. He had seen death too often not to know it now.

Wild with fury at the horse thief, Bull Calf shook his fist in air. "We will follow on our three horses. We will overtake him and cut his throat. We—"

Kioga raised an admonishing hand.

"Hear me, elder brother: Let him go. It is not far east where the north-running rivers lie. We will march there in two days. We will take the boat. We could go little farther on horse anyway."

The old chief still smoldered, but soft words had put out the blaze. Bull Calf and the others brought in Four Bear's body, and prepared both their dead for burial. . . .

The sun rose on a camp that mourned.

Yellow Bird and She-Runs-Fast, wives of the dead men, painted their faces black with fat and charcoal, and cut their long hair. On their blankets the Indians laid the dead. Upon their faces they painted the marks of tribe and clan, that the spirits, soon to depart, would be recognized by the souls that awaited them in the Hereafter.

Then they sang unto their dead in eulogy, and bade them farewell. On a high scaffold built of drag-poles which the thief had left behind, they laid the bodies beside their weapons.

Two days later, Captain Mitchell skipper of the river-streamer *Athabaska*, rubbed his eyes at a picturesque sight confronting him on one bank, where a band of Indians waited, as if fresh from the past of a century ago.

If Captain Mitchell hesitated to accommodate the motley band, in Kioga the Indian migrants had an able spokesman. Persuaded by this tall fine-looking leader who spoke perfect cultured English, Mitchell weakened. And he gave way entirely when Snow Hawk offered to pay for the passage of all with American funds. With all aboard, the *Athabaska* steamed on.

Canoes, lumber, and sledges lay piled on the steamer's deck. Chained to the boards were numerous husky dogs, mingling their howls with the lowing of a few northbound cattle. From aft came the whinny of a hand of woodcutters' horses. A strangely mixed company of Indian half-breeds, miners, trappers, and fur traders strode the decks. A black-robed priest moved about silently.

Presently, strolling about the deck, Kioga came upon an excited circle of miners, trappers, and woodsmen. Within the circle a huge bear of a man was engaged in pinning an opponent's shoulders to the boards. After his victory, the Snow Hawk observed the passing-over of certain objects to the victor—a process whereby the giant had already acquired considerable wealth.

A typical brawler was the winner. Gigantic in stature, overbearing in manner, and with the strength of three average men, he was a formidable antagonist, and not a little drunk. He was tolerated by captain and crew for his titanic labors at the woodpile, whenever the steamer paused to fuel up. And as usual, he was boasting.

"*Je suis* B'tees Belleau, stronges' man on this *rivière*. I have kill' grizzle-b'ar wit t'e naked hand. *Pardieu,* but I am strong fella! All this I have win." His broad self-satisfied gesture included dogs and harness, skins and traps, on which the gaze of the losers dwelt moodily. To some this meant a year's labor lost, to others loss of income for the coming year; for without traps furs cannot be easily caught. None of this was lost upon the watchful Kioga.

The boaster's exultant glance fell at last upon him who sat with swinging foot upon a large crate. The pride-inflated Belleau did not like the cold indifferent gaze of the other. And as he was convincing himself of this fact, Kioga, weary unto boredom of the man's incessant vaunting, arose and prepared to go forward in search of a modicum of peace and quiet.

Perchance something of his detestation of the other had been discernible. Certainly the Snow Hawk was not one to veil his feelings in awe of any man. Howbeit, he had not gone two steps when in arrogant tones the great Belleau challenged him loudly.

"*Vous, là*! You sneer at B'tees?"

Slowly the Snow Hawk swung round, meeting Belleau's furious gaze coolly.

Quick and straight the answer came, thrown directly into Belleau's teeth.

"And if I laugh, what then?"

Because Belleau was the true bully, he stood openmouthed before this direct reply. Then, not daring to allow another to front him down, he recovered, glaring upon Kioga. And now, reading him as through a transparent piece of glass, Kioga could not conceal a little smile.

"*M'sieur*," began Belleau ominously, "I am B'tees Belleau. It is not safe to laugh in my face. I have kill' a man for less. But you—ah, *je vous pardonnerai* if—" Here Belleau's cunning eye moved to the belongings of Kioga's companions "We will gamble, you and B'tees—*non*?"

A moment Kioga stood thoughtful. He did not wish to become involved in any unpleasantness which would delay his party; but suddenly, on the echo of a dog's barking, another thought entered his mind. To Belleau he made answer all innocently:

"Gamble? For what, Belleau? Our horses and gear against your dogs and these things you've won?"

Gleefully Belleau rubbed his hamlike hands together. This was to be easier than he had expected. "*Oui, bien, oui!*" he agreed eagerly. "Whoever lift the mos' heavy weight, she is win—*non*?"

"You're right—no!" interrupted a bearded miner whose pistol and holster alone remained to him. "Look-a-here, Belleau. Keep this square an' above board. It's his specialty—lifting," he added, turning to Kioga. "You can't beat him at his own game."

Belleau bristled indignantly. "I have the honor, *m'sieur*. I am play fair the game. *Mais* the American may refuse."

Kioga acknowledged the miner's interference with a nod, but he did not refuse. "Will you hold the stakes?" he asked of the miner.

"Shore enough,'" was the instant reply; "but you might's well hand it all over to him on a silver platter."

The grumbling miner separated the stakes: Belleau's dogs, gear, and winnings of the day on the one hand, and on the other Kioga's horses, and most of the band's trappings.

Upon these preparations the Indian migrants looked with keen anxiety. Though they had seen Snow Hawk manhandle a steer, this Belleau seemed inhumanly strong. As for the crew and the pasengers, these were all anticipation. The American could not win, but it was refreshing to see Belleau bearded once in his life.

A lifting platform was improvised, a crude affair consisting of two sections of thick log upon which to place either foot. The platform itself was the gangplank, girdled with strong rope so arranged as to be raised by a single central strand, having a great knot at its end. Upon the platform were placed two iron drums of gasoline. Between these was set a huge box containing machine parts and other heavy objects. Finally Belleau called a halt, and threw off his shirt.

Clambering up to a position straddling the weights, he seized the knotted rope in both hands and tried his strength. The weight would not move. One box was taken off, and Belleau tried again. With an effort that brought sweat to his brow he succeeded in raising one end of the platform. The wager called for a clearance all around sufficient to roll a six-inch log beneath.

Dripping with sweat, Belleau strained, tugged, and struggled; yet he had to order the removal of another box before he could complete the lift. The log rolled beneath. Baptiste's grip slipped. The ship quivered as the weights struck the deck. But Belleau's confidence was unabated, for never had man in all Canada raised such a weight as that. Grinning triumphantly, he turned to Kioga.

"Your turn, *m'sieur*," he sneered.

Forth stepped the Snow Hawk, shirtless, a moment to estimate the weight on the platform. Beside the bearish Belleau, he looked almost slender. But among the onlookers, experienced in gauging a man's powers, there were eyes hard to deceive. Eyes that took in the depth of chest and the extraordinary thickness of the lower-back muscles—twin indices of a man's strength. "By God, there's a man!" muttered someone softly.

Now to the astonishment of the beholders Kioga threw back the boxes Belleau had removed. Baptiste's dismay was only momentary. Then he laughed, jeeringly. It is one thing to load a platform; it is another to make a lift.

Lightly the Snow Hawk sprang upon the wooden supports. Bending, he laid hold of the rope below the knot. Putting strain upon it gently, he centered the combined strength of loins, thighs, and back, with a gentle ripple of muscles tensing under the taut skin. Again Bapsiste laughed, long and loud.

But the laughter died in his throat. For in that instant the platform cleared the boards, rising swiftly in a single movement. He whose duty it was to roll the log beneath stood in amazement, forgetful until reminded of his task. Swiftly he rolled the log beneath with space to spare. Not until then did Kioga lower his load gently to the deck, and step down amid a spontaneous cheer—from all save the great Baptiste, who sweated even more profusely now than after his earlier exertions.

After his own effort, Kioga showed no more than the natural flush of color coursing through the muscle-groups involved. But Belleau's face burned scarlet, as he mingled profanity with his protests.

"*Sacré enfant de garce*! I have-a been cheat'!" he roared.

Whereupon the bearded miner silenced him.

"Then git up thar an' lift ag'in! Ain't nobody stoppin' ye, is they?"

So again Belleau climbed up and heaved and groaned and strained, but the result was a foregone conclusion. He was overmatched, fairly beaten at his own game—and none knew it better than Baptiste Belleau.

So came Kioga into possession of fifteen big Northern dogs, in good condition, together with their harness, as well as all the other gear Belleau had gained from those against whom he had wrestled. These latter Kioga returned to their respective owners, traps and all.

And the ship was troubled no more by Belleau, who slunk ashore at the first opportunity.

With the steamer making good headway, it seemed that the migrants were at last well on their way to the Arctic and destined to gain it without further mishap. But during one night came a terrific explosion from amidships. The steamer quivered no longer to the spin of her paddle wheel as she settled heavily upon a sandbar in midstream.

Serious damage was done to the boiler, it seemed. Two weeks or a month might pass before repairs could be effected, Kioga learned with regret. They dared not wait, indeed, and he settled the matter by arranging with the captain for purchase of four large canoes, into which the band loaded its possessions, a supply of food, its dogs, and equipment.

Then, amid the hearty farewells of other passengers, Kioga and his strange party were away, this time in one of the world's most ancient means of transport, bark batteaux such as Alexander Mackenzie used when first he broke the trail they were now following toward the Arctic.

Beyond view of the steamer, it was not long before the band shed their clothing to paddle again naked to the waist in the heat of midday sun. But this was feasible only where the going was swift. Elsewhere, and at every pause, they were greeted by eddying swarms of ravenous Northern mosquitoes, whose blood-hungry millions were omnipresent in camp or at portage. Smudge fires nor brushing kept the mosquitoes away; but plastered with clay and in motion upon the river, the band was comparatively free from attack.

Several days passed thus without notable incident, save that their progress was swifter than at any other time in their journey. Then one day they encountered a stretch of fast water, the only alternative to which was a long laborious portage—with the mosquito hordes ready and waiting.

To Kioga, accustomed to run the foaming roaring streams of Nato'wa, the face of this rapid was as an open page, with no dangerous exposed rocks. The run was made in safety by three of the craft, and the fourth was passing safely through. Kioga's canoe brought up the rear and mishap occurred to it, because of the stern-man's ignorance of watercraft.

From his crouch in the bow Kioga had permitted his bark to head almost straight upon an upthrusting rock that split the current ahead. Long experience on treacherous waters had taught him that if he but kept his canoe straight, one half of the current would bear it safely round the rock.

Mistaking Kioga's deliberate act for carelessness, the stern-man dug his paddle deep, attempting to steer the craft out of the fancied danger. One half of the current thus caught the bow to the left, while the stern, responding to the after paddle, was seized by the other half of the current. In an instant the canoe swung broadside, was carried full upon the rock, ripped, smashed, and broken in two, precipitating its occupants into the water.

Perceiving that both of his companions were able to attain the shore, Kioga salvaged such floating objects as came within his reach. The canoe itself rushed on its way, a total wreck. The canoe could be replaced. But the loss of one part of her cargo was a serious matter. Somewhere near the fatal rock, scattered beyond recall along the bottom, lay their ammunition. Such guns as they had were now practically useless.

Luckily, each man fortunate enough to possess an old rifle still carried a few cartridges with him. With these, as time passed, they shot some migrating ducks, but little more.

Now daily their supply of food was being reduced by the inroads of many mouths, human and canine, for the dogs too had to be fed. They took trout and whitefish and *inconnu*, and with these they fed the dogs, but Kioga and his band caught nowhere near enough on their poor hooks and makeshift lines.

That night, at the camp-fire, Kioga addressed his men.

"We have come many miles. Let us sleep well, and on the morrow hunt. Before sunrise the hunters will seek what may be found along the river woodland. Those remaining will fish in the stream."

Grunts of approval came from every side, as the remainder of the band awaited Kioga's selection of those who were to hunt.

"It is true we have little ammunition," he told them quietly. "But we have several bows and many arrows. The bows are old and the arrows warped. We cannot make the bows younger, but the arrows will straighten, and we can make more. We are forest men. These are our weapons. We will not fail, if we be cunning hunters."

"Strong words." Old Bull Calf laughed in delight at the prospect of an old-fashioned hunt. "There is a saying among my people: 'Any bow to a good hunter.' Tomorrow red meat will fall to the arrows which our ancestors made. And now let us sleep."

But to Kioga had come the thought that it was too much to expect these warriors to kill, when both weapons and skill were dull. Of his own skill he had no doubt. It was but a year ago, more or less, since he had put down his strong hunting bow.

A stiff breeze blew, giving them surcease from the torturing mosquitoes. It was very still. In the south an immense orange moon rose slowly. It was the prowling hour, and the Snow Hawk was also restless. He rose in the quiet of the night and tried several of the warped bows. One broke at a pull of the cord. Another cracked, and he laid it aside. Of them all he selected one of horn and sinew, reinforced it, and tried his aim by shooting at a tree trunk nearby. The shaft wandered in flight, but struck true enough. Selecting a handful of the straightest shafts, he would have returned to his place beside the fire, but his pulse was beating swifter. The touch of that primitive weapon had awakened an instinct even more primitive, and he stepped silently beyond the fire's light, where in a moment his eyes expanded to the gloom. Forward he moved to the river, and pushed off alone in a canoe. A moment he bent, cupping water not to his lips, but to that keen nose of his, upon which he had learned to rely from boyhood to lead him to meat. He snuffed but a little. The moist nostril perceives what the dry overpasses.

Then, keeping to the stream, he pushed along its surface for several miles. At a wooded bank he tied the canoe and stepped ashore. A twig snapped softly under his foot. A little impatiently he paused to remove his moccasins, wondering if his skill in the stalk had suffered during his stay in civilization. The faintest scratch next reached his ears. No other human ear could have detected it. But Kioga had the ears of an owl. A twig had rasped against fringed coat or leggin. He removed both; and almost naked he slipped along now, silent as any other prowler of the night.

One by one he ignored the telltale taint of others who moved within the dark around him. With discriminating nostrils he sought the scent of the greater deer, perhaps even a caribou if luck proved good.

Suddenly a wisp of scent came, then was gone. Rigid as a hound at point for but that instant, in another moment the Snow Hawk was in full stride, traveling fast upon a thread of scent, which in the unraveling would lead to meat. And soon upon an expanse of moonlit mud he saw a long, oval unmistakable spoor—the trail of a moose, of all deer the most magnificent, cunning and formidable, a prey worthy his subtlest skill.

One quick glance told him the quarry had an hour's lead, that it bled a little, from wounds inflicted perhaps in battle with some vanquished wolf. And as he went, great slashes showed in the moist earth, stamped there in rage or pain.

Swift before, his speed was multiplied now, for he raced as he learned to do in his crippled boyhood. Here swinging rapidly hand-over-hand, borrowing of every springy limb its resiliency in propelling him forward. A sudden check, drawn and tense, as the Snow Hawk listened, looked, and savored the air into which he moved. Then a lightning freeze to rigidity, as across the clearing the quarry moved in full view!

Belly deep in tall lush grasses, an indigo etching rose against the red-umber sky of early dawn. There the stately quarry passed in ghostly silence—yet not more silent than the Snow Hawk followed.

Beast of the marsh, uncouth, unearthly in dimensions, its vast shovel-like antlers spreading six feet across, hanging with marsh-plants, and swaying amid the vapor-columns blown from its wet nostrils; from its shaggy rich-brown sides the muddy swamp-waters adrip; from its neck, below the ugly muzzle, the strange bell-like dewlap grotesquely pendant and swinging. It was Muswa to Kioga—not the ponderous Muswa he had hunted in his own land, but a giant as giants go on the continent of North America.

Quick to the string he fitted an iron-headed arrow. Swift to his jaw he drew, and loosed the goose-winged bolt away. Straight in short trajectory it flew; and as the deer dropped its head beneath the water in search of the succulent marsh-plants it loved, the arrow grazed the horny crest.

The mighty armament threshed erect. With bulging eyes and heaving flank the startled moose turned broadside to the silent hunter. Again the humming of the bow-cord. As by magic, the moose bore in its side the feathers of an arrow. Another leaped and sped true, and yet another still, before it could leap aside. Five giant bounds the beast then took, before espying Kioga in the act of nocking a fifth arrow.

Of a moose this much is known: He is one of those few who stands and gives battle to the human hunter. Wheeling now, implacable of mien, grunting savagely and with the whites of its eyes showing, the bull turned on its tormentor.

In that instant the quick eye of Kioga glimpsed the old scars of wolf-fangs on the animal's brisket. There were white hairs on the grotesque muzzle, attesting age and cunning. And there was fury in the blazing eyes as the bull charged. But ready and waiting stood Kioga, until the glittering frost in each spadelike horn showed gemlike and gleaming.

Then, like the flicker of heat lightning, he leaped aside. Close past his flank the left antler flailed; then the moose wheeled to lash out with the deadly fore hooves. But the man-figure had leaped upward, as in the flying mount, and was locked to the shaggy shoulders, high up behind the beating tines of the antlers—and striking swiftly with his knife.

A moment Muswa shuddered, quivering with pain and fear. Twenty incredible bounds he took. Then he collapsed beneath the hunter.

It was not the first such wild ride Kioga had survived. Upon such a beast as this he had first dropped from above, to learn his strength and taste the primeval thrill which comes when the quarry sinks beneath the body-weight pounce of the ambushing hunter. Now again his blood ran swift and hot with the ardor of the kill.

But in a moment he turned to practical business. With deft strokes he divided the great carcass and bore head and all four quarters to the river. Returning he retraced his steps to the canoe, in which he picked up the moose, and turned back to camp.

Smiling Woman was first to note his return. The immense weight of the moose sank the craft almost to its gunwales. Above its prow the immense head was raised, the antlers spreading out to either side. The effect was as of some strange amphibian creature, swimming out of the distance. And astern, covered with blood, Kioga knelt upon his clothes and slowly worked his craft ashore, the orange fire of the rising sun at his back.

Such a shout arose as only leaves the throat of hungry

men. The cooking fires were quickly kindled. With sharp blades the women cut up the meat, impaled it upon peeled twigs, and set it to cook before the coals. Soon rose the rich aroma of roasting moose-loin to thrill the senses of men long starved for the diet of their hunter-ancestors.

IV

The days passed; the miles reeled off behind; and the dense forest along the river gave way to the sparser growth of the higher latitudes.

In the Indian camp one night old Sits-in-Sun had been turning strips of meat to dry over the smoking fire. She went away for a few moments, and returning, clapped one hand to her mouth.

"Sits-in-Sun is afraid. What is it?" asked Kioga gently.

"I turned meat here a moment ago. Now—a piece is gone!"

"Thieving jays swooped down to steal, Mother."

"No," replied the aged woman, casting affrighted glances about. "There is a hungry mouth among us who have meat."

Soothingly the Snow Hawk reassured the old woman. But she shook her hoary head. "I am old: I know—we have offended a spirit. Tonight I will make an offering to charm it away."

True to her word, Sits-in-Sun that night gave of her best dried meat, placing it just outside the illumination of the camp-fire on a stone. Sometime between the still small hours and dawn the offering vanished. No trail led into or out of the camp, as the suspicious warriors quickly ascertained. Impatient at the delay occasioned by this incident, Kioga at last remonstrated with his band.

"There are thieves of the air and thieves of the earth. A wolverine, or mayhap a fox, has stolen the offering. Let us waste no more time on this, but break camp and take to our canoes. The sun rises high. The journey is far. If an evil spirit follows, it will become lost on the rivers."

"You cannot lose a spirit thus," muttered old Sits-in-Sun.

"Spirits can walk on water, fly in air, and pass through holes smaller than the eye of a needle. *Ai-i*, this is a bad omen."

No further untoward events occurred during the day, however. And at nightfall, drawing their canoes upon a sandbar, the band kindled its fires, eating again of the diminishing moose-meat.

Near the end of the meal Kioga was first to glimpse the approach of a deep-laden canoe bearing a single occupant, who sat startled, with uplifted paddle, staring at the warlike band. As they returned his wave, he appeared to regain his composure. His paddle dipped and the canoe touched the pebbly beach.

The newcomer was a swarthy, square-faced man, wearing a weathered mackinaw coat. His heavy woolen trousers were tucked into high hobnailed boots, from one of which a knife-handle protruded. He had not shaved nor combed for many a week.

Accosted by Kioga, he shook hands, introducing himself simply as John Smith, trapper and prospector, with a glance that discouraged further questioning. He carried his rifle constantly under one arm. His quick black eyes leaped curiously from face to face among the Indians, and dwelt overlong on the young girl Pretty Eagle, who sewed on a skin amid the older women.

Then he sat down unbidden with his hosts, took up a chunk of meat in one hand and ate greedily, wiping his greasy fingers on his coat, already amply soiled by previous wipings.

"Goin' north?" he asked at last.

Kioga nodded affirmatively.

"Mind if I wander a way with ye?"

In all truth, Kioga liked nothing about the stranger; and he was about to refuse the company of the newcomer, when he chanced to glimpse Sits-in-Sun, standing stiff and pallid with fear. In an instant he knew what was in her mind: The man had eaten so much that she associated him immediately with the hungry "spirit" of the previous night. To her mind, refusing the trapper their company would endanger the success of their journey, for the spirit might actually dwell in the person of John Smith.

However absurd the Snow Hawk may have thought such a belief, he did not wish to cause the old woman further worry; and after all, he had nothing tangible against the other man. Therefore he simply nodded, raising no objection to the trapper's company. . . . He was to regret his softening.

The trapper's "spirit" was of a different nature than metaphysical.

Returning next day from a short exploration of the neighboring wilderness, Kioga found several of his younger braves in a stupor, while others laughed loudly and talked boisterously, with loosened tongues. John Smith had been distributing liquor among them, in return for certain desirable properties of theirs. A quick glance discovered him examining his new acquisitions, obtained in trade for the whiskey.

In ten strides Kioga was beside the guide with uplifted ax. The man leaped aside, but the stroke was not intended for him. Instead it fell upon the whiskey keg. And then, without hesitation Kioga went to the man's canoe and began cracking each keg open.

Furiously the trapper saw his contraband seeping away in the sand. He seized the prow of the canoe to thrust it out of harm's way—with the result that the falling ax-blow struck the frail craft itself, ruining it. Now he snatched up his rifle, then caught himself in hand—fortunately, for had he so much as leveled it, any one of four ready knives would have slit his throat.

Thinking to divest the man of his gains, Kioga reflected that when sober the Indians must resent the trader as much as the trade. So without a word he turned his back, while the trapper, white with rage, glared his hatred.

In point of fact, in he who called himself John Smith the worst dross of two races was run into a common mold. Though a primitive passion swept him now, native cunning overcame it.

Red dawn found the camp astir, packing for the day's journey; the Kioga, as was his habit, prepared to reconnoiter a little way ahead. At the beach he heard a light footfall behind him, and turned to see Pretty Eagle approaching. He greeted her courteously in the Indian figure.

"A beautiful day begins."

"May it end as beautiful," said Pretty Eagle, glancing behind her; then she spoke swiftly. "The half-breed, he is drinking again. Beware of him. He bears you ill will, Kioga."

The Snow Hawk smiled. "He is the least of my enemies," he told her quietly. "Fear not. My eyes have not been closed."

As he paddled away, her eyes followed him. Lowering a container, she then dipped water from the river. Turning to retrace her steps, the dark eyes hardened, for the trapper was close at her heels. With flushed face and averted gaze she would have passed, but he would not give her way. Boldly he leaned closer. His strong breath reeked in her pale oval face.

"I go away soon," he said. "Come on with me. I know how to treat a girl right."

Infuriated by the insult, the girl dropped the water-bag and reached for the slim knife in her belt. But his fingers fell upon her wrist, twisting brutally.

"Eater of carcajou! Let me go!" she panted fiercely. "I am not for you, swiller in rum!"

"You see only the white dog."

"Fool! Shall I rouse the camp?" she threatened, struggling in his grasp. But fired by her nearness, he would not let go.

She threatened anew.

"Him you call the white dog has fangs. He will hear of this."

Silent and unnoticed, a canoe drifted upon the scene. Thinking on Prety Eagle's words, Kioga had but turned a bend, before returning, the better to maintain watch on "Smith." An instant later the trapper, crushed to his knees, stared death in the face, while steel fingers choked the breath from him. When he recovered consciousness, the trapper found his head ground into the wet sand while Kioga kicked water into his face.

"If I told the band of this," Kioga said to him, "they would cut your eyes out. No more of this, or it will cost you dear. You stay with us this last day—because we need your labor. Tonight, you go!"

Toward nightfall, alert to find a camping-place, Kioga ordered the canoes to drift. Absorbed in searching out a safe passage among the underwater rocks, he was leaning forward, eyes upon the murky river bottom, when behind him the volcano that was the trapper erupted suddenly into action.

Warned by the inner voice to which he never turned deaf ear, Kioga drew back even as a deafening concussion made his eardrums ring. A red groove along his forearm suddenly filled with blood. The trapper, who had been middle man in the freight-loaded canoe, had struck without warning, drunkenly heedless of consequences, knocking one Indian unconscious with his rifle, then firing at Kioga.

As the Snow Hawk wheeled, the half-breed was clutching at something which twined about his neck from behind, his rifle slipping into deep water. ... In the dusk Kioga was a second determining the nature of the trapper's assailant.

Suddenly he saw; and, seeing, understood much that had been a mystery in the last several days.

A thin brown arm clutched John Smith about the neck, while its mate, flourishing a small steel blade in the other hand, struggled in the half-breed's grasp. The man shifted his shoulders sharply, throwing his young assailant across the canoe.

And that assailant was Tokala the Fox, appearing as out of thin air in their midst!

Five yards separated the two drifting craft. The breed's fingers had closed on Tokala's slim neck, throttling the shrill battle-yell. With his tortured back crushed down upon the gunwale, the boy struggled manfully. But in another moment his back would have been broken.

Then it was that Kioga's heavy paddle, hurled spearlike, struck the man in the back of the head, knocking him asprawl into the stream. Released, Tokala fell back into the canoe.

A few feet away was the shore. Leaping knee-deep into the water, Kioga snatched the boy into his arms. White-faced, with cruel red marks on face and neck, little Tokala lay lifelessly against his arm.

And as the Snow Hawk turned to step ashore, the trapper rose unsteadily behind him with upraised knife, the intention plain to plunge it into Kioga's back. Then, on feathered vanes, came swift check. A sharp hiss, as of a breath indrawn, preceded the *whick-k* of a striking arrow. Transfixed through the neck, Smith fell, coughing blood. A long-drawn cry rose quaveringly. An instant later the active old figure which was Bull Calf jumped ashore with *coup*-stick ready.

Tokala had had the honor of counting the first *coup*. But Bull Calf was intent on being second and struck the fallen man a light blow. Immediately following came Bets-His-Shirt to count third *coup*.

The Indian who had been struck by the trapper's gun was brought to, and his injuries bandaged. And that night Tokala, the little stowaway, faced a solemn-faced jury of his elders, demanding an accounting of his presence.

Little by little Kioga gently drew from the boy a halting confession. He had secreted himself in the *parfleche* box with the knowledge and consent of Smiling Woman. Each day she had brought him food and water. Each night, with her connivance he had emerged like a jack-in-the-box to loosen his cramped muscles. He had slept, he blushingly confessed, in

41

the young women's tent, returning to his voluntary prison before the camp was yet awake.

One night, unable to resist, he had stolen forth and taken a piece of meat from Sits-in-Sun's rack. He was also the spirit who had appropriated her spirit offering. The mystery of Smiling Woman's medicine-box was solved.... His story told, the small stowaway darted a fearful glance about the circle of the chiefs. Never a smile on those stern brown features! Glumly Tokala stared at the ground, the picture of pathos and complete dejection, awaiting judgment.

Came then the voice of Kioga, stern and slow, to the councilors.

"He has told his tale. What shall his punishment be?"

Lower fell the head of Tokala.

"It should be severe," answered Bets-His-Shirt.

Rounder grew the stooped little shoulders.

"The punishment should fit the offense," added Bull Calf. "Let Kioga set the penalty."

The Snow Hawk cleared his throat.

"So be it. Tokala, you have disobeyed your chiefs. You must be punished. The chiefs have said it. Therefore—"

Tokala's heart withered in his small bare breast.

"First," continued the Snow Hawk, "stand erect like a man and face the council!" The boy's dark head snapped up, misery and resignation in his eyes. "Second: you shall take this hook and line and catch ten thousand fish in the river. Not for your belly, but for the dogs. From this hour they are your care. Do this work well—and mayhap the offense will be washed out. I have said it!"

A moment Tokala stood thrilling to the meaning of the sentence—no return to hated civilization, no punishment worthy the name, only work—a man's, a hunter's work! He felt tears close to his lids. He reached forth, snatched hook and line, and then ran, as if a *wendigo* pursued him, toward the river.

Behind him the solemn councillors contained themselves for but another moment. Then a roar of laughter sounded through the camp.

Smiling Woman, called to defend her deception, took a defiant attitude, a woman's privilege. "Did I not tell you the *parfleche* box contained what had belonged to my brother? Did I not say it was *wakan* to him? *Ai-i*, what have I done that is wrong?"

Again the chiefs laughed, long and loud.

So came Tokala into an honored place in the band, having

aided the Snow Hawk in battle and counted first *coup* upon a fallen foe—a feat entitling him to wear, at ten years of age, an honor of the first grade, an erect eagle-feather in the scalp-lock. Bull Calf took it from his own warbonnet and placed it in Tokala's hair.

V

While Kioga and his band journeyed northward toward the Promised Land of Nato'wa, another expedition was in preparation in the seaport of San Francisco. Quietly berthed in her dock, a small two-masted auxiliary schooner had undergone overhauling in preparation for a journey which would have startled science and aroused the attention of all the world.

The *Narwhal* was a ship with a past, and carried her prow high, as befitted one who had fought the Seven Seas and defied the Arctic. Beloved of many men in the course of a long career, changing her name for several owners, she had been faithful to all—as she would be true to her master of the present, who from her forward rail conned her lines with critical affection.

Stalwart, a little austere, was Dr. James Munro, traveler, explorer of far places, savant. Like his ship, Munro had been weathered and tried by many a storm, emerging fit and strong into the prime of middle life. The sum of his labors, and monument to his fame, is that collection of Indian relics housed in the museum which bears his name; and you will find him quoted everywhere as the foremost authority in his special field—the strange mysterious race known as the American Indian, of whose customs, history, and language he probably knows more than any other living man. And he delighted above all else in visiting the people he loved, and pitied for the tragedy of their destruction by the white race.

His knowledge of their languages and customs gained him access to the lodges of red men on two continents. But it was by means of a peculiar hobby, his mastery of sleight-of-hand and conjuring, that he had won his way into the hearts of scattered bands round many a distant camp-fire. And the name Swift-Hand, spoken anywhere among them would bring a smile and sudden unexpected animation to faces habitually stoical.

Munro's long search for the missing *Cherokee* had brought him off into the far North. There he had met Kioga the Snow Hawk, and had come into possession of the wrecked *Cherokee*'s strange history and a knowledge of the amazing discoveries made by its owner, Lincoln Rand. Now, in the prime of maturity, when many men would have sat with pipe, dog, and book at a warm fireplace, a new and magnificent adventure fired his imagination: He would seek this newfound land of Nato'wa, verify the findings of its discoverer Lincoln Rand, and explore it further.

Slowly Dr. Munro climbed down the forecastle hatch and vanished below. Through the galley, he moved aft into the main cabin, which had accommodation for several persons around a great table under the reinforced skylight.

The ship's interior reflected the scientific nature of her previous employment: There were devices for making depth-soundings; wire nets on long cables for trawling the ocean bottom; depth thermometers and other instruments and tools used by the geologists. Everywhere on the walls were harpoons and their lines, ice-axes, picks and shovels, and various other tackle. The *Narwhal* was equipped with every modern device, lighted by ship-generated electricity, heated by oil. A double sheathing protected her from the formation of inside ice, during extreme cold, due to breath and cooking steam.

Passing through the engine room, Munro entered a large after cabin, whose walls were hung with more harpoons, ropes, and rifles on appropriate racks. This was the chartroom, containing also maps, sextant, chronometer, and compasses, in addition to two-way radio equipment.

Adjoining this were Munro's own personal quarters aft, enriched by many colorful and interesting articles. Surrounded by his choice little wall-library, he now took his ease, scanning the list of his crew. In most respects it was a personnel of which to be proud:

Barry Edwards, his Canadian assistant, was tried and proved and had been with him on the Northern floes when he went to the rescue of those abandoned by the whaler *Bearcat*. His engineer Lars Hanson was a resourceful and able man, an American-born Swede, a competent sailor of immense good nature. An expert in marine engines, his knowledge, added to Munro's inventive ability, had given the *Narwhal* an engine capable of burning whale oil if the need arose.

The mate, Peter Edson, combined the virtues of first-class carpenter with his other qualifications, which were above reproach. Of Dan La Salle he was sure for Dan had been of the party which survived the sinking of the *Alberta*— a competent wireless operator, his efforts as an amateur had saved life when the *Alberta* went down. He would be valuable as one who had knowledge of the highly dangerous torturous channel in the reefs through which they must approach Nato'wa. Dan was absent on a quest ashore for news of Kioga, but was expected soon to rejoin the ship.

At the name John Henders, Munro paused to speculate. This man held the important place of cook; and as a cook, Munro held nothing against Henders; but he had come aboard drunk on two occasions—and Munro made a note to replace him at first opportunity.

One other member of his expedition gave Munro further perplexity. This was Beth La Salle, sister of Dan and like him a survivor of the *Alberta*. Munro had earlier experienced grave misgivings concerning her presence, but she herself had dissipated his concern.

Having no other close kin than father and brother, she had long dwelt in a man's world, and her disarmingly frank way with the crew had both attracted favor and then discountenanced familiarity by reason of its impartiality. Knowing and trusting every man but one of his crew, Munro feared not for her personal safety. But that a civilized young woman could adjust herself to the long darkness and complete isolation of the Arctic, he could not be sure.

Elsewhere on that ship, the object of Munro's thoughts gazed out into the dusk, inhaling the smell of tar and fresh paint and new yellow rope.

Beth La Salle stood above the average height for a woman. Diana herself was not formed on more gracefully supple lines, nor the huntress more agile. Her mouth was beautiful—and resolute. She wore practical masculine garb in a manner possible to few women, with dash and decided grace.

No anemic clinging beauty was Beth La Salle, but quick and surprisingly strong. There was young athletic strength in her walk now as going below to the quarters adjoining Munro's, which she was to share with Dan, she took pen in hand and drafted a letter to her well-loved Aunt Margaret. She wrote:

Dear Aunty Mag:

Your letter reached me today. There's a lot I never told you about what happened after the *Alberta* left port, months before she sank. As you know, Allan Kendle went north to shoot specimens of Pacific coast animals for the Museum. Unfortunately we 'lay to,' as the sailors say, to pick up a load of shipwrecked men, who later proved most ungrateful guests.

They mutinied, disabled the ship. Storms drove us far offshore and into ice-filled Arctic waters. After passing through dangerous ice and dreadful reefs, we finally grounded on an unknown coast. Shortly afterward the mutineers attacked the crew, nearly killed Allan, and carried me off as hostage. In searching for me later, Allan was captured by wild tribesmen inhabiting the coast, which was not that of an island as we had thought, but evidently an unknown land.

In a quarrel one of the mutineers killed another. It looked pretty bad for your little Beth. Suddenly, from nowhere, came rescue by one I took for a demon, half-naked and streaked with war paint. Oh, but I wish you could have seen him knock down those cut throats! I shall never forget it, nor all else he did for us later. And we were the first white people he had ever seen.

While returning me to the ship he rescued Allan from the fire-stake. We three escaped with a hundred savages yelling on our heels. Sometimes it seems impossible that we passed through such horrible experiences and lived to tell of them! But nothing was impossible to our new friend. He spoke and wrote English. We learned he was the son of white parents, shipwrecked here long ago. His name was Lincoln Rand, but he was known to the natives as Kioga the Snow Hawk. He had lived long among them and was high in their councils—until we came. Our rescue earned him their enmity.

Kioga found us meat, guided us safely through the reefs, found more meat when the ship sank and all looked black. Then the terrible thing happened. While Kioga was out hunting one night, the whaler *Bearcat* came up and took us aboard. Your weakling niece was unconscious. Allan deliberately encouraged the *Bearcat* to sail, leaving Kioga behind. Dan protested; but Captain Scott, with sick men aboard and in danger of being beset by the ice, steamed away. We knew nothing of this until much later. When I came to and learned of Kioga's abandonment, I never suspected Allan of such a brutal deception.

But Kioga didn't die. You couldn't conceive of such a man dying! He was picked up later by Dr. Munro, the famous scientist, and taken aboard the *Narwhal,* bound for San Francisco. Knowing that one word from him would result in my breaking off with Allan, Kioga never even let us know he was alive. He believed I loved Allan, you see. A few days before Allan became ill, Dan discovered that Kioga was alive. He told me just as I was leaving to be with Allan through a crisis in his illness. I wrote a hurried line, telling Kioga I would see him the following day; Allan's sickness prevented it. Kioga attributed my delay to indifference. Oh, if he only knew! In delirium Allan betrayed himself. After learning *that,* everything was at an end between Allan and me.

On the *Narwhal,* from which I write, we await Dan's return, hoping that he will have found some trace of Kioga. If he is unsuccessful, we sail for Juneau or some other northern port to lie up for the winter. In spring we set out in earnest. Munro will be going on an explorer's adventure. Dan has always wanted to go back to the newfound land. It fascinates him. As for me—Kioga risked his life for us, fed us when we hungered, abandoned his people to be at my side, and finally sacrificed himself, as he thought, for my happiness. Can I do less than follow him?

You ask me what I feel for this man Kioga. I can only answer that when I heard he had been abandoned, the sun grew dark. Nothing matters on this earth but seeing him again.

The ship is ready to sail north. Dan will be with me, so you needn't worry. I hope to see Dad in Alaska and bid him good-bye. We shall reach Nato'wa, God willing, find Kioga, and make a safe return. Until then, bless you, dear, and remember kindly,

Your affectionate niece,

Beth.

Leaving the ship in darkness and alone, Beth mailed her letter and was boarding the *Narwhal* again when out of the darkness came a hail.

She turned, with swiftly beating heart, recognized the voice.

"Dan! Is it you?"

"Me, all right," came from the dock. A tall shadow followed the voice down the gangplank. A moment passed while they embraced; then the girl pushed the newcomer away and searched his face in the glow of a side-light. Her voice was tense with an emotion he understood.

"Dan—any trace of Kioga?"

"Traces enough!" he began, checking her rising excitement with a negative wave of the hand. "But it's contact we wanted, Beth, not traces. No use me telling the whole story twice. Let's find Munro, and have it over in one telling."

Greeted cordially by the scientist, in the privacy of Munro's own cabin, Dan recounted his experiences since first he had begun his search for the missing Snow Hawk.

Unsuccessful in his early efforts, he had finally unearthed a few clues in a Western cattle-town near the Canadian border. A half-breed had told him a tale of a mounted Indian band that had started northward under the leadership of a stranger who corresponded roughly to a description of Kioga. Then came reported discovery of a burial rack, bearing two blanketed bodies—new corpses but painted in the manner of long ago. A long-distance call established the fact that an Indian band had left the crippled river steamer *Athabaska*, and had proceeded northward by canoe.

From another quarter, from reliable sources, came a news report backed up by actual photographs. They were pictures of an elevated burial scaffold, bearing the body of an old chief, wrapped in a blanket which flapped in the wind. From the scaffold hung a painted medicine-shield; and nearby crouched the body of a woman, which had not decayed, but had mummified. Beside the dead woman's body lay a knife, a bone needle, and a piece of dried meat.

Milestones. Milestones all, marking the path of the strangest caravan of this century.

"All evidence," concluded Dan, "of something. If I don't miss my guess, Kioga went that way."

"And with him a band of reservation Indians," mused Munro, "—old men and women who remembered the old way. One by one they died away. And yet—I don't quite see—"

"The Canadian police?" interrupted Beth suddenly.

"Exactly," began Munro; but Dan covered that point with an observation. "Great organization. But not omnipresent.

The North is full of Indians and breeds, roving around hunting and fishing. Canada treats 'em with a decent consideration. You can't expect a handful of men to know everything that goes on in an area of that size. Can't be done. If any Mountie does know they passed through his territory, he hasn't said so."

The girl sat in silence.

"Sorry, Beth," said Dan, covering her hands with his own. If she was disappointed, she concealed it. Rising—

"We haven't been idle while you were gone," she said quietly. "Come and look over our treasure chests."

Munro followed them into the adjoining cabin, where Beth knelt and opened a long chest displaying an assortment of objects such as has not been taken into northern seas since the first beginnings of the fur trade.

There were little boxes of blue, red, and yellow beads; packages of needles; yard on yard of bright-colored cloth; awls, hatchets, steel knives, iron packets of brilliant powdered paints; bright-hued kerchiefs; little music boxes that tinkled pleasantly when raised from the table, and tin harmonicas and flutes; small dolls with movable eyes, and toys that flashed forth sparks at the pressure of a thumb lever.

Stored away in the lazaret was a watertight box filled with assorted fireworks, pinwheels, Roman candles, firecrackers of all sizes. There were also aromatic packages of tea and tobacco and small bottles of cheap cologne.

At sight of these supplies for the Indian trade, something deep within the younger man stirred. His eyes had looked upon the splendid forests of Nato'wa, whose little-known shore his feet pressed. His blood had stained its savage ground, drawn by the attack of a wild animal whose claw marks in his side still ached on wet days. All that was young and venturesome in his nature anticipated their return to Nato'wa. He turned to Munro.

"When do we start, sir?" he asked.

Munro laughed at his eagerness. "We were only waiting for you, Dan. We sail on the tide."

At Juneau the *Narwhal* interrupted her northward voyage for a few additional supplies—and to hire a new cook; for Henders, the man they had shipped at San Francisco, had shown himself too fond of liquor to warrant risking him on their long and hazardous voyage. The search was delegated to Dan La Salle.

It was the noon hour when he landed, and not far from the

schooner he came upon a crowd of dockhands and stevedores gesticulating angrily before a wall of high-piled merchandise. Wrathful epithets crackled on the salty breeze. Approaching the scene of hostility, Dan peered between the heads of the agitated dock gang.

A stranger figure never trod the waterfront than he upon whom Dan's curious gaze alighted: Not over five feet four the stranger stood, dwarfed in the circle of his persecutors. Brown as coffee was the homely face below the brim of a dusty soft hat. From under the wavy brim a most peculiar pair of eyes looked calmly forth upon the world, and found something therein to twinkle at. Like most else about the man, the eyes did not quite match, and one bushy brow was but half the size of its neighbor, a scar marking the spot where once its remainder had flourished. The nose was remarkable for its size and straightness, above sweeping lank moustaches. For the rest, from skinny, wrinkled turkey-neck down, he was a most unkempt, disreputable specimen of mankind.

All of this Dan's eyes absorbed in a swift glance, as he sought the source of a high-pitched chatter that rose defiantly above the barrage of profanity. Suddenly a long prehensile coil flicked its length about the little man's neck. A black spidery hairy hand appeared from behind one ear to seize his shirt collar. Its mate flourishing a fistful of good American currency, proceeded to stuff the greenbacks into the stranger's breast pocket. Whereafter the diminutive monkey continued spouting fury and indignation from safety behind its nondescript master. At a word from beneath the moustaches, the little animal became abruptly silent. Without formality the stranger then introduced himself to all who cared to listen.

"Shore as my name's Flashpan, us-all better be a-movin' on."

The voice like his person, was unusual, coming cracked and alternately strong and whispered.

" 'Taint nowise healthy hereabouts for us, or for others," he added meaningly, producing a long-barreled pistol of ancient vintage, and cocking it audibly with an agile thumb. "Naow, gent'men," he continued, "cl'ar the road!" Then, to the monkey on his shoulder: "B'hold the ways of men, Placer, and be thankful the good Lord made ye a monkey. The heathens like to cleaned us out with marked cyards; yet when we turn the tables and get it back, they cuss; and what's worse, they repent not."

At this point one of the angry dockhands would have laid

hands upon the little man from one side, but a black dog of Northern breed leaped up and clicked menacing white fangs an inch from his throat. An instant later the entire mob, closely pursued by this grim Cerberus, took to its heels, leaving the diminutive stranger in command of the field.

He who called himself Flashpan eyed them quizzically a moment, spat with incredible exactitude ten feet across the dock into the bay, and thrust his weapon back into his rope belt. Through his fingers he sent forth a shrill whistle. Back came the great dog with wagging tail. Bending, Flashpan swung an immense packsack, hung with pick and shovel and cooking outfit, to his back, upon which the monkey sprang instantly.

Thus, like a scrawny Atlas bearing the earth upon his shoulders, Flashpan prepared to continue his journeyings anew, when his bright all-noticing eye chanced to glimpse the *Narwhal*, tugging at her dripping lines. Checking, he lowered his immense burden and its agitated occupant to gaze yearningly upon the stout craft.

"Handsome, isn't she?" said Dan by way of scraping acquaintance.

"A beauty, son," replied the ancient. "I mind me, son, of times I've sailed aroun' the globe on such a ship, an'—"

"Ever cooked?" interrupted his young listener.

"Aye, cooked," answered the Ancient Mariner, looking surprised. "Sharks' fins in the Chiny Sea, an' birds' nests on the Yangtsuey; curry-rice in Injy and spaghetti in It'ly; sourdough biscuit on the Yukon an'—"

How much longer this recital would have continued history knoweth not, for at this point Dan interrupted:

"Look here! We need a cook on the *Narwhal*."

With shrewd eyes the little man looked from Dan to ship and back, gulped, and with an effort that swelled veins on neck and forehead, managed: *"No!* Ye do?"

"Suppose you come aboard and have a talk with the captain."

"Wa-al," began Flashpan, a doubtful eye roving from his dog to his monkey. "Y'mean all three of us, I s'pose."

Flashpan recalled his dog from eager investigations about a rat-hole in the pier. "This here is Nugget," he explained to Dan. "Call him that account he was a lucky find, and gold clear through. Now this monk, here, his name's Placer, account he's uncertain, kind of an unknown claim, an' y'never know what he'll do. C'mon along, Nugget; we're boardin' the *Narwhal*."

"For our records," said Dr. Munro when Dan had presented his find, "I must ask you a few questions."

Flashpan doffed his hat with a sweep. "At yer service, Cap'n."

"How old are you, Flashpan?" Munro began.

The new cook squinted with concentration and spat reflectively through an open porthole. "Round'bout ninety-eight 'twas when I come of votin' age and sold my first ballot," he recalled.

"Pretty old for this job," said Munro thoughtfully.

"Old but tough," returned Flashpan with a look of secret alarm.

"But this may be a dangerous voyage."

"Dead shot with rifle and pistol," returned Flashpan swiftly.

"We-el—"

"Cook like a Frenchman, I can," persisted Flashpan. "Been around, I hev. Seen a-plenty of this here world, aye. Of an adventurin' disposition, Captain, sir—fancy-free and a-ra'rin' to go!"

"Not married, then?"

Flashpan wiped aside a suspiciously quick tear. "Mighta been a widower, Cap'n, if I'd married her—which I didn't."

Munro smiled. Flashpan gestured roundly, confidently. "I accept the berth, Cap'n, sir," said he.

"Hold on!" laughed Munro. "What's your occupation?"

"Prospectin', sir. Had me pick in five countries, not includin' Africky. Picked up a twelve-ounce nugget other day up Dawson way. Kept it fer a souvenir—fust one in nigh onto twenty year. Chicken feed," he pronounced disdainfully; then with hope: "Strike it rich someday, mebbe."

"What about the monkey?"

"Placer? Oh, he'll stand the cold. Why, he got away from a circus down Iowy way in a snowstorm—had fur like a seal when I caught him."

"All right," decided Munro, "I think you're the man for us. Now as to pay—"

With a gesture of superb disdain Flashpan waived the trifling matter. "Never earnt a dollar in me life, Cap'n," he declared. "Been diggin' fer gold nigh on to forty year. An' I got enough here"—he slapped a clinking bag at his waist—"and in other places," he added mysteriously, "to live comfort'ble. But it's the lookin' I like, sir, not the findin'," he confided. "Never mind the pay, sir. Jest lemme go ashore wherever we be, and try me luck, is all I ask, sir."

Late that night, Henders crossed the gangplank unsteadily and went down the forward hatch. At the galley door he paused to rub clouded eyes and look again! Upon a table, dressed with loving care in miniature pirate's clothes, swaggered a long-tailed monkey in shiny boots. He doffed his tiny black hat, then cursed the intruder roundly. By the stove, eyes gleaming, sat a huge, bristling dog. A moment Henders stood lost in liquorous amazement, then ventured to enter his galley. On the instant its guardian bared his teeth and warned the man back with a growl.

"My own galley," hiccuped the cook, wonderingly, "an' y'wont let me in, eh?" He drew back his booted foot to kick.

"Hull on, thar!" came a commanding voice from behind. Turning, Henders found a pair of quizzical eyes regarding him from the pantry, and saw a strange figure wearing a cook's apron. In the figure's hand was a meat cleaver.

"Who're you?" he demanded thickly.

"I be Flashpan, cook on this wessel. What're you-all doin' in my galley?"

"*Your* galley?" repeated Henders. Slowly he dropped a hand to the cabin-house top, where he had seen a belaying pin—a weapon. His fingers fumbled for it. With a curse he realized it had disappeared almost under his eyes—and glancing up, he saw an active simian fleeing aloft, bearing away the belaying pin.

From aft came the laughter of the crew. The ex-cook in fury brandished a hamlike hand at the vanishing thief and cursed Flashpan obscenely, demanding: "D'y'know who I am?"

Imperturbably the new cook leaned back, then with a sudden show of ferocity jumped forward, flourishing his cleaver. Startled, Henders retreated to the gangplank, teetering as he sought to balance himself. Then he slipped—from the arms of Bacchus into those of Oceanus. The chill sobering waters closed gently above his head.

When he rose into view, "I know ye now," cried Flashpan. "Wipe the seaweed from yer ear! An' when ye've cooled off a bit, Neptune, ye'll find yer truck on yonder dock. And come no more aboard the *Narwhal* or I'll carve ye into Christmas beef!"

So, by cunning, and force wisely expended, Flashpan came into despotic domination of the *Narwhal*'s galley. It was soon apparent that this was all for the best. Upon their hooks the once dirty pans hung glistening like mirrors; fresh paint covered the long-neglected shelves, from which newly washed cups swung to the ship's movement.

Dan, passing the galley, fell back in amazement.

From his pack and from an old leather trunk which Flashpan had brought aboard, a multiplicity of objects had emerged to decorate that culinary stronghold: A brace of pistols hung above the stove, flanked by a bowie knife in a long sheath, and an old Sharps rifle with ornately carved stock. On a nail several bullet-molds hung by strings. A pair of spurs jingled above the door, surmounted by a horseshoe.

However bizarre his ideas of decoration, Flashpan proved his cook's skill at the first meal. Biscuits, brown and feather-light, appeared in magic quantity from his oven. Roast fowl, cooked to a turn, steamed upon the great oaken cabin table, and the cheering aroma of coffee, brewed with masterly touch, arose.

After dinner, in a hoarse but not unpleasant voice, Flashpan demonstrated another side of his character. Accompanying himself upon a battered guitar, produced magically from that all-encompassing trunk, he sang:

> *Oh-h, I been cook on a four-wheeled schooner,*
> *A cook on the lone prairie-e-e,*
> *I've cooked and I've fried, an' dang near died,*
> *In many a far countre-e-e,*
> *But who'd have knowed, that afore it snowed,*
> *I'd be cook on a schooner at sea!*

Some hours later, on the rise of the tide, the *Narwhal* moved from her wharf and soon rode the first long swell of the high seas. Thus in a vessel hardly larger than that in which a Genoese discovered a New World four centuries and more earlier, Munro set sail into the white sanctity of the Arctic, whose grim gods have guarded its secrets from the beginnings of recorded time.

With a last salute to land from her air-whistle and a blast on her patent foghorn the *Narwhal* went forth at sundown upon her Odyssey. Her red and green side-lights burned brightly. Her iron prow clove the waters with a gentle hiss. Her new rope creaked and her sails bellied out full of the wind that snapped the flag being lowered from her truck.

Aft at the wheel Dr. James Munro leaned upon its spokes, a different and younger-looking man than he had been ashore. From somewhere he had produced a fringed buckskin coat, ornamented with colored quillwork, gift of some faraway Indian friend. He made a fine picturesque figure garbed thus.

On the rail near the forward cabin-house, Beth La Salle gazed into the mysterious distance, recollection strong within her. An immense full moon hung as if suspended from the crosstrees like some great brass gong waiting to be struck. Under such a moon she had last seen the man she loved going out into the Arctic night. . . .

A little later when Dan came on deck, and would have spoken, Beth raised a hand for silence. From the bow came the strains of a guitar. In the shadow of the foresail, with his pets worshipfully mute at shoulder and knee, sat Flashpan, beating time with a hobnailed boot while in his hoarse voice he improvised words to a nameless but swinging melody:

Swing ho! Swing ho! We're a-sailin' for treasure,
We'll sink our shafts deep in a far new countree.
Sail on! Sail on! There's go-o-ld without measure,
For men who will dig in the far new countree!

VI

Night and day Kioga drove his men now, for a visible skin of ice covered the river; but at last the thickening ice cut through one of the craft. That marked the end of river travel. Nature, hitherto neutral, was now leagued against them.

With deep regret Kioga saw his canoes drawn upon the bank and hidden in the brush. For all the toil of the portages, the going had been swift where the rivers were deep. Henceforward, it would be even more toilsome, as they continued the northward march on foot. When the march was resumed, none was without a share of the vital load. The order of Indian march was maintained as before, save that now the dogs drew the travois. Thus, for a week, with ice in the rivers and the snow not deep enough for sledge travel, they moved very slowly—and at a time when haste was vital.

But the time was not wasted. About the camp-fires there was great activity. Of branches steamed to shape, and strips of moose-hide, they made long snowshoes. Of driftwood, found near the river, they made sledge-runners. And while Tokala watched with fascinated eyes, the Snow Hawk plaited several strips of moose-hide into a tapered lash some fifteen feet long. In the firelight the resulting whip was a beautiful russet brown and it coiled from Kioga's hand like some sinuous snake.

During that night it snowed heavily, and in the morning the dogs were harnessed. Upon the sledges were laid the belongings of the band, lashed securely against the inevitable upsets. Upon their feet the Indians fixed the ready-made snowshoes.

Then, with a shout and resounding crack of Kioga's whip, they were off, the dog-teams first, hitched in tandem for easy passage through the woods along the river. Before the dogs went two strong young men on snowshoes, taking their turn at breaking trail. Behind the sledges came the remainder of the band, scattered along. Well-provided though they now were in equipment, they must be alert to kill meat. The dogs would eat in two weeks all they could haul, and their back-loads of dried meat were necessarily light.

For Tokala, this journey was pure ecstasy. Into his healing lungs he drank the clean free air of the open hills. Behind him he had already put all thought of the poverty and deadly labor which had scarred his short life. By night no more the close quarters of airless dormitory, but above his head the illimitable vault of heaven, hung with the blazing northern stars. And in the north sky at night the unspeakable beauty of the aurora, warm green, pale yellow, sheerest silver, moved from east to west like a host of invisible warriors, bearing a forest of flashing spears.

Each evening the women put out cunning snares and caught many small furbearers; white foxes, hares, a few mink and weasels. Late one afternoon, poised upon a ridge fifty yards away, a golden-eyed lynx, gray-white and beautiful, watched them pass. From Kioga's ready bow leaped a slim swift shaft which struck the snarling cat through eye and brain. Of the lynx meat they ate at the sunset meal, and found it very good. The richly marked skin was added to that of some white foxes, and a fine outfit made for Tokala.

The sick boy was showing improvement. The puny frame had straightened. A delicate color came and went now in the once pallid face. His endurance had also grown, and whenever duty permitted, he ran beside the mighty Snow Hawk.

And into those eager little ears Kioga told many a tale of his own exciting boyhood!

Tales of a lithe brown-skinned boy, hotly pursued over hill and dale by the gaunt wolves of Ga-Hu-Ti, forty in a pack; of hairbreadth escapes from tiger's claw and snow leopard's fang; of strange adventure on the foaming rivers of mysterious Nato'wa, in the thunder of her mighty cataracts. Tales that are told about the lodge-fires of those distant Indian tribesmen, of coastal Nato'wa.

He told Tokala of how Mokuyi had given him a bear-cub, Aki; and of how Aki had led him among the bears, with whom he spent years of his early life, returning to the village possessed of a woodcraft surpassing the cunning of the subtlest hunter. He told of how Yanu, the fierce old she-bear, had spilled her lifeblood defending him against his wild enemies; of Aki, faithful guardian of his childhood, upon whose shaggy belly oft his head was pillowed. Of Mika the silver-coated, a white-toothed puma raised from cubhood, with whom he had hunted in concert, so that no beast in all the wilderness was safe from their onset; and of many another fierce pet that shared his friendship in those days.

And at sunset of the day he had killed the lynx, he tossed a surprise into Tokala's lap, a half-grown lynx kitten, one of a litter he had discovered hidden away somewhere. Indeed, life had become very good for Tokala the Fox!

Each day, now, the party drew closer to its first objective, the Arctic Ocean. And Tokala—who could know little of the terrific difficulties and dangers of the journey over ice and stormy waters yet before them—dreamed eagerly of this promised land of Nato'wa which Kioga so vividly described. . . .

And now gaunt famine dogged their trail; for the game which had sustained them disappeared. Only whitefish, caught on the bone hooks through a hole in the ice, sustained them. Came a day when even this source of supply failed.

They ate bark and tender twigs. From the rocks they took an occasional bit of *tripe de roche*, the wild plant which has sustained many a starving party in the North. A dwarf variety of Labrador tea was found also, from which they brewed a spirit-lifting draft. But it was not enough.

Great age, combined with near-starvation, struck down old Bull Calf in his ninety-third year. Sits-in-Sun found him dead, wrapped in his blanket, facing the southeast. Just as the sun rose, her cracked and quavering voice rose in the mourning-cry. All day the aged crone wept, bewailing her dead; nor at nightfall would she be comforted.

"Threescore and ten summers have I been his sits-beside-him woman. He loved to dress my hair. All those early years I rode at his side, bearing his shield. Together we lived the old life and saw the buffalo pass. We shared the poverty given us by white men. We learned of Nato'wa, land of the Indian. But—*ai-i-i,* too late! Bull Calf has gone away. I will walk no more, but sit beside him as before, so that if a time comes that he wakes, he will find me there."

"Mother," protested Kioga, "we do not wish you to die."

"My son," she answered solemnly, "I am Sits-in-Sun. I have spoken."

The Snow Hawk said no more, but aided by several of the band he erected a tall scaffold of new-cut limbs. Upon this, after singing and eulogizing, they laid the remains of Bull Calf, swathed in blanket and with face painted. Beside him they placed his pipe, his knife, the quiver and bow with which he had hunted in his youth. And upon his burial scaffold they hung his cherished shield.

Unnoticed by old Sits-in-Sun, Kioga laid a bone needle, a skinning-knife, and a few personal things at her side, along with a piece of dried meat. These were to accompany her on a journey, longer than this march had been, for he knew she would never rise again.

The band then quietly withdrew, leaving Sits-in-Sun chanting the old death songs of her tribe. As they turned a bend in the river and looked back, she still knelt immobile. A fold of the dead chief's blanket flapped in the sad wind. Sits-in-Sun did not move. The shield swung gently, flashing in the sunlight.

The following days diminished the weakening party by several of its number. Crow Man, sixty-nine, passed to his ancestors, and Three Scalps, who could not bear to see him go alone, followed a little later. She-Is-Swift gave up the ghost one night at dusk....

Faced with the task of providing meat for all these famished mouths in a land named for its scarcity, Kioga's eye often fell upon the dogs. But if he slew them, he knew, they must leave behind much that was valuable. So long as strength held out, he determined to avoid loss of a single dog.

One night camp was pitched in a copse of dwarfed trees. Scooping away the snow with snowshoes, the men cleared a circle and helped the women raise a wigwam of branches chinked with snow.

Speech came seldom, and gloomily then. Those who could, sat erect, warming themselves at their tiny fire—a precious core of heat, since it constituted all they had been able to find of dry wood. The Barren Ground is well named.

They looked at one another, at the discernible sag of the cheeks, the emaciation which drew the transparent skin tight from cheekbone to cheekbone. Their skulls seemed barely covered. Their hair hung down like black snakes, and they appeared so wild and terrible, that they no longer looked at one another.

The dogs, as if possessed of second sight, evaded the men, huddled together outside the tent in a hollow and moved wraith like about, howling, fixing the camp with their gleaming eyes. They too were waiting the end. They too were hungry.

Then to Kioga came Wounded Knee, who gazed long into the fire, ere speaking in these words:

"My eyes are dim, Kioga. But I see straight. And this is what I see: We old folk hold you back." Kioga made as if to interrupt, but the old man checked him with hand upheld. "Hear me, my son. We have talked, we old ones. We have counseled together. And this we say: Leave us behind. Go on alone, else our children will never see this land of Nato'wa. We wish our children to live, that they may reach this land of happy hunting."

Snow Hawk thought a time in silence before answering.

"Elder brothers, hear my words: We younger ones have good ears. But we cannot hear what you have just said. We hunger. But we are men—and men of our people know how to starve. If we find no meat tomorrow, we will find it the next day. I say again, we have good ears; but we cannot hear the words you have just spoken."

Kioga turned to the younger men, as if to seek confirmation for those for whom he spoke. A deep "*Hau! Hau!*" answered him.

Wounded Knee said no more, but returned to the circle of councillors, who numbered four, the last of the very old people.

A little later Kioga drew his blanket about his eyes to seek an hour's sleep. With a start he awoke, and it seemed that he had slept but a moment. He glanced over toward where the old councillors had sat, then came erect. He saw they were not lying with feet to the blaze as customarily.

The four chiefs were missing. Rising, he went to the entrance of the lodge, which flapped, and pushed aside the skin.

White glittering granules of snow sifted in, and his breath was like steam in the bitter cold. Outside, all was black, the snow hissing down venomously.

He felt something fluttering against his face, and reached forward to seize an upright stick. Taking it inside, he found it to be the feathered *coup*-stick of Wounded Knee.

Waking his hunters, Kioga told them: "The councillors have gone out alone." Then he rushed out, ten braves at his heels. The snow stung like shot, blinding them. There was no way to follow a trail. So said the braves, but Kioga did not hear. He was already far out on the unseen trail; for to his ears had come a sound, faint but familiar, which he followed.

It was a death-song, rising monotonously on the whistling wind, and fading. A little way he went, then checked. The chant came from an opposite direction, toward which he turned—only to hear it from a third point. Then from yet fourth came that deep chanting, fainter now, bewildering, coming from every direction.

Kioga paused, shouted the names of the councillors. The driven snow stung his palate. He called no more, for now he understood. Turning back, he sought a scent of smoke, found it, and on its thread returned to the camp. Inside lay the hunters, hardly able to move after their few exertions. And from without came only the moan of wind, the slash of snow. If the Snow Hawk went out again, and were lost—all these within the lodge were as dead, for none but he could now move about. And so he sat gazing at the door through which the four old men had passed. . . .

The storm abated. Morning dawned clear, brilliant, sharply cold. A little rested, the braves accompanied Kioga slowly out. They found the old councillors—at widely separated points, frozen stiff and buried in snow. They found them easily, by the markers over their icy graves. Above each man—except Wounded Knee—fluttering bright red and yellow and blue in the reddish morning sunrise, was an upright *coup*-stick. Wounded Knee was never found. He had left his *coup*-stick before the lodge where Kioga found it the previous night.

Wise councillors, cunning councillors! Knowing they would be followed, they had separated, singing their death-chants as they went, the better to discourage pursuit. Weary at last, one by one and alone, they had dug deep their *coup*-sticks and squatted down, never to rise. They had sacrificed themselves for their people, that these might carry on unhampered. Wounded Knee, Bets-His-Shirt, Chases-the-Cow, Iron Horse:

four brave, old great-hearted men, tottering into Eternity in the best tradition of their race!

All that day in the hunger-lodge the pleading drum of Moon's Son, young medicine man and self-appointed visionary of the band, beat with growing weakness. Stupor had claimed some of the lodge's occupants. The teeth of Tokala chattered with cold and weakness. The shadow of death lay across that lone lodge of starvation, waiting to creep in when the diminished firewood should at last be exhausted.

And that afternoon as if in answer to the singing of Moon's Son, and across the graves of those who had died that food might go farther, appeared the vanguard of the migrating caribou herds. First a small band, loping slowly along, then scattered groups, later small herds, then larger, until at last as far as the eye could reach they came, the clattering of their antlers creating a roar that could be heard for miles.

With the coming of caribou the cruel gods of the North must have smiled, for of all who heard the animals pass only Kioga had strength even to come forth and look at them, then throw wide the lodge-flap that others might see and perchance take strength from the sight. And it was a cruel game starvation played with those who watched the Snow Hawk.

With dragging feet he pursued the active animals, saw them coming on every side, smelled the mellow scent of their endless numbers, and heard the clack of antler and hoof on the hard snow. Never hitherto had he taken account of his strength. Always, like the flow of a mighty cataract, it had been there, in boundless tide when needed. No man had ever successfully challenged it; and no beast in far Nato'wa was his equal, when to strength he added his cunning.

But now Kioga knew his weakness. He who once could have run a caribou down in fair chase now crept upon the herds in vain. Those who watched lost heart.

Kioga had fallen, and now lay quiet.

Then of a sudden Tokala shouted weakly. Moon's Son's drum picked up its faltering beat, which rose to a swift tatoo, at what the medicine man saw.

Forth from the Snow Hawk's prone position went his bony hand. A caribou bull, wounded in battle with a fellow bull, had stood bleeding on this spot. Kioga was crushing the frozen nourishment in his teeth. Little by little some of his strength returned. At length he slowly took up his bow and nocked an arrow. He drew the cord. He held his point upon the nearest bull. The string twanged, loud and vibrant. The bull leaped high, breaking its neck in its fall, and lay dead, pierced through the heart.

Again and again the bended bow, the musical note of plucked cord, the jar of the recoiling arc, as the feathered reeds whipped forth, dropping each a running caribou until the hunter's quiver lay empty at his hand. But twenty fat animals lay dead in the snow.

Soon the lodge was filled with the aroma of simmering roast ribs and tender brisket; plump tongues were hung to smoke; heads were roasted whole and the fatty nose-gristle eaten first.

It was a great feast. The bones were full of rich marrow, and there was so much meat that already the dogs were gorged to repletion, and struggling to devour yet more. When they felt able, the hunters went forth now and shot down caribou as long as their arrows held out, then pulled them free of the dead animals and shot again.

So from starvation to luxurious living Kioga's band went in one day.

And over the old councillors the feathers fluttered. . . .

Now the sun rose above the southern horizon upon a happy camp. The brown caribou-skin lodges hugged the snow under blue plumes of smoke that rose vertically and feathered away southward. The dogs tussled and wrestled and lolled about, tongues hanging contentedly.

Treachery, self-sacrifice, famine and surfeit and death had visited the camp many times. But returning to the tents next night, Kioga heard a thin wail. Entering, he learned that Grass Girl, wife of the delighted young Moon's Son, had gone out to bring in meat and been absent overlong. Uneasiness gripped the women until she was seen returning slowly with a back-load of meat, steadied with one hand, while in the other she tenderly bore her first born—a healthy, screaming boy-child. With the easy *accouchement* of the native mother, she had been delivered of her child beside a caribou carcass. Life was balancing the scale.

The little newcomer was given its secret name. What that name was I cannot tell, for the baby-name is never spoken, lest evil spirits annoy the child. But to the warriors Grass Girl's son was thenceforward known as Plenty Meat.

VII

The caribou horde had come and passed south. But the sledges were loaded with dried meat, and the dogs so glutted they scarce could walk. Preparations were being made for a quick departure with early morning. In his tent Kioga was whetting his arrows sharp and affixing a wrist-strap to the whip when a sudden violent clamor from the dogs sent him bounding forth, whip in hand, pausing not even to don his caribou-skin coat.

The melee raged fiercely a hundred feet from the tents, in full view under the silver flood of the moon's light. The unlucky dogs contended with foes more dread than one another. Two white wolves, doubtless having scented fresh meat, fought silently among them. Gaunt from long running, trained to leather hardness by their pursuit of the vanished caribou, their onset was in marked contrast to the resistance by the sluggish dogs, gorged with meat and further hampered by the dangling traces.

One of the dogs already lay twitching, mangled and torn, and as the Snow Hawk bore down upon them, the male wolf of the pair, with three snaps, ripped open another dog in an instant.

Rushing from their tents, the Indians now learned the true function of that long lash which the Snow Hawk carried. It was as much a weapon as a bow. Even as they watched, forth sang the unerring plaited thong, quick as a cobra's strike, and as deadly almost, to draw blood and leave a deep gash wherever it touched a wolf. The dogs, with courage renewed by the presence of an ally, attacked more boldly, and to better effect. The wolves, their fighting edge dulled by the scourging of the lash, suddenly turned tail and were away, dogs in pursuit. But the heavy dogs were no match for the speed of their wild brothers, and soon returned to camp, to lie about licking their wounds, of which one died during the night.

The party proceeded next morning at somewhat reduced pace, owing to the loss of two dogs. Well on their way, one of the wolves was found dead, frozen stiff on the plain. The body was cut up, thawed out, and fed to the dogs.

It was only a few miles to the Arctic Ocean now. Fed and clothed, the band moved steadily on, several of the men aiding the teams, especially that which drew the sledge heavily loaded with *dépouille*—the pure backfat of the caribou.

They came, that night, to an abandoned Eskimo camp, where they slept, and on the morrow changed their course, running on smooth shore ice now. Hitherto they had run the dogs in tandem, but now they changed to the fan formation, and with the dogs thus hitched abreast made better time. Several days found them in the area near which Kioga had first encountered the scientist Dr. James Munro after his abandonment on the ice.

The Snow Hawk was mindful now of how his hazardous journey to the mainland had been interrupted a year earlier when a white bear, marauding by nature, and hungry besides, had destroyed his camp. Accordingly he cautioned his hunters concerning the risks attendant on ice-travel, with emphasis on the huge white wanderers which have clawed and despoiled their way into the diaries of every Northern expedition. From this time on an alternate sentry guarded the camp at all hours.

The sentry it was who entered the snow-house that night with word that a sledging party had halted a mile distant, whether with hostile or friendly intent he could not determine. Seated before the oil-lamps with Tokala, Kioga drew on his furs and emerged—to see a band of Eskimo at some distance, pointing to the camp and evidently at disagreement among themselves on some point.

Gesturing, Kioga observed that his greeting was returned by one of the strangers, who pointedly threw aside his weapons and, holding aloft both hands, advanced halfway toward the camp. Acting in like manner, Kioga came to within a hundred paces of the man in the semidarkness. The Eskimo shouted something in an unknown tongue. Having no other alternative, Kioga called back a greeting in English. Little expecting to hear an intelligible answer, he started when English syllables, far from perfect but plain enough, fell from the lips of the Eskimo.

"We Eskimo. Kamotok, me. Look for seal; no find him yet."

At utterance of that name of the Snow Hawk strained his eyes across the ice, then hurried forward. The Eskimo, suspecting treachery, turned to move away, when the Snow Hawk checked him with a question.

"Where is Lualuk, of the one hand, Kamotok?"

In surprise, the Eskimo wheeled.

"Who are you who know Lualuk?"

"I am Kioga, friend of Dok-Ta-Mun," answered the Snow Hawk, using the name by which Dr. Munro had been known to his Eskimo dog-drivers.

Kamotok's subsequent actions, under constant watchful observation by the curious members of Kioga's band, startled the Indians. He shouted aloud in his excitement, threw back a few words to his friends at the sledge; they instantly hurried yelling across the ice in the wake of their leader, who was rushing upon Kioga.

The Indians snatched up their weapons and ran to meet the Eskimo, ready to meet force with force. But when they arrived on the scene, to their amazement, they found Kioga the center of an enthusiastic mob. Kamotok was pumping his hand and plying him with a hundred eager questions, with the Snow Hawk laughing at their enthusiasm and answering as fast as he was able, while one-handed Lualuk anxiously awaited an opportunity to speak.

Having made his Indians known to Kamotok's people, and allayed somewhat the Eskimo distrust of Indians—their hereditary foes—Kioga next invited the Eskimo to their lodges, where all partook heartily of the prized backfat of the caribou.

Influenced by this good cheer and the friendship of their leaders, round-faced Eskimos and lean-jawed red men were soon at ease in each other's strange society. From Kamotok—whose long assistance to the American scientist had given him his working knowledge of English—the Indians learned why Kioga was so highly esteemed in this remote corner at the top of the earth. Lualuk held forth the stump of his hand and jabbered something at Kamotok, who turned to the migrant band.

"He say, tell you Kioga kill Club-foot."

"Who was Club-foot?" piped up Tokala the Fox, who had drunk all this in, in silence. The Eskimo grinned down at the boy. "White bear, ver-ry big. Bite off Lualuk's hand. Kioga kill with knife. See!" He showed the boy a strip of bear-skin sewn into his right glove. "I take this from that big Club-foot. I am lucky all time—kill plenty seal now. Nanuk—him ver-ry strong. Not so strong as Kioga!"

Thus, from the lips of an Eskimo, the band learned a little

more of the strange career of their friend and leader the Snow Hawk.

Thereafter Kioga talked long and earnestly with Kamotok, of ice conditions north and west, and of the possibilities for seal- and walrus-hunting. He learned much; but of the area which most concerned him Kamotok could tell him nothing, for there were lines beyond which the Eskimo never went, and of any large land north of the Siberian coast the man was completely ignorant.

But the information Kioga received concerning the Eskimo method of hide boat-making was invaluable, and the gifts from the generous Eskimo band almost as much so. Among these were a few lamps for burning seal-oil, to light and warm their igloos on the way; two ice-axes; several fine sealing-harpoons, one with a steel head; and several lengths of seal-hide rope. Out of his great good will Kamotok would have included his prized rifle, but this the Snow Hawk would not accept. Thus far their primitive weapons had kept them in meat. Deprived of his gun Kamotok might perish, and many of his people with him.

In return for these gifts Kioga emptied his pockets of their coins, a small initialed penknife, a gold watch, and sundry other little articles. These he deposited before the glistening eyes of Kamotok.

"For you and your people, in return," he said. "And now, we have one other end. For five good strong dogs, we will give as much caribou fat as your men here can bear away on their backs."

Kamotok turned to one of his hunters, and spoke a few words. The man's face was wreathed in a great smile as he agreed eagerly. Turning back to Kioga, Kamotok said simply: "It is done."

Both sides were well pleased with the arrangement. With fresh dogs, the Indian band could make up for those lost. The Eskimo, to whom nothing is so necessary as animal fat, were delighted.

The following morning the Eskimo saw the departure of Snow Hawk and his strange band, and looked with wonder after him who spoke of a land of which they knew nothing.

Once again possessed of fast strong dogs and well-equipped for their forthcoming battle with the ice, Kioga and his party drove their animals onward. They spent the night in comfort beside their seal-oil lamps in the shelter of a snow-hut lined with caribou-skin, and built like the Eskimo dwellings they had left.

Only by adopting the ways of people who made the ice their home could they hope to survive where so many others better equipped and prepared, had perished. Accordingly their dress was now adapted to conditions on the ice. All but the most necessary sledging equipment was discarded, until in the end they retained but the Eskimo minimum: meat, fur bags to sleep in, and the weapons and clothing on their backs.

Within their well-made igloo of snow-blocks, men and women and dogs alike slept together to take advantage of the common warmth. Again they were entirely dependent on their hunting weapons for meat, for of provisions, they would carry at most but two weeks' supply. Where the ice was broken up by wind or pressure they took an occasional seal with the harpoon. Kioga taught the Indians how to be constantly alert for seal-holes in solid ice—those under-ice chambers, gnawed from below, through which the seal breathes. Thus they had an occasional if precarious source of fresh meat. Nothing was wasted, nothing thrown away. The seal-skins became part of their garments. The bones were ground with blood and made into thick, nourishing soup; the least palatable parts were fed to the dogs. And the seal-oil kept their lamps alight. Thus they existed on the frozen desert, beneath which in frigid water lie the bones of many whose expeditions were far better found than this wild nomads' camp.

One morning the band had harnessed the dogs, preparing to hitch them to the sledges, when with an excited clamor the animals suddenly took off at a furious pace. Struggling vainly to hold them back, Tokala was dragged along behind, sprawled on his little fur-clad belly and gripping the trace, twisted round his wrists.

Almost as soon as the dogs, the trained nostrils of the Snow Hawk drank in the scent.

"Bear!" he cried over one shoulder as he picked up an ice-ax from the sledge and bounded after the dogs. "Bring harpoons and bows!"

Hard on the heels of the huskies pressed the Snow Hawk, overhauling them at last amid a jagged mass of rough ice, at the center of which, in a depression surrounded by gleaming pinnacles, stood an ice-bear of the breed known as Nanuk, the tiger of the Arctic.

Its short heavy ears were screwed back. Saliva dripped from the yellow bared incisors and froze instantly like spun glass. The close-set little eyes blazed diabolically in the triangular head, which almost touched the ice, effectively covering the long cream-yellow throat. Beneath the long high quarters the bulging muscles rolled as Nanuk swayed upon the rigid pillars of his broad and shaggy limbs.

Before him, with eviscerated belly yawning to the sky, lay the dog who had ventured too boldly; and straining away with terrified yelps were two others, still in the traces which bound them to their unlucky fellow, from whose carcass the bear's immense red-stained paw pressed the dark blood.

His gaze already darting about seeking Tokala, Kioga had advanced to where the dogs ringed the bear at a respectful distance. And then the Snow Hawk, to whom fear was unknown, felt his blood run cold.

Prone before the bear, within range of the curving claws of that massive hairy forepaw, lay Tokala the Fox.

For an instant Kioga thought him dead, then realized that the boy's eyes, wide and staring, were fixed in dread fascination upon the bear. He called a quick low warning: "Tokala—lie still and as if dead. Do not answer me. But when the arrow strikes in and the bear turns—jump and run!"

An iron-headed shaft already strained against Kioga's cord. Came a twang as the bow hurled its bolt. The bear grunted a muffled roar and snapped back at the wooden agony skewering his loin. Another arrow sank into its side, and at point-blank range Kioga pumped yet two more deep into the feathers.

Tokala had now risen on hands and knees. For the first time Kioga realized why he could not jump and run as instructed. His foot was caught and twisted up in the dead dog's trace. As the bear wheeled in a circle, snapping and tearing at the arrows, the boy's movement caught his eye. Pausing only to smash an attacking dog into a pulp, the bear rushed upon Tokala.

Simultaneously Kioga resorted to the sole remaining means of saving Tokala—his long sharp knife. In two bounds from behind he was fastened to the bear's shaggy shoulders. The plunge, plunge, of his dripping blade checked the beast in mid-charge, just as the first of the Indians topped the nearest ice pinnacle.

Shaking itself within its loose thick skin, the dying animal reared and fell back, seeking to crush its assailant. But as it fell, Kioga writhed from under and laid hold of the forgotten ice-ax. One mighty chop upon the skull, quick as the fall of a meteorite, and the bear sank down, prey to the frenzied worrying of the dogs already swarming over the lifeless foe.

Shouting and gesticulating, the Indians scrambled excitedly

down into the little amphitheater of ice and surrounded the Snow Hawk, who knelt beside Tokala, feeling the boy's ankle.

As soon as the women came up, the clicking knives were busy again, separating the bear from its heavy skin. One of the warriors plunged deep his knife, and reaching in, drew forth the bear's heart, of which he ate a small piece and handed it around among the others. Thus, by the logic of the Indian hunter, they partook of the animal's courage. The long claws were cut off and later strung on rawhide, which in turn was sewn upon Kioga's parka.

Again the dogs were well fed, this time upon bear-haunch; while the Indians regaled themselves upon the thick bear-liver cooked in a seal-oil flame.

The Snow Hawk, as he ate, thought back a few short months to a time when he had walked in the busy marts of civilization. And he who had eaten ten-course dinners, drunk from priceless crystal, and wiped his lips on snowy napery, now bit off another piece of bear-liver; and when he had finished, he licked his fingers and quenched his thirst with melted Arctic ice. He had but one regret concerning the material things he had put behind: and that was for the tingling shower of a modern bathroom. Neither he nor his companions had bathed for many weeks.

Level ice, once attained, offered no obstacles to the rapid passage of the Indian band, now hardened by exposure and strengthened by an abundance of meat. When an occasional fissure yawned before them, they unhitched the dogs and made them leap across, or in the case of those which balked, threw them over bodily, whereafter the sledges were hauled across. But hummocky ice gave them exhausting work smashing a way through with their ice-axes. Men as well as dogs here strained against the sledge-traces; and where the ice towered about them on every side, shutting them in, they traveled by dead reckoning or by watching the stars.

Even worse peril than ice itself was its lack. One night clouds shut out the stars and a milder wind blew, softening the surface. Where the sledges had slipped along easily before, they now sank deep and the dogs likewise floundered up to their bellies in soft slush. Some of the meat was transferred to back-packs but much more had to be abandoned. During that night, while taking a rest enforced by sheer weariness, the dogs became restless and whined uneasily, awakening Kioga.

He was soon conscious of movement of the ice underfoot, and of an occasional ominous crunching which passed nearby and moved into the distance. Wind and unseasonable warmth were combining to break up the ice on which they moved—the field on which they had slept was in perceptible motion, and it was no time for sleep.

"Throw the meat from the sledges," was the first order Kioga gave. "We come soon to open water, where there will be meat in plenty." In view of the unexpected breakup of the ice, he knew now that they were not many miles from the warm currents which temper the climate of Nato'wa.

With the sledges lightened, they pushed on anew. Everywhere fissures now appeared, with open water between. Where these were very wide, they moved along the edge until they found a cake or pan of ice sufficiently large to bear their weight—then ferried across the watery lanes. It was unmitigated toil now, but none complained.

At the edge of an open lane, Kioga finally called a halt to allow the stragglers to come up. And now the wind changed again, frost set in, and two inches of ice—enough to lock in the floating pans, but not enough for safe sledge-travel—formed on the surface. Their situation was critical. The wind was bitterly cold. There was nothing left of which to make a fire. They hungered terribly from the toil of this endless march; and the meat was all gone.

But in the North those who turn back are almost always lost. Push on they must, trusting to Kioga's judgment that they must soon come to the open water—and seals. Kioga ordered the dogs harnessed again and turned to his drivers.

"You, Buffalo Child, drive three hundred paces to the south. You, Crow Man, as many toward the north. I, with my team, will take the middle course. The women and aged will go first, scattered, that we may see them safe." Turning to these: "Most swiftly and do not once stop. If mishap befall one, let all the others continue on their way. For if one fall through the ice, surely two would break it in the more easily. If it be the will of the Great Ones, we shall pass; if not—Give me your hands, each one. We have come far together."

Quietly all shook hands. Then, one by one, well separated, the women and the old man moved fanwise out across the thin field. When they were well past halfway over, the teams drew apart, and to the crack of the whips and the shouts of the drivers the sledges started cautiously over the ice. Thus, for perhaps half the distance to solid footing—when of a sudden the dreaded cry echoed from mouth to mouth:

"Run! *Run!* The ice breaks up!"

Obedient to orders, those in the front hurried on as fast as their limbs would carry them. Old Four Braids, unsteady at best, went through to the knees, but dragged himself flat along the ice, rose and continued on. Under the sledges the thin ice was quaking and sagging. Wild with fear, the dogs galloped with the lashes hissing over their heads, and the "*Hai! Hai!—Hai! Hai!*" of the drivers beating into their ears. On Crow Man's team one dog slipped and was dragged a hundred yards before he could attain his feet. Buffalo Child, feeling the ice going beneath him, ran safely away to one side, decreasing the weight in the area of his sledge, which slid swiftly on, passing into a zone of comparative safety.

Kioga alone, with his lesser team of but four dogs, where the others numbered five, seemed in difficulty. To the Indians who could pause and watch, the flat sameness of the ice appeared to be sinking in a long concavity where the weight of the sledge, man, and the dogs bore upon the thin skin blanketing the sea. They could hear the pistol-shot reports of his moose-hide lash, and his low appeals to the dogs, straining every sinew to obey. They saw him, without pausing, dash piece after piece of its load from the sledge, until it was quite empty save for Tokala, who rode white-faced, clutching his lynx kitten to his breast.

With horror they saw disaster creeping upon the fast-moving sledge. Just behind the Snow Hawk in the wake of the sledge the ice was cracking in his footsteps. Once he went in with one leg, but seizing the sledge drew himself along behind it so that his pounding feet might not strain the ice again. Then behind the sledge itself, like a scratch which follows the diamond drawn across glass, there appeared a continuous break in the ice.

Kioga bent, grasped Tokala by the wrist, swung him back, and with a mighty toss flung him skimming along the ice, still clutching his lynx kitten, into the arms of waiting Indians.

But under the pressure of his exertion the sledge grated harshly and went under astern. Checked, the dogs piled up, fell in a tangle. Seawater welled up from every break in the sagging skin-ice. Kioga slashed at the traces with his sharp knife to separate dogs from sledge. And then, with a great splash, it happened.

The sledge sank like a stone, dragging man and entangled struggling dogs into the hole which had claimed it. The yapping of the animals was quenched in seawater. Silence reigned over the tragedy spot. Only the squeaking of the small ice about the hole marked the sinking of man and team.

Came the wail of a heartbroken boy, shrill and distinct on the frosty air, as Tokala the Fox shouted again and again the name of Kioga, his idol.

A moment suspense and the realization of dread tragedy held every soul in thrall. Then of a sudden Tokala glimpsed what the rest overlooked, and his shout of discovery broke the spell.

Ranging across the ice was a limp wet length of leathern whip-thong, one end lapped twice about an icy pinnacle where it was swiftly freezing. Even as they watched, the lash snapped taut. Out of the steely sea appeared a wet and soggy mitten, followed by the streaming face and head of the Snow Hawk.

In an instant the Indians had grasped the lash and were straining to draw him upon solid ice. This was no simple feat, for he had hold of the dogs' trace. But many hands accomplished the seemingly impossible. When Kioga attained his feet, he in turn dragged three half-drowned, coughing dogs to safety.

The sledge, however, had gone to the bottom and taken one dog with it. Thereafter it was not an easy task to dry out Kioga's sea-soaked clothing in the heat of their tiny oil-flame; but after a delay of several hours it was done. Preparing to start anew, the Snow Hawk was attracted by the howling of the dogs he had saved. They had dropped to their bellies to rest and were frozen to the ice beyond all possibility of self-liberation. Ensued another delay while the band chopped them carefully free, tended and bound up their sore feet and removed some of the ice from their coats. Finally they were moving again. . . .

Ahead was sound solid ice, across which they presently marched, well lighted on their way. The Dance of the Spirits—the aurora—was throwing its flickering witchery over the floes, tinging cold ice with hues of warm copper and greenish-blue. In the southeast the slow dawn was heralded by a deep red glare; and with the passing of hours the sun slowly rose, like a spinning metal disk emerging from intolerable flame. With its rise the ice became a wonder-world ablaze with varicolored fires, the frosty floes gleaming like sheets of gold, resplendent with a gem-work of blazing rubies, amethysts, and emeralds. Before the spectacle the band fell silent.

But the glory soon passed, curtained in full glory by ever more frequent waves of mist, dark, leaden-hued, thick almost as smoke from a prairie fire. Through this the band moved with all caution for several days until they came again to open water. Here they camped to take inventory of their resources.

Though they had three bows, an ice-ax, one harpoon, and a length of line between them, all else including arrows, tomahawks, and most of the meat had been thrown aside in their flight across young ice. Their little meat was soon gone; to return was impossible. The only alternative was to seek a pan of ice large enough to bear their combined weight and chance all on ferrying across the watery lead. Upon this plan, as set forth by Kioga, the band agreed unanimously.

Soon the mists rose a little, permitting them a glimpse of the sea. At what he saw, Kioga's heart gave a mighty leap.

Seals sported in the ground swell nearby. From afar came the reverberant roaring of a sea lion herd swimming rapidly northward. A hundred yards away a whale showed its fluke, sank, leaped suddenly clear of the sea and fell back resoundingly, creating a wave that washed up on their floe. By these evidences the Snow Hawk confirmed his earlier conclusion that they were on the edge of that great warm Arctic current which, so far as is now known, surrounds the land of Nato'wa. Far across it, below the horizon he knew, were the barrier reefs which gird that impregnable land with a labyrinth of rocky treachery.

To a modern naturalist, the very presence of sea lions would have seemed anomalous, thus far north of their ancient harems on the Pribilof Islands. But an all-wise, all-provident Creator alone may set the hour of a species' extinction. Nature decreed that the sea lion, and his fellow-unfortunate, the almost vanished sea otter, should forsake their oldage southward migration to find haven from Man the Destroyer, and a breeding place in the warm currents about Nato'wa.

Morning came after a night of rest, and they were preparing to carry out their plan to ferry across the open water, when Tokala the Fox ran into camp with startling tidings.

"We are already drifting," he panted. "The main ice is far back!"

It was true. Their floe had become detached from the solid field, barely visible in the distance southeast. Their course therefore was north and west with which they found no fault. That night, however, their floe divided itself, like some gigantic amoeba, into several lesser floes; and shortly thereafter a dangerous situation disclosed itself to the band. It was Grass Girl, the mother of Plenty Meat, who voiced it thus:

"The ice is cold. The water is warmer. Our camp is melting out from under us. Beat your medicine-drum, oh my husband, that the ears of the Great Ones may know we pray to them. For if we come not soon to land, we will leave our bones in the ocean."

Moon's Son obeyed, thumping his medicine-drum all night, and in the morning its sound was still to be heard across the steel-blue waters. Kioga heard it as he surveyed the newest inroads of the sea upon their floe. About its edges spongy ice fell away at a thrust of his harpoon, and at central points the floe was badly honeycombed. They dwelt today upon a little world of ice which was disintegrating under them.

Perhaps the Great Ones above did hear; or perhaps a pack of three great killer whales was to blame for a small herd of sea lions taking temporary refuge on the far end of the floe. Kioga stole upon these, their barking and roaring a thrilling medley in his ears.

Within throwing distance he rose. Swiftly he hurled the harpoon with deadly force, straight through the nearest bull's heart. Five cows struck the waters simultaneously and escaped. But a young bull, startled by its companion's downfall, bolted back from the bleeding animal, and by a stroke of good fortune Kioga was enabled to cut it off, pounce upon and dispatch it cleanly and quickly with a few knife-thrusts.

A shout to the band brought everyone running. The kills were dragged to camp and the skins separated from the meat. With the thick flipper-skin the women renewed the worn boot-soles of the band, sewing it on with sea-lion sinews. The heavy slabs of fat replenished their supply of fuel-oil for the lamps; and the hungry dogs fought over great chunks of meat tossed to them from the ample supply now available.

But with the ice-ax Kioga was breaking up the sledges carefully and measuring the skins with his eye.

VIII

All day the Snow Hawk worked with ax and knife, cunningly joining together pieces of sledge-wood, bound with seal-skin strips and shaped into ribs for a canoe. These he affixed to a longer keel-piece and before the eyes of the Indians a kayak took form. Over the frame he drew the raw sea-lion skins, pulling them taut as a drumhead about the curved ribbing.

Meanwhile the women worked upon the intestines of the sea lions, slitting, flattening, and suppling them. Of these strips sewn together he fashioned a crude decking for the makeshift kayak. With more care a finer craft would have resulted. But haste was vital, a fact pointedly indicated by the constant breaking away of sections from their floe. Kioga knew, of course, that all could not seek safety in this little craft. If it served him in driving sea-animals within reach of the band's weapons, it would have done all he expected of it.

Having completed his work he made a brief tour of the little island of ice which was their home. Convinced that it would hang together for several days more, he then lay down for a few hours of well-earned rest, and refreshed, rose at dawn with the others, prepared for an arduous day, filled with excitement and peril.

The kayak, which he had left afloat the night before, having leaked not one drop, presented an interior dry as a chip. A paddle was made of sledge-wood. Upon the covered deck he laid the harpoon and turned to his Indians. They awaited his words at the edge of the floe, the only ice visible now on all the flat expanse of sea.

"Hear me, warriors," said the Snow Hawk. "Yonder a band of Awuk's people swim. If we had time to wait, they would soon come to lie upon our ice. But there is not time. I go, then, to invite them here. See that you make them welcome with your sharp spears. Awuk and his folk are stupid. Avoid the cows if with young. Creep slow and silent among the great bulls farthest from the water. Kill swiftly with well-aimed strokes, that many may die before the rest become alarmed. Keep the dogs hidden and away.... I go."

With that the Snow Hawk embarked in his kayak, moving quietly away from the floe. An hour passed. He circled far out around the little walrus herd, then slowly came upon them, gently thumping his hollow canoe with the flat of the paddle. The herd, cautious but not alarmed, moved away toward the floe. Thus by imperceptible degrees the strategy was wrought, the walrus moving a little, Kioga pursuing leisurely. At last that which he had anticipated transpired. One at a time or two by two the walrus flung themselves on the floe, where the Indian hunters lay in wait.

It proved to be not a hunt but rather a slaughter. Wind

and sun favored the Indians. The breeze blew from the walrus and they blinked their none too keen eyes in the rising sunlight. With lances improvised from sledge-wood to which their knives were quivered in the death-struggle before the rest took warning. Then such a bellowing as seldom rives the silence of those waters echoed across to Kioga's ears. Several more of the gigantic visitors fell, lanced to the heart.

Kioga meanwhile approached with extreme slowness, having taken in tow the first evidence of land, a small tree of many branches, which he recognized as one of a variety which grows on the coasts of Nato'wa. He brought it along not only to encourage the band, but also for its tough resilent boughs, which would be sore needed in the construction of a craft large enough to bear all to safety.

Within hearing of the Indians on the ice, he was suddenly aware that their shouts contained not the jubilation of successful hunters, but frantic notes of warning. The voice of Tokala rose shrilly above the others.

"Behind you! Look back!"

A swift rearward glance revealed to Kioga the cause of their alarm—a school of four orcas, the dread killer whales believed by Eskimo to be the reincarnation of land-wolves. A moment the Snow Hawk watched narrowly as they approached swiftly, side by side, their immense black dorsal fins erect, a sinister spectacle. Even as he watched, an immense sea lion leaped frantically from the sea in their path but too late to avoid the closing of great jaws armed with row on row of deadly teeth.

With the pack-unity of wolves the orcas paused to do murder, while Kioga bent every energy toward reaching the floe with his clumsy tow. A hundred yards lay between him and safety when the orcas moved again through bloody foam in their relentless formation. As they approached, the analogy was plain again—water-wolves, an ocean pack bent on rapine, their back-fins slashing the water like great blunt glaives.

No man in a kayak saw they, but a long seal-like shape, basking as it were at the water's surface near the floe. In a body they sounded, and for a long minute there was a silence. Then the sea seemed to erupt killer whales ten yards from the Snow Hawk's tiny craft. Full length from the water leaped the orcas, like immensely enlarged salmon. From each rounded head a snowy plume of spray jetted hissing up. As one animal they fell upon the frail skin cockleshell, smashing it to shreds amid a smother of foam and the lash and thrash of mighty fins and broad thick-muscled tails.

But blood was not let in that fearful assault. No fool was Kioga to pit his lesser muscles against beasts like these! On the instant of their reappearance, with their spouting loud in his ears, he abandoned the kayak, stepped upon the tree drawing abreast of him, and balancing like a wire-walker, darted its length, ankle-deep in water. As he approached its thick end, the blunt white-chinned snout of an orca jutted forth between him and the floe. Too late to pause—the tree trunk was settling under his weight—he executed a mighty leap, full upon the slippery back of the blowing orca, and flung his line to the ice. As he alighted, half blinded by the animal's steamy blast, he drove the harpoon deep within an inch of the palpitating spout-hole.

Simultaneously the whale thrashed the sea into milky froth. And that had assuredly been the end of Kioga, but for the presence of mind of Moon's Son the medicine man, who took three quick turns of the line about a ridge of ice. As the orca sounded, the weapon was torn from the wound, and Kioga, still gripping its handle, was hauled to safety.

Already the others were sinking on the blood-trace of their stricken fellow—a grim trail that ended in cannibalism a mile distant. Whereafter, well-gorged the remaining three killer whales were seen no more.

Again under the moon's light, the sounds of ax were renewed. From the tree the Snow Hawk hewed away the excess branches, leaving only several at regular intervals on either side. Bent up from the bole, which was to be the keel, the branches were as ribs, stayed with hide ropes and bound at all points of stress by hide thong. The sharp knives had had their way with the tough walrus-skins. Men and women alike labored with bone awls and needles, drawing thread larger than the hole through it was forcibly pulled, to bind the interlocking seams together in a watertight union. So the umiak skin was assembled.

Slowly the craft took a form at which an Eskimo would have laughed—unless he too lived on a world that melted swiftly away beneath his feet! When it was completed many hands moved it to the water's edge, and lowerd it gently.

Seawater welled through the skin bottom. But the dismay of the Indians was short-lived. As the skins became water-soaked the seams swelled. No more brine was then admitted. But the work of construction was done none too soon.

Nearby another great chunk of the floe cracked away with a splash.

A short journey convinced Kioga that the craft would bear them safely across open water at least to the reefs about Nato'wa. On the morrow, men, women, dogs, and children took to their rude ark, bearing meat, and water in skin bags, to last a week. Thus they left the floe behind them.

Favored by wind and current, within a few days they found themselves within sight of distant shoals extending to the horizon at either hand. Meanwhile they had collected another proof of land nearby, a sapling. This, when trimmed and rigged with their gut tarpaulins, became a tolerably effective mast and sail, giving them additional headway.... By dawn of the next day they coasted within sound of the waves roaring over the rocky reefs.

At the bow Kioga scanned the rocks. Many times he had come hither from the mainland, through a channel known only to himself, which he had discovered by observing the routes taken by the sharks infesting the coastal bays of Nato'wa. His eyes sought the landmark which he had last seen when he piloted the yacht *Alberta* through the inner labyrinth toward the open sea. He saw it at last, a ragged pinnacle of basalt, forming a natural breakwater, behind which he guided his unwieldy craft and its load of weary human freight.

This would be their last opportunity to rest before the final harrowing barrier was conquered and the real shore attained. Rest they did on the narrow reef beside a huge roaring fire of crackling driftwood, the resinous smells of which were delicious after long weeks in the reek of a smoky seal-oil flame. But impatience to reach their goal brought them early awake. With dawn even the dogs seemed eager for action. Lightening his craft by every possible ounce, Kioga stripped it to the barest essentials.

Fending-poles were made of driftwood. Then, with an eye to the swift inrush of the tide, the threading of the deadly reefs was begun in a growing mist. In a light canoe Kioga had often made the perilous passage in three days. In the stiff-handling umiak, deep-laden and slow to respond, they were forced by fog to camp on another rocky reef, subsisting on clams dug from the rocks. The dismal mists rolled thicker on every side. Immense tidal combers dashed cold spray over the huddling band.

It was a small thing which sent their spirits soaring. In the midst of foreboding, with a weary flutter of mist-wet wings, a little wind-battered bird alighted upon the wet rocks. Such a show of indomitable cheer as it then made must have raised the hearts of condemned men. Its song was a subdued twitter, suddenly bursting into a series of ear-piercing whistles, repeated with swelling throat. Five times it ran its rapid score with comic fearless earnestness. When the Indians laughed, its crest drooped as if in embarrassment. Then it took flight and fluttered shoreward through the mists.

But with it went also despair. As the mists rose slightly the band again put off. Vigorously they fought the great waves which would have hurled their craft upon the rocky ridges, turning it safely a thousand times with their fending-poles.

The thousand-and-first time disaster fell like a lightning bolt. An invisible reef was suddenly uncovered by a wave in the trough of which the umiak rode, to graze it with a sickening rip of the walrus-hide bottom, through which the seawater boiled.

They could no more than let her pound against the nearest reef and abandon as swiftly as possible, one helping another to the rocky ledge whose underwater spur had scuttled their craft. It seemed they had come all this way only to meet their end within striking range of their goal. But the winds calmed; the mists dissipated. The sea came to rest. On the southern horizon the sun rose to but half the size of an immense fiery orange before slowly beginning its descent. But by its glorious slanting beams Kioga saw the receding tide had uncovered more of the ledge on which they stood—and showed it to be in reality a little rocky peninsula joined to the mainland. They could wade ashore!

Towering, forbidding, inhospitable-looking as a castle's wall, a great cliff reared into the sky beyond, its battlements gilded by the vanishing sunlight. In the calm bay below the cliffs a host of wildfowl rose in a honking cloud as a pair of fisher-eagles swooped in upon them, striking right and left. On a little beach bordering the bay lay the wrecked umiak, round about which sandpipers darted with stiffly mechanical rapidity, like wound-up toys, concerned only with making the most of the short daylight hours in filling their little crops.

A long moment the band looked upon these evidences of land-life, stunned by the reality of what they had striven toward, all these long arduous moons, and endeavoring to maintain composure. Then suddenly a choked sob escaped Grass Girl, holding her babe against her breast. Others of the women wept hysterically. The men of the red-skinned migrants, deeply emotional beneath their stoic veneers, did strange things.

Old Crow Man stood silent with outstretched arms, great tears rolling unheeded down his seamed cheeks. From rock to wet rock leaped the younger men, some to throw themselves bodily down to kiss the wet sand, others to kneel and filter its particles upon their heads and shoulders. Tokala the Fox capured, shouting gleefully about the beach, his lynx kitten still on one arm. The uncertain dogs picked their way cautiously ashore, pausing to sniff new scents or prick up their ears at new sounds; while one, nipped astern by the claw of a gigantic rock-crab, chased its tail in a spinning circle.

Kioga, however, knew too well the dangers of this wild coast, to tarry; and after their moment of thanksgiving, he led his band along the cliffs toward an ascending path.

The eager dogs, excited by fresh scents on every hand, roved in a scattered group a hundred yards in advance. The band had, in fact, barely gained the up-trail when what the Snow Hawk sought to avoid came to pass, with such suddenness that he was powerless to intervene.

Heedless of several summonses to return, the yelping dogs had gathered around an old bone-pile, long since picked clean by the scavengers, and were here sniffing about. Of a sudden a score of lean gaunt shadows materialized as if from nowhere, rounding a bend in the cliff wall like silent specters; and in their wake flew and circled a noisome band of croaking ravens and lesser crows.

Of all the fierce living things in the land of Nato'wa, none is so much to be feared as these coastal felons, the Direwolves who respect nothing that walks on two legs or four.

Running in such close formation that a room-sized rug would have covered the pack, at the moment of glimpsing the dogs their tactics changed. The inner segment described an encircling movement, cutting off the dogs' retreat toward the cliffs. The outer, without pause or hesitation, rushed foaming on the prey.

Now these were prime giant husky dogs in fine condition, many of them little less than wild themselves. Yet against the leather-tendoned, trap-jawed beasts which attacked, they were as suckling puppies. Came the deadly snick and slashing snap of fangs on fangs, mingling with the ferocious snarling of the cornered dogs, fighting for life itself. But from the gaunt destroyers there came no vocal sound. The Dire-wolves of Nato'wa speak but once, before assembling, and do their killing in grim silence.

One of the dogs, indeed, made good his escape from the first rush. But the leader of the second segment laid him out twitching, half his throat bitten away by a single rabid chop of the jaws. From sight, to attack, to finish, it was over as appallingly soon as that. Not one dog survived when the wolves crouched down to their hot feast, pausing now and then only to slash at the impatient ravens hovering in black impudent clouds about their ears.

From a safe height in the cliffs, wherefrom they could hurl great rocks in case of attack, Kioga's band looked upon the scene which symbolized the gloomy savagery of this untamed land as word of mouth could never have done: the faithful companions of their long march were no more. Forewarned against the grim realities of the wilderness round about them, the Indians finally continued their climb, scaling the cliffs. Atop the ramparts they built a shelter of rocks wherein to sleep the night. And here Kioga warned his party at length as to the precautions to be taken against the prowlers of darkness.

"Take no risks," he concluded. "Keep your fire hooded. The Shoni scalp-hunters may be abroad. Wait patiently within your shelter until I return with meat. Be alert to admit me when I call from the darkness."

With that the Snow Hawk melted into the gloom as silently as a leaf grows. Over his head the sky was intensely black, shot with the great Arctic stars, glittering like silver. Kioga, grateful to be home, drank in the tonic piny air until it seemed his chest must burst.

At the edge of the evergreen forest he paused to listen.

Moving aground a little way on the animal trails, he sensed something looming up before him, and at a touch of the shaggy bark knew it for an immense fallen tree bole. Upon this he vaulted lightly, stealing along its slanting length.

Now he paused to probe the dark with widened pupils. Two shining mirrors flashed yellow light, went out. He knew that a puma prowled nearby—and on that he remembered Mika, the great savage panther he had raised from cubhood, and hunted with by the light of the Arctic moon. He recalled Aki the bear, that shaggy bulwark of protection who had defended him from a hundred foes.

He kept moving onward, into the wind now, and over terrain which had not known his tread for many moons. His course took him straight along the lip of a ravine, deep in which a tiger spoke in husky earth-shaking tones, and thence inland, skirting the base of a mountain. Soon he caught the scent he sought—an acrid, faintly sulfurous smell. Following this, he entered a little valley in whose shelter the forest was yet thicker. Here he came to that place frequented some time in its life by every beast in the forest for fifty miles around—the hot springs. In these curative fluids torn tissues find comfort.

Searching out a certain pool, Kioga found it occupied by a huge old grizzly bear, splashing joyously about in the moonlight, bellowing with enjoyment. Sloughing off his furs, upon the aged bather Kioga waited patiently, standing like some naked god amid the spinning vapors. When the bear emerged, shaking water over a radius of many square yards, Kioga gave him time to leave, before depositing his clothing on a convenient ledge. Then he enjoyed that which he craved more than red meat itself—a hot cleansing bath, his first in many weeks. In this forest luxury he reveled for half an hour, emerging refreshed and with skin aglow, to plunge himself in cold running water nearby. Then he returned to his clothes.

As he bent above them, a few branches overhead moved, and a beam of moonlight revealed an intruder.

Coal-black of body, but with mottled whitish triangles running down its six feet of muscular back, a rock-viper lay coiled in the dry warmth of his cast-off furs. Its peculiar taint rose to his nostrils like the very emanation of death.

Frozen to rigidity, with hand still outstretched, the wits of the Snow Hawk sped like lightning. To move would but draw its strike, and he would end with the deadly thing fastened to his flesh.

There was nothing to do but wait—and hope it would mistake him for a part of the scenery. As he waited, in the expectation of death, there flitted past his ear a pygmy owl, uttering its curious *kr-r-r, kr-r-r, kr-r-r*.

Like a flash of light the snake lashed out at the little blur of feathers. Quick as the strike came, the winged elf evaded it, and perched indignantly on a ledge nearby. And in that fraction of a second Kioga's fingers snapped upon the snake's clammy neck just below the head. The koang whipped itself round his arm, no mean antagonist even now, with its twenty pounds struggling to get those fangs home. But fingers with the grip of blacksmith's pincers held it securely. Then with his knife he severed the head from the thrashing body. He cleansed the knife and buried the head under a foot of earth. The remainder he left to the pygmy owl whose coming had probably saved his life.

Then Kioga forgot his close brush with extinction, as all wild things forget what is over and done with, and bethought him of his Indians, who would be waiting for food. Naked as he had emerged from the sulfer-bath, he prowled forth into the dark again.

It was winter in Nato'wa indeed. But the heat in this timbered valley, warmed winter and summer by the hot springs bubbling in it, soon brought the sweat springing through Kioga's pores.

In every direction the breeze bore the scent of meat. And so, on a rock ledge affording a moonlight view of an animal trail, Kioga crouched in ambush with knife between teeth, awaiting the coming of game.

Soon came one of noble mien and careful step, its tenpoint antlers edged with droplets of condensing mist. A study in sepia and quicksilver, all unsuspecting the elk moved under the hunter's perch. One step it came, and two; another, and then—down pounced that lurking shadow.

An instant of plunging blade to hilt in the creature's side, another seizing the horn, with lightning twist dislocating the spine—thus, without sound died Kioga's prey, struck down by a master killer.

Leaving the viscera for the scavengers, Kioga bore his kill back to the springs, donned his furs, and turned back toward the rocky shelter which housed his band, just as the sun rimmed redly over the southern horizon.

Suddenly there came to him upon the now frosty breeze a sound—the ground-vibrating temblors of a tiger's roar. To you or me, one roar would seem like another. To Kioga's ear, long familiar with the forest's many voices, this much was certain: Guna had encountered prey. And in all the forest few willingly miss witnessing the red drama of a tiger's killing—Kioga least of all. He turned aside, approaching the stream along which Guna doubtless prowled.

To the Snow Hawk that deep-chested challenge brought no slightest quiver. But at a further sound—somewhat like a kitten's mewing—he started, almost as if with fear, and threw aside his new-killed buck.

To another, hurrying along the stream's bank, sheer terror came. It was Tokala the Fox, armed with a great unwieldy club that was more a burden than an arm in his small hand, who paused quivering as the tiger spoke. Hours since, he had slipped away from the Indian camp, seeking only the highest felicity life held for him—to be at the Snow Hawk's side. Lighted until now by the aurora, unscathed save by the devil's-club which had lacerated him when he sought protection from preying beasts behind its sharp bayonets, still in one arm he bore his cherished pet the lynx kitten; and it was the voice of this little creature that had caught the tiger's ear—and Kioga's.

And now Tokala's eyes fastened in dread fascination on the movement in the undergrowth whence rolled that terrifying sound.

From a thicket there slowly emerged into the light, stripe by stripe, a beast of splendid majesty. A massive orange-colored head adorned with black crossbars came slowly into view. A pair of black-tipped, thick-furred ears surmounted it. Eyes with the glow and heat of yellow fire seen through glacial ice fixed the boy, lighted with baleful menace.

Now Guna rose grunting to a half-crouch, a magnificent beast of the long-haired breed in full winter coat, richly girt by sable stripes about the glistening rufous sides. The furry cylinder of its tail was motionless save at its twitching end as the animal quivered before launching its bounding rush. The quill-like whiskers angled backward from the wrinkled lips, whose upward twitch exposed the deadly knives, those four long, curving yellow seizing-teeth.

In that tense moment the Snow Hawk attained the river's bank above and behind Tokala, with ready arrow and bow half drawn. In one glance he foresaw the frightful destruction to which Tokala stood exposed. Tokala bravely raised his club, as with short grunting roars the tiger launched its rushing charge.

Simultaneously the Snow Hawk drew in advance of the beast and loosed two lightning shafts in quick succession. One arrow took Guna squarely in the eye. The other but pierced a hinder leg. Bellowing in pain, the tiger sped on. A short twenty paces lay before its prey. The animal was closing in a mighty spring.

Then from its blinded side came catapulting one whose lightning onslaught was as ferocious as the tiger's own. Tokala and the fading stars looked upon a scene plucked from some prehistoric page in man's forgotten past. Man and beast collided obliquely with a force that all but tore the Snow Hawk's arms from their sockets. Gripping the tiger's ruff with one hand, with the other he stabbed his keen blade repeatedly into the muscled neck, savering the great artery.

The roaring tiger reared, shaking itself like some great dog within its loose thick overcoat of fur, great jets of blood spraying the river sands. But powerful legs linked him round the loins like iron chain. All deliberately, yet with the practiced quickness of many a like encounter, Kioga planted his steel in other vulnerable ground—working it deep behind the ears, where skull meets neck.

A roar ear-splitting in its volume foretold the end. Grimly Kioga made good his hold, not daring now to drop away, lest in its paroxysms, already begun, the tiger rend him apart.

Two shuddering leaps the tiger took, then crashed down upon its back, bearing the Snow Hawk also down, to strike with stunning force against the hard-packed sand. Then all was dark, and Kioga knew no more.

During all the crowded moments of the encounter Tokala had watched in terror mixed with amazement, half disbelieving that of which his own eyes now assured him—that even Kioga had triumphed over so fierce a beast as this. Feverishly he clubbed the tiger on the skull.

But now he saw the Snow Hawk pinned, bleeding and silent, under the huge striped body. Twice he whispered the Snow Hawk's name and went unanswered. With all his strength, dragging at one mighty forepaw, Tokala sought vainly to move the giant carcass. Then hastily he fled as he had come, along the stream bank, back to the Indian rock-camp, to bring Kioga aid. . . .

Rousing a few minutes later, Kioga threw off the tiger's pinioning weight. Looking about for Tokala, he saw only footprints in the sand and surmised the boy had gone for help. Perhaps it would be needed, for as he bent to pick up the deer he had earlier thrown aside, a stab of pain ran through his thigh. Nevertheless he shouldered the needed meat and limped on Tokala's trail. What with frequent rests to massage his injured leg back to normal, and pauses to make sure that Tokala's tracks had not strayed, he was more than an hour reaching the cliffs.

He would eat with the band, thought Kioga, and then reconnoiter near Hopeka—the Indian village where once he had ruled supreme as war-chieftain of all the Shoni tribes. He wished to learn their exact sentiment toward himself. For because of his rescue, more than a year ago, of white captives from the storm-driven yacht *Alberta*, whom the Indians had been tormenting at the torture-stake, Kioga had incurred the wrath of his people.

At Hopeka he expected only hostility. But whatever he found, he could perhaps enter the village and appropriate weapons with which to arm his own band. Failing that, there was still his cave, several marches distant, where were hidden weapons enough for fifty men, all hammered out long ago on his own hidden forge. . . .

Approaching the shelter on the cliffs, he noted that the Indians had evidently taken his instructions to heart, for they neither exposed themselves, nor was a fire visible. As agreed, he called out:

"*Ai-yah*! Meat, brothers. Come with sharp knives!"

There was no answer. Laughing at their caution, Kioga added:

"Perhaps you are not hungry. Perhaps—" But he said no more; for at that moment he suspected what made him drop his burden of game and rush to the rock shelter. There was no sound within, but as he crossed the threshold, his foot came in contact with something soft—a human body, which he drew toward where the dawn light might shine on its face.

What he saw need not be dwelt upon. He was looking into the face of Moon's Son, who would beat his magic drum no more. He had been at least an hour dead, to judge from the body temperature, which the Snow Hawk noted subconsciously as one to whom death was no uncommon sight. From the terrible ragged design left by the blade, he judged it had been a bone knife wielded by a Shoni braid-collector. And Moon's Son had been scalped.

A swift glance about in the increasing light indicated a surprise and a short struggle. The trail further said that the attackers had hurried their captives off in a northerly direction. Even now the victorious warriors would be embarking in their canoes and regaling the luckless captives with picturesquely pantomimed accounts of the tortures they would surely undergo.

Two courses were open to the Snow Hawk. He could trail the Shoni braves while the spoor was hot—or anticipate their arrival at Hopeka, the village nearest this point on the coast and capital of the Seven Tribes, and there try to free his friends. He forgot the pain of his injured leg, as circling northward he took the paths that would bring him to a river debouching into the Hiwasi, which flowed past the gates of Hopeka.

Arrived at a likely spot, well screened by overhanging tree limbs, he lay in wait, this time for nobler prey than deer.

IX

From time to time canoes passed the Snow Hawk's waiting-place, lighted by pine-knot torches smoking at their bows. But half visible in the lowered dusk, Kioga recognized them by their lines. Some were deep-laden with trade goods or tribute exacted by the Shoni from the tribes near the mountain passes and defiles miles in the interior. Such things might be bartered at the native bazaars in return for skins, weapons, feather-work, or for the skillfully made fur clothing for which the women of Hopeka are famed.

Other craft held couriers bearing messages from outlying villages, or visitors traveling from one place to another. Well favored are the Shoni in the possession of their skein of waterways, which are at once their highways of conquest and avenues of trade.

None of these did Kioga molest, until there came one craft at which his watching eyes lighted up. A small craft, it was manned by a strange figure decked in all the garish trappings of a witch doctor. He wore an eye-mask, designed to frighten the beholder, an all-enfolding robe of deer-hides falling almost to the ankles and marked with mystic medicine-signs, and a headdress of raven tail-plumes tasseled with strands of human hair. Of the shaman's features, hidden by mask and paint, little was discernible as he paddled, muttering incantations into the Snow Hawk's hearing.

What happened then was hidden by branches overhanging the river. The incantations ceased as if choked suddenly off; several large ripples spread out to midstream; and the canoe did not at once reappear. Perhaps the medicine man communed with some dark spirit imparting strange secrets.

But soon the craft came forth, and in it there still sat a figure in robe and feathers and mask, as if nothing uncommon had happened. Indeed, the paddler seemed possessed of fresh strength, for the craft all but flew onward now, and came soon into view of Hopeka.

Beached before its gates lay hundreds of canoes, among

which the eyes of the lone paddler roved swiftly as if in search of someone known to him. Then he pushed boldly ashore, felt the sand hiss under the prow, and stepped forth, carrying a war-club which had lain beneath a thwart.

He observed that the sentries were inattentive to duty, for he approached unchallenged. Something important must be transpiring within the walls! With the war-club he rapped on the gates.

"Who knocks?" came a startled query from within.

"Look on me," answered the newcomer loud and sternly, "and say if you know not my name!"

There was a subdued colloquy between two startled guards before one climbed to gaze down from atop the lofty palisade and cry out to his fellow sentry: "It is Raven's Tail the sorcerer! Open the gates!"

The huge log barriers fell apart, but just wide enough to admit him they called Raven's Tail, who strode haughtily in, masked, with head carried high and robe close-wrapped about him. The gate was hurriedly pushed shut.

"Wherefore such caution, sentinel?" asked the supposed shaman of the sentry standing respectfully by.

"A Wa-Kanek band was seen in the north by all report, oh Dealer-in-Magic."

"Better, then, to be more vigilant," was the sharp answer; then: "Where were your eyes when I stole upon the gates?"

"You have been absent long, oh Raven's Tail. As I hope to die a warrior, I knew you not," came the sentry's answer lamely.

"And in my long absence has naught of importance happened?"

"Does not a shaman know all that may occur?" asked the second sentry with the faintest trace of sarcasm. This brought the gaze of Kioga sharp upon his face; whereat he paled a little. And the other sentry answered:

"The Winter Festival will soon begin. The trading opens thereafter. There is talk of choosing a new warrior-chief."

"*Ahi!* Then Kioga—" began the supposed shaman, and paused, for the sentry had stiffened, as did his companion.

To the Snow Hawk there was no surprise in this. He well knew that the men who did the fighting had small regard for the shamans who fomented war—though superstitious fear, carefully contrived by the medicine men, usually kept open expressions of hostility quiet.

Perceiving that the sentries were watching him suspiciously, he was about to move on, when Brave Elk answered his earlier question with one of his own, cunningly designed to trip him.

"Knew you not, oh shaman, that Kioga the Snow Hawk is gone away in disgrace these many long months?"

"I know everything that has happened, or will happen," returned the masked one sharply, as if in rebuke.

"Then," demanded the irrepressible Brave Elk, as was his right according to Shoni custom, "give us some sign of your great medicine."

The masquerader turned slowly, riveting the speaker with a steady stare through the slits in the mask. Then he spoke gutturally and with emphasis designed to awe the man and others who had gathered to hear the oracle speak.

"Naught of importance has happened lately, so you have said. But I tell you that before the moon has risen, the torture-fires will be kindled. The cries of your victims will wake the forest. And beware—I repeat, beware—lest the Snow Hawk fly into your midst—for of such a thing my omens have spoken! *Hai-ya!*"

With that he wheeled and mingled with a band of tall and dignified warriors stalking about the village muffled in beautiful skin blankets and crowned with fillets of handsome feathers indicative of their deeds and office. Everywhere he went, a way was cleared for him. . . .

Soon the jaws of the sentries dropped, for it come to pass as Raven's Tail had foretold. A hail from the river was heard. Sentries manned the walls to scan the waters whence it came. Then fierce and shrill above the mounting noises in the village came the bloodthirsty cry: "*Ai! N'taga tui choka!*"

Prisoners for the stake! Sacrifice for the sacred fire!

All other pursuits were put aside. The populace crowded eagerly toward the gate to view those destined as sport for the licking flames. Foremost among the villagers was a figure in robe, mask, and blanket.

The great gates swung apart. Flanked by their burly captors, the Indians of Kioga's band came wearily in, bloodstained and disheveled. All who lived were there. Grass Girl with her babe mourned Moon's Son, whose scalp adorned the belt of a Shoni at her side. The others glanced hopelessly about, stunned by the size of the village and the fierce expressions of its inhabitants. Little Tokala shrank back fearfully from the masked face grinning down on him as he was pushed along.

But the frightful creature followed, as Tokala learned by frequently looking back over a shoulder—followed and noted where the captives were imprisoned and the position of their guards; he observed that they were given food and drink, and that would-be molesters were driven off. But at last, to Tokala's intense relief, the shaman went away.

Having heard a mutter of drums on the ceremonial grounds, Kioga knew that the prisoners would be safe, at least until the Winter Festival was over, a matter of many hours, in which time much could happen. And so he proceeded toward where the drums had begun to roll, and took up a position behind and to one side of the great assemblage. Now and then a passing warrior greeted him—sometimes with hostile bearing; but none questioned his identity.

Swiftly the keen eye of the Snow Hawk darted among them all seeking a glimpse of noble Kias, friend of his boyhood—tall, lean, powerful Kias, who had fought at his side in the battle at the Painted Cliffs, where under the Snow Hawk's leadership the Shoni tribes had turned back the raiding Wa-Kanek for the first time in the memory of living men. Nowhere could Kioga distinguish that familiar figure.

But among the chiefs regnant sat Menewa, beloved of his people in the Tugari tribe, whom Kioga recognized instantly. Then his eager glance cast about for a glimpse of one he would never forget—Heladi, daughter of Menewa, she who had brought his fierce wild life its one interval of peace and calm—and a love which he had denied with unwitting callousness. Heladi was nowhere to be seen. Had she met the sudden death of the raider's knife, or fallen into the clutches of a tiger when bearing water into the village?

X

Kioga the Snow Hawk, disguised as Raven's Tail the sorcerer, went back through the village. He moved in the general direction of the prison-lodge, wherein the boy Tokala, and his American Indian fellows, lay straining in their bonds and wondering in bated tones what their fate was to be, while the two guards squatted outside, grumbling at their ill-fortune in missing the opening of the Winter Festival. A bit of one guard's complaint reached the oncoming Snow Hawk's ear during an unexpected lull in the distant music.

"We watch. Others worship. Is it just?"

Came his fellow's answer grimly: "Think of that when the fires roast the prisoners' toes, warrior!" Then the speaker hissed suddenly for silence as the headdress of Raven's Tail came into view.

Calmly the newcomer squatted between the sentries, who did not venture to speak.

"The hour of the dance comes near," quoth Raven's Tail, "and for those who long endure, great gifts await."

The sentries eyed one another uncertainly as the shaman continued: "They give away the Snow Hawk's robes this moon. Each one will have the worth of fifty scalps. Ah, that I were but a younger man. Ah, that my bones were light again, as yours!"

The eyes of the sentries glittered with resentment and suppressed eagerness. "Of what use," muttered one, "is strength to us who sit and listen?"

"For five moons have I prepared," complained the other. "My muscles are like oak. To what end?"

Turning to Raven's Tail, the first sentry spoke again. "Oh, sorcerer, tell us this: Shall we gain nothing of the contest dances?"

Added the other: "Is there no spell will hold the captives fast?"

A while the shaman seemed deep in thought. Then: "There is an incantation known to me. And yet—strange that I cannot now recall it!"

The sentries exchanged knowing glances, undeceived by this old parry of the deceitful medicine men, who set a price on every magic wrought.

"Would this fine blade its recollection aid?" asked one.

"And this broad beaded belt *ahi*?" added the other.

The sentries saw the gleam of the eyes behind the mask, glancing as the bribes laid down by them before the supposed shaman. Then, as if possessed suddenly by a waiting spirit, Kioga leaped to his feet. "I hear a voice," he exclaimed, "speaking in a strange tongue. It is the incantation. I will utter it before the prison-lodge."

And in that strange tongue the Snow Hawk spoke to those within in English—utter gibberish to the listening sentries. What he had to say was quickly said. The effect upon the prisoners startled the two guards, watching their charges through the lodge door. Those who had sat erect slumped forward in their bonds as if in sleep. Several began to snore; whereat Raven's Tail, doubtless exhausted by this display of magic power, dropped again into a squat.

One of the sentries entered the lodge, kicking and prodding the prisoners with his foot. None moved. Stupor had evidently claimed them all. The voice of Raven's Tail came faintly: "It is done. They will not stir until the spell is broken. That none may break it, I will sit and watch."

Yet again the Indians exchanged glances, and reached some mutually satisfactory conclusion. A moment later they vanished toward the dance-ground, where soon the dancers would compete for the tribal rewards of endurance. . . .

For perhaps half an hour the Snow Hawk sat immobile before the prison-lodge, to make sure that all village eyes were occupied with other scenes.

The stirring music of the Shoni was beginning, to which no man can harken and think of other things. Their link with the American Indian is established; but in their music, as perhaps in no other way, the tribes of Nato'wa have far surpassed their continental cousins. In all the known earth there is no such music as this, to one of whose many forms Kioga now listened with bated breath.

Faint on the still night air it came, in subdued yet thrilling paeans. Higher it rose, then faded into seven muted measures—the opening bars of the Hymn to the Sun, marking the beginning of the Shoni Winter Festival. Beneath it boomed the undertone of the speaking drums, timed to perfection with the deep bassos of the Old Men's Society. In slow rhythmic measures it gathered volume as the elder tribesmen, from far assembled, gradually joined their voices in the prelude. Came then a pause, spaced with silence. Now began the round response of the female litany, interwoven with the rising surge of the warrior-accompaniment; followed by the mid-organ tones of the children's orisons. Another pause, while the solemn monotonous incantations of the medicine men picked up the ceaseless rhythm. And then—like a thunderclap—the full rolling swell of all the tribespeople burst echoing on the ear, surging through the forest aisles and along the misted waterways in majestic intonations. Seven times repeated it was, in ever-rising volume—the thrilling hosannas of the Shoni. Herein was something of the solemnity of the Roman High Mass, and of the drama of Wagnerian music, with the added quality of antiquity. For the Shoni religious music, as sung thus by all the people, is the voice of a race—a red race, which was old when ancient Egypt was an infant sprawling along the Ageless Nile.

All in the village faced the south, where the worshipped sun had long since vanished. Even the sentries, gripped by the thundering majesty of the Hymn to the Sun, grew lax as the rituals proceeded according to the primitive liturgy of this little-known race....

At length, persuaded that the prisoners were for the moment forgotten, Kioga rose abruptly and darted into the longhouse, the village music muffled by the bark walls.

In the semidarkness Tokala drew back as a slim knife played at his ankles and wrists. A moment later Kioga identified himself, pausing to hug the boy to him before whispering loud enough for all to hear:

"It is no time for greetings. Listen well, Tokala: I will prepare a canoe for your escape. Take this knife and release everybody. Let all rub arms and legs, that the blood may flow. If someone comes, lie quietly as before, as if asleep. If he grows suspicious, several attack and bind him tightly. But do not kill, for these are my people, among whom I have a few friends left." Then turning again to Tokala, Kioga spoke with a gravity fitting the occasion: "You are called the Fox, little brother. Be quick then, and cunning; for much depends on you. Listen for my signal. When you hear it, if all is yet well, knock twice on the lodge-pole, thus—"

Wide-eyed and quivering with a sense of the importance of his assignment, Tokala proudly accepted the knife and, as Kioga turned away, at once went to work, sawing at wrist and ankle bonds.

As the Snow Hawk reached the exit, the whispered voice of Grass Girl came to him: "May the gods of our fathers accompany you!"

"And may the devil watch over Raven's Tail and keep him unconscious," muttered Kioga as he vanished quietly into the outer dark.

Into the nearest bark house he prowled, to feel with sensitive agile fingers for the weapons which would hang along the walls.

He emerged shortly, loaded with several bows, many arrows, a spear, and a few round-headed clubs. Now the purple shadow of the palisade received him; and over it, one by one, he tossed his burden of weaponry. He paused to listen for any suspicious sound as his eye sought the top of the barrier towering twelve feet from the ground, a wall to hold in even an athletic man. With one quick lynxlike spring Kioga seized its rim, and with a lithe twist of waist and hip was up and over, to drop softly outside the palisade. The village sounds came muted now, through the log wall.

All depended on haste, but haste controlled by caution. One wrong move would throw the village into wild uproar. In that brief moment atop the palisade he had observed the sentries, intent upon ceremonies at the dancing arena.

Staking all on speed, the Snow Hawk slipped beneath and uplifted a great canoe from the sands. With a thwart resting upon his shoulders, and one eye ever upon the sentry lookouts near the gate, he moved it a few yards. Then he froze rigid, on perceiving that the sentry had risen to throw a glance toward the river. He could see the man's plume flutter, and it seemed that his eyes had fixed that motionless craft. A moment later a second watcher rose by his side, to peer out.

It seemed to Kioga that the pound of his heart was echoing thunderously in the hollow canoe, and must surely be heard. And when both sentries vanished suddenly, he was doubly certain that discovery was at hand. But the gate did not swing wide. The pulse of music continued unabated.... Again he moved onward, this time without interruption, dropping the canoe lightly to the water, throwing in paddles, springing in himself. He was quickly out of sight, and in a little time had concealed the craft under overhanging vines on the bank.

Back at the prison-lodge, Kioga heard Tokala's signal of safety responding to his call. Without a word he gestured to his band to come forth, and maintained watch while they filed silently in the direction of his pointing arm, merging with the obscurity there at the palisade.

Ten minutes later Kioga stood with his band at the canoe, giving directions as to the route they must take upriver, and distributing the stolen weapons among them.

"You will meet few Shoni canoes," he assured them. "Most of the war-boats are assembled here in Hopeka. But Wa-Kanek raiders—enemies of these Shoni—have lately been seen hereabouts, so it is reported. Beware of them also. Paddle north and west. You will come to a cleft in the cliffs. Wait there three days. If I do not come, go across the mountains to the plain called the Shedowa. There you will find horse-tribes such as your own American people once were."

From a birch nearby Kioga stripped a section of bark, and with knife's point etched on its inner side a crude map, by means of which the band were to be guided. Then, taking farewell of them once again, he hastened back to the village, entering as he had left, secretly.

As Raven's Tail he prepared to seek the news and gossip of Hopeka, by means of which to shape his future conduct. As warrior-chieftain of the Shoni tribes he had once wielded a power second only to that of a ruling chief. How far he had destroyed the esteem in which once he had been held remained to be discovered.

Nearing the ceremonial grounds, he heard the music deepening. The hour of psalmody and solemn invocation was past. Instrumental music had now replaced it. All the village walls threw back a strange and pleasing rhythm—not the primitive discords of monotony which passed for music among many of the American tribes, but a complicated score, played from memory, on instruments curious and varied.

Here a group of maidens sat, in their laps the lutelike *abalis*, whence at the pluck of slender fingers leaped chimes of soft guitarlike sound. There seven flagelets piped all as one, twisting their quiet notes into a rope of melody. A quick and birdlike warble spilled from twenty wooden flutes, answered by the reedy skirl from a dozen primitive pipes. Yet all of these were but the overtone for the two primary instruments of the Shoni people. One of these is a development of the drum, long, vari-chambered, and yielding forty-three notes.

These notes the drummers now evoked in rich combination, by quick beats of skin-covered sticks after the manner of an xylophone; while other musicians played the Indian harps, whose nine strings of variable pitch are attached to turtle-shell resonators. From these the several players struck forth deep harmonious chords, pursuing the after-beat of the music with a hesitant mesmeric rhythm all their own.

Thus from primitive beginnings the Shoni are working toward that modern descendant born of a hunting bow and man's fertile imagination—the grand piano; and toward the organ too, whose first ancestor may have been a leg-bone whistle shrilled through the lips of prehistoric man.

XI

With the quickening of the music's tempo, Kioga felt his sense of apprehension also quicken. Every moment brought nearer the ultimate discovery of the prisoners' escape and the possibility that Raven's Tail would recover his senses to interrupt this danger-spiced game the Snow Hawk played beneath the very knives of his enemies.

Yet he must learn more of the trend of politics among the tribes—if not as Raven's Tail, in whose guise he had walked so securely, then by risking to appear as a simple warrior, trusting in the darkness to aid in his disguise.

His eye cast round for one whom he might relieve of a suitable blanket and appropriate warrior's finery. A feast-lodge stood nearby. Into it a minor village witch doctor was stalking in warrior's garb. Ten steps took Kioga to the door and in, the bear-skin falling softly into place behind him.

The shaman felt along the bark wall for a pipe, not hearing the silent footfall at his back. As he turned, a gasp of surprise was audible—not more. Fingers sinewed as with wire closed upon his neck. A moment he struggled with his attacker, but his resistance was as nothing to the muscles of the Snow Hawk.

Ringed ever closer by the danger of discovery, Kioga worked with lightning speed, gagging and securely binding his captive with rawhide thongs snatched from a wall-peg. Then he substituted the man's blanket for that belonging to Raven's Tail, donned the other's headband, and prepared to quit the lodge.

Suddenly he was possessed by the spirit of deviltry. He would reopen his old feud with the medicine men with an appropriate prelude. In a moment he had propped the bound captive erect against a lodge-pole and tied him fast. About the man he flung Raven's Tail's robe, its mystic markings well to the fore. Upon the captive's brow he placed the gaudy headgear, and across the eyes tied the hideous medicine-mask.

He ran a spear between arm and body, pointing front, and on a last inspiration, stuck the pipe in one side of his mouth.

An instant for pausing to grin appreciatively at his handiwork—then he entered the street again, whereon were scattered many people moving toward the dance-arena. But no one now avoided him, as with blanket drawn up about his eyes, the color of which alone might have betrayed him, he joined the throng.

Nearby a witch doctor dealt a brutal blow to a child that thoughtlessly ran across his path. A warrior on Kioga's left eyed the shaman with ill-disguised anger, but kept his peace. To this warrior Kioga addressed his words.

"It was not thus," he muttered tentatively, "when Kioga was war-chief here."

The man started. "*Ahi!* You knew him, then?" he asked.

"Quite well."

The warrior leveled a quick glance at Kioga.

"I also. He was very brave," he declared.

"As to that, opinion differs," answered his companion. "The shamans liked him not."

The voice of the warrior dropped guardedly. "The shamans! They care for none but those who do their will. They control everything. 'Tis even said,"—his voice was still lower—"that the Long Knives have formed again."

"*Ahi!* That is news!" ejaculated the Snow Hawk, startled. When he had gone away a year or more before, the power of this secret organization had been virtually dead. Many of its members had fallen to Kioga's own avenging hand—his answer to their plotting and brutal murder of both his Indian parents. Single-handed he had all but crushed the society, which was organized for treachery and the overthrow of government. Yet, taking advantage of his absence, from its remainder, like some diabolical djinn, it had sprung back into existence.

But the warrior was speaking again. "How news?" he asked in some surprise. "Where have you been, that you knew not of these things?"

"In a strange country, among strange tribes far to the south," answered Kioga not untruthfully, ere pursuing his original theme. "But where are those who were loyal to Kioga?"

"There are other ways of dying than in battle," was the significant reply. "Many have drunk their death. Others have been found with an arrow in the back."

"What of Kias, once called Kias the Deaf—who fought beside the Snow Hawk in the battle of the Painted Cliffs?"

The warrior reflected. "Many moons ago Kias went away with a war party. More than that I know not, though some say—" Here his voice paused, his gaze resting suspiciously on a figure nearby.

Half turning, Kioga saw a fierce and arrogant personage decked in the gaudy vestments of a shaman. The hands which clutched the figured cloak about him were scarred with self-inflicted unhealed knife-cuts. His face was a living horror, its upper lip cut quite away in some boyhood knife-brawl, exposing all the upper teeth. His uncombed hair hung lank and uncouthly about the broad but bony shoulders.

As the Snow Hawk watched, the man moved slowly away.

"They hear and see everything. Even the earth has ears," muttered Kioga's companion, following the witch doctor with his gaze.

"Who was he?" inquired the Snow Hawk. "I thought I knew them all, but here is one who is strange to me."

"He is called Shingas the Half-mouth. Old Uktena spoke against him in the council. Two days later Uktena died. Some say his son Kias also died that way, since he was not here to mourn Uktena. You may remember Mokuyi and Awena, kin of the war-chief Kioga."

"Well do I remember them," said the Snow Hawk softly.

"They were murdered," continued the other. "'Tis Half-mouth's boast that he had a hand in that too. —Why do you jump, warrior? Did a wasp sting you?" he remarked half jokingly.

"The wasp of memory," Kioga agreed quietly, controlling that sudden access of hatred which had tightened every muscle in him at the words of his informant. "The killer of Uktena and of those unhappy dead has gained a foe in me."

For the first time the other sought to see beneath Kioga's paint and his muffling robe. "Who are you, warrior?" he demanded suddenly.

"If I reveal it, will you guard my name?" asked Kioga.

"By my hope of a warrior's death," the brave assured him.

Pausing where a fire's light might briefly shine on his face, Kioga lowered the blanket.

In but the short instant, then, that his companion looked upon his features, all jocularity fled. Narrowed grew his eyes as Kioga's own engaged them. He sucked in a startled breath, then fell back a pace in his astonishment, and essayed to speak. "It cannot be—and yet—it is—"

"Your promise! We are watched!" Kioga reminded him; and as the man composed himself and corrected all but his sudden paleness: "Tell me, warrior. How many feel as you? How many loyal would rally to the old call, if I uttered it here, now, upon this crowded street?"

Bitterly the warrior made answer. "Not twenty tomahawks would flash at the Snow Hawk's signal. A year ago he deprived the Shoni of captives. He left his tribe ungoverned and without farewell. Before that all loved him. After——" He shook his head regretfully. "The medicine men keep memory of those offenses alive, and make them look greater."

"They were great enough," conceded Kioga unhappily. "But what's done will not undo." Pausing, he offered his hand to the warrior, who wrung it without a word. "Tell no man that I was here," he admonished. Then drawing his robe closer about him, he struck quickly off by a side lane through the village.

As he approached the arms-lodge, wherein were kept spare weapons of all kinds for use in any emergency, the odor of cooking meat reached the Snow Hawk's nostrils. A brief investigation revealed a spitted haunch of venison slowly roasting and dripping its sizzling flaring fat into a bed of red embers before a neighboring lodge. He paused, cut himself a liberal slice in the absence of his unknown hostess. Of some corncakes set out to cool, he took several. From a woven basket he scooped up a fistful of dried plums, then went on, munching as he went.

And in the shadow of another lodge an old woman crouched concealed with her hand clapped to her mouth in mingled wonder, fear, and gladness. A little girl-child close in her arms would have spoken, but the old woman hissed an admonition. "Silence! If these old eyes do not play tricks it was—*ai*! may the Great Ones Above grant it was—Kioga the merciful. The Snow Hawk is back! The house of Seskawa is honored. He has eaten of our food."

Kioga emerged from the arms-lodge with a stout bow and several arrows. At the dance-ground to which he next returned, he paused to watch the naked dancers, their skins glistening like wet copper, their muscles writhing as they flung themselves through the arduous measures of their dance, to the incessant, maddening beat of the tom-toms.

Turning away, Kioga was about to avail himself of every last moment in which to test village sentiment toward himself. But as he moved against the crowds which came toward the dance-arena, he suddenly checked. A tall young native woman was approaching in the throng. At sight of her his heart leaped with pleasure, relief and something more perhaps, for she was passing beautiful.

Her hair was black as blackest ebony, worn in the double-looped coiffure identifying her as of the Wacipi, for whose women's favor men of many tribes go courting. Round each dark twisted braid a beaded deerskin band was bound, redly gleaming in the firelight.

Across one shoulder hung a bird-skin robe, no smoother than the taut young breast it partly covered. Her arms were ivory, braceleted with burnished copper; her feet warm-shod in doe-skin moccasins, quill-worked in rectilinear designs. She wore her garments as a mountain wears a morning mist, lightly. She moved with the grace of a savage leopardess, all suppleness and undulance.

Her name—Heladi—sprang to the Snow Hawk's lips, but went unuttered. In one slim hand she bore a fan of priceless feathers, his gift to her more than a year ago. In one earlobe there glowed a burning ruby in a setting of ancient workmanship. That had come from his own store of treasure, found long ago buried on the seashore sands and locked now in the darkness of his hidden cave, which had been sanctuary for him in other days.

Closer she came, clothed also in reserve, eyes proudly looking straight ahead, until she was not three arrows distant. Fearful of betraying himself, Kioga drew back.

Men were not wont to draw away from her. The sudden movement caught the young girl's eye. Her proud glance turned upon the tall and stately warrior close before her. A second it seemed that he would pass unrecognized, and then—in full stride she halted. He heard the startled catch of her indrawn breath, saw the dark pupils of her eyes dilate with wonder, joy, and amazement, as the color drained from out her lovely face. Her lips had shaped to utter some greeting, when suddenly she stiffened. As swiftly as it fled, her self-control was back. With upraised fan she hid her features from the curious round about and went along her way, albeit a little uncertainly, like one who rocks beneath some heavy blow.

As she passed, a harsh and furious cry came from near the village gate, near which a wildly gesticulating figure, struggling in their grasp, harangued the guardians of the gate, laying curses upon their ancestors and unborn children.

With a last glance after Heladi, Kioga drew near, harkening to the man's furious words, before clearly seeing him.

"Fools! Fools! Fools!" shouted the newcomer, beside himself with fury. "Do you not know who I am?"

"You are an impostor," replied one of the guards. "Raven's Tail entered here these many hours ago."

"*H'yah*! There was the impostor!" screamed the true Raven's Tail.

"You lie," declared the other guard scornfully. "Did he not predict that prisoners would be taken? Did not the prediction come true? Do they not now await the fires, in the prison-lodge?"

Almost as if in answer a discordant bedlam rose in the direction of the prison-lodge. Someone was voicing the discovery that the prisoners had made their escape.

Came then a voice from among the warriors crowding near the gate.

"Raven's Tail guards the feast-lodge. Look and you will find him there!"

As one, twenty braves leaped to verify the words. Their leader rushed into the feast-lodge, but drew back at the prick of the spear held by the tied-up captive. His shout and those of his followers brought the contest dances to a sudden end. New voices swelled the clamor.

Emerging from the feast-lodge came the braves, supporting between them a figure still garbed in the terrific robes and mask and headdress which had always made Raven's Tail conspicuous.

"Did I not tell you?" demanded the gate guard triumphantly, dealing the unhappy Raven's Tail an extra buffet.

"Seize him!" shrieked the luckless shaman at the top of his lungs, pointing to the wearer of his sacred vestments.

By now the village was in completest uproar. And the confusion was unresolved until tall Shingas the Half-mouth pushed his way through the crowding villagers, to peer first at Raven's Tail, then at his accuser.

Waiting upon his judgment as to identities, the noise quieted a little. Whereupon Shingas proclaimed in his near-gibberish that Raven's Tail was indeed Raven's Tail, a fact whereat the guardians of the gate trembled in their blankets. For their offense was double in that they had admitted allowing in an impostor and thereafter subjected the true Raven's Tail to gross indignities!

In another moment the crafty Shingas, leaping from event to event, made an admission seldom heard from members of his primitive cloth. "We are all fools, deceived by an impostor. Bar the gates! Search the village! Strip every warrior of his robes!"

His exhortations came just too late. That same voice which had earlier spoken from the throng was raised anew.

"Stand we here while the prisoners all escape? Let us give chase, and search the rivers north and south for them!"

The four culpable guards—two from the prison-lodge, two from the gate-were all too eager to be gone, that they might escape respectively the wrath of their chiefs and the wrath of Raven's Tail. Fifty others besides—impetuous would-be young warriors, eager for honors—followed the guards out to the canoe-racks on the sand. On the instant two longboats forged northward and two lesser craft cruised oppositely.

In one of the latter, the Snow Hawk rode in the stern position.

This craft skirted the shore in cautiously rounding a bend, passing into the darker shadows there. When it emerged, the stern position was vacant. Kioga had transferred himself apelike from canoe to overhanging limb, and thence ashore, making his northeasterly way through the gloom of the forest primeval along the beaten game-trails.

For perhaps half an hour he traveled without incident other than an occasional brush with some minor prowler of the forest. It was his intention to visit the cave which had been his haven during all the years of his boyhood outlawry.

He was following silently along the Hiwasi River. On either bank the undergrowth defied human progress. But Kioga's passage was not so easily barred: light as a gibbon, he swung actively along by the strength of hand and wrist beneath the river overhang.

He might have climbed higher into the midway a hundred feet aloft, where none could view his going; but the wash of a war-canoe had caught his eye some distance ahead. He would determine who the warriors in it were, and whither they went, and if among them there were those whom he might call allies.

Swift forged the longboat north upon the river, propelled by the brawn of many arms. But when Kioga chose to hasten, none but the swiftest craft might hope to keep him in its wake. In fleet agility he overhauled the canoe as if it were an anchor and concealed himself where it must skirt the shore, the better to view the occupants.

But none were there on whom he could rely. They were searchers all, from Hopeka, doubtless seeking traces of the vanished prisoners.

Intent upon the warrior-laden canoe, Kioga did not see a little figure limping wearily along in the direction of Hopeka on this side of the river. But of a sudden the foremost paddler hissed. As one man the others held their birch blades deep. He who had signaled snatched up his ready bow, snapped a shaft against the waiting cord, and took aim.

For the first time Kioga glimpsed the figure at whom the arrow pointed; it was Tokala, little deserter from the Indian band, footsore and exhausted, but doggedly seeking a way through the tangle to be at the side of Kioga his idol. And upon Tokala's heart a cruel-barbed arrow was trained.

Whether the man's intent was to loose or merely cover the boy with his aim, Kioga did not pause to ask. As a jaguar springs from green concealment, in one great bound the Snow Hawk leaped upon the warrior and bore him under, capsizing the war-craft by the fierce impetus of his pounce.

A moment, while the startled Shoni braves floundered in the icy river; then swift the action, loud the yells of excitement as they closed with the long-sought Snow Hawk, like wolves about an encircled tiger. While it endured, this was a Titan's struggle that Tokala witnessed, fought out waist-deep in the cold Hiwasi.

Empty-handed, Kioga struck at his armed assailants, lightning blows that rained down wherever an opening showed itself, and felled a man with almost every blow. Twice and again the warriors' clubs glanced from his shoulders, and five men lay helpless from his swift assault. Then—it was over.

A well-aimed swinging club brought the Snow Hawk stunned, to his knees. Upon him fell many hands, binding him fast with cords from the hunting bows.

A wild triumphant yell announced the thrilling tidings of Kioga's capture. Others of the Indian party seized Tokala, exempted now from further peril by the overshadowing reality of the famous Snow Hawk's downfall.

Pausing only to revive their injured companions, the warriors were soon forging downstream again.

XII

Alone in her lodge the Shoni maid Heladi sat—she who had known and loved the Snow Hawk, and seen him vanish from her ken in the company of strange whiteskins many moons ago. Though Heladi had long mourned him as forever gone, the memory of him had remained with her. And now today the unbelievable had happened. She had looked into eyes whose glint she would never have mistaken for another's. The Snow Hawk had come back! To her?

A thousand questions clamored in her mind for answers. Why was he returned? Who were the captives whose release he had undoubtedly engineered? Where was Kioga at this moment? He had surely known her. Would he return? When—

A clamor at the village gate caught her ear. She left the lodge again, not without assuring herself that her woman's knife reposed in its sheath at her back.

Now rose such a shout as made the forest echo. With beating heart Heladi turned in that direction, pushed her way through the crowded warriors. A path was made for her, for she was a highborn, the daughter of a ruling Wacipi chief, and the Wacipi are the most advanced of all the seven Shoni tribes.

Heladi's heart turned cold within her at what she then saw. It was the Snow Hawk, assuredly enough—all covered with drying blood and dragged along unresisting by several warriors—a dead man, from his appearance. Behind him came the boy Tokala, struggling impotently in the grip of a grinning brave who grasped him by the hair, half dragging, half carrying him.

Death had this young girl seen a thousand times when the war-men came home from battle bearing their slain. But never had she thought to see the Snow Hawk thus. She sought to draw closer, but in the surging throng, many of whom followed the warriors bearing Kioga to the prison-lodge, that was almost impossible, even for Heladi.

Her glance therefore turned after the boy Tokala. She saw him at last, still furiously struggling to gain the side of his idol. The young men had formed a rough circle about him and were making sport of him, tossing Tokala repeatedly back when he sought to squirm through their legs or break from the ring.

Again and again the desperate child flung himself at the cordon of sinewy brown arms. He bled from the nostrils. An ugly blue bruise had raised below one eye, bumped by an Indian's elbow. Suddenly his grim persistence was rewarded. Snakewise he managed to writhe under a brave's arm and darted from among his baiters. But then his strength, already sorely tried, ran from him. His knees trembled with near-exhaustion. In one direction hostile laughter greeted him. In another a medicine man raised a threatening tomahawk. Behind him the persecutors were in pursuit.

But before him, with eyes all aflame with indignation stood a young woman—beautiful in her feather robe. And so, because there was no place else to turn, Tokala laid aside his boyish pride and stumbled toward Heladi. He heard her broken incoherent words of pity as she dropped on one knee to receive him. His stoicism was breaking fast. Through vexing but unrestrainable tears he dimly saw her outspread robe, glimpsed the ivory paleness of her skin, and flung himself against her with an impact which made Heladi gasp. The next he knew, his arms were round her slender waist, his cheek against her heart, whereon he sobbed unrestrainedly now. But none save Heladi would ever know, for the warm covering of her robe concealed him from other eyes.

Her words to the boy's tormentors came swiftly, like the bitterest juices of sarcasm and irony from acrid fruit.

"Brave warriors! Mighty hunters! Ten eagles against an unfledged nestling! How many enemy scalps you must have taken to win the right to bait a child! Who is so brave will seize him now from Heladi?" With flashing eye the girl defied them; and seeing that none answered her, and that some looked at the ground in embarrassment: "Back to your dancing and boasting!" she mocked on. "Tell the chiefs and people that ten hunters ringed one deer and could not hold him! Sing the praises of this small unknown. The hour has brought you little else to boast about!"

Then, touching the dark head of Tokala, she spoke in tones that none who heard might misinterpret: "I take him as my brother. Hereafter hurt him at your peril."

In such manner came Tokala the Fox to be adopted into

the Seven Kindred Tribes of the Shoni Nation. His erstwhile tormentors went away crestfallen. And because they were not mean at heart, but only savagely impetuous, many of them did indeed sing the praises of the deer who had broken through the hunters' ring.

In the lodge of Menewa, Heladi bathed Tokala's hurts. She gave him to eat and drink—of corncake, spread with fresh wild honey, and of nourishing venison broth, and the tender breast of a mountain pheasant. And when at last the weary boy fell asleep with his head in her lap, she laid him upon her own low couch of soft new panther-skins. She covered him well and went out into the village, moving toward the prison-lodge wherein Kioga was slowly regaining consciousness.

He had little hope of succor. Aware that on the morrow he would likely be put to the torture, he resigned himself to death; and having resigned himself, sought to rest in preparation for the ordeal to come.

For a time there was a silence; then Kioga heard voices outside, one a woman's. A figure lifted the skin and entered, wrapped in the shadow of the prison-lodge. The smell of sweet herbs mingled with the delicate pleasant scent of one he well knew identified her to Kioga. He whispered to her softly, in the Shoni "intimate" dialect.

"Heladi! How come you here?"

A hiss of surprise escaped the shadow at his side. "Oh, eyes that see in the dark," came her murmured reply. "The guards were changing. I came as if to bring you water. I am not recognized as Heladi, who once sang of love to the Snow Hawk." Mockery, cruel and biting, now filled her murmuring voice. "What did the white-faced woman do, that you return to us? Would the white-face have brought you—this?"

Kioga felt the cold touch of a copper knife, but did not reply.

"Tomorrow the stakes will bear thee," said the girl. "Does the Snow Hawk feel no fear?"

"I dread but thy taunts, Heladi," answered Kioga. "For the rest—I do not fear to die."

"My taunts?" wondered the girl dully. Then with quickening words, recalling the white girl she had seen Kioga with: "Ah, yes! When the fires come to your eyes and your hair lifts in flames, then my voice will rise above the rest."

"But sing my death-chant, oh northland songbird, and I will die with glory," returned Kioga, parrying her every mockery with a softness born of a deep affection and regard for her.

Fiercely she began anew: "Will you not ask for the knife? Will you rather take the flame, the piercing spear, the smell of thy roasting flesh? Say but one word, and I give thee a quicker death."

"No, Heladi. Upon the stake I will hang and in the fires burn. I will die at the hands of my own people, with honor. Not like a coward in the night by the gentle thrust of a woman's knife. My thanks, Heladi. But leave me now, that I may rest and face my hour with courage."

A choked sound came from the girl, and her rounded arms slipped about his neck, holding his head a moment against her breast, as she said brokenly: "My heart is ice. But have I waited all these moons—to see thee burn? *Ai-i.*"

Her little cry of horror and yearning broke off suddenly as a footfall sounded without. Quick deft movements of her sharp knife cut the bonds at his wrists and knees, releasing the torturing constriction of the long thongs. Swift fingers slipped away the bonds, and as a feathered head was thrust into the lodge, she melted into the shadows of one corner.

It was the guard, come to play at cat-and-mouse with the blood-caked prisoner. He bent jeeringly above Kioga, kicked him in the injured side, and drew his knife threateningly.

But of a sudden his brutal chuckle was cut short as a lithe form flew at his throat. A gasp, twice repeated, echoed in the confinement of the barken walls. Came then a hoarse low cry, thick with the bubble of air through fresh blood and filled with the horror of the death rattle—then a heavy impact as the guard's head struck the floor, its feathers brushing Kioga's face. An instant Heladi stood with eyes blazing down on the fallen man, like a tiger mother who had defended her own; then she knelt again.

A few moments since, she had been a woman fired by love. Now she was a young girl chilled by horror and awe of what her knife had wrought—but untouched by fear. For a space the Snow Hawk's arms were about her comfortingly, and there she would gladly have remained, though discovery and death found her thus. But Kioga's admiring words awakened her to the reality of their danger.

"*Ahi.* Sister of the lightning! It was a noble blow! How still he lies!"

She shrank a little from looking at the dead guard. "The gate is open," she said. "Within the hour they will come for you. I can do no more. May the warriors' god watch over thee."

"What of Tokala?" he asked her.

"I have taken him."

Quick as thought came Kioga's reply: "What of thee, Heladi?"

"What of me?" she returned on a quiet note. "I am turned traitress. It will be known, for Child's Hand saw me coming here. All will turn their heads from me. But I do not wish to live. I will walk into a tiger's mouth." And with a lithe movement she drew away from him as if to go. But he caught her hand, turned it up, and pressed his lips against the cushioned palm. She quivered at that, then snatched her hand away. There was a rustle. He called her name softly, twice. But Heladi was gone.

The path to liberty was clear. In ten leaps he could be at the palisade, over and away, as free as that owl hooting derisively from beyond the log wall!

But in that moment his exultation was checked by what the girl had said of discovery by the shaman, Child's Hand. That she might dare perform her threat of self-destruction, he felt certain, knowing the steely nerve of these Wacipi women. Yet knowing also the medicine men, he knew too that worse might befall her.

She had freed him. If he escaped, it would be at cost of her replacing him for the torture. All her father's power might not save her from that.... He leaped for the door, a plan in his mind. He must escape; not only his own life was at stake, but the safety of the American Indians whom he had brought to Nato'wa was in his keeping. And Heladi should accompany him, at any cost.

But it proved too late. He heard many voices—village warriors announcing that they had come for him. Another time he would have made a break for liberty, but he dared not now, lest he be slain before the lips of Child's Hand were stopped. Perhaps some other way would yet offer itself. He returned and sat down beside the dead man....

A warrior's head protruded through the doorway, then drew back with a swift yell of warning. In a moment ten warriors reinforced the man as he tore aside the skin, revealing the interior to the others in the light of his torch.

Calm as a graven image, Kioga sat at ease, cross-legged upon the earth. Beside him, inert in death, lay his guard. The bonds which had enwrapped him on their departure lay at his feet.

The Snow Hawk's voice, weighted with stinging contempt, struck at them:

"Come, women! I offer no resistance. Is the stake driven? Is the fire kndled? Why do the warriors wait? Do eleven armed men fear the wolf whose teeth have been drawn?"

Yet another minute's hesitation held them, as if they feared that he might yet by another miracle escape. Then, as one, they closed with a rush, seized, raised, and pinioned him anew, and led him toward the ceremonial circle.

Kioga's eyes went to the moon's reddish disk, half-risen above the southern peaks and swollen to bulging immensity. When black sky showed between it and the mountaintops, his ordeal would begin. Only then, according to Shoni belief, can the worshiped body obtain view of the ceremonies by which a life is sacrificed to it. . . .

Uproar announced Kioga's approach. In the too-brief interval remaining, he prepared to die as he had lived, violently. . . . The moon rose higher. The drums quickened, and the singing grew louder, fiercer, shot through and through with savagery, as the warriors danced ever closer, brandishing their knives. As Kioga watched, all of the moon became visible, and presently a thin line of sky appeared beneath it.

Simultaneously he felt a sharp prick. A drop of blood ran down his arm, from a crease cut in it by a knife. The torture had begun; the Snow Hawk steeled himself.

Next he felt his hand seized from behind. Some lever was introduced under the nail, pulling it apart from the raw quick. Into the bleeding flesh a thorn was thrust; and so, one after another, with all of his ten fingers.

Jeered a shaman, piercing the flesh of Kioga's arm with a pointed stick:

"What will the council say when I tell them who slew your guard? *Hail.* A true arrow that, to make the brave Kioga flinch!"

Laughing in wicked triumph, Child's Hand made way for others.

The Snow Hawk's eyes swept the village. Here were they he once had ruled, now clamoring for his scalp, egged on by his enemies the Long Knives, led by certain of the witch doctors. Yet there were friends among them; a familiar face came before him. He knew this new tormentor to be Brave Elk—he who had defied him when he masqueraded as Raven's Tail.

"You too?" he asked the man a little reproachfully.

Dimly amid the din of shouting and singing, he heard the man's words, uttered as he bent near, playing a tomahawk about Kioga's face: "Thirty braves wait my signal to rally at your side."

"You are well named, warrior," returned Kioga with suddenly gleaming eyes. "But thirty would die instead of one. It is folly. I will endure yet a while. There are two things, however, I would ask of Brave Elk."

"Only ask, and they are yours," returned the loyal warrior.

"Kill for me the shaman Child's Hand," snapped Kioga.

"It shall be done. What else?"

"Your tomahawk—and swiftly—should they put out my eyes," said Kioga. The warrior drew back in something like horror. The Snow Hawk's gaze held him commandingly.

"It shall be done," repeated the man. A masked figure, a village witch doctor, shouldered him aside, brandishing a copper instrument, flattened at its end, which he thrust into a pot of reddish embers. While it heated, he fixed the Snow Hawk's lids back with a devilish contrivance which hooked into either brow and held up the eyelid.

Now he stirred the embers and withdrew the glowing copper rod; and grinning evilly, had brought it up before Kioga's face, when of a sudden the Snow Hawk brought his last full strength to bear in one mighty effort to burst his bonds. And seeing some of the cords breaking asunder like threads, the cowardly shaman drew back.

Then from one side Shingas the Half-mouth came to his assistance, aiming a heavy blow with a war-hammer. Had it landed squarely, Kioga must have been a corpse in his cords. But in his haste Shingas swung too far back. The hammer struck between the torture-pole and Kioga's spine, at the neck.

With the weapon's fall, it was as if Kioga lost consciousness—yet not entirely so, for though the sight of his torturers seemed to melt suddenly from his view, as a curious numbness crept along his head and neck, oddly enough he could hear all that transpired round about him. The poignant agony of those thorns embedded in his fingers' quick was undiminished. Nor did he lose the power of other perceptions. And what he heard a moment later seemed the fantasy of delirium.

For at a sudden wild yell, Half-mouth sprang back in quick alarm: The brave beside him was tearing at an arrow quivering between his ribs, his eyes rolling, the muscles of his face working terribly beneath its paint as he fell.

Instantly Shingas's gaze flew to the village gate, where he saw that which struck terror into his craven's soul: Two sinewy figures had dropped from the palisade top, had struck down the surprised sentries, whose eyes had been fixed on the torture, and had thrown wide the ponderous barrier to the inrush of a horde of yelling naked fiends.

Long lulled by that sense of security over their enemies which had been born after Kioga's great victory, the Shoni had for some time neglected to maintain their old system of scouts and outposts, and had left themselves open to their old raider-foes the Wa-Kanek, from the vast plain west of Natowa's coastal forests.

But something of a surprise also awaited the Wa-Kanek, in the presence here of so large a force of armed men. And the Shoni reaction was swift. Already the two Wa-Kanek warriors who had thrown the gate open were martyrs to their boldness. One, transfixed by a Shoni spear, hung pinned to the palisade, writhing in agony above his fellow, who, at his feet, resembled more a porcupine than a man, because of the arrows that protruded from him.

The swift hissing shafts of the villagers cut into the irregular ranks of the invaders, as from every point of cover they raked them. Already the gate was choked with the fallen, beyond all closing against the remaining horde, which trampled on its dead in gaining ingress.

Swift raged the battle back toward the torture-post, which it passed and enveloped. With clubs and tomahawks, knives and spears, the Wa-Kanek warrior-fanatics rushed in, covered by a whistling barrage of fire-arrows and flinthead shafts from their rear. With like weaponry the Shoni fought back.

Already here and there the incendiary bolts of the enemy had fired a bark lodge, from which the frightened occupants scattered screaming. All about Kioga the battle raged hottest. In his ears was the thud of club meeting yielding flesh and bone, the fiendish yells of savage embattled men, merciless and bloodthirsty, who asked nor gave quarter. A hard-hurled tomahawk struck an inch from his ear in the torture-post—a strayed throw. In the heat of fury two savage adversaries fought it out to the death almost against him, unwittingly injuring the Snow Hawk even as they slashed one another. And then some secret friend had the forethought to remove the hooks swiftly from Kioga's eyelids, and to slash his remaining bonds.

He slipped lower within them, until he was on his knees,

all but helpless, victim of the numbness and restricted circulation caused by the tight-drawn cords.

Yet though he heard and felt the bloody progress of events, no single detail did the Snow Hawk see. That darkness, somehow associated with the numbness in his neck and upper spine, was with him still. And presently on receiving a glancing blow from a club aimed elsewhere, he sank into darkest oblivion.

The battle stormed on, passing him. And due to the unexpected numbers of Shoni war-men assembled for the Winter Festival, it was not the slaughter the Wa-Kanek had contemplated. The village lines held; the Wa-Kanek forces wavered; and because it is the nature of Indian warriors to retreat if the end be not quickly achieved, the raiders then withdrew, smashing many Shoni canoes as they left, to take counsel of chiefs and medicine men somewhere on the rivers.

Fearing some trap, the Shoni pursued no farther than the riverbank, though their invectives, insults, and arrows followed the retreating enemy until these were out of hearing and arrow-range.

Returning then, the Shoni gathered their dead and the dead of the Wa-Kanek raiders, which lay thickest about the torture-stake. A hasty separation of the two was then made, against the expected moment when the Wa-Kanek would return the assault. As is their custom, the Shoni loaded the enemy dead in several longboats, and accompanied by a shaman, pushed off downriver. Not until the craft were well away did the villagers discover that in their haste they had permitted the body of Kioga to go with the others.

Arrived at what is known variously as the Caldrons of the Yei, the Haunted Whirlpool, or the Unti-Guhi, the shaman began the superstitious rites which mark the donation of human bodies to the river-gods. . . . It may have been the cold water playing about a dangling wrist which brought the Snow Hawk back to consciousness. But whatever it was, the cracked monotonous drone of the shaman's voice was the first thing he heard as his faculties began to serve him. He opened his eyes, but the same utter darkness was still with him. He saw nothing.

Some moments passed before he fathomed the astounding fact that he was a dead man, among other dead men, his soul being prepared for sacrifice to the river, even as his body had been preparing for sacrifice to the fires. The droning voice ceased. Kioga heard the splash of bodies being pushed into the flood. For the first time he tensed his muscles secretly, and found them responsive, though every movement gave him pain.

Now, closer by, he heard other sounds—the sickening rip of hair from skull as according to custom the shaman incised and tore away scalp after scalp from the dead who had not been already scalped by individual conquerors—communal trophies of the tribe. The man was working just beside him. He, Kioga, would be next.

At this same moment one of the canoe-men called a name to which the knife-wielder answered. That name was Child's Hand, the shaman who had seen Heladi enter the prison-lodge in her attempt to free Kioga—Child's Hand, the sole possessor of the girl's deadly secret.

Kioga felt the man's clawlike hand at his brow, straining the skin taut that the blade might better do its work. He heard Child's Hand utter a sudden subdued exclamation of astonishment at this piece of good fortune—to secure the Snow Hawk's hair, which would be a priceless relic if only the entire skull went with it. The Snow Hawk felt his hair released and his chin forced back. In a moment would come a quick slash, and— But Kioga did not wait for that.

Like the head of a Nato'wan viper, the Snow Hawk's waiting hand darted forth, the fingers clenching into the shaman's cordy neck. One quick, eel-like writhe, and Kioga had flung himself into the river. A moment the resisting shaman gripped the canoe's gunwale, playing havoc with the craft's trim. Then, overbalancing to the drag of that mighty arm fastened at his throat, he went down kicking and squirming, to disappear beneath the troubled surface, as silently as any body he himself had ever consigned to the waters.

Came a shout from the stern paddler. "*H'yah*! The pole-hook! Child's Hand has fallen into the river!"

But though they watched, the shaman did not reappear. Somewhere beneath the water Kioga was seizing the shaman's scalping knife and plunging it into the man's own heart. Then releasing the dead man, he struggled with his remaining strength to attain the surface. The rushing currents had already swept him swiftly beyond view of the red canoe-men, and for a moment he faced the likelihood of being caught into the maelstrom of the Caldrons.

Then a crosscurrent snatched at him, and upon a rocky ridge he was hurled with a force which drove the little breath out of his lungs. There he clung, fighting with every ounce of his little remaining strength to make good his hold, to hang on, that he might live.

Given an inkling of what the next long months would bring, perhaps the Snow Hawk would have strained less eagerly; perhaps he would have preferred the swift oblivion of drowning to that which he must yet endure. Fortunately, though many lay claim to prevision, few men are gifted with it. The Snow Hawk, having regained a little strength, painfully dragged himself ashore. Listening to be sure none of the Shoni were in pursuit, he chafed his cold and stiffening limbs until the blood flowed. Then, rising in his nakedness, he who had been so sure of foot stumbled toward the thickets, groping his way from tree to tree until well concealed from possible view on the river side.

How dark the forest seemed this night! How cunningly the ground-vines caught at his uncertain feet! Branches seemed reaching from nowhere to strike him in the head. But still he groped onward, following as best he could the southward trail, away from Hopeka.

A strong scent came to him suddenly. T'yone the wolf was straight downwind. So close was he, that Kioga caught the beast's snarl. His foot was on a stone. Picking it up, he hurled it in the direction of his old enemy, and heard it strike, with a thud—heard T'yone's retreat and knew the animal must have been exactly where he had looked. And yet— why had he not glimpsed the yellow fire of the wolf's eyes?

With a dread suspicion which he scarce dared harbor, he sought a certain animal-trail known to him, which would lead him to a cliff-ledge wherefrom he could put his growing apprehension to the test. A half hour of uncertain climbing brought him to the well-known spot, where oft he had lingered to watch the moon's slow rise. He reached forth, found the familiar cleft wherein to secure his feet. Unmistakably this was the place. The air was clear and cold—his nose and skin told him that. The moon had risen before he hung upon the torture-stake, and would be flooding the valley with a silver glow; yet he saw it not. He passed a hand slowly back and forth across his face, shook his head and tried again— but in vain. He rubbed his eyes, felt them very gently with his fingertips, and all seemed well, save that the brows were tender where the shaman's torture-hooks had pierced them.

Then, nearby, he heard a winter-bird give liquid voice, as only it does when the moon is in the full. And that, perhaps, was when the Snow Hawk realized the stunning truth.

No more for him the swift wild dash down the mountainside. Never again the lightning pounce upon the unsuspecting deer. No glimpse from this day onward of a leopard's spots, the Northern Lights, the sun reflected in a deep blue pool, a woman's smile.

Hitherto lightning's incarnation, henceforward he was of those who are brothers of slowness, who carry staffs and feel their way along. He who had been the soaring hawk was now the earthbound mole, destined to burrow unseeing on his tortuous way. He would walk that circle of darkness in which the sightless move. And in the end he would be a heap of bones in some man-eater's den.

For long the Snow Hawk crouched on the ground, meeting such a situation as few have been called upon to face. At last, descending tortoiselike from his high pausing-place, he groped for and broke for himself a long slender stick wherewith to feel his way....

Morning, marked but by an hour's flush in the southern sky, found him still unseeing as he picked his way toward the so-called Tsus Gina-i the Ghost Country of the Shoni, Somewhere in those unplumbed depths the Snow Hawk's lair was hid. Could he but attain that refuge, he would be safe so long as he could obtain food and drink.

But even with the thought the grim laws of survival were coming into play. A gaunt panther, who at another time would have given Kioga a wide path or lived to rue it, paused before the Snow Hawk with lolling tongue and polished fangs adrip. On detecting Tagu, the Snow Hawk flattened against a tree, a snarl upon his clean-cut lips, as he instinctively fell back on savage bluff to keep the panther at a distance. It was successful—this time. But though with that snarl Kioga had warned Tagu away, there were others who by some dark instinct came to an awareness of the Snow Hawk's plight. Of these Pack-skull the Grim and his voluble brother crows were a few. From them others learned of it, and in turn broadcast their knowledge. For so it is in that world where the law of fang and claw is the only law. Know you not with what subtle cunning the wolves wait on a sick and ailing bull, and how the meat-birds draw unto a living thing, with prescience of its end? When, before, would a raven have dared to sit croaking at Kioga's very elbow as one did during his every pause on the way to his cave, while others wheeled heavily about over his head, wondering if they too dared?

Already the pangs of hunger assailed Kioga. Of what use now the fine primeval adjustment of those fox-keen nostrils? Scent the prey he did—a deer nearby. Stalking, he heard it move away. He heard it snipping a twig, sprang at the sound with sudden hunger tearing at his vitals. He crashed into a thicket of devil's-club from which he picked himself up bleeding anew, and much wiser as to his present limitations.

The pain in his swollen fingers was agonizing. With his teeth he had drawn out the torturing barbs; now he held his inflamed hands in the water of a brook to cool. Such slivers as still skewered his flesh here and there, he then drew forth.

For several hours he made his slow way along, judging his course as best he could from memory, and listening intently for the sound of a waterfall, which at last he heard and was able to locate himself after a fashion. Unless he erred, a stream flowed a little way north of here, which eventually passed through country little known even to the Indians. Once within those confines—whose every trail and stream and cave Kioga knew with the intimacy of an entire boyhood spent there—he would at least be able to move with greater familiarity, and far less risk.

But he was not there—yet. And on the still forest air there came to his ears a long howl with a note of sadness which but made it the more terrible. In the middle of its utterance he heard that which sent him rushing on, heedless now of the blows he sustained from branch and stone and unexpected fall—a sudden bubble of sound in the interrupted howl—then the sirenlike, triumphant, uprushing rocket of grim music, bursting at its apex into a dozen yapping notes. It was the signal *"Come to meat!"* by which Kioga knew his trail was found.

He was confused by the apparent hopelessness of his situation. But only for a moment did he run; then his old cunning reasserted itself. Never by headlong flight could he deceive these slant-eyed pursuers. If best them he did, it would be by wit and wile superior to their own. If his sight was gone, his woodcraft at least remained.

Pausing in his tracks, he worked grimly, quickly, and stoically with his sharp knife. Waiting the few moments he dared wait, he then continued on, slower and more haltingly than before. He heard the heedless crash of brush that betokens a pack rushing hot on the blood-trail, and the whines of famished eagerness with which the wolves quartered the spot he had so lately quitted. Soft as might be now, he moved toward the water. Echoed up the short deep yelps of bafflement, heard but rarely from the pack in force, just as the Snow Hawk felt against his face a cold clean breeze off water.

The howling rose in volume as the wolves vented their full discomfiture.

Kioga moved across the sand, feeling with his stick for what he sought—a log thrown by the spring freshets high upon the bank. At a likely seeming log he paused, bent, assured himself that its weight was not beyond his reduced powers. After a moment, marshaling his strength, he dragged it toward water, pushed it into the quick current, and threw himself upon it.

The rattle of clawed feet sounded behind him on the sands, followed by the snoring growls of the panting killers as the prey floated to midstream. There Kioga was safe. The Nato'wan wolves, like their distant relatives the white wolves, take to deep-running water only in a life-or-death extremity.

The Snow Hawk was safe for another reason: he had confounded T'yone's gang with the very thing it sought, his rich red blood, a great pool of which he had let from his own veins, temporarily blunting their capacity for further scenting—and it is primarily by scent that wolves run down the prey.

A pint of blood—a high price for one in his condition to pay for the moment's respite in which Kioga had accomplished his escape. But with that price he had bought life itself, which surely had been forfeit had he taken measures less extreme. Calculated in those terms, the purchase cost was not so great, thought Kioga as the great round log bore him from the danger zone downriver into the trackless Ghost Country. When the log grounded at last, he knew he had gone as far as this stream could take him, for at this point that particular stream separates in a hundred directions, losing its identity in a gloomy swamp.

XIII

To one less amazingly endowed with keenness in his other senses, Kioga's situation must have seemed hopeless indeed. Yet it had come to him, as he felt his way along, that he need not despair. His passage from the river along familiar ground was eventless, though managed at but a fraction of his normal racing pace. At the base of the cliff he found without difficulty the old narrow trail he had climbed up or down thousands of times. And halfway up the cliff's face, his seeking fingers encountered the stout door of interlacing branches, plastered with river clay, which long ago he had erected to bar out wind and storm.

Another moment to manipulate the cunning latch with which he had equipped it; then the door of sanctuary swung inward. The quick ear of the Snow Hawk caught the faint murmur of running water—the spring which bubbled in the depths of his comfortable haven. Stepping in, his cold bare feet sank ankle-deep in the soft rich skins which covered the stone floor. He passed onward, to slake a raging thirst at his private spring. Then, cold, hungry, and utterly exhausted, he flung himself down, rolled up in the thick-furred skin of a great tiger, and fell asleep. . . .

After a few hours, however, the pain of his wounds awoke him, and he rose shivering. Here and there he groped about the spacious lightless enclosure, his fingers informing him that all was inviolate. Spears, bows, and tomahawks hung upon the wall. There were several whips of various lengths; ropes hung in neat coils, and in one corner stood a sort of three-pronged grapnel-like object, little larger and much less cumbersome than a club, to which he would later return.

There were other things he would have lingered over, but he was cold. In his rude stone fireplace there remained the charcoal and dry sticks of a dead fire. Just beside it he found a handful of loose bark, his firebow and its spindle, which later he adjusted into the notch of its tinder-block. Taking a lap round the spindle with the bow's braided thong, a few quick strokes sent a wisp of woodsmoke up to his nostrils.

He pressed the fluffy bark against the kernel of ember his drill had generated and gently blew until he heard the crackle of a little flame. Upon this he cast a handful of dry sticks, which igniting, formed the basis for his fire. He quickly built it up to roaring dimensions, piling on billets from the immense store in his cave, and comforted himself in the warmth of his blaze.

His next thought was of food. Moving a few steps, he reached into a woven basket to find therein some pieces of old dried meat. Of this he ate sparingly—for he knew not where the next meal was coming from. There should be two large baskets, he recalled, groping about. Ah! Here was one, filled with kernels of dried corn. Enough, he estimated from memory, to last him several weeks.

But a sudden scurrying sound disillusioned him of that, and when he set the basket down, several families of wood-mice scattered about. The squirrels had got into his other basket and finished off its store of acorns. Scarce a handful remained of what had once been at least a bushel. These were serious blows, but with hunger partially satisfied by the dried meat and partially disregarded, Hawk turned to other things.

His hands passed over the stone anvil whereupon he had beaten many an iron or copper head for his weapons. He paused upon touching a thick bear-skin which covered a trunk-sized chest, bound with rusted and broken iron bands. Throwing aside the skin, he raised the creaking cover, and plunged his hands elbow-deep into an assortment of fiery gems, large, small, and of a hundred shapes and varieties.

He could not see the chatoyant glitter and sparkle of this priceless hoard, nor enjoy the cold radiance of the small halo which arched above the open chest. These things are for the eye alone. But he could remember that exciting day, years since, when he had dug this treasure from a sunken hulk long buried in the coastal sands.

His hands now went to a rock shelf high on the wall. Carefully he took down book after familiar book. From these well-worn tomes, salvaged in his boyhood from a wrecked steamship, he had educated himself as best he might—building on what his Indian foster-father had taught him of speaking, reading, and writing the English tongue, with a bit of charcoal for chalk, and the inside of a barken lodge for blackboard. His touch played about corners and backs slowly, but without opening the books. Of what use to look within them now?

From the wall he took down a length of rawhide rope, plaited by his own hand in the so-called four-braid, of which he unlaid a length of a few feet. With his knife he then cut off the several lengths of leather and made them into slipnooses. Arming himself with a war-tomahawk, and covering his nakedness with fresh moccasins, *azain*, and warm Indian hunting-shirt, he set forth into the forest again, climbing down the steep path he had utilized in coming up.

Over certain well-beaten animal-trails he pulled down tall and springy saplings. To these he affixed his snares, tying the resisting treelets down by means of cords and twig triggers so delicately adjusted as to send the snare jerking upward at a slight touch. Five of these, in various places, formed his trap-line, which he left returning to his cave only after he had notched each sapling with the tomahawk for identification later.

For several hours he labored at the creation of a digging

implement of iron, for an even more ambitious plan had entered his mind: He proposed to dig a pit, and mayhap at one stroke of fortune take a month's supply of real meat!

But that, thought the Snow Hawk, was a problem for the morrow. Tonight he would visit his trap-line, which he did. One snare dangled empty. A second and third were unsprung. A fourth, operating at his own touch, jerked his hand into air with startling force. He reset the sprung snares before going farther.

But in the fifth cord he found a reward. A fine plump hare, victim of sudden neck-breaking death, hung limply.

Kioga dined that night in royal style, all things considered; and banking his fire for the term of his rest, rolled into his good furs and slept the clock around.

Waking rested, he finished off the remainder of the hare and gave thought to his proposed pit. Faring forth, he felt the soft gigantic snowflakes of winter on his cheek. With his mind occupied by new problems, he gave little further thought to his blindness. In a day, two days, a week, doubtless his sight would return; for were not his eyes open and whole—apparently quite uninjured?

Though his lost sight had been one of the most important of his faculties, infinitely valuable, every other faculty remained intact. To these in his extremity, he appealed.

King of his remaining faculties was the wonderful subtleness of his smell-sense, wherewith, by moving into the wind, he could detect and evade part of the dangers lurking everywhere about him. His hearing was of the most exact acuteness. For such a savage as he, the very air was alive with wireless messages of scent and sound. Moreover, through much of the arctic year Natowan forests are wrapped in semi- or total darkness. His early life had been spent roaming constantly about in these glooms. Therefore he was no stranger to that little-known faculty that has been described as sense-of-obstacles.

So, as he now went about, it was with the aid of no new ability that he instinctively dodged things in the path. Indeed in this forest, with all its obstacles, he was safer than on a desert or plain, where there is naught to reflect sound to the sightless one.

At a likely spot Kioga paused and attacked the frozen earth with his crude iron pick. In an hour his labors had advanced to a point where a pit six feet long and several deep yawned open. The end of the day found him laying thin branches and rubble across the deepened pit, which the falling snow rapidly concealed. Then he turned caveward. At his snares two more hares awaited. Resetting them, he continued on, to spend the next few hours repairing an old fish net. This he later took to a stream nearby, stretched it across a channel, weighted its lower cords, and departed, new ice among the inshore willows tinkling elfinly, like musical glass, as he trod on it.

Next day, hampered by the depth of snow, he approached his game-pit with bated breath and keen ears. At a series of repeated snorts and savage batterings as of horns against earth, he unslung his bow, held two arrows in his hand and a third against the string, and advanced. An intentionally broken tree-marker informed him that the pit was but ten feet ahead. Even as he listened again, the captive in the pit began a new thrashing of horns, tossing clods of earth and sticks into Kioga's face.

A change in the breeze brought him the thrilling scent of living venison. Here was meat to satisfy every demand of the most ravenous. His pit had taken its first toll!

He snatched back the string and loosed an arrow straight down into the hole. He heard the unmistakable sound as it sliced into the beast's body. With the remaining arrows likewise deep-imbedded, he heard the creature's struggles presently cease. Waiting until certain the end had come, he lowered himself carefully, passing his hands over the new kill.

Its size exceeded his fondest hopes. It was a fine buck, weighing all of two hundred pounds, the antlers perfect, the hair coat smooth and still warm. With as little exertion as one might employ to raise a house-cat, Kioga lifted the heavy animal out of the pit. One deft slit down the belly allowed the abdominal contents to roll out. Repairing the disturbance of the pit, he then recovered it, in hopes of another victim in the near future. Shouldering the meat, he went home. . . .

Flushed with his triumph over the problems of blindness, which he had thus far met and solved, Kioga had returned to his cave and borne his fresh kill within. Feeling for the door in order to close it, he heard a sudden blast of wind rip past the entrance of the cave. The suction caught at the great barrier and crashed it shut. In closing, its bar caught the Snow Hawk a terrific knockout blow on the side of his head. He went down like a riven tree, knew a moment of complete unconsciousness. Then he awoke to a fresh awarness of that grim and painful reality of his affliction which comes to all the newly blind.

He would hereafter be the sport of his own carelessness,

prey to the slightest moment of forgetfulness. He learned these tragic inferiorities of his state at costly price. His accident laid him up for two long days, during which it seemed that his temples must burst with pain. And though he grimly rejoiced in his temporary triumph over the terrific dangers of his position, his heart was torn with anxiety for those dear to him. What of Heladi—and Tokala? What had befallen Grass Girl and the other Indians whom he had brought from the security of America into this wild land?

XIV

Back at Hopeka village, immediately on the repulse of the Wa-Kanek raiders, Heladi was one of the first at the scene of Kioga's earlier ordeal.

Already the wounded had been borne to one part of the village, where the women were administering curative herbs and applying soothing poultices to their wounds, while the shamans chanted magic songs over them, to aid in the cure. Among these Heladi moved rapidly, pausing but an instant before each to assure herself it was not he whom she sought. With mounting dread she turned toward the silent rows of the dead. But of all the horrid death-masks Heladi looked upon, none bore the faintest resemblance to the Snow Hawk.

As she stood bewildered, it dawned upon her, when two of the returning longboats discharged their warriors, that some of the enemy dead had already been taken out on the river. And walking purposely past a group of those who had manned the death-craft, she overheard snatches of their talk about the peculiar fate which had overtaken the shaman Child's Hand.

Had it been any other than he who bore the dangerous knowledge of her presence at the captive Kioga's side, she would have passed off the shaman's death as accident, or as another treachery of which the village had heard so much of late. But with Heladi, the wish was parent to the thought that Kioga might have had a hand in this. Uncertain and fearful, she turned toward her lodge.

One night a week later, paddling silently into view of Hopeka, with a contingent of twenty brawny braves, came one of fierce and haughty mien, who was secretly feared by the shamans and marked for eventual quiet disposal by the Long Knife society's plotters.

This was Kias, lifelong friend of the Snow Hawk, and one of the very few remaining alive who had dared to defy the shamans in open council. Kias it was whose father Uktena had paid the death penalty for a like offense. And Kias wore this day a deer-skin blanket, blackened in memory of his father who had died so strangely, with suspicion pointing to foul play.

That excitement greeted Kias's coming is certain. The news traveled swiftly, particularly in those quarters frequented by the Long Knife society's membership. Timed less providentially, the arrival of Kias and his band might have occasioned the society less concern. But at an hour when the shamans had all but established themselves masters of the Seven Tribes, the advent of opposition, particularly in one so skilled in the Indian arts of rhetoric and eloquence as the quick-tongued Kias, was an unhappy visitation.

In his turn Kias had instantly observed the general excitement. Quick to inquire into this, he learned the amazing truth—that his friend and former superior the Snow Hawk had indeed returned. To one who owed his tribal position and his very life to Kioga, this was startling information, the more so since Brave Elk, his present informant, attested it. It was also Brave Elk who was able to tell him of events preceding Kioga's own capture, including the adoption, by Heladi, of the boy Tokala. At mention of this Kias turned to Brave Elk quickly.

"Heladi—daughter of the Wacipi chief—is it she of whom you speak?"

"Even so," replied the other. "She cares for the boy who came with Kioga."

"It may be, then that they will tell us more of this," said Kias thoughtfully. But he was too shrewd to seek out Heladi directly and involve her in the far-flung web of the Long Knife espionage system. He called instead at a neighboring lodge, headquarters of a band of bachelor warriors who called themselves the Arrowmakers. Here for a while he tarried, to break a long fast and ponder how he might talk with the girl secretly....

In the interim the welcome news of his coming reached the Wacipi maid. Here, she knew, was a bold and trustworthy spirit, known to be sympathetic toward his former master, scornful of any suggestion that he disavow allegiance to the Snow Hawk. Cautioning Tokala to remain indoors, it was Heladi who sought out Kias, to acquaint him with all the recent happenings and enlist his aid.

Unsuccessful everywhere else in her search, she turned at last toward the fire-lit bazaar, located near the bachelors' lodge. Despite the recent excitement and the sacred ceremonies of the season, trade must go on. For the Shoni, unlike most American Indian tribes, had developed a regular system of barter and exchange.

Articles strange and picturesque adorned the rude stalls erected for display of various wares. From deep in the farthest reaches of the peak-country came these magnificent glazed earthenware specimens of red, yellow, and blue pottery. Copper ornaments and combs of bone and metal lay among chains and glossy disks of the reddish metal. There were necklaces of animal-claws for trade, and polished pendants on leathern thongs, and labrets for those who wore them, and earrings and quill skewers with which to pierce ears or nose. There were dried pigments for war and ceremony, powdered in little wooden bowls. There were whole skins, worked in colored quill designs, ready for conversion into apparel, and great squares of native woven stuff of split reeds, made to shed water from the wickiup. Moccasins of many varieties, shell-beaded, lay about; elsewhere were shown flints for arrowheads, and little pressure-tools of bone for chipping flint; carved bone whistles, small musical instruments; cups and spoons of mountain-goat horn heated, shaped, and polished; piles of hardy dried fruits from the far mountain confines heaped up on shallow baskets, themselves valuable for their water-holding closeness of weave.

And on racks behind the stalls, adjusted so as to catch the eye, the most beautiful and priceless of all Shoni handiwork—the feather robes—were displayed. They hung there in all their iridescent splendor, their folds filled with highlights and areas of gleam, like rarest Oriental rugs. Of these, many were as much as ten feet square, yet so light a child might carry several and scarce feel their weight.

Such were the Shoni bazaars, filled with dark-skinned children stuffing themselves with the free maple sugar dispensed liberally by the toothless old hags presiding over the stalls.

It was here that Heladi came upon Kias, and approached him with a haste which drew attention from certain watchful eyes whose observation had been better avoided.

"Kias," came her greeting, "the hour has been doubly long seeking you."

"Heladi!" he answered her, as he shot a few quick glances round about to see if they were observed. "Know you not that I am always watched and spied upon? You peril yourself coming to me openly."

"Since when has a daughter of the Wacipi feared danger?" she demanded a little haughtily. "Have you had the news of Kioga?"

"In part," was the reply. "But tell me what you know else."

And so, in the shadows of the bazaar she told him, filling in many interstices in the structure of his information. When she had done, "And the shaman Child's Hand—returned he no more to the village?" asked Kias.

Heladi shook her head; whereupon Kias grinned suddenly. "But for that," he asserted, "I should agree that Kioga is dead. But there is something in the shaman's end that rings of the old days, before the Snow Hawk was made chief. Do not give up hope."

Meanwhile, left to his own devices in the lodge, Tokala the Fox wandered restlessly about. And it was not long before he ventured to peep out at the lodge door.

The village was full of scenes at which the lad's little Indian heart beat the quicker—men of war stalking about, heralds moving with messages from lodge to lodge. As he watched, a strange and interesting figure moved past—a village magician known as Walks-Laughing, a harmless sort of creature to whom few paid attention. Scarce had the curious creature meandered past, mumbling, than Tokala was following on his heels, dodging from lodge to lodge, hiding whenever Walks-Laughing turned. In this manner both spanned half the village, the magician gaining no more attention than usual, Tokala passing for one of the village children.

Attracting lukewarm notice where some young men had congregated, Walks-Laughing finally paused, reached into his skin-wrapped bundle, produced several stones and began to juggle them swiftly from hand to hand. He proceeded next to devour the stones, which seemed to multiply as rapidly as he swallowed them.

The matter-of-fact Tokala, who was busy keeping count—which he lost at the seventy-sixth swallow—this was surpassing wonderful. Wide-eyed and openmouthed, he hung back waiting excitedly for the magician to burst.

Others, however, less naïvely gullible, were loudly laughing at the display. Among these were several children Tokala's age, but wiser in the ways of the village, one of whom chanced to see the little stranger intent upon the magician. Now, among little red-skinned roughnecks, just as elsewhere in the children's world, there are always those who delight in pursing and tormenting a stranger from another part of town.

Before Tokala realized it, he found himself confronted by a lad some years older and a head taller than himself—evidently the gang-leader and local bully. Behind him stood a score of children of various ages.

The taller lad reached forth, seized Tokala's nose and twisted it cruelly. Tears of anger and pain sprang into the Fox's eyes. At that moment, from the direction of the bazaars, came Heladi's lithe figure. Beside her, intent upon her serious words, a tall warrior strode beneath his blanket. The Fox saw Heladi suddenly check, pointing, and saw the warrior's eyes raise. They were witness to his second disgrace!

Suddenly something in Tokala snapped; with every ounce of his limited strength he lashed out. His little fist sank into the solar plexus of the bully, whose jaw dropped as he gasped for breath, sank to his knees, and lay *hors de combat*.

No less astounded was Tokala, ringed round by his lesser annoyers. But the Fox recovered more quickly than they, and fell tooth and nail upon the nearest. Triumph filled him with fighting fury. Not all the village children would have been a match for him then. A moment's resistance, then they fled, leaving Tokala the Fox supreme in his mastery, standing alone on the field of action.

Aware that this time, at any rate, he had naught to be shamefaced about, he held his head high. Seeing him standing proud and defiant, one of Kias's mettle could not but be instantly taken with a keen liking for the Fox.

Heladi addressed Kias.

"He is called Fox," she said. "Kioga brought him here."

"Rather call him Wolf, for his courage," answered Kias as his hand went round the boy's shoulder. "The friends of Kioga are the brothers of Kias."

Tokala caught the gist, if not the entire substance, of that, and as they moved on, he strutted along erect and with a great show of indifference to the gaze of his recent persecutors. At the lodge of Menewa, Kias prepared to take his leave.

"What will you do?" Heladi asked him as he bade her good-bye. Kias was thoughtfully silent a moment. Then:

"I and my men will go downstream—on a hunt, that we may add meat to the village store. You understand?"

"Yes," said the girl quietly. "And may you find him you go hunting."

Some hours later, armed for the hunt, Kias and a number of trusted braves congregated about a spot where their canoe lay beached undergoing a minor repair. They were observed of several observers. For one thing, the guardians of the gate watched them with mild interest. More intent by far than these, however, were a pair of glittering eyes that from the face of the shaman Half-mouth focused upon the band, cold with hatred, suspicion, and fear.

Word had reached Half-mouth, via the primitive grapevine system of his own invention, of two things: The peculiar death of Child's Hand was one; the other concerned the unwelcome arrival of Kias, whose appointment as a kind of roving ambassador to the Seven Tribes—made by Kioga and ratified by the council—had long been a thorn in the shaman's side.

To a companion at his side he addressed a few quick words. The man nodded, and accompanied by two others standing near, set out, well armed and carrying several quivers of arrows, to attend to a small matter of bloodletting. They did not leave by the main gate, but by an auxiliary and little-used exit which Shingas barred behind them.

Yet another pair of eyes, and these the brightest and quickest of all, witnessed the preparations of Kias and his men. Also, by lucky chance, these same eager orbs, watching from a vantage point in the south wall, fell upon the silent shadows that were Shingas and his cohorts, prior to the recent separation.

Now Tokala was a child, a mere boy not yet eleven years of age, ignorant of the motives which move men to murder, and totally unaware of these primitive politics. But he needed no guile to make him realize that the secret departure of Shingas's armed men boded ill for Kias.

A little time ago Tokala had almost regretted stealing away from Heladi's lodge. Now he felt more than justified; instead of climbing back to the ground within the wall, he hung down by both arms outside, shut his eyes, and let go.

Tokala was not, remember, such a boy as the Snow Hawk had been, all rawhide and rubber and coils of springy steel, but a recent invalid by no means possessed of his fullest powers of strength and endurance. He fell the twelve feet with a jar that hurt his ankles cruelly. After a moment, biting back the pain, he limped softly along the palisade, always in its shadow. At a point where the forest threw an even denser shade, he parted from the village and attained the near bank of the Hiwasi River, where it turns southward after passing Hopeka village. On a sandy spit, covered with sheltering brush, he crouched, awaiting the coming of Kias and his band.

Presently the fast longboat, laden with its silent red men, came forging by. Rising to hiss sharply, Tokala saw in dismay the warriors lay aside their paddles, seize their bows, and train the sharp arrows on his position. Nevertheless he dared to hiss again. The canoe came slowly inshore, broadside on.

Tokala rose and called Kias's name.

At once the leader of the band struck down the weapons of his fellows nearest him, and springing knee-deep into the icy stream, met the boy halfway with the query: "What do you out here, Tokala?"

In halting Shoni words the Fox told all he had seen and overheard of the plot to destroy Kias and the band, and also of the place named for the killing. Turning this over in his mind, Kias then signaled the canoe nearer, lifted Tokala aboard, and gave the order to paddle into the shadow of the overhang, where he laid his plans to outwit Half-mouth's assassins.

At first he was of no mind to permit Tokala to remain, owing to the risks to be run. But so insistent were the boy's entreaties that Kias finally gave way on condition he keep well hidden behind his own war-shield at the moment of meeting. To which Tokala eagerly agreed. Kias now divided his men. A third of them took to the forest and stole forward to the place named by Tokala as the point of likely ambuscade. The canoe, after allowing them time to reach that point, continued on.

Never, perhaps, did a heart beat swifter than Tokala's as the craft approached the danger zone. Already the overhanging cliff, sharply watched by Kias and his men, was looming into view, fully visible in the floodlight of a brilliant moon.

Slowly the longboat crept nearer, keeping to the concealment of the overhang. When within fifty yeards Kias gave a signal. Shooting forth into midchannel to take advantage of the swiftening current, the warriors bent to their blades. Fast as an arrow the craft fled between the rocky walls, rounding a bend in full view of the place of peril.

So swift was their pace and so sudden their appearance that the ambushers were taken unawares. An instant later two huge boulders, precariously poised on the bank above, toppled into the stream. A split second sooner, and the canoe had been smashed in, but now the mighty splashes merely broke over the stern.

Then a wild long-drawn yell from above echoed along the river as Kias's men took the ambushers suddenly from the rear. Two of Half-mouth's allies hurtled to destruction in the waters below the cliffs. To make doubly sure of them, the canoe-men pumped their bodies full of their waiting arrows.

The third and last foeman fought savagely and to the bitter end near the edge of the rocks high above. Forced to the very lip of the gorge, he finally turned and with a despairing shriek flung himself far out, as if seeking to crush the canoe below with the impact of his own body. A covey of arrows flew forth, of which half a dozen found him in midair, and he fell twisting and turning, dead before he struck the rocks.

Thus ended the first open engagement in what was to be one of the grimmest struggles for supremacy in all Shoni history. And not by the wildest stretch of his imagination could Kias have divined who were destined to be his strongest allies in this lengthy mutiny.

Picking up his successful scouts, Kias continued on his way, arriving finally at the point where enemy dead were commonly thrown into the river. At this spot the Indian band quartered every inch of bank on either side, searching minutely by torchlight for the hoped-for evidence that Kioga might have survived to make his escape from the charnel-boats. Soon that hope dimmed, for at the point where Kioga had actually escaped the currents, every possible trace of his passage was washed away.

At the very last it was not Kias, nor any of his practiced trackers, who came upon a trace of Kioga, but little Tokala himself. Bending suddenly, he picked up something from the grass and rose with a little cry of triumph, flourishing an object he remembered well indeed.

It was the only trinket Kioga had withheld from the handful he had given Kamotok the Eskimo—a copper circlet which had belonged to Awena, his Indian foster mother, in the long ago. But it was enough. With renewed efforts the band finally found a trail—an erratic, uncertain, meandering trail, ending upon the sandy bank of a stream some distance from the Hiwasi. The clawed tracks of wolves had all but obliterated the man's traces. From the age of the several marks Kias drew the conclusion that Kioga must have fallen to—or only just evaded—the ravenous pack. And from this point they failed utterly to pick up the trail again, and perforce they gave up the attempt.

XV

Somewhere to the north of Bering Sea a two-masted schooner scudded before the wind in a smother of spindrift. Close-reefed, lying steadily upon the port tack, the science-ship *Narwhal* fought through a gale with a weather-proof ease that bespoke care in design and seaworthiness and hull. Of canvas she carried only a storm-jib, sheeted flat aft, to prevent broaching to.

Dr. James Munro, whose property and responsibility the *Narwhal* was, kept a weather eye on both ship and gale's progress. Fair weather and an eagerness to be away had induced him to turn his ship's prow into the Arctic in midsummer and assail the Polar Sea at once. Contrary to Beth's expectations as expressed in the letter to her aunt, the *Narwhal* never did touch at Alaska, being beaten from land by an off-shore gale of several days' duration.

Finding himself several hundred miles in the direction he wished to go, and far from land, with ideal weather and a strong wind, Munro consulted first with young La Salle and his sister. His decision to head straight for the Arctic met with the eager concurrence of both. Though they had anticipated meeting their father ashore at Nome and bidding him farewell, a stop would conceivably involve almost a year's delay. By continuing on, taking advantage of two or three months' open water in the Arctic Sea north of Asia, they might, with luck, reach the strange coast of Nato'wa before the end of the year. At worst they would be ice-beset—for which they were prepared—and in a position to strike northward with the ice break-up the following year.

Having gained their agreement, Munro crowded on sail, cut his engines to conserve fuel, and made good northing at the rate of seven knots an hour, according to his entries in the logbook for those days. Soon thereafter he sailed his ship between the continents of North America and Asia, into the Northern Sea.

To the scientist's great satisfaction, Beth had taken readily to life on the *Narwhal*. The men, trained in Munro's scientific work, vied with one another in little acts of gallantry.

But of them all it was the cook Flashpan who most openly laid his old heart at the girl's feet. Early at dawn coffee and buttered hot biscuits awaited her before she had yet risen. At noon and suppertime she was first to be served. Come midnight, and if she were still up and about, a hot broth would be found mysteriously awaiting outside her door.

In return Beth gave Flashpan of her willing attention, to the immense satisfaction of the strange little man. Into her sympathetic ear he poured a thousand tales picked up in his worldwide wanderings, caring not for the doubting smiles of the crew.

"Such language, Flashpan!" ejaculated Beth, this day of the gale, covering her ears in mock horror. A deep flush rose behind the miner's straggly beard.

"'Scuse me, Miss Beth," he begged, gulping in embarrassment. "I fergit when I'm excited. But if you'd of seen me when I rushed in, swinging' me sword, an' cuttin' down them thar heathens like stalks o' corn! I tell ye, gal, that was a engagement!"

A while Flashpan sat lost in recollection ere a doleful expression overspread his face. "But that was in me younger days, an' I ain't so young anymore. All I c'n do t'git around now."

Dan was seated nearby, striving in vain to tune out a roar of static from his radio receiver. "Flashpan," he said, without trace of a grin, "tell us about the time when single-handed you turned back the forty native riflemen. Remember—with Robertson at the siege of Chitral?"

The old prospector flashed a look of heartfelt gratitude at Dan, cleared his throat, settled himself, and for the twentieth time retold his tale. A master raconteur was Flashpan, confident in his powers of elocution. He swashbuckled up and down the dining cabin, pausing to embroider his story with accounts of bloody details—in all of which he seemed to have been in the thick of the fight.

Flashpan was both storyteller and actor. But he was more than that. For on such a ship as this, on such a cruise, it is vital to the successful expedition that its members remain in an agreeable frame of mind. Flashpan did his share in keeping spirits high, with the aid and abettance of his shadow the quick-fingered monkey. Dan provided music from the radio, static allowing, and edited the ship's little paper—the *Narwhal Pole-Star*. Sometimes too, Beth sang to Flashpan's guitar accompaniment, or devised games for special occasions. And among the most fascinating hours were those donated by Dr. Munro himself. A skilled conjurer, wonderfully adept at advanced magic and knowing all the oddities of natural phenomena, his exhibitions commonly rounded off the recreational periods.

One night, during such an exhibition, all those off watch had gathered amidships. Their favorite feat of legerdemain—the vanishing of a bowlful of water—had just been performed for the tenth time.

No less mystified than the humans, Placer the monk sat with head hung sidewise and mouth agape in ludicrous amazement. But of a sudden, in the midst of that hush, the little animal leaped frantically chattering upon the table and thence to the shoulder of his master. With both arms entwined about Flashpan's neck, he gibbered steadily, his frightened eyes fixed upon a closed port against which the passing seas streaked forward. An instant later Nugget, the great guardian of the kitchen, lifted his head from the prospector's lap and voiced such a mournful howl as oft bespeaks premonition of tragedy or death.

Silence fell upon the little group of humans. Vibrating like the strings of a double-bass viol, the rigging sent uneasy tremors down into the ship's interior. Great waves rushed past, each dealing the rudder a heavy blow whose vibrations quivered through the cabin. The beams groaned. It was one of those moments when the ablest skipper knows the ghost of a fear for the stanchest ship.

"*Hist!*" Flashpan broke the silence, holding up a lean hand and speaking in bated tones. "Did ye hear that?"

"Hear what, man?" demanded Dan a little impatiently.

"There 'tis again."

"The wind," whispered Beth.

Flashpan's eyes grew big. "No; 'twas a banshee that wailed. Look at Nugget and Placer. They heard it—'tis an evil omen. God save us, amen!"

Indeed the great dog, fangs exposed, stood with stiffened tail. The monkey had taken refuge under Flashpan's coat.

Suddenly to the straining ears in the cabin came a faint sound that sent Munro leaping up on deck: A human voice from somewhere out in the gale. Fearing that he had miscalculated their course and was running on land, Munro strained his gaze through mist and foam over the starboard bulwark. Close behind him came Dan, and it was he who first descried the source of that hail. His cry "Rowboat ahoy!" brought all hands up.

There, amid the tossing waves, alternately rising to the foamy crests and falling in the troughs, they glimpsed a small boat, taking water from every comber. Two men were visible, one of whom waved feebly, ere collapsing into the bottom of the skiff.

Then began the arduous task of attempting rescue, complicated infinitely by the sudden erasing of the wind, followed by a raising of the sea into irregular dangerous hills. It was a vicious sea in which to maneuver, but by putting out bags containing fish-oil Munro managed to slick down some of the worst water to windward and ease up closer to the small boat.

Below, Flashpan prepared hot soup and coffee, to be ready for them when the men were brought aboard. Beth laid out Munro's first-aid kit and made up bunks to receive the unfortunate sailors.

Ten minutes later the seamen were safe aboard, their boat in tow, while the *Narwhal* proceeded onward. . . .

When they had recovered sufficiently to give account of their plight, the men told a story full of discrepancies. On being pressed to clear up certain parts thereof, they retreated behind a mask of surliness.

"We're here, safe 'n' sound, ain't we?" said one, who had given the name of Branner. "What's the third degree for?"

"He ain't been a seaman long, usin' that tone to a master," muttered Flashpan to Edson, the mate. "I got a idee he followed more'n the sea in his lifetime, by gum! Burglin' would go better with that face. An' now, I wonder, where did I see that rascal afore?" Still wondering, Flashpan disappeared aft.

"Number One rule on this ship is civility," remarked Munro to Branner in a sharp tone which he never used with his own men. "That is, if you expect to stay aboard."

One of Branner's companions, who had given his name as Bucky Slemp, growled at him: "Pipe down, Bran, an' learn to respect your betters."

A head shorter than his gigantic fellow, Bucky looked a nefarious little man. A thin foxy face, with an accompanying air of sly cunning, advertised one of some intelligence. Clearly, he dominated the other two by virtue of a glib tongue and a cold blue stare. As for the third man, he spoke seldom, habitually staring at the planks underfoot, avoiding the gaze of others and answered in monosyllables. He called himself Mitchell.

Slemp now undertook to tell of the foundering of their fishing sloop and of taking to the lifeboat from which the *Narwhal* had rescued them. And until he was interrupted, his story sounded plausible enough. But Flashpan, returning forward at the beginning of Slemp's recital, fixed the man with a gimlet eye and twisted his moustache with a dubious air, obviously designed to attract Munro's attention.

"Something on your mind, Flashpan?" asked the scientist.

"Eh!" ejaculated Flashpan, as if surprised. "Oh, aye, sir! That they is. Been sleuthin' round a bit, I hev. Got a idee we-all have met 'fore this!"—indicating the rescued men with a curving thumb. "C'n I ask 'em a few questions, Cap'n?"

"Go ahead," agreed Munro.

For a moment or two Flashpan's eyes were intent on the deck.

" 'Twarn't in the Klondike, we met," soliloquized Flashpan. "An' I ain't been down Californy-way nigh onto twenty year. So that's out." He paused to scratch his grizzled jaw reflectively. "But I mind me of a time when I shot a man fer stealin' my pardner's poke up on Gold Crick. Got away, he did. But seems to me I recolleck wingin' him in the ear. An' if I'm not mistaken, one of our friends thar has a nick in his port listener."

Munro glanced at the head of Branner, and the latter paled.

"What I'm wonderin' is what were ye all doin' in these parts." Pausing, suddenly Flashpan snapped his fingers.

"Oho! I got it: Ye were seal-poachin' in the Pribilofs."

The effect of his words was instantaneous. Mitchell, the silent, denied his guilt volubly. Branner's bravado evaporated, and even the cold-eyed Slemp lost arrogance.

"You've got nothin' on us," he finally asserted with a feeble show of defiance.

"Mebbe not," answered Flashpan disarmingly. Then, squinting: "How long did ye say ye were adrift?"

"Ten days," repeated Slemp warily.

"Three men, ten days—and no food, you say. An' all of ye strong and healthy. Next ye'll be tellin' me that's red ink on the bottom-boards of yer boat."

Mitchell went green about the lips, at that. The unperturbed inquisitor went ironically on: "An' them holes in the tiller an' sternsheets warn't made by bullets, nohow! An angry narwhal punched 'em in, I presoom. An' ye carried sealin' knives to pare yer fingernails with!"

By now the men were watching him in cold dismay. Then suddenly he spun round, driving home his questions with swift jabs of one bony forefinger: "Who—or what—did ye pitch overboard 'fore we picked ye up? What have ye been eatin' to keep so strong and healthy? Will ye tell the truth, or—"

"It's a lie!" cried Branner in hoarse appeal to Munro. "We didn't kill him! He got a bullet in the head, and—"

"Or will we hold ye for the Coast Guard?" interrupted Flashpan.

The features of Slemp were a study in cold venomous hatred. While Flashpan had been speaking, he had quietly laid hold of a spare turnbuckle. But Dan struck down his arm before the missile was thrown.

Flashpan struck an accusing attitude.

"I hold that ye're guilty of robbery, murder, an' illegal poachin' on the Government seal preserves, an' what other crimes I cannot say."

"Whatever they may be," cut in Munro, "we'll know when Dan picks up the Coast Guard's signals. Meanwhile, lock them up in the forecastle."

But what with delays repairing the radio aerial broken by strong winds, and thereafter continuous Arctic static roaring into the ship's receiving apparatus, communication was never established between Government craft and the *Narwhal*. Faced with disastrous delay if he put into port, Munro decided to sail on with his unwelcome guests. Though he liberated them to avail himself of their seamanship, he assigned each to a separate watch, and allotted them bunks among his own men. Thus he thought to keep them apart and under constant supervision of his own trustworthy crew.

Indeed, the extra hands were welcome on the following day, and thereafter. For that night, with a change of wind, the occasional ice-pans were crowded into great fields. For the first time on this voyage the *Narwhal* came to a standstill. But Munro was of no mind to remain in that condition. Half an hour later the thunder of dynamite twice rolled across the floes, and through the immense crack thus opened in a large pan, the ship passed at fair speed, her iron-sheathed prow grinding through whatever it came against.

From the crow's nest Dan scanned the sea ahead and called out the location of open leads.... And so the days passed in unremitting battle, men's flesh and brawn, and ship's iron and wood, against the mightiest force on the surface of the sea—ice.

Wind was now both ally and their foe. It filled the sails, but also acted upon the pack. The day came when solid ice stretched to the far horizons. And here, in a vain effort to continue, all but a few sticks of their dynamite was expended. Once more, for the last time, the wind befriended them, and the grinding of a moving pack commenced anew, providing the ship with an open lead a hundred yards wide, through which she moved under power and sail. But morning found the *Narwhal* beset in earnest, already showing signs of rising as the ice-pressure increased round about her.

"We're caught, boys," Munro told his men. "Unship the rudder and get the screw up. Come down, Dan." And to the shipwrecked sailors: "Lend a hand astern."

So came the *Narwhal*'s progress to its end, save for the variable drift of the pack itself, which would soon end in a complete freeze-up. . . .

Two months passed thus, without noteworthy incident. At rest in her frigid bed, the *Narwhal* gradually rose higher, her bare poles towering up into the velvet sky where the stars hung like disks of wet fire, and the aurora inflamed or cooled the vault with alternating rouge or argent hues. Much of their time was occupied in learning the Indian sign language, against the hour of their arrival among the aborigines of Nato'wa. And they ventured occasional hunting expeditions on the ice. But game was almost nonexistent on this frozen desert.

And their astonishment was therefore the greater when one night, in midwinter, when darkness was with them around the clock, there came two figures of men trudging out of the east. More surprising still, however—one glimpse of the fur-clad men sent Munro forth with outstretched hand to greet them. For one was Kamotok, his former companion on many scientific cruises in these northern waters, the other Kamotok's cousin Lualuk, with whom the scientist exchanged cordial greetings.

"The hunters are far from the home snow-house. How is this?" he asked in their own tongue.

"Seals are wary to the east, Dok-Ta-Mun," replied Kamotok, and then told further of how he and Lualuk had driven too far out, been caught by a sudden thaw and carried far from land into the moving pack. Delayed by the roughest kind of ice, they had been two weeks traveling a few miles. Preparing to spend a lean winter on the ice and eat their dogs if nothing else came to their harpoons, a snowfall had given them a better traveling surface. Judging their position by the stars, they struck due south for the coast of Siberia, the nearest land. Then they had struck the trail of one of the hunting expeditions from the *Narwhal*, and had followed it for a time out of curiosity. Then bursting star-shells, sent up to guide another exploring party back to the ship, had attracted Kamotok's eye. Changing their course slightly, they had thus come upon the *Narwhal* fast in the ice.

"Welcome, then, Kamotok," answered Munro. "But why does Lualuk quiver like a harpooned Awuk?"

"He has news. Someone's friend was here. He who someone rescued from the ice, long moons ago."

"Kioga? Here?" demanded Munro with a start. "When?"

"When the sun was going away. There were many with him—men, women, a newborn, and a boy of ten winters."

Munro translated this to Dan. The younger man eyed Kamotok a little dubiously. The Eskimo, far from taking offense, produced some of the objects Kioga had given him, along with the caribou backfat, in exchange for the dogs. Among these objects were several which even Dan recognized as having belonged to Snow Hawk.

Munro stood turning these things over in his hand, like Dan almost unable to comprehend that his young friend had actually led an Indian band safely through the very land of famine and across the ice in the few months since he had received Kioga's note of farewell.

"It doesn't seem possible," he mused.

" 'Taint possible!" cried Flashpan.

"You never met him, Flashpan," interjected Beth, who stood to one side. She continued with a little thrill of pride: "If there were only one man on earth who could do it, that man would be Kioga."

"Shore, Miss Beth, shore!" said Flashpan, instantly deferential. "Leastways, we know he was hyar. But he's made tracks. Whar to?"

"To Nato'wa," said Munro quietly.

"Aye—Nato'wa!" shouted Flashpan, suddenly starting and setting his moustache more askew than ever. "Whar gold awaits the eager Argonaut, where a man's pick c'n bury itself in raw yellow ore a foot deep, an'—"

"Flashpan!" Beth reproved. "Won't you ever think of anything but gold?"

"Not till I fill your hands with nuggets, lass, an' lay the sacks of dust in little piles afore yore lovely feet! Until then I can think of little else!" And with that he slouched away, to look into the distance with unseeing eyes.

Meanwhile Munro and Kamotok were conversing once more.

"Someone goes on a long journey?" suggested the Eskimo.

"North and west, to find Kioga," affirmed Munro. "Would someone accompany us?"

"It is a place of devils," discouraged Lualuk of the one hand. "Our people never go there. Lualuk's people will need much meat this winter."

"There is no abler hunter than Lualuk," replied Munro courteously, but observing Kamotok closely. "But is there no one else who would wish to go?"

A while the Eskimo sat in thought. For many years he had worked with this white man he knew only as "Dok-Ta-Mun." A genuine friendship existed between the two men; and like many of his race, Kamotok was a genius when it came to handling motors and tools. Furthermore, though superstitious at heart, he possessed the prodding virtue of curiosity. Finally he spoke, abandoning his own dialect for his own peculiar version of English.

Mebbeso takalook. Long tam sit around, thinkin' of someone who went away last year. Mebbeso I com 'long."

So it was agreed, and Munro congratulated himself on having the services of this expert dog-driver and his team. But Lualuk could not be induced to go; and after receiving a bag of gifts, departed later that night. . . .

A day later another of many sledge journeys was undertaken, using the ship as a base. These trips were for the purpose of locating, if possible, the warm ocean currents, somewhere in this frozen desert, upon which Munro calculated to reach his goal. Unhappily the ice became increasingly broken, with vast areas passable only at the cost of heartbreaking labor by both men and dogs; and in consequence no very great headway was made.

One night Kamotok went out alone to survey the ice in hopes of better traveling conditions. Several hours later he had not returned. Munro had all but determined to go forth with Dan to make a search, when the dogs from the first sledge, with a salvo of howls, signaled the approach of Kamotok's team. To the amazement of those in the ship's company, on Kamotok's sledge were two human creatures, so unkempt, tattered, and emaciated as almost to deny their humanity. Helpful hands were at Kamotok's sledge at once.

"My Lord!" breathed Edwards, as he helped Munro with

one of the men. "He must be all bones! No weight to him at all."

"Starvation and hardship," was Munro's opinion as he examined the men in the warm cabin. "Not dead yet, but near it."

Indeed the men were in the final stages of emaciation, pitiful bony skeletons when stripped of the rags that still covered them. Between their bearded lips Munro forced brandy. Later they were fed, a little at a time, on thin broths concocted by Flashpan and administered with a spoon. Thereafter, in his capacity as ship's barber, Flashpan shaved their faces, revealing men who were living cadavers, marked as by frightful suffering and unspeakable ordeals.

For days the men were unable to speak, living like animals from one feeding to the next. Then slowly their features began to fill out, until one morning Dan, who had been studying them intently, beckoned to Beth.

"Doesn't that man's face look familiar?" he asked in a whisper, eyeing the girl narrowly to get her reaction.

"When he turns his head under the light—yes!" answered Beth suddenly. Then: "Oh, heavens, Dan! After all these months—could they be the sailors from the *Alberta* who deserted when she sank?"

"Looks like it to me," muttered her brother.

"But how could they have lived, more than a year, on this ice?"

"The *Bearcat* left a cache of provisions and clothing and weapons for Kioga, when we sailed without him. You forget that."

"Forget!" said Beth in low tones that echoed some of the horror of that terrible long-past hour when circumstances had forced the abandonment of the man she had even then begun to love. "I'll never forget that night, Dan."

Young La Salle covered her hand with his. "I'm sorry, Beth. It was I who forgot. You were unconscious at the time, and couldn't have known."

When the two men became at last in condition to talk, their story confirmed Dan's opinion. In addition to the provisions in the *Bearcat*'s cache, they had come upon a walrus which Kioga had earlier slain. On this they had subsisted, short-rationed, for several months, living in a snow-hut in continual hope of rescue. A few seals had fallen to their single rifle, but many more had escaped into the sea after being shot. Despite their modern gun and ammunition, they had been handicapped by their ignorance of how survival is managed on ocean ice. In the end their cartridges ran out. The Arctic night began to fall again. The meat was soon devoured, then their gloves, belts, and the uppers of their shoes. Starvation followed and something like madness, and at last unconsciousness.

In this state Kamotok had come upon them. Adding to the horror of it all, even now in their sleep the two men screamed the name of a third sailor, whose flesh had sustained their strength when in their extremity they had broken that age-old taboo which forbids man to eat his own kind.

What with the advent of these twain, in addition to the other men taken from the small boat, the quarters on the *Narwhal* were crowded indeed. Had the extra men been of his choosing, Munro would not have felt concern; but already the fine comradely spirit prevalent during the early weeks of the cruise had been dampened by the churlish behavior of the newcomers, who were not slow to join forces in a rebellious bloc.

Munro's diary speaks, at this point, of their resistance to authority. With this he coped by penalizing insubordination with deprivation in the matter of food—a very effective cure—for the time at least. But if mutiny came—what then?

So the winter wore onward toward spring. For those with eyes to see, there was beauty on the floes when the moon uprose round and full to silver the jagged pinnacles of ice and cast long shadows from the *Narwhal*'s masts upon the fields nearby. The aurora was seldom absent in its endless transfiguration of the sky.

With spring came the long-hoped-for snow—upon which, with Kamotok, Munro set forth in a northwesterly direction, setting out meat caches along a line of march across which he hoped at last to sledge to the water which is kept constantly tempered and free of ice by the warm currents flowing about Nato'wa.

One morning after an all-night drive with dogs and sledge, he was successful, and his eye fell upon a lofty ice-peak ahead—the apex of an iceberg imbedded in solid field ice. The vast track forced through the smaller ice by the frozen colossus was still visible. By this token Munro knew that he had almost found his goal. For icebergs are the product of glaciers, and glaciers originate on land and hereabouts land could only mean—Nato'wa. A day's journey farther on, he was confronted by open water above which hung heavy fogbanks born of the meeting of frigid and warmer currents.

Returning, he informed his men of the discovery, and again the *Narwhal* was prepared for the day when the ice would release her upon the last stage of her epic voyage. Nor was that moment now long arriving.

XVI

The great ice breakup began with a disquieting rumble as of distant thunder, continuing for hours, to the accompaniment of the dogs' uneasy howling. The *Narwhal* shifted in her cradle of ice; and tense hours began for all on board as they watched the great plates of ice, forced together by terrific pressures from afar, forming into great rocklike uplifts fifty and sixty feet high, mighty barricades of white solidity. The thunder was a constant uproar. The dogs, wild with terror, trembled in their kennels on the ship's deck. Open-water pools began forming beside the stern-posts.

In anticipation of the breakup just ahead, Munro again had recourse to dynamite, and cracked up several hundred square yards of ice about the ship. But his operations were interrupted by a severe blow, accompanied by snow. Shift and shift about, the men came below decks, alternately warming themselves and eating, then going aloft to watch the action of the ice grinding and groaning about the ship's hull.

A crisis came. Breathless with excitement, Edson rushed in. "Berg bearing down through the small ice, sir. Coming head on, and we're right in her path!" he reported.

In two bounds Munro was on deck, and one glimpse was all he required, before his command rang out: "Stand by! All hands stand by to abandon ship!"

In another half hour, at its present rate of relentless progress, a spur of the berg bade fair to take off the partly canted *Narwhal*'s masts and gouge out half of her side. And as the great berg came grinding on, powered by wind and current, and slowly smashing and crushing through the broken pack, each man save one leaped to his emergency post.

Casting an eye over his crew, "Where's Flashpan?" demanded Munro. For the moment there was silence, while Dan went below. "Not down there," was his report.

Of a sudden Beth's cry rang out: "There he goes! Look!"

Far out on the heaving ice they could now see their prospector-cook, his long moustaches flying in the wind, leaping like a mountain goat along the quaking footing until he came abreast of the relentlessly grinding berg. In one hand he carried a short coil of thin cordlike stuff, in the other an ice-chisel and small ax. For a moment he vanished behind the spur, then appeared scrambling along its top. Working swiftly with ax and ice-chisel, he hastily drilled several holes in the body of the spur next the berg. Into the holes he could be seen rapidly dropping cartridges of dynamite, which he rammed home with the handle of his ax, placing on top of each charge the primer with its length of fuse, and pouring from his pockets a tamping of sand.

The coolness with which he worked at his perilous task moved those on the *Narwhal* to give him a rousing shout of encouragement in his self-imposed task of dynamiting the ice-spur from the main floe, in the hope of minimizing the peril to the ship. Now he was cutting the fuses, and Munro shouted a warning.

But Flashpan paid no attention. He struck several matches, sheltered them with his body, then applied them to the fuses. With a composure which attested an icy nerve, he waited to be sure all were alight. Then with an agile jump and a shrill yell of triumph he dropped out of sight, and soon they saw him running for life back the way he had come. . . .

On came that ponderous white mass, lifting the thick ice-floes upon its mighty forefoot. A mere fifty feet now separated the berg from the *Narwhal*, whose people—all save Munro—were abandoning ship. It was clearer than ever that the spur would tear out the ship's vitals from stem to stern.

Then—on ears the heavy concussion of the detonated triple charge burst suddenly. Shivered to icy shards, the entire spur slipped away from the mother berg, leaving a cavity, and falling heavily into the rubble at its base.

Its center of gravity disturbed, with ponderous slowness the berg began to roll. With Flashpan it was now a race for life, and he was scampering with all speed at an angle away from the direction of the berg's roll. From about the *Narwhal* the others were shouting encouragement. But as the berg shifted the ice beneath Flashpan heaved. He put forth a burst of added speed, but the tilting of the berg upheaved the floe upon which he ran, and the little man was flung bodily in air and pitched sliding and rolling a dozen yards amid the jagged pinnacles to one side. Beth covered her eyes and prayed.

An instant later the ship quivered to the impact of ice being forced against its side. The chill of the iceberg's slow passage was with them a few minutes as the crew boarded her anew, the danger past. But the frozen juggernaut was forging forward through the wreckage of its own creation, and the *Narwhal* floated free in the berg's wake.

While the crew were putting out an ice-anchor, at the risk of life and limb Dan leaped down to the ice and rushed over to where Flashpan lay as one dead among the jagged shards of ice, his face and chest streaming blood. Picking him up, Dan bore him alongside and handed him aboard the *Narwhal*.

As Beth knelt at his side, taking the grizzled head tenderly into her arms, the prospector's eyes came open. His attempted grin was a painful grimace, but he was still his gallant self.

"Don't worry over me, gal. Y' cain't kill an old turkey like me. Not with dynamite, leastways." But soon thereafter he became unconscious; and for several days Death waited outside the door of Munro's cabin, in which he had been honorably installed. But a week later the injured man was hobbling around and at the end of two weeks he was performing his dexterous miracles with flapjacks in the galley again. . . . . .

However unwelcome the close passage of the iceberg, it had at least cut a wide swath in the solid pack, into which Munro instantly turned his ship, the gainer by almost a month in time. They cleared the pack without serious damage, running with the wind behind the drifting berg almost to open water.

Here fog, that great destroyer of shipping schedules, delayed them for many days—but they were days filled with wonder. For all about them disported the wonderful teeming life of these strange mild northern waters. Sea lions and walrus abounded in mighty herds; orca spouted almost under the *Narwhal*'s bows. Two polar bears were shot from the gunwales, roped aboard by means of snatch-blocks, and their skins pegged out beyond reach of the dogs to cure. The greatest peril no longer was ice, but the floating derelicts with which this area is plentifully encumbered.

The days were slightly longer now, adding to their enjoyment of the sights in this strange sea. They came at last into view of the basalt pinnacles which mark the entry into the Nato'wan reefs. Stripped for action, with hatches battened down tight and all shipshape aboard, the *Narwhal* entered upon her final battle with her old enemy the sea.

Following the chart which Kioga had drawn for him long months before, Munro gave his engineer one bell for "Slow ahead," and nosed his ship gently into the so-called outer labyrinth, which comprises many miles of treacherous reefs, overcast by intensely heavy banks of smokelike fog.

Forward could be heard the *splash-splash* of the sevenpound weight as a seaman cast the hand-lead and called back his endless depths: "By the mark, nine," and, "Mark underwater, nine," and again: "By the deep, seven!"

Beth and Dan stood amidships, recalling the circumstances under which twice before they had threaded these deadly waters. Of the first occasion, when the yacht *Alberta* hammered her way through to pitch on shore, a battered leaking cripple, Beth dared not think at this similar hour. But of the *Alberta*'s second passage outward, she thought oft and again. Then the ship had been guided by Kioga, who knew the channel well; and she recalled how her fears had seemed to vanish when he stood at the forepeak, shouldering full responsibility for the ship's safe passage. For all her confidence in James Munro, how different she felt now as the *Narwhal*'s bow grated along some submarine ridge!

But for the first day this was all the damage the *Narwhal* sustained. Like others before him, Munro was amazed at the range and swiftness and irregularity of the tides, which added immeasurably to the difficulties of navigation. He made quick cross-bearings when visibility permitted, and in this way roughly charted his course—but only very roughly under the circumstances. Several times they came to emergency anchorages.

But on the fourth day a serious mishap occurred with a suddenness that added to the danger. The *Narwhal* was proceeding at a small boat's pace under power and a rag of foresail, when of a sudden came that dread tearing grind and stoppage which spells the beginning of disaster. Instantly Munro gave the engine room four bells. But though the screw was quickly pulling full speed astern, the *Narwhal* would not come off her rocky perch. An instant later Flashpan popped up out of the forward hatch like a strange jack-in-the-box, shouting that the ship was taking water near the chain-locker.

In answer to that, "Man the collision mat!" shouted the mate. Every man available jumped to obey. The mat was quickly drawn over the hole and held there by passing lines under the bow. The leak was checked. Then began the exhausting labor of lightening the ship forward. But as fast as heavy objects were shifted astern, the falling tide nullified the work. Mindful of the tidal drop the day before, Munro said to his mate:

"It's now or never, Edson. Break out those boxes in the hold. Quick, man! Get that heavy stuff all astern while there's still time. What you can't handle fast—over-side with it! We've got to lighten her forward at any cost."

All hands were now concentrated on the task. In their haste the men dropped and smashed the radio storage-batteries, and Dan heaved them into the sea, with other objects too heavy to get aft with the requisite speed.

At length the *Narwhal* lurched, listed, and then grated off the ridge. There was not time to repair the damage forward, but the pumps would take care of that. Fortunately no further important injury was sustained during the three-day passage of the inner maze.

Early one morning when the fog lifted, Munro pointed out a Gibraltar-like shape in the distance. With varied emotions those aboard the *Narwhal* strained their eyes to see the newfound land, each reacting in his own way.

"Land, ho! *Land!*" shouted the men of the crew, with the enthusiasm known only to those who have been long at sea.

Quivering with suppressed excitement, "Eldorado!" muttered Flashpan, imagining a seam of gold in every mountain.

"Somewhere here—Kioga!" breathed Beth, with swiftly beating heart.

Eager thoughts also rushed through young La Salle's head: *Adventure—exploration—wild tribes*! He felt his blood surge swifter, for it was his second visit to this savage shore, and the first was burned forever into his memory.

"Nato'wa—a new land!" murmured Munro, scientist and explorer. "A new frontier!" Somewhere upon this nearing strand lay the remains of the woman he had once loved, and of the two closest friends of his youth. His task it was to affirm the astounding discovery of a great new Northland, made by Lincoln Rand a quarter of a century earlier. More than that, he must amplify his meager knowledge of this new frontier—an adventure so strange and extraordinary as to surpass and crown the many exploits of his life.

Slowly the *Narwhal* clove the unknown waters of the coastal reefs, welcomed inshore by a host of ivory gulls funneling above her to topmost spars. Rarely a vessel's hull enters here intact to ground upon the rocks of Nato'wa. The

Cherokee, early in this century, was such a one. The American yacht *Alberta* was another. Both, by strange chance, were cast upon these shores in a span of twenty-odd years, with living men aboard. But the *Narwhal* was the first ship in all known history to enter the coastal waters of Nato'wa under her own power. In so doing she joined the famous company of ships which have borne men to discovery down all the ages, from the hollow log of antiquity to the cedar triremes of old Tyre and Sidon, and the Viking longships and Old World caravels which went forth to seek the unknown.

The *Narwhal* had certain advantages. Her skipper had knowledge of a new land in the North, and therefore a goal. He had a rough but accurate chart of the only channel deep enough to admit a ship of any considerable draft, and aid in reading it from Dan, who had been here before. For the rest, a rare combination of favorable weather conditions, added to the born explorer's indomitable will to conquer adverse conditions, had aided the *Narwhal* to accomplish the impossible. . . .

The vapors of morning rose mysteriously from the gloomy waters of a hidden cove as Munro gave the engineer one bell. The engines ceased. Slowly the *Narwhal* lost headway, with the leadsman still heaving the weight and calling depths. A few minutes later there was a scraping sound as the *Narwhal* passed over the last ridge. The black cliffs loomed up. Munro ported his helm. The *Narwhal* came about in three fathoms, with the idle among her crew hanging over bulwarks and from rigging, peering anxiously through the mists.

Without realizing it, all aboard had been speaking in low tones as if fearful of breaking the breathless silence of this wild and menacing place. Munro likewise gave his orders quietly.

"Stand by port anchor. Stand clear port chain."

"Aye—all ready, sir," came the mate's reply.

"Let her go!"

A brief roar of chain in hawse-pipe, and a splash as the hook went under. Then: "Twelve fathoms as the water, sir," said the mate.

"Good enough. Hold chain," returned Munro. He heard Edson clap on the stopper forward of the windlass and drop the pawl on the riding chock. Ten minutes later, with all shipshape and the *Narwhal*'s boat riding alongside, Munro prepared to go ashore. . . .

In all the excitement, vigilance over the five castaway hands on board had become relaxed—a most unfortunate oversight; for no sooner had they opportunity than the seal-poachers and the deserters from the yacht *Alberta* joined heads below, in whispers hatched a plot to seize the ship. Acting instantly upon their scheme, Slemp and Branner slipped aft below decks. Opening the arms-cases, they removed the contents, and after secreting some weapons on their persons, carried others forward. What they could not carry they consigned to the sea through an open port. Then carefully closing the boxes again, they awaited a moment favoring their intended piracy.

But behind them, emerging from a dark corner, whence he had observed all with intense simian perplexity, Placer the monk approached the boxes, peering through the cracks with a wrinkle of anxiety between his sparkling eyes. For several minutes he climbed over the cases, ridden by the twin hags of uncertainty and curiosity, both intolerable to any monkey. Then, possessed of a brilliant idea, he excitedly fled forward like some grotesque caricature of a human dwarf. He would take this portentous matter up with the master who knew all things.

Bursting in shortly upon Flashpan, below to inspect the forward timbers, Placer chattered volubly, tipped his hat, tugged Flashpan's apron and induced the little man to go with him aft.

"What mischief have ye been into now?" wondered the cook irritably as he followed to where Placer danced on the ammunition-chest. Then suddenly glimpsing new marks of tampering about the nails—"Oho!" muttered Flashpan. "Oho, sez I! No monk did this, me lad! What in the o' tarnation—" A second Flashpan stood thus, eyes slitted; then he hastened on deck.

On the ship's landward side he saw Slemp and his confederates near the boat-falls, and the tattooed hand of Branner passing rifles from the nearest porthole into the boat. Then he understood. And running swiftly astern, he dropped a quick warning to Munro.

"Mutiny, sir! They've rifled the gun-box! They're passin' rifles into the ship's boat. What'll I do, Cap'n?"

Munro's thoughts moved like lightning. Then quickly: "Act as if nothing were wrong. I'll post our men to tumble them into the boat and cut it adrift. Even with guns, they'll be at a disadvantage. Too late to try to stop them—they'd open fire the minute they knew we'd waked up. You go below and cover them from the galley port. Then I'll send the other boat and bring 'em back."

Flashpan dropped below. He heard the sudden activity and surprised shouts as Munro's men went into action. Seizing his pistol, he rushed to the port in time to see a boathook shoving the boat off, with its five momentarily bewildered mutineers picking themselves off the bottom. When they recovered enough to produce their arms, not a man was visible on the *Narwhal*—all had taken cover behind bulwarks and deck-cabins. Thrusting his pistol through the port, Flashpan ordered the rebels, in a clear loud voice:

"Drop them guns, and raise yore hands!"

In consternation two of the men obeyed. But the remainder, desperately aware of the consequences to come, seized the oars and sculled frantically away from the ship. The report of Flashpan's pistol rolled out, its bullet splintering one of the oars. Undeterred, the man plunged a rifle-stock deep, paddle-fashion, and though a second shot brought a yell of pain from Slemp, in another moment the boat passed round a great rock, out of the line of fire.

On deck Munro accepted the situation calmly enough.

"A rush might have been better on our part. But none of our blood has been shed. Let them go. We're well rid of them, and we still hold the ship."

So it was that at a moment when their services were most required, the discontented among Munro's men, laden with the choicest of the *Narwhal*'s remaining weapons and provisions, deserted. South along the coast they went, building a fire before an open cave wherein they spent the night, well barricaded.

Morning found them up at break of dawn; noon found them still arguing as to a future course. All agreed the *Narwhal* must be boarded and captured, but none on the method to be employed.

Their endless plottings terminated strangely. Branner was arguing in defense of immediate violence, when of a sudden he stopped and leaped to his feet, staring at something along the shore. Wheeling, Slemp reached for his gun. The others stood tense, eyes riveted upon a strange figure approaching down the shore, followed by a band of painted Indians, bearing spears war-clubs, and skull-breakers in their hands.

The leading figure paused. At a signal his followers likewise halted, spreading out to hem the seamen in. Then the leader shambled forward again, a ragged unclean deer-skin flapping about his unwashed knees, around which leggings of hide were fastened with twisted leathern thongs. His hair was black and lank, his beady eyes glittering snakelike as he moved softly up to the uneasy seamen. What manner of man he was could not be ascertained beneath the smears of paint which hid his features.

Almost instinctively Slemp drew back, before falling naturally into bluster.

"Ahoy! Stand where you are! Who are you, and what d'ye want, sneakin' up on us with your hoodlum gang!"

The newcomer's voice was no wholesomer than his person, his vile English no more reproducible in print than the aura of evil that hung about him. But the weight of his words was this:

"I'm called Mad Crow," he boasted. "These men of mine would cut your throats if I waved my hand. How do you come here?"

"By ship—how else?" returned Slemp, bold to assert himself a little more. The caricature of a man showed excitement. "Where does she lie?" he demanded tensely.

"Along the coast somewhere," replied Slemp shiftily, wondering how he might turn this man and his band to account in capturing the *Narwhal* the while conceding him nothing in return. "Well guarded by twenty guns," he added deceitfully.

"Guns or no guns, we'll have her!" shouted the other in sudden animation. "It won't be the first time I—" But there he checked himself, flashed a glance at Slemp and his men, then was silent. But the slip was not lost on the other man, nor the signs of fear prompting its repression. Slemp made mental note to fathom it at another time; meanwhile he wondered at the anomaly of such a creature, obviously from the outside world, dominating this band of red-skinned warriors.

"Maybe, if we c'd get together," began Slemp as if considering it for the first time, "we c'd take the ship and sail her out to sea. She's a fine craft, well provisioned an'—"

But the other interrupted him there. "Any rum aboard?" he asked with feverish eyes.

"Barrels of it!" lied Slemp; and then, suddenly: "By God, you're a white man, sure enough!"

"Aye!" shouted the other. "White of skin and black of heart. Pirate and murderer and worse than that! But square with them what's square with me."

"Where are we, and what are *you* doin' here?" asked Slemp.

"Stayin' because I can't get away. I don't know where I am, nor does anyone else. But I got friends!"—indicating the silent savages standing around. "They think I'm crazy, and fear me for it. 'Tis the way of the bloody heathens. If I ain't crazy, I soon will be in this God-forsaken place!"

"Been here long?" pursued Slemp in his crafty manner.

"Too long! Came on the *Alberta*, devil wreck her, 'long with a gang o' shipwrecked cutthroats she picked up on the high seas! Wolves got most of the others—and a bit of me besides." Now for the first time Slemp noticed that the man's one arm was off above the elbow. He recalled talk he had heard aboard the *Narwhal*, of how some of her company had been wrecked upon this unknown coast before.

Doubtless this man, whom the Indians had named Mad Crow, was one of those pirates who had been driven from the *Alberta* more than a year ago. To the sharp-witted Slemp, here was one of his own kind, a conscienceless rascal whose tolerance was well worth cultivating. And so he made his proposition.

"Take us to a safe place, where we c'n get our heads together. It's not often I meet a man I like as well as you, my hearty," he said cunningly flattering.

And so it came about that this one-armed renegade joined forces with Slemp and his men in an unholy alliance. Followed by the Indians, the white men tramped into the forest.

Flashpan's pistols and old hunting rifle, and Munro's revolver and rifles, were all that remained of firearms after the theft of their other weapons. Arming the men with boathooks and axes, who were to go ashore, Munro stepped down into the boat beside Dan and Beth. He gave the order to pull for shore; and as they went, the sun was half risen behind them, a dull rust-red ball dimly seen through the hanging mists.

When the boat's prow grated on the rock-strewn shore, Dan leaped up, eager to step on land. But Beth's restraining hand fell on his arm. He saw that her eyes were on Munro as she whispered: "Wait, Dan. Let him go first."

A moment Munro stood poised. Then with a spring he was on *terra firma*, bearing the American flag and staff, which he planted upright in the ground. In fringed buckskin, hunting-shirt open at the neck, bareheaded and with eyes alight, he was indeed a commanding figure that might have sprung bodily from some old historic painting. He stood there transfigured by this proud moment of triumph over wind, ice, and wave.

The Stars and Stripes were unfurled. Then in tones that echoed bell-like in that misted haven, Munro spoke history:

"In the name of God and Country, I claim this new land of Nato'wa, and all that it contains, for the United States of America."

As one man, the others of his party bared their heads in a moment of solemn silence. A spontaneous thundering cheer burst from the watching men on the *Narwhal* and was returned by those ashore.

And out of the following stillness, from some far escarpment in the forested hills nearby came an answer—a deep and ominous howl rocketed skyward from the quivering throats of the Dire-wolves.

XVII

In the days that followed his accident, blind Kioga, like many another wild thing, lay close hidden in his comfortable lair. Inaction was his chief enemy now, for it bred thought; and thinking revived the keen agony of his anxiety for Heladi, and for the American Indian companions for whom he felt responsible. . . . Thinking, too, brought back memories of Beth La Salle and of his former way of life. That way madness lay.

Accordingly he filled every moment with some task. He shortened the handles on what few tools he already possessed, made of stone or iron. In the course of his toil he soon found himself able to manipulate ax and hammer without need to see them. And he learned the strange sensitiveness of the tongue in checking the operations of his fingers.

Also, in snare-line and pitfall Kioga threw up his cunning defenses against the slow death of starvation, drawing on every resource of his active brain to forestall the likelihood of foodless times. The forest near his cave was fairly lined with pits and traps. But he dug no more, after the day he fell into one of his own traps. . . .

One day on visiting his snares Kioga found, suspended by a foreleg, a three-month-old tiger cub very much alive. How it came there, whether wandering from the mother and becoming lost, or bereaved by jungle accident, he never learned.

But there it hung, bawling noisily. It was but a matter of seconds to drop it into the leather sack in which he collected his smaller prey. He took it home, liberating it in his cave. And now there were two mouths to be fed. But Kioga found compensation in the pleasure of the little beast's companionship.

As the weeks passed, the sightless warrior lived from the net and the snare, moving always upwind, armed ever with lash or spear. Sometimes he carried bow and arrows, but as a rule only when a captive in a pitfall required killing.

His heavy twelve-foot whip served him well, for with it he controlled a diameter of nearly thirty feet at the center of which he stood. Such a whip is manipulated half instinctively, for sight is not necessary to its control; and many were the smaller marauders he lashed off from the plundering of his trap-line.

So passed that lonely winter, its circle of darkness unbroken for the sightless hunter by star's gleam or aurora's flicker. With its passage the Snow Hawk gradually increased the area of his range. And wherever his moccasin-prints were to be seen, the round pugs of a half-grown tiger-cub showed beside his trail. Nor had ever living man so exhaustive a knowledge of his immediate habitat as had Kioga. He carried within his mind a kind of mental map whereon obstacles of all kinds were marked by repeated experience. Many were his mishaps, but never twice at the same spot. For each misadventure threw up a danger sign on the mental photograph on which, by imagination, he followed his own progress.

Blind men have before climbed the steepest rocks and found their way in the complexity of great cities. But the civilized blind may fall back, as a last resort, upon their seeing fellows. Kioga had no such last resource.

When the Snow Hawk fared off his customary route, he must blaze the way for his return by notching tree trunks with his tomahawk or knife, or by breaking chest-high branches and allowing them to hang, so that he might touch them on his return. But he finally abandoned these crude makeshifts for a superior device.

Since boyhood there had hung on the wall of his cave several medicine-rattles, pebble-filled gourds used by the medicine men when they sing over the sick. He chanced one night to knock one of these rolling to the floor, and traced it almost immediately into a corner by its sound. Thus was born the germ of another stratagem against his affliction.

When again he went off the beaten track, at intervals he

strung up bits of copper in pairs, where the wind might blow them together, setting up a continual metallic tinkle. By this sound he could hear his way back again. A dozen such signals might well enable him to extend his wanderings for half a mile on a quiet day. In other bad places he ran cords along the worst part of a trail, using these to guide himself.

If in all of this he surpassed what a civilized blind man might do, he owed it to a previous intimate knowledge of the area which he now roamed, to his lifelong habit of going in semidarkness, and to his matchless powers of scent and hearing. Without these last he must have perished the first week.

One night during a storm it seemed to Kioga that he saw the flicker of lightning against the blank backdrop of his blindness. But of this he could not be sure, for no thunder followed. Again, weeks later, on hearing the crackle of electricity above his head, he fancied he saw a meteorite fall. Whether true sight, or one of those optical phenomena common to every eye, he could not tell. And these illusions—if illusions they were—disappeared, replaced by the darkness to which he had so wonderfully adapted himself.

The sense of nearby obstacles, scent, and touch, all these enabled him to find his way about. Trifling variations, bumps of many kinds, slopes and declivities—all these and numberless other signs were carried to his brain by his moccasined foot's mere touch, telling him the nature of the ground he trod. Thus to some extent he could locate himself automatically, free of the need to seek unseen landmarks whereby to know his whereabouts.

Here muscular-memory was his tool. You may close your eyes and write out a legible sentence; the hand remembers every movement. You may mount a familiar flight of stairs by night, and know instinctively and without counting the steps when the landing is reached. The limbs become automatic registers retaining memory of an oft-performed act, just as does the writing hand. And by aid of muscular-memory blind animals move about with sureness. So with Kioga.

He had in his lean and striped companion yet another aid. If those lonely mountains in the Ghost Country could speak, many a tale would they tell of the blind warrior preceded through the forest by a tiger's whelp with eyes of phosphor fire. Between man and beast there was some inexplicable bond; where one went, the other was sure to be found. And when the moon was bright, sometimes the wilderness denizens paused on their hunting rounds to watch the startling spectacle of a man and an awkward young tiger eating from a mutual kill.

But snowfalls were the bane of his existence. The blue-white beauty of evergreens, banked high with the thick soft blanket, he could see only in imagination. Worst of all, snow dulled sound; and sound was a vital asset to him. For whereas we live in a world of visible things, Kioga dwelt in a world of sonorities. In like manner snow obliterated the lesser irregularities of the ground, on which Kioga depended to feel his way through his moccasin-soles.

In the beginning he thought by counting his steps to memorize his position better. But the effort to coordinate voided the instinct, leaving him worse bewildered than before. Thereafter he trusted to the inner voice.

But many were the times when Kioga, the sure of foot, sprawled clumsily upon his face, his fine optimism smashed to earth by the crushing conviction that his blindness was to be permanent. For long he fought against this dread specter. But it grew upon him. And at length this man who had asked little of his Creator, relying always in the hitherto sufficiency of his own mighty strength, sought a high cliff, wherefrom to address the Great Unknown, in accordance with the tradition of his adopted people in their times of deep trouble.

Garbed in his finest robe and most valued headdress, he ascended to the heights. From under his robe he drew his calumet, feathered and hung with tassels of fur. Into this he tamped a pinch of native tobacco, grown and held sacred by the Shoni. From a round box he drew forth a smoldering nugget of fire, pressing it against the tobacco. Six puffs only he took, blowing smoke to the four compass points, once upward to the sky and once earthward. This ritual concluded, upon the cliff he then laid out his offerings. His finest bow was there, among others of the most valued products of his cunning fingers, along with a much-prized volume from his little library.

Now in the tones which his Indian foster mother had taught him long ago, he sent up his simple request in the soaring chant of the Shoni supplicant:

> *Oh Great Ones! Hear me now.*
> *I am Kioga—a warrior who sees not.*
> *By your grace I live and bring these gifts.*
> *Oh you who look upon my misery,*
> *Give me but leave to see the stars again.*

Then a while he waited, head thrown back and arms upstretched: waited for the sign that did not come—the downfalling scream of hawk or eagle, the hissing crackle of a meteor, or aught else that might be construed as a favorable omen that the gods would grant his request. And so for day after day, impoverishing himself of all he valued, until, dejected and unanswered, he felt his way down again, like some stricken miserable animal returning to its den.

To make matters worse, his fierce companion of the past months did not answer his summons. The tiger-cub had now answered a wilderness call too strong to resist and probably would never return. Thus utter loneliness was added to Kioga's other trials. . . .

One day in spring, in the Moon-When-the-River-Ice-Breaks-Up, Kioga was returning, spear in hand, bow at back, from a steambath in the vapors of a mountain hot spring. As was by now his well-established habit, he was coming home to his lair by way of shallow creek navigable only in the lightest of canoes. The creek was almost clear of its winter ice, and at a certain rock he paused, turning to begin the short ford which would bring him to the opposite bank. He was halfway across, moving without sound into the wind, when of a sudden, strong and pungent, came the scent of wapiti. So warm and nose-filling it was that without an instant's hesitation the Snow Hawk's spear-arm flew back and then forward as he hurled the weapon straight ahead.

The throw was one of those lucky accidents which occur now and then in the life of every hunter. Kioga heard the impact of iron against flesh, and felt a shower of sand kicked up as the stricken animal bounded in its pain and surprise. Throwing hesitation to the winds, he flung himself in the direction of the sound, lest it escape and bear away his spear. And it happened that his spring was timed with the fall of the wapiti, upon which he dropped with knife bared and plunging for the lungs. And as the Snow Hawk ended the deer's struggles, a silent canoe, bearing the figure of a woman, drifted round a bend.

It was Heladi, who had seized upon this first opportunity of setting forth in search of him. She had come far on the twisting streams, defying alike a natural fear of the so-called Ghost Country and the danger from tigers who haunt these streams and have been known to drag men out of their canoes.

On the verge of admitting failure, Heladi had seen Kioga make his kill, had seen him hurl the spear with all the certitude of a man in full command of every faculty. In another moment she would have called his name. But as he rose, drawing forth his knife, his gaze fell upon her, there where she floated not ten yards away. With her heart in her throat, Heladi waited eagerly for his greeting, looking straight into those glowing deep-set eyes.

Yet for all their fire, she had the feeling that she was unseen, for his glance did not engage with hers, but roved uncertainly off to one side. How this might be she could not conceive; for proximity, light, and all else were in her favor.

Unable longer to control herself, she raised her paddle in greeting. From its edge there flipped off a dozen droplets which, falling, made a faint watery sound.

Quick as a flash, at that sound the Snow Hawk wheeled. As she drifted a little to one side she saw that his eyes did not follow, but remained staring intently at the spot whence the sound had come. His head was slightly tilted, and every feature strained in an obvious attempt to see and hear. Yet it was as if some veil were hung between them. Unsuspecting the truth, the girl yet felt nameless fear clutch suddenly at her heart.

Now, slowly and without a sound, Heladi lifted one hand, experimentally. Kioga plainly did not so much as notice her movement. But inadvertently then, her paddle touched against the gunwale. Simultaneously Kioga's hand flew back, with a lightning movement. Heladi saw the light glint on his knife as it sang toward her, turning twice in air. She sat rigid with utter horror as the sharp heavy blade leaped past, a fraction of an inch from her side, on a level with her breast. What with the force with which it had been thrown, it sank halfway to its quivering hilt in a branch overhanging the stream.

The distance between them was constantly increased by the slow current. Heladi watched, then, in complete fascination, the man's strange actions. She saw him move forward tensely to where she had been, and listen. She saw his nostrils quivering as he whipped out an arrow, fitted it to the bowstring and loosed it, to lodge somewhere in the soft bank. Again, a long moment he stood tense. Knowing that he was alert for the slightest sound, Heladi was yet silent—silent because in that moment she understood, and paled at the knowledge, as at something too dreadful to admit.

He quartered the stream, back and forth. Finally he found the branch wherein his knife was buried, and retrieved it. He felt about a longer time for the arrow, but though it was within easy reach, his searching fingers missed it repeatedly. At last he abandoned the fruitless search and circled back to his deer. Shouldering it, he bore it easily along the path, which he touched intermittently with the extended bow as he went. Before turning into the forest, his perplexed eyes once again crossed Heladi's unseeingly.

And then, of a sudden, she saw him drop his deer with a crash and come bounding back, his face as white, almost, as the snow still lying in the wooded hollows. She heard him call her name:

"Heladi!" and yet again, "*Heladi!*" She knew that those acute nostrils must have borne to him some faint suggestion of her presence; she could only imagine from the deeper lines etched in face and brow, the agony of mind he suffered, knowing that he had not recovered that swiftly sped arrow.

His bow went forth, reminding the girl of the extended feeler of an eyeless insect, using its palpus in lieu of eyes.

With new and terrible intentness he went over the ground time and again, repeatedly passing and repassing within a yard of the missing shaft. With a stick he measured the depth of the water. He would be calculating, Heladi supposed, whether or not a canoe could have passed here. Then he returned, and this time brushed against the feathers of the rigid arrow. With the indrawn breath hissing through his teeth, he satisfied himself that it was embedded not in a woman's soft flesh but in wood, from which he cut it with his knife.

The watching girl saw him draw a hand across his brow, leaving the marks of his fingers through the cold sweat that bedewed it. He whose endurance was that of a wolf, in this moment showed a terrible weariness—the exhaustion not of body, but of nerves and of mind.

And because she knew, by some faultless instinct, that he would not wish her to come upon him thus—a pitiable groping creature, he who had once strode a conqueror through the forest—she kept her silence. All that made his present life tolerable was the belief that he had concealed his infirmity from every other living soul. Let him think his nostrils had erred in reporting her. Though her heart yearned to him, filled with her pity, she held herself in iron check, making no sound. For of all things else, Heladi knew that that pity would soonest crush the spirit of the proud war-chieftain, once a leader of his people. . . . The antlers of his deer vanished slowly in the thicket, as she watched.

Crushed by what she had seen, awed by the knowledge that even in his blindness he could hunt, exist, even thrive where any other man must surely have perished, Heladi comforted herself in the knowledge that she had done nothing to break the fine lonely pride which sustained Kioga in these terrible hours.

But from her canoe, Heladi removed the little basket of food she carried. It was not much to give—but it was all she had. This she placed carefully in the very center of the trail, where Kioga must find it if he returned.

Thus Heladi let Kioga go unspoken, though it wrenched her heart to do so. Returning to Hopeka village, she told no one of what she had seen, not even Kias, nor her confidant, Tokala. But from that day forward each sunrise found Heladi at the south wall, addressing in the Wacipi dialect the sun she worshiped, chanting her petition for the safety of the Snow Hawk.

Back in the forest, bearing his kill to the cave, Kioga was shaken as a result of his momentary fear that he had slain Heladi. But finally he concluded that his nose had deceived him and that no one had in fact been present on the sandbar. He blamed his nerves for the betrayal.

Nevertheless that joust with the unknown had left its mark; and the spirit of the Snow Hawk was at its lowest ebb since the first hours of his blindness, as he hung his deer outside and entered his cave; and then, as if to enhance his mood, the unbearable happened.

Seeking surcease from his dejection in manual work, Kioga was casting about for his hammer, wherewith to beat out a few copper arrowheads. His hand, moving among his other implements, came upon an object which momentarily puzzled his sense of touch.

Turning it over and over, he instantly deduced that it was a circle of metal, perhaps of his own manufacture, forgotten moons ago. Of a sudden he detected the engraving on its flattened surface. Remembering then, he felt as if some cruel and heavy hand were pressing his spirit against the ground. It was the silver bracelet which had belonged to Beth La Salle. He recalled how he had brought it to her here, as an earnest of his good intentions, proof that he had visited the ship *Alberta* to ascertain the welfare of her people.

Dejection the Snow Hawk had known well, of late. Hopelessness had been his daily companion. But now he plumbed despair. What he had long put from his mind came picturing forward in vivid detail. He thought of her whose laughter had rung in this rock-bound fastness one happy day;

and of her smile and her lithe beauty, and her eyes that had looked into his with something more than interest before this same fireplace. And of a sudden this, his sanctuary, became the lair of desolation.

On a fierce impulse, he flung the bracelet aside, and fled that place with all its reminders of Beth La Salle.

Down the rocky path he went, like one hag-ridden, to pass through the forest, fording shallow streams when he came to them, swimming across those too deep for wading, however cold they were. Along half-forgotten trails and precipitous ridges and through ravines Kioga went, recking not of a hundred falls and bruises sustained on his way.

And in the going, what with his headless haste, the Snow Hawk passed far beyond the outer limits of his accustomed range. Nor did he come to his senses until, paradoxically, he took leave of them, falling into a narrow fissure between two rock walls, where, stunned, he lay slowly recovering his wits. . . .

Rising, Kioga would have retraced his steps. But what had become a simple matter on familiar ground was now an impossibility. For the first time in his life the Snow Hawk was completely lost.

The fine optimism of his first blind weeks was gone; the hope of ultimately regaining his sight was gone. In another week, thought Kioga, he too would be gone. But he was past all caring now. He moved forward in a world that was suddenly as strange as Mars. When the trail sloped upward, he followed up—what matter in which direction it went?

Thus he passed along an unfamiliar treeless slope, knee-deep in melting snow and loose sliding rubble that bruised his feet. That he was at a higher altitude he knew, for the air knifed his lungs, and his heart beat faster. And that was well; upon some lofty pinnacle he would lay his tireless body. There, as close as might be to the unseen stars, he would leave his bones in blessed isolation, like the wilderness hawk he was.

But this was not to be. For as he trod upon a softened bank, the snow gave way beneath him. Thrown upon his aching knees, he felt the earth suddenly shift, moving beneath him. Rocks and earth caught at his heels as he lifted his feet, and the downward movement of the shale on which he tried to stand was perceptible now.

He had witnessed this thing a hundred times from afar, this slow beginning of mountain landslides. It might end as suddenly as it began, checked by an upthrusting ridge. Yet almost at once he knew it would not. The slide was gathering momentum, with a mounting roar.

Instinctively Kioga threw himself flat to distribute his weight, and rolled sidewise, striving to twist away from the main moving body of the churning slide, onto the area of slower moving rubble which he knew would be right next it. Though he welcomed death, he had lived a mole too long, and did not wish to die like one, underground. But his own momentum set the side-current of shale and stones moving more swiftly, and upon the churning masses of rock, earth, and snow he was tossed about as the slide attained its swiftest pace.

He could hear the cracking sounds of the lesser trees being shorn close off; then the smash and crash of greater monarchs breaking off and uprooting as the monster slide roared downward, bearing on its tossing crest a million tons of splendid hardwood forest. Somewhere very near a mountain goat bawled piteously and almost unheard, caught like Kioga in the rocky maelstrom whirling to a distant level.

About the Snow Hawk's ears the flying pebbles whistled like bird-shot, drawing blood sometimes when they struck him. The roar of the slide ahead was deafening now, but suddenly ended in a silence far more ominous—for the moving mass of stuff was slipping over a cliff, to maim and kill all in its path in some cañon or valley far below.

Rising erect, that he might meet his death face to face, Kioga braced himself. An instant later came the thunderous rumble from the distant depths. He felt himself uplifted as by some mighty force as the slide on which he was borne so irresistibly poured over the brink into the cañon's gloomy darkness.

XVIII

Having planted his flag, laid formal claim to Nato'wa, and made an appropriate entry in the logbook to commemorate the historic event, Munro and his party explored as much of the coast as daylight permitted, before putting back to the

Narwhal. Assuring himself that the tide had fallen as far as it would fall, and that therefore they might safely spend the night at this anchorage, the scientist finally gave the welcome order to his men to turn in for a needed rest.

He himself, with Dan and the mate Edson, went on watch while the others slept, and in turn were relieved by the second watch a few hours later. Dan and Edson retired gratefully. Beth was sleeping the sleep of complete exhaustion. But there were two on board to whom sleep would not come.

Flashpan, in the privacy of his galley, and superintended by the monkey Placer, was feverishly polishing his old cavalry saber, oiling and reloading his pistols, and sharpening his bowie knife to a razor edge against the eventualities of the morrow. Now and then he put out the galley light, and drawing the curtain, peered cautiously shoreward through the galley port, as he muttered Hood's lines:

> *Gold! Gold! Gold! Gold!*
> *Bright and yellow, hard and cold,*
> *Molten, graven, hammered and rolled:*
> *Hoarded, bartered, bought and sold;*
> *Stolen, borrowed, squandered, doled,*
> *Heavy to get and light to hold.*

Returned from his eager glance ashore, the little man then hammered a wedge into a fresh new pickax and filed an edge on his ancient shovel.

Astern in his own cabin Munro tossed restless on his bunk, fully dressed. Unable to sleep, he finally rose, turned on a reading light and picking up the logbook, tried to write. But after a few trials he put it down and sought to calm his mind by reading. Chance brought his hand to Dixon's *Vanishing Race*, which he perused a little while before deciding to go on deck for a breath of air.

He came aloft by way of the main cabin companionway. Aft he could see Barry Edwards, a vague shadow standing near the binnacle. Forward, a faint cough apprised him that Lars Hansen was wakeful in the cabins. The scientist paused, struck a match and puffed at his pipe in its glow. He was repeating half aloud the last sentences he had read before laying aside his book a moment before:

> We are standing at the center of a mighty circumference. An Indian world revolves for the last time upon its axis. All the constellations which gave it light have

burned out. The Indian cosmos sweeps a dead thing amid the growing luster of the unfading stars of civilization and history. . . .

The solemn centuries look down upon this day. Look down upon the sheathed sword, the broken *coup*-stick, the shattered battle-ax, the deserted wigwams, the last red men mobilized on the plain of death . . . their muffled footfalls reaching beyond the margin of an echo.

Words, these, born of the Last Great Council, held by the American Indians on Washington's birthday in the year 1913. Thinking upon them, "I wonder!" murmured James Munro.

And scarce had the words passed his lips, when from the nearby shore of this grim new Northland there came a sudden answer. At a brisk hissing sound James Munro instinctively stiffened. An instant later the pipe flew from his lips, clattering into the scuppers. Came a thud—sharp, quick, venomous, as something struck into the deckhouse wall.

Not a finger's-length from his mouth, its feather-vanes still vibrating, and imbedded to its barbs in the wood, an arrow quivered—an *Indian* arrow, with ownership-marks painted round its shaft in red and blue design!

Already Edwards and Hansen, attracted by the sound of Munro's rolling pipe, had come amidships. Edwards, glimpsing Munro's startled features in the light of the sputtering match, was first to speak. "Anything wrong, Doctor?"

The match went out. "Don't strike another," said Munro calmly. "Nothing's wrong, Barry. But I've just had a close shave."

"Close shave? How, sir?"

"Two inches from my chin—what do you feel sticking into the cabin-house?"

In the darkness Barry Edwards reached forth to touch the shaft. An indrawn gasp of astonishment from the Canadian. Then: "It's an arrow, sir! Came down from above, by its angle of entry, I'd say."

"And so saying, you'd be right, Barry," returned Munro in that dead-level tone he used when most stimulated by excitement. "We're welcomed to Nato'wa! Pass the word around and wake the men. But don't let a light show. We've got to find a more sheltered mooring than this."

So, in the silence of the dark, the *Narwhal* cautiously warped her ghostly way along the coast, following the route Munro had worked out while exploring it in the ship's boat earlier that day. It was slow going, and dangerous to ship and crew, for no other coast on earth is so rugged and honeycombed as Nato'wa's. But at last, just at full high tide, the ship was worked into a little cove barely large enough to receive her. Rock walls ran precipitously up on three sides, well above the mastheads. Atop these a mat of ground-vines swung from ledge to ledge and hung downward, screening the vessel from casual view on the landward side.

"Snug's a bug in a rug," declared Flashpan admiringly, as Munro lashed the wheel; and indeed the *Narwhal* was securely berthed in one of those natural rock-girt basins wherein the tides are least felt. In a little time the ridge over which she had entered would be bare, its base sloping seaward, leaving the ship landlocked; for the deep hollow of the cove was never emptied of its water, nor did it change its level, save with an exceptionally high tide. Only at the full swell of the tide could the ship be worked out of her haven. On the other hand, the encircling walls which imprisoned her were also a protection from the swift storms which whirl seaward from this birthplace of the winds.

Such a storm now roared from inland with a fury that brought more than one prayer of thanksgiving that the ship was safely cradled in this impregnable berth. In the fury of the blow Munro glimpsed another reason why Nato'wa had remained a land apart down all the ages: no bottom to hold an anchor in such a wild wind. What with reefs, fog, uncertain tides, and a polar ice-barrier to be overcome, little wonder that Nato'wa is as primeval now as in the day of the prehistoric elephant.

Elsewhere enormous waves rose towering up to crash against the rocky cliffs and foam bubbling back; and the sound of the winds boomed and roared incessantly as for two days the elements warred with one another. But for all the fury of the tempest, in her sheltered berth the *Narwhal* rode at ease. Only the rain, slashing down upon her battered hatches, evidenced the fearful violence of the blow—that and the coming of hundreds of storm-driven seabirds seeking haven on her bare spars. . . .

In his comfortable cabin Munro matured his plans for exploring the interior of the new land. As broached to his men, his ideas met with certain invited criticisms, chiefest among them being the danger of encountering a superior force while themselves practically unarmed. To this, Munro answered:

"Hostile savages are here, beyond a doubt. But this is my idea, if it comes to hostilities." And with that he laid before them the details of a carefully conceived procedure, which was based on the likelihood that they would be able to locate the Indian village known as Hopeka. As he spoke, the faces of his listeners brightened, smiles appeared, and Flashpan clapped his thigh with enthusiasm. And so the plan was put into execution.

Several of the chests and the lazaret were opened. Certain of their contents were removed to a big wicker basket. From among his men Munro selected Dan, Flashpan, and Hansen to accompany him in search of the Indian capital.

Edson the mate and Barry Edwards were to remain aboard with their only serviceable rifle, and see that all went well; and Kamotok was to stay and tend the dogs. But when Munro urged that Beth La Salle remain on the comparatively safe ship, she answered quietly: "Remember our agreement, Dr. Munro." It was her first and only reference to the fact that she had paid part of the cost of the *Narwhal*'s expedition in exchange for the privilege of sharing their risks in the search for the Snow Hawk.

The scientist thereupon raised no further objections....

With Munro in the lead, the party began the exploratory journey inland. Flashpan wore his pistols in his belt and carried his pick. "Jest on the chance," was his reply to good-natured chaffing by Dan. "Y'never know. Might find gold anywheres hereabouts."

Dan was armed with a harpoon; Hansen had his double-bitted ax, and a supply of nails and baling-wire. Between them Dan and Munro carried the wicker basket.

From what Dan remembered, and what he himself had learned from Kioga, Munro knew better than to seek a river navigable from the coast. None such exists on this part of coastal Nato'wa. Instead the little party struck inland north and west until they came to a winding river. On its bank they felled trees and wired them together into a serviceable raft. Loading their little equipment on the raft, they were presently poling upstream against the current, scanning the river closely in anticipation of contact with the red-skinned inhabitants.

But though they saw as yet no Indians, many another living thing did they raise on their journey along this wild mysterious river, green-walled and darkened by the towering trees. The undergrowth was a veritable tangle, passable only behind axes or on the perilous twisting animal-trails. The air was crisp with the scent of pine and hemlock, mingling with the rich odors of earthy decay and the lighter fragrances of countless ground-flowers struggling for existence with jungles of tall ferns, overhung in turn by towering rhododendrons, and guarded by a thorn-armed warrior-plant they named the devil's-club. Over every sun-touched spot a lush tapestry of wild flowers was spread.

Deer and elk sprang back from drinking-places as they poled past. Wildfowl rose in clamorous clouds to settle again behind the moving raft. Among these was a dense flock of passenger pigeons, driven to this last sanctuary by white men, whose scientists call the species extinct. From behind a cluster of purple clematis the black-marked face of a snow-leopard appeared, regarding them icily out of its cruel eyes. And a great panther, flame-orbed, was barely glimpsed as she stole along a fallen tree bole, a shadow among shadows— then a sleek young tigress lying near a kill, plying a sinuous tongue on the flank of a cub but a few months old.

Finally, a thing that brought a gasp of admiration from Beth: Upon a broken stump near shore a variety of dragon-flower grew, its downy golden sheath giving way to petals as pure white as new-fallen snow. On Munro's order they drew near shore, that Beth might pluck it. But the watchful Flashpan struck up her hand just as she stretched it forth.

Close below the bloom another type of beauty lay—coiled with jaw agape and poised to strike: a water snake, plump, triangular-headed, revolting—yet handsome withal in its gaudy markings of black and red.

And so it went. Here a thing fair and fragile, and right beneath a deadly horror, made by the same Creator; the sinister and the beautiful side by side—but with the sinister oftener prevailing; for this was Nato'wa, surely the last unconquered wilderness, and probably also the first....

It was Munro's initial acquaintance with the wondrous fauna and flora of the new land. He began now the first of hundreds of sketches and drawings that were to enliven that remarkable notebook of his.

Until this moment no sign had they seen of living men in this strange land save that arrow sent out of the dark to graze Munro's cheek on board the *Narwhal*. Now a low warning from Beth found the men alert.

"Don't look now," whispered the girl tensely, "—but I saw someone move, on the bank just ahead."

Flashpan reached for his pistol. "A Injun?"

"I think so," answered Beth guardedly. "I only saw his head—*there!*" Her voice came sharply now. Focusing upon the bank, the others saw a grim and ghastly painted figure rising slowly, like some supernatural being from the netherworld. His dark and glittering eyes looked on them with a surprise equaling their own. For a moment this savage conned them, and they him, ere with a lightning movement he whipped an arrow close over the canoe, and dodged behind a tree trunk.

A shot rang out, and Flashpan stood gun in hand, searching for his target again. But a rustle of leaves and crackle of trodden twigs told them that the terrified Indian had fled.

"Ol' Betsy shore does need a cleanin'!" complained Flashpan as the raft continued on downstream.

So the white explorers came slowly upriver toward Hopeka. Unlike other discoverers in other ages, they sought not conquest but knowledge, not war but peace. And surely never did an exploring party present more picturesqueness.

Forward with plunging pole stood Flashpan, laboring like one possessed to keep the rude craft headed straight, and swearing fine round oaths at the constant interference of the restless monkey prancing around the raft. Amidships sat the young white girl, striving to recall landmarks from the time she had come this way before. Laboring with Dan and Hansen astern, Munro clad in his buckskins reached and pushed rhythmically as nightfall came upon them.

They were rounding a bend in the darkness when with a hiss Flashpan ceased poling and pointed. Every eye in the party fell startled upon the towering palisade of Hopeka, their first ocular evidence, dimly seen, of actual human residence on Nato'wa. Unlike the tent-circle of the nomad plains tribes, here was a permanent village of major size strategically located. Though far from impregnable, it was defensible in time of war, and evidenced one other variation of the Nato'wan tribes from those of continental America.

And as they came into view, from the opposite direction a longboat, laden with a dozen warriors, sped southward. For a moment both craft floated silent, the whites fascinated, the Indians utterly astonished—like an allegorical painting depicting the first meeting of modern and primitive men. Then from the longboat a strange cry went up, to be returned from the village walls. The quick staccato of the Shoni tongue shot back and forth, laden with information and warning. The gate swung open, and armed warriors darted out to man their canoes, of which a dozen were almost instantly afloat and bearing down upon Munro's unwieldy craft.

Munro gazed momentarily at these fierce-featured savages of fine physique, with the keen interest of the anthropologist who has realized a great hope. Unmistakably these men were of that mysterious race called Indians; and here one of the oldest enigmas in science was becoming solved, the known past of mankind moving back through the ages. But Munro's interest became alarm when quick arrows cut the water roundabout and thudded into the raft.

"Redskins, shore enough!" cried Flashpan, drawing and cocking his pistols, coolly deliberate. "Jest say the word, sir. I'll snip the top-knot off'n the fust one."

"No shooting, Flashpan," admonished Munro sharply. "Not yet, anyway." Then to Beth: "The box—quick!"

The girl threw open a wooden case within the chest itself. Into this Munro reached, while Dan—well drilled in his part beforehand—struck a match. Applying the end of a long sticklike object to the flame, Munro pointed it above the heads of the on-forging war-boats. A moment's pause, while the red fire fizzed as if from the end of his hand. Then—a soft puff and away went a ball of blue fire, arching over the nearest canoes. Then another of red hissed skyward, and another, and yet another as the Roman candle hurled its molten balls aloft.

Quick to catch the spirit of the occasion, Flashpan had stuck a pinwheel into the raft's side and applied a light. The wheel spun faster and yet faster, throwing out its whorls of fire and sparks. Nor had Beth, Dan, and Hansen been idle. From the raft there suddenly sprang skyward half a dozen varying effects to scatter their brightly colored stars. These were yet bursting when bundles of firecrackers, tied to the river-poles and held aloft, were spitting and barking; while Flashpan applied six-inch cannon-crackers to the nearest flame and hurled them gleefully in air, to crack with amazing volume of sound, rolling across the water like gunfire—and all this in but that single moment of time.

One crowded moment of such display was more than enough to check the advance of the Indians. The hissing shafts fell no more. In their amazement and bewilderment the savages had forgotten to loose them, and sat as if paralyzed by the blinding pyrotechnics.

Meanwhile, roused from its sleep by the noise and excitement and brilliant lights on the river, all Hopeka was crowding to the gates and overflowing in colorful force upon the sandy riverbank. Cries of awe and pleasure and wonder greeted each brilliant eruption of a red-tailed rocket.

On the river itself the warriors only drifted, as the raft moved slowly shoreward, offering no barrier to its coming. And for this moment Munro had reserved the most brilliant of his fiery theatrics.

At every corner of the raft pinwheels now spun, interspersed with those long-burning "sparklers," throwing out their incandescent glitter. Fore and aft several flares burned with silent rosy glow. Amidships a tin of prepared combustibles threw up a blazing shower, volcano-wise. And as these burned lower, Munro prepared the grand finale—his largest rocket, to which he now touched a match.

The fuse fizzed; the rocket leaped on high, exploding soundlessly into a veritable cascade of blue, yellow, green, and purple lights, which burst and burst again with wondrous coruscations into separate fan-formations of falling stars. And amid those falling stars Munro, followed by his little party, set foot upon the sands before the village of Hopeka.

All that he had hoped for of his display had been achieved. They enjoyed a momentary exemption from further hostile acts. To hold this gain, he would need to draw on other resources; but the worst moment was past, the ground prepared for planting the seed of friendship.

The populace, warriors included, were silent in awe, curiosity, and fear. No injury was offered Munro as he stepped forward with upraised hands toward a band of several elderly chiefs pushing their way through the throng.

Before the others could speak, Munro had anticipated them. He began to talk in the Shoni syllables as he had learned them from Kioga. He conveyed his peaceful intentions. In the name of the Great Ones, he asked of the Shoni a bloodless reception for his friends and himself.

A moment the chiefs stood silent, startled by the strange white man's fluency in their own language. Then one of the older men stood forth imperiously.

"Come in peace," was his greeting. "And tell us why you are here. Tell us the meaning of these miracles you have just performed. For the night was day, and we were blinded as by the sun."

"We come from a far place, where the sun lives in winter," answered Munro. "Such miracles are common there. Men fly in the air and walk afar beneath the seas. Their lodges are like mountains. Their skins are white, like snow. Their numbers are like the needles of the pine tree. Of those people am I. Men call me"—and here Munro gave the name by which he is best known to red-skinned men on other continents—"men call me Swift-Hand. For behold! What I have, I have not!" And at this point the scientist smoothly caused a round stone to vanish from one hand, before their watching eyes. The chiefs gasped, for though the Indians of Nato'wa are not the gullible innocents which the first American explorers met, the wisest of men may be deceived by the magician's hand.

When Munro's interlocutor smiled, another seed was sown. "As Swift-Hand we will know you," asserted the elderly chieftain. "Hopeka welcomes its white-skinned visitors."

Having negotiated for their safety thus successfully, Munro gestured to Flashpan and Dan to bring the chest they bore between them. Obeying, followed by Beth and Lars, they were conducted through Hopeka's gates toward the ceremonial ground.

Pausing at an open spot, Dan and Flashpan had set down the wicker chest, when the prospector bethought himself of one until now overlooked.

"Placer!" he roared. "Placer! Where are ye? Come to me, monk!"

Suddenly, with a startling noise, the cover of the chest flew up. Out in one flying bound, like the djinni from Aladdin's lamp, came the screeching Placer. But the effect his appearance had upon the whites was as nothing to the terror into which it threw most of the Indians. No one of them had ever hitherto dreamed of such a creature as Placer. The women, children, and most of the men fell back, some with fear, others in amazement.

Indeed, garbed as a miniature pirate, still full of the fear which had prompted him to hide when the fireworks began to fly, Placer was an incarnation of Fright. Glimpsing Flashpan, he bounded upon his shoulder, only slowly to be calmed by the miner's soothing voice.

One by one the Indians took courage and approached, showing keen interest in this little exotic from another clime. Placer soon returned the interest in his own peculiar way, springing suddenly atop the shoulders of a medicine man nearby to do a little investigating on his own. Before the horrified shaman—a man of much decorum—decamped without dignity, Placer proudly flourished aloft his war-cap and medicine-rattle.

It was long before the Indians would approach where Placer sat. Only later did Munro learn that they at first believed him a deformed little man, turned monstrous by the scientist's magic. But soon, aware that little physical danger attended nearness to the monkey, the villagers were again crowding about the chest, wherefrom Flashpan produced toys and dolls for the naked children swarming about his knees. The tooting of tin flutes and the sound of tin harmonicas blown without regard to harmonics mingled with the shrill cries of the children struggling over possession of these delightful new trinkets. So another stone was laid in Munro's plan to gain tolerance for himself and his people by the giving of gifts.

While distributing these trifles in the top of the basket Flashpan had exposed the more desirable objects just beneath—the colored cloths, glittering steel knives, beads, and needles. By now the more arrogant of the warriors had had some of their awe conquered by the strangers' manifest goodwill. One in particular, a forward and bold young witch-doctor, presumed upon his position to dip suddenly into the chest and come up with a handful of choice articles. But he had reckoned without Flashpan, who realized that to allow the man to succeed in this first act would embolden all the others.

Hardly had the Indian risen, flourishing his new acquirements, when the miner's hand dropped upon his wrist. Little knowing with whom he had to deal, the Indian laughed derisively at the notion of this little man attempting to wrest away his new gains. Then the amazing grip of Flashpan began its work. A quick and unexpected twist caught the red man off guard and forced him to one knee. Caught in an unfavorable position, his superior strength availed not. Then the fingers at his wrist began tightening.

Munro, tense, was watching sharply. The outcome was of great importance to their prestige—a vital thing among Indians; but recalling an experience of his own with the mighty grip of Flashpan he smiled grimly. Of a sudden the shaman's stoicism broke in a grimace of pain. The trade articles slipped from his hand back into the chest. Flashpan let go as suddenly as he had taken hold. The savage described an undignified twisting fall, amid the smiles of his own people.

Rising furiously, he walked a few paces away, then whirled suddenly and in a blind passion snatched a tomahawk from the nearest hand, making as if to hurl it at Flashpan's head. Simultaneously the miner's hand moved, flashlike. As by some magic there was a pistol in it—which exploded once.

Munro held his breath. But Flashpan had but fired at the tomahawk. The weapon flew from the startled Indian's hand to a spot near the palisade, leaving only its broken handle in the grasp of its wielder.

The savage rose, bewilderment on his face. The loud report, the acrid smoke of the gun, added to his throbbing swollen wrist and the superstition that this little man must be invincible, put an end to his hostile acts. He vanished forthwith into the crowds, followed by Indian laughter. All unknown to himself, Flashpan had already acquired prestige enough for several men among these red-skinned peoples—and with Munro, too. But the glance of the vanished shaman had boded no good. Flashpan had humiliated one of the most active members of the Long Knife society.

Throughout this episode Placer the monk had been moving from shoulder to shoulder among the Indians. The whites could scarce forbear smiling at the uneasiness with which these bold and fearless people suffered the attentions of Flashpan's long-tailed pet, who paused at each scalp for investigations which were unsuccessful, for the Shoni are a very cleanly people. Discouraged, Placer finally desisted, and curling his tail about him, sat down upon the chest.

That night another incident occurred which was to affect the villagers in their estimation of these white visitors.

In the lodge of weeping Seskawa, an old woman who had long inhabited the village, a child lay dying from the bite of a poisonous snake—not of the cowled koang, whose bite is almost instant death, but a lesser viper, allied to the copperhead, as Munro's examinations of the killed snake later proved.

Seskawa appealed in frantic grief to the white scientist; and accompanied by a few chiefs and many curious, Munro went to the old crone's lodge, where two medicine men were in attendance.

One was in the act of exorcising the poison from the child by chanting magic-songs. The other held one end of a long tube made of animal leg-bone between the child's bluing lips. Frequently he sucked at the tube, appeared to draw something into his mouth. Thereat he made wry grimaces, ground his teeth savagely, spat ostentatiously into his cupped hands, then made a great show of tearing something limb from limb.

Observing him, Flashpan scratched his head. "By the bones of Beelzebub! What's he a-doin'?" he demanded of Munro. In a whispered aside came the answer: "He's drawing out evil spirits, and chewing them up fine. But the poor patient is almost dead."

After a while Seskawa with righteous anger drove the medicine men from the child. Kneeling at its side, Munro felt of the pulse. It was imperceptible. The blue-red puncture marks of the snake's fangs showed in the badly swollen leg.

Munro's first act was to apply a tourniquet above the swelling to check the spread of the venom. Then he deeply cross-incised the fang-marks with a scalpel from his first-aid kit.

Behind him the witch doctors gasped at what to them was medical heresy.

After he had applied suction with a suction-bulb from his kit, Munro took a vial of permanganate crystals, sprinkling these sparingly into the open cut where the fangs had gone in. Then came a hypodermic of the serum his forethought had provided—which might or might not counteract the venom of this strange snake. So, moving the tourniquet slowly in advance of the swelling, and continuing his treatment with wet antiseptic pads, for several hours Munro worked over the all but lifeless child. But though the swelling subsided, the boy seemed little nearer life than before.

As a last resort Munro removed his shirt and held the child against his skin so that his warmth and strength might assist nature. Thus the hours passed, old Seskawa watching with dull sorrow, convinced that her great-grandchild was doomed.

But Munro knew better. He could feel the current of life moving softly through his patient's veins, and caught the strengthening flutter of the little heart. At midnight a shrill ear-piercing cry rose from the lodge of Seskawa. When the populace gathered round, the old woman threw open the entrance, that all might pass in and witness the reality of the child's resurrection. Then she cried the praises of the scientist throughout the village. And men said of James Munro: "He has performed a miracle." But the discredited shamans found his success not to their liking and went away muttering jealously.

Among themselves the whites spoke freely in English, little thinking that there was one among their red-skinned listeners who could comprehend their words. Nor did Tokala the Fox betray himself. Who knew but what these whiteskins had come to take him back to civilization and the hated reservation? A dreadful thought—but it did not prevent Tokala from being on hand when gifts were being passed out, or from starting a furtive friendship with Placer the monkey.

Lingering near the visitors' lodge he overheard much of their talk. Hearing then the Snow Hawk's name, at once he was all ears. And gradually, adding two and two together, he realized that here were friends seeking Kioga. The more he learned, the harder he listened, until his fearless presence won their attention.

"Here's one, at any rate," said Beth to Flashpan, slipping an arm around the boy, "who's not afraid of us." With that she smiled on Tokala, showing teeth that compared favorably even with Heladi's. The Fox, returning the smile, shyly slipped away.

On his way rushing home, Tokala met a man he knew and loved for a hundred lessons in shooting the arrow and throwing the knife. And unto Kias, newly entering Hopeka from a river journey, the boy told all he had overheard near the white men's camp. A while Kias thought on this. Then: "Perchance these be more friendly men than those of our skin," he said. "Yet if their tongue be not ours, how shall I talk with them?"

"They know the language of the hands," said Tokala.

"It is good," averred Kias. "Go, then, and tell Heladi."

Parting, each went his opposite way.

XIX

In a distant part of the village the excited Tokala flew into the lodge of Menewa to bring Heladi tidings of the white men's coming. He told her about each of the men he had seen, describing them in detail. Finally he spoke of the white-skinned woman who accompanied them—whereat Heladi looked up abruptly, stiffening with a sudden premonition.

"The white woman," she demanded of Tokala, "was she slender, with hair like dark wild honey?"

"Yes."

"Had she eyes the color of—of—"

"Gray—like the morning sky," offered Tokala as the girl hesitated. Then: "But why do you look at me so, Heladi?"

"It is—*she*!" whispered Heladi, scarce hearing Tokala's question, and heeding it not. She was recalling a painful scene a year ago: Kioga, accompanied by a wounded white man whom he had rescued from the stake at the cost of his standing among the Shoni, sat in a moving canoe. A lovely white woman, rescued from the renegade white men, sat before him. For these two Kioga had sacrificed all he held dear. For this woman he had all but destroyed himself. After an absence of long moons, he had returned with something changed within him—because of which Heladi hated this white-skinned young woman of bitter memory.

"*Ai!* It is she!" she repeated. But certain as Heladi was, she put aside her needlework. "Come, Tokala. Guide me thither. I would look on these white-skinned ones. I would know if—she—is more beautiful than Heladi."

Impetuously the boy hugged her. "No one could be, elder sister," he assured her with boyish adoration, in the English they sometimes used.

"We shall see," said Heladi quietly, laying aside her work. "Hand me my knife. And bring your spear."

And with that the pair set out for the whitemen's lodge.

Seated in a new lodge which the grateful Seskawa had vacated for their benefit, the whites ate of the feast provided by their red-skinned hosts. Their meal was interrupted by Flashpan's low, awed whistle as he poised a deer-rib chop in one hand and gazed up the street.

All eyes followed his to where an Indian girl moved down the lane between the lodges. Close beside her strode the lithe young dark-skinned Tokala, a lynx kitten, half grown, straining in his grasp.

"Wal—cut my braids!" exclaimed Flashpan. "A chorus gal!"

"By Jove!" breathed Munro. "She's better than that."

Even Hansen grunted a grudging agreement, and Beth caught her breath. "Oh, Dan! How lovely she is!"

Dan alone answered nothing. But in his eyes was something more than tribute as he looked upon this lithe Wacipi maid. Serene and outwardly composed, but for the flashing eyes that leaped among them, briefly stabbing each in turn, he would never forget her as he saw her this first time. For in that moment, while his gaze dwelt on her, Dan's whole life had changed.

One other too watched, suddenly tense with recollection. And as the eyes of Heladi met hers, Beth knew a moment of something resembling fear—fear that was quickly banished by admiration of the Indian girl. How lithe she was! What queenly poise, what bearing of a princess! And princess had Heladi been, indeed, did Shoni ways permit. Surely no man could look on her with unseeing eyes—and Kioga had known her well.

In Beth, Heladi saw her for whom Kioga had sacrificed all; and despite an instinctive antagonism arising out of this, primitive and civilized woman found one another of keenest mutual interest. Though whole worlds stood between them, they shared one thing in common: Both loved the Snow Hawk.

For long the eyes of these two women were locked in gaze, in the quick appraisal of their sex. Each in the other saw a threat to her own happiness.

Nor was this hostile tension lost upon Tokala, watching from Heladi's side. Though there was something here he did not understand, his loyalties were all with Heladi. To the white girl's smile this time he turned a face of stone.

But having held Beth's gaze those long full moments, Heladi turned to James Munro, he of the resurrected child, the magic hands, the performer of miracles. Munro could not but wonder at the strange expression in her face and eyes. So also had Seskawa looked—old Seskawa, whose great-grandchild had lain at death's door. It was as if this girl's eyes spoke at once of hope and yet of terrifying fear, probing him deep, weighing, betraying some strange deep yearning.

And so indeed it was with Heladi. The white medicine man had restored life to a snake-bitten child. Might he not restore sight to one who was sightless? But not yet would she voice this thought. Another time, soon, when the eyes of others were not on her, she would come and bring the white man gifts and lay her plea before him. Until then the secret of Kioga's blindness would rest with her alone.

As she turned away, one she had noticed but fleetingly now stepped forward. Regarding her speechless until this moment, swayed by the strong appeal of this primitive beauty, young La Salle, in his limited command of the Shoni tongue, sought to bid her stay. But the words seemed to stick in Dan's throat. There are times when silence is a stronger pleader than speech itself. Perhaps this was one such time; for as Dan's eyes bespoke the feeling in his heart, Heladi's glance held his, as with interest. And as she slowly turned away, he saw what set his pulses leaping. A little smile playing round her mobile curving mouth.

After Heladi had gone, many others came to gaze at the white visitors. With danger to their persons no longer a matter of great concern, Munro looked about him with the interest of the student of races.

He saw in the Shoni a tall, handsome, cleanly, and healthy race. But many were terribly disfigured by their contacts with the wild beasts of the forest.

Mortality from this cause was great. Tigers' depredations only last week had terrorized two smaller villages, and had caused their abandonment, the inhabitants coming to live in fortified Hopeka. With his own eyes Munro saw a panther speared down from a perch atop the palisade. It had been seen before it could hook its claws in the body of a child, hanging in its cradle-board just out of the animal's reach against the wall.

For this fierce boldness of the greater killers Munro blamed the Indian custom of scaffold-burial, which, as in other lands, breeds man-killers among tiger, panther, and wolf by developing their taste for human flesh.

As is the way the world over with mountain peoples, the Shoni were proud, arrogant, fearful of none; given to periodic marauding against one another solely to acquire prestige. And their social system was therefore a fertile soil for the malcontents to dig in.

In the conversations to which Munro listened, there was frequent talk of the war-chief Kioga. To these the scientist attended closely. Tales of the Snow Hawk's fate had lost nothing in the telling. Some there were who said he had been of those dead given to the water-spirits; others swore that even at this moment he was assembling a war-force to subdue Hopeka. Rumors from everywhere amply attested the amazing renown of Munro's young friend.

In the throng of red men the eye of Munro watched continually for the one who, of them all, might most probably know Kioga's fate. Oft had Kioga told of Kias, who had been friend of his boyhood and close ally in later years. But the name had escaped the memory of the scientist now; and he knew he must seek him not openly but in roundabout fashion; for of the undercurrents eddying in Hopeka he had become aware. He must wait, fathom the dark intrigues which filled Hopeka with strange unrest, and not till then inquire too persistently. No time, this, to show his hand!

His patience was rewarded. There came to the scientist's lodge a tall figure close-wrapped in a deer-skin blanket. The newcomer had come to Munro for treatment of wounds. One arm was hung in a crude sling, stained with blood. But when Munro would have drawn off the wrapping, the visitor gestured at the lodge.

With an imperceptible signal to Flashpan to guard against possible treachery, Munro followed the Indian within. Pronouncing his name, Kias identified himself as the friend of the missing Snow Hawk. And from Kias, Munro learned the strange circumstances under which Kioga had returned to visit his people.

For the first time Munro had a clear picture of the troublous days confronting the Shoni tribes. For the first time he felt a foreboding of danger to come, a sensation that not all the world's diplomacy could avert the coming struggle for dominance between two forces within the Seven Tribes.

In this first talk with Kias was born in Munro's mind the need for a strategy of his own to protect his party and himself against the possible rise of bloody insurrection. Here, in Kias, was one of strong and fearless mold. How many more such might be found?

"Not twoscore," Kias assured him gloomily. "Men follow those whose force is greatest!"

"Here as elsewhere in the world," mused Munro. "But let us watch and listen. It may be we shall gain allies."

"If only Kioga were here! There's a name which would raise our numbers! With one hand he would crush the Long Knives. Around his torch a thousand men would rise."

"Then let us seek him," said Munro.

"To seek him is no use," answered the Indian heavily. "The wolves fed full. Kioga is no more." Whereupon he told Munro what he had seen on the river sands that night when with Tokala he had gone out to disprove or affirm the Snow Hawk's death.

"Blind, Kioga may be," said Munro. "But dead—I cannot believe that."

"Where, then, went he?" asked Kias.

Significantly Munro made answer:

"Where goes a wounded tiger? Where goes a wolf with broken bones—a bear whose eyes are arrowed out?"

"To the home lair," said Kias. Then suddenly comprehending, he rose quickly up, tense and eager. "*Ai*! If he lives, he will be near his hidden cave, of which he often spoke."

"And where is that cave?"

"Long journeys hence," the Indian replied, lowering his voice. "Somewhere in the forests of the Tsus-Gina-i—the Ghost Country."

"You fear the dead?" asked Munro, eyeing Kias narrowly.

"I respect them," was the answer, "but I do not fear. Where Swift-Hand would go, there I will lead."

"Well spoken," commended the white man. "Tonight we'll think on this. We need canoes and men to paddle them. We need a cause for leaving Hopeka, lest suspicion be aroused."

"No," denied the other. "You need but ask the chiefs. They'll dare not refuse the worker of your miracles. There are warriors known to me who will stand with us. Men of my mother's clan, good fighters all. Two stanch canoes will bear us."

"Good! Tomorrow we will talk again." Then, smiling: "Will your wounds trouble you this night?"

Grinning in return, Kias affected anew the fiction of an injured hand, thrusting it back in the sling. "It will pain me when the sun comes up," he answered.

"Until then, good resting," said Munro as Kias left the lodge.

XX

On the next day Kias came again as agreed and plans were laid for the search for Kioga. But one other thing required doing. Questioning the Indian further, Munro found that Kias recalled his white friends of two decades past. But as to their place of burial he could tell Munro nothing; nor would the scientist ever likely learn. Long since, the wall logs which had been blazed to mark the spot had been replaced with new. And none could tell where Mokuyi, Indian companion of those first white visitors to Nato'wa, lay at rest.

But near the coast, back in a wood which had rooted close to the sea, Munro later came upon the decaying framework of a half-finished little ship. On its bow, weathered dull, a nameplate still clung. It bore the single word, *Cherokee*—and a dead hand had added the Roman numeral *II*.

This was the vessel, its completion interrupted by massacre, in which Lincoln Rand the first had hoped one day to make his way back to civilization with an account of his strange discoveries in Nato'wa. But like its builder, *Cherokee II* was a thing of the dead past. As Munro removed the nameplate the entire structure collapsed upon itself.

Unable, then, to erect a suitable monument over the graves of his long-mourned friends, Munro instead cut their names and an inscription of their discovery on the face of a cliff. This cliff overlooks what the scientist named Rand Bay, and is the first thing the eye falls upon when entering the little cove.

Standing a while with bared head beside this tribute to two men he had respected and one woman he had loved, Munro finally turned from the things of memory back to the grim realities existing all around him. . . .

The prophecy of Kias proved truth. What with the prestige Munro had gained, he was more than welcome in the longboats of his Indian hosts, coursing up and down the river highways. On a great slab of rolled birch-bark he began to map what parts of the area he visited. Rand Bay was the first name writ thereon. The forested mountains through which the Indians paddled were called the Buffalo Back Range, and are so marked on the chart he lettered. Thus was begun the great culminating scientific work of this illustrious scholar.

But for all his inquiries, there was none could tell him even vaguely the area of this new land. As large almost as a continent it might indeed be, and still fall within the blank spaces on the Arctic map. A veritable geographical fortress was Nato'wa, inestimably rich in natural resources, yet incapable of being carried by storm—a land and a people which might endure as long as time, when other nations had destroyed one another.

Into the Tsus-Gina-i none would go save those of Kias's band. One morning, accompanied by Beth, Dan, and Heladi, the search-party set out upon the canoe-voyage into the forbidden territory. It was slow laborious toil against the currents, swollen by the season's thaw since Heladi had come this way. Many days found them still struggling for their goal. But their labors, at least for the white people aboard, were rewarded by the wonders in the changing panorama. The swift streams they followed broke off into the wildest tumbling rapids, and milk-white cascades of inspiring beauty.

In the valleys the timber grew to the very edge of the water, overhanging everywhere beyond the banks of the rivers. Mighty forest trees sprang majestic upward from the eternal green twilight about their colossal bases, to sway their lofty capitals in the sun. Between their solid columns the ribbon of the river ran in deep religious silence, the canoes but black shapes in purple shadows, laden with men and women in colorful costume.

The Indians of Kias's band scarce dared speak aloud this morning as they dipped their silent paddles in a river of sepia and moved into the growing dawn. Slow sunrise came to crown the rain-wet trees with halos of flame. Then down the fluted trunks the sun's light moved, lighting the cinnamon boles slowly until they glowed like red-hot ingots heating toward incandescence in a smelting furnace. Never had Numidian marble richer colorings than these heroic stems, which seemed to support the very sky upon their tremendous columns.

And far below gazing up at them, a handful of ephemeral beings called men. All of their little earthly spans together would not equal the early childhood of one such tree.

Their crowns gilded by the suns of seven thousand years; springs bubbling from their roots to slake the thirst of tiger and elk and panther—such are the wonderful forests of the primitive Tsus-Gina-i, on countless miles of which James Munro gazed. Little wonder the Indians thought the souls of the departed lingered here!

So they paddled onward, the sound of running waters ever in their ears. And on their way it was Munro's good fortune to look upon a waterfall known only to the Indians as Tominga, the Enchanted Cataract. As a traveler in many lands Munro had seen them all. But not Niagara, nor Tequandema, Roraima, Iguazu—nor Victoria nor Kalambo—no one of these compares with Tominga, the greatest known waterfall on this rolling globe. All of one entire day Munro observed it, wondrous yet appalling in its unspeakable voice and power.

Born of earth-heat and an unknown glacier, the vivid waters of Tominga drop full two thousand feet over red and yellow granite cliffs, themselves having a breadth of near two miles, into a chasm which is the cataract's only outlet. Its roar may be heard for twenty leagues. Its volume is the source of thirteen rivers, of which the Hiwasi is but one. The motion-picture photographs taken by James Munro indicate a fall of almost inconceivable magnitude.

Thereafter fierce rapids forced a dozen portages upon them; but at length the tremendous rumble of Tominga died behind them, and they came at last to the point where Heladi had earlier seen the Snow Hawk. Here, with his skilled trackers, Kias set out to locate Kioga's old trail. A day of unavailing labor followed. Exhausted by the labor of search in such impenetrable wilderness, the Indians—all but two—returned at sundown to the party's bivouac.

At midnight the last of the band, save one, returned with a curious report: Of the Snow Hawk's trail he had seen nothing. But at the end of day, attracted by a peculiar metallic sound, he had turned into the forest and found a strange object, which he now tossed before the others. It was a rawhide cord, from either end of which bits of metal hung, and struck against each other.

"What could it be?" wondered Beth, examining it intently. At that moment Kias chanced to glance up and meet Munro's gaze. The same thought had entered the mind of each. But at the girl's question, both remained silent.

"We ought to know tomorrow," said Dan, himself as mystified as Beth.

Next day, proceeding to the place where the object had been found, the Indians examined the ground roundabout. Then one of the braves hissed for silence; and in the hush that ensued a delicate tinkle was faintly audible to every listening ear.

Moving toward the sound, they found another cord, with metal bits attached. Then again another sound and a forward march, and so for several hours, following the metal indicators one by one, just as Kioga had done in guiding himself from place to place.

The band soon came upon the body of their missing companion, roughly covered by forest mold, sticks, and branches. Nearby, the tracks of a huge snow-leopard told a grim tale; and a portion of their unlucky companion had been eaten. Placing the remains on a scaffold, they continued on, at another time to return and bring the body home to Hopeka; for to linger now would have been to invite the same danger that had laid Metumpa low.

They had not gone far in the green silence when suddenly the underbrush close by was sharply agitated. Kias, in the lead, dropped in his tracks coincidentally with a twanging note, as of a bow discharged. The others leaped behind cover, arrows at their strings, alert for expected ambush by him who had driven the shaft which skewered Kias's thigh between knee and hip. They waited tense a moment, then let fly arrows at the spot whence the shaft had sprung.

While the others covered them, two went forward to scout the thicket from the flanks, intending to kill whoever lay there in ambuscade. Munro, meanwhile, attended Kias, breaking the arrow and drawing the ends from the wound. For the stalwart red man, such a hurt was a thing to laugh at. Kias explained that he had willfully dropped in anticipation of another arrow, not from the shock of the first arrow's impact, which little more than cut the skin.

Summoned by the others, Kias and Munro went to the thicket, into which the Indians were staring. No body lay there, riddled by their arrows. Their shafts had merely struck into nearby trees, whence they now protruded. But fixed to a rigid base was a sprung bow whose slip-trigger and trip-cord told its story of adjustment by a cunning hand. The touch of Kias's foot had sprung the bolt.

Dan's brows were knit in puzzlement. "Those copper signalers—and now an automatic bow," he muttered thoughtfully. "Damned queer. I wonder—" But with that he paused, eyes narrowing.

"We'd best go slow," said Munro quietly. "The next arrow might do a better job."

Well for them that they did go more slowly. Twice in the ensuing hour Kias detected and sprung an automatic bow; and once another, undetected, whipped its whispering death across their path. A little chill crept over Beth along with the unpleasant thought that at any moment one of them might fall pierced by a concealed arrow.

Before noon they came upon the Snow Hawk's traps and snares, some dangling empty, others weighted with game on which the ravens perched, devouring. And that night the absent hand struck among them once again. This time it was Mengawa, the Tugari. One moment the party saw him on the trail ahead. The next he had vanished with a startled yell, as if swallowed by the earth. Rushing up, they found him lying stunned at the bottom of a deep pit, which had been skillfully covered over with a latticework of forest trash. Mengawa was easily revived. Not so the failing courage of the superstitious warriors.

"We tread upon a spirit's hunting-ground," said Mengawa, glancing about uneasily.

"Twice the *wendigo* has warned us. Metumpa lies dead; Kias had his blood drawn. Mengawa fell into a trap. It is time to listen to the warnings of the spirit."

Grunts of agreement came from the other braves. Thus, for all Munro's cajoling and persuasion, to superstition bowed savages who would have laughed at odds of ten to one in open battle.

Of all the red men, only Kias would go farther.

Reduced to five, the little party continued on, the tall savage leading, Munro coming after him, then Beth and Heladi, with Dan bringing up the rear. Luckily, the trail was warming now, for exhaustion was coming upon the white girl.

It was Kias who found a fresher print close beneath a towering cliff and traced it to a ledge running up its face. Following the narrow path, he came at last to the well-hidden door which, yawning wide, betrayed Kioga's cave. A signal brought the others climbing slowly up.

With quickening heart Beth recognized the place, the ledge,

the ponderous open door. A moment, waiting and calling the name of Kioga, before Kias entered, the others at his heels, fearful of finding nothing, more fearful still of that which might be found.

Embers still glowed when Kias blew on them, and in a moment a flame lighted up the interior. For the first time Kias, Heladi, Dan, and Munro looked upon the hidden aerie which had sheltered the Snow Hawk during all his amazing boyhood, and also in the latter days of his cruel affliction.

But Beth looked on this familiar scene with tightening throat. In this picturesque retreat her first regard for Kioga had begun, to grow, later, into the love which had sustained her through all these arduous hours, when even the men had approached complete exhaustion. How empty the cave seemed without that superb figure seated before the blaze, as he had sat long months ago when he brought her here to inviolable shelter!

As the talk of the others came to her ears, she began to observe the peculiar things they commented on—the sawed-off tool handles, the lack of food, the depleted store of books and weapons, the objects scattered in jarring carelessness upon the floor. The open door indicated sudden departure, and that not long ago, judging by the heat of the embers on their arrival. But all were too far gone in weariness to follow on at once.

Pondering the riddle that Heladi could have answered, they all spent the night in Kioga's cave. When morning came, Kias again took up the search, quartering the ground like a bloodhound on a trail, and running it finally to earth and through the wilds again. Soon upon the mountaintop they found Kioga's pile of offerings, books, bows, the very cream of his possessions. For what, Beth wondered, had he made such sacrifices? And Dan, watching her pityingly, wondered how long it would be before she guessed what he had only lately realized.

Following the freshening traces across stream and beach, then upward toward still greater heights, they came to where Kioga had left his footprints in the snowy banks, so clearly that even Beth could make out the traces. And then—trail's end! The earth gouged out by landslide, its swath plain-marked to the edge of a cliff below. From where they stood they could see down—far down—to where a hill of rubble lay, with mighty trees protruding from it like matchsticks from a pile of sweepings.

For an instant Beth did not grasp what to all the rest was

crystal-clear. Then suddenly her eyes flashed up to Dan, at whose grim expression her face drained white. Munro was pale too, and so was Kias under his Indian mask. From Kias, Beth's eyes came to Heladi's, burning like coals, then fell away again trying to thrust aside the truth.

A little cry, struggling for life in the white girl's throat, stopped at her quivering lips. For in that moment she realized that not only she was suffering. Rigid and stricken, Heladi stood beside her, sharing Beth's own realization that from this last track Kioga had stepped into the path of annihilation. Strong as only an Indian woman is in time of heartbreak, the girl's eyes alone betrayed the pain that filled her.

"Looking back again to the fearful scars left by the landslide, a single question escaped Beth, voicing all her protest against this tragic happening:

"He walked—right into it. Oh, Dan—couldn't he see?" And then she paused.

Almost with the words, sudden realization came, and with it all that hitherto had been a mystery was clarified.

"That's just it," her brother was answering softly. "He couldn't, Beth."

"Perhaps it's best—this way," Beth managed at last haltingly. "Better than to go on—blind and all alone. It must have been—quick."

But there imagination broke her. Vivid and terrible the image was before her of the Snow Hawk walking here. One moment in all the flush of his splendid strength, and the next—cut down like a mighty tree and hurled into this dread abyss.

These tearless men before her, iron-grim as men oft are when least they wish to be, could say nothing to assuage her grief. There was only one who knew Beth's heart in that moment. Distrust and fear and animosity were gone between these two. It was Heladi's slim arm, strong as steel for all its slimness, that sustained the exhausted white girl on their slow dejected return to the cave, and Heladi who soothed her through the long and restless night.

Returning to the scene of the slide, Dan and Munro searched vainly for some trace of Kioga. They found no remains save of a few dead animal creatures, on whom the ravens were performing their dreadful office. They turned again to Kioga's cave, low in spirits. . . .

When it came time to quit the cave, Beth begged leave to remain a while alone. And in silence broken only by the crackle of the dying fire, she knelt a moment, touching the things that belonged to the Snow Hawk. From among them she selected a copper ornament bearing the marks of his tools, and hid it in her dress. Then from her finger she drew her only jewel, ring given her by her father years ago, and placed this beside her hand. On a strange impulse she then wrote with the stub end of a pencil upon a piece of clean white birch-bark peeled from a log near the fireplace. Her note began without salutation and read thus:

I came all the way from America, with Dan and James Munro, to tell you what I should have said before, had you not left us so suddenly. Since fate willed I should never see you again alive, I take this means of telling you, instead. I have loved you from the first, and will to the end. I leave this note and ring. Though you will never read the one nor wear the other, it will always comfort me to know that you would find them here if you could only return.

She ended the letter with her signature. Rolling the bark into a thin cylinder, she thrust this through the ring and placed both atop the Snow Hawk's bookshelf. A few little things—a handful of arrowheads, a boy's knife, and a whittled top—caught her eye and stabbed at her heart. For these too had belonged to Kioga the lad. Pain seemed to be choking her. Wheeling, she hastily followed the others down the trail, which she saw but dimly through a blur of unshed tears....

The return to Hopeka was accomplished in a tenth the time it had taken to fight a way up the swollen streams. And no villager who saw but remarked upon the great change in the white girl, who smiled no more; and in Heladi, whose heart was on the ground.

"Shore!" exclaimed Flashpan fiercely when he heard the news. "Shore, Miss Beth, that's too bad. Hit shore is—" and gave up trying to say more.

But there was one, bright-eyed and expectant, whose childish queries for news of Kioga were not easily answered. It fell to Heladi to tell him.

"We sought him a long way, Tokala."

"And he is coming back?" demanded the eager boy, searching Heladi's face for the happiness that was not there.

"The tomahawk is sheathed," she told him finally.

A grimace of perplexity wrinkled Tokala's cheeks. "You did not find him?" he asked, puzzled by her strange words.

"The hunting-bow is laid aside," came the Indian girl's voice, her eyes still evading his. Slowly the Fox drew back, his smile vanishing as half-understanding came. He spoke this time in another tone. "Heladi! He—" The unbelieving rise of his inflection was like an arrow in her breast. Slowly, then, she looked at him, and answered: "Yes."

Tokala the Fox sucked in one great deep breath, exhaled it jerkily. Then he wheeled, very quickly, and began to walk away, but stumbling as he went, might have fallen only for a strong hand that caught him. A moment later a great scientist did not disdain holding a small Indian lad's head against his hunting-coat, that none might see how hard he was taking these tidings.

XXI

When Kioga asked succor of his gods, they had not answered him. But when, rushing to destruction on the savage landslide, he faced his end without fear, they took pity. Or else it was the merest chance, and not the special providence which watches over the helpless, which saved the Snow Hawk.

For within twenty feet of the lip of the gorge he was snatched into the snowy backlash close beside the main body of the slide. Hurled into a spur of solid rock, he jarred to a smashing stop against its base, and crushed down by the mass of cold earthy stuff, the discard of the landslide, lay buried a while as one dead.

He returned to consciousness of the fact that his entire body was one vast ache, multiplied by a dozen pressures where branch and stone weighed down on him. He lay twisted and bent almost double.

Close by, a huge thing roared and heaved about, and the strong acrid odor of a bear filled Kioga's nostrils. Trapped like himself, the animal exerted all its powers to reach the light dimly showing through the interstices of its prison.

Unhappily the digging claws flung back the displaced materials into Kioga's face, speedily accomplishing what the landslide had failed to finish. Seeking to prevent being thus buried alive, Kioga found himself able to move, a thing surprising in itself. And by laying grip upon a root near his hand, he contrived to loosen the earth's hold on his shoulders and draw himself into a semirecumbent position. Then before the rubble could settle upon him again, a prodigious effort freed his legs.

Well above, his fellow prisoner was laboring to good advantage, slowly boring upward from the mass, and leaving behind a space into which Kioga presently crawled. Writhing and twisting ever upward, he soon found the air coming clearer. Pausing to fill his aching lungs, he redoubled his efforts when the rubble began to settle around his knees. Blood from the injured bear rendered his handholds slippery. But now he could hear the mighty animal shaking itself on the surface. Then, coughing, it shuffled off to a distance.

Ten minutes later, Kioga himself crawled exhausted from his living tomb, to rest where the sun was on his face. Thus for a time, recovering a modicum of strength; then sounds of rending and tearing came to his ears.

The wilderness undertakers were at work round about him, their cawing and muttering a thing of horror. The shadow of great black pinions sailed back and forth across his face. The victims of landslide do not long lie unattended. What the ravens and vultures leave the crows flock down on; the foxes share the feast; and ultimately the bone-crackers come—those gaunt carrion-wolves which ghost about wherever flesh is to be found.

What the vulture-kind light on need not be carrion. Life may not be extinct before their work begins. But helplessness—that must be patent, and well they know how to judge it!

So now, with Kioga, near whom a great king-vulture settled, its great beak pointing gougelike toward his eyes. Two more then came, eyeing the lone figure with knowing gaze, and others of their kind came soaring in until a hundred perched near, waiting the first one's move.

Well the Snow Hawk knew his danger. Ears—but mostly nostrils—told him that. Movement alone would not drive them off. All that held them back now was the illusion of his open eyes, as it were watching them. Did he but move, they would be upon him, the first lightning jabs straight into the muscles at the small of the back, below which lies the kidney fat—then a few quick rips to lay bare the spine with its creamy vital marrow. Thereafter—but there is no thereafter when those knowing probes once began their grisly work.

So Kioga stirred not, save that his fingers slowly closed about a loose thick branch below his hand. Listening for the informative drag of tail-feathers when the leading vulture should bend above him, he waited, readying. All was silent round about him now. But those eyes, fully two hundred, red and angry, watched him. He heard the sickening sound when the leader waddled up to closer range. Down came the bald hideous head, its spade divided for the deadly stabbing pluck.

And midway, with force enough to crush a leopard, Kioga's club flew up to meet it, smashing the vulture back among its fellows, carrion like the things it had grown upon. Leaping up, Kioga next flailed about among those nearest, knocking a score from their scaly legs and clearing a larger circle. Then he hurled whatever came to hand, stones, limbs, and clods of snow, blindly but to good effect, and shouted at them: "Begone, H'ka! Away! *Hai-yah*! *Hai*!"

The meat-birds were confounded. Slow to rise in their heavy takeoff, the exodus was soon begun. The funeral squadrons settled lower down, near the cliff, and a mighty protesting chorus echoed along the landslide from the beaks of a thousand lesser crows and ravens, cursing at the disturbance.

Again with the aid of a stout staff, painfully and slowly Kioga picked his way down the strange mountainside. His headless fever of an hour ago was gone, and he was the Indian stoic again, neither courting nor evading his end, which he felt must be near, but merely accepting what was thrust upon him, enduring the pain of his hurts in silence.

But when the acrid smell of a sulfur pool reached him, he paused to find it and lie for several hours in the hot curative waters. Out again to dry off in the mild spring breeze, then off to wander anew without aim—but not without direction. Even at darkest midnight he knew when he moved from east to west by the evidence of the tree foliage, which always freshens earliest on the slopes, where the returning sun first strikes it.

When his staff indicated a break in the trail and no bottom could be felt, another expedient served him: He dropped a pebble, listening for its fall; it struck instantly, and therefore another ledge was just below and it was safe to lower himself. A mile farther along he came to another break in the path. Another dropped pebble. This time he heard nothing, and turned back, knowing that a precipice yawned before him.

And so until daylight, guided by the direction of streamlets, the echoes of his whistle from cliff to crag, and finally at dawn the feel of the sun on his left side.

In a grotto formed between two great rocks he slept, to wake ravenously hungry. And when he came to the path of another recent landslide, he roved its edges in search of newly killed animals carried down from the upper heights.

Soon he found fresh deer-meat which a wolverine had musked down for future use. No other animal in the wilderness would touch such rank fare. Yet Kioga fed off the wolverine's kill, and stayed to exhaust the remainder before moving down toward the denser valley forests.

At the bases of fallen trees he poked around with his staff, unearthing the nutcaches of local squirrels, devouring again.

He who had once scorned all but the choicest loin cuts of fresh-killed meat, devouring the leavings of carrion-eaters! Robbing squirrel hoards, grubbing for edible roots and bulbs, eating bark, weeds, grass—whatever, in short, his nostrils led him to! Even those squeaking creatures he once had thrown aside when Yanu tossed them into his boyish lap were welcome now, in the pressure of need to satisfy the cravings of appetite. Haunting deadfalls and snowslides, vulturelike, for what might be found to gobble down—to this had the proud Snow Hawk descended—from foremost hunter of a hunting people, to the level of the foulest feeders in all the wilderness!

But the worst was not yet. One day when the pickings had been slimmer than usual, Kioga came upon something seemingly dead and reaching hungrily forward to tear away his own preempted share. But of a sudden a sickening revulsion swept over him. For what he had seized savagely upon a hastily flung away was circled by a leathern wristlet, the bowstring-guard of an Indian warrior. As he would have moved away, he was checked by a human voice, speaking from depths of misery.

"Who touched me?" it questioned in dull tones.

"I," answered the startled Snow Hawk. "Who speaks?"

"I am called Black Shield by my people, the Wa-Kanek."

"How comes it then that you speak the Shoni tongue?"

"I have lived a captive among them for many winters," came the voice again, hoarsely. "My heart hungered for a sight of the scenes of my boyhood. I was escaping to the plainsmen, my people."

Reaching forward, toward the voice, "Let me uncover you of stones," said Kioga.

"Touch me not!" said the other sharply. "Every bone in my

body is broken, and my eyes have been blinded. Can you not see?"

"I too am blind," said Kioga quietly.

The other sighed. "I give you pity. How came this to be?"

Thereupon Kioga, happy to hear the voice of a fellow being again, told him how he had survived the winter through.

"This is most wonderful," said the other after a pause. "By what name are you known?" When Kioga told him, the dying warrior gasped painfully. "The Snow Hawk, war-chief of the Shoni tribes! What shall you do?"

"I shall soon come to the end of a path."

A while the other thought on that. Then: "At my waist—my knife—I have no more need of it. Take it!" To humor him, Kioga did so. "Now promise me one thing," said the other.

"What is that?" said Kioga.

"Where I am going, if this may be, I will speak on your behalf before the Great Ones. If they give back your eyes, promise me that you will carry this knife back to my mother."

"With these hands, if my sight is returned," said Kioga solemnly, "I will place it at her feet."

"All my boyhood life—I had been called coward," whispered the other in a voice noticeably weaker. "I feared other men, and horses, and the darkness. Men laughed at me. But now, at the end, though I am crushed and going to die—I am of strong heart. Tell her—that."

"The Black Shield is a brave man," said Kioga with conviction. "How shall I know his mother?"

"Her name is—" Kioga bent to catch the failing words. But that was all. The young Wa-Kanek was dead.

After burying Black Shield as best he could, the Snow Hawk took up the knife and turned away, unable thenceforward to bring himself to touch unknown flesh of any kind....

Nightfall after this strange experience found him wandering among the lower forest tangles, searching for a place to spend the night. In his descent, forgetful for one moment, he trod on empty air.

Even as instinct warned him of a misstep, the lightning contractions of his tiger-muscles hurled him across a bottomless crevice. Blindly he caught at the nearest handhold on the rocky wall to which he had bounded. He chanced to catch a protruding root of a cliff-hugging tree, and hung there swaying. And as he swayed, there came to his nostrils warning of another's nearness. Maintaining his grip on the root, he found a toehold lower down, and slipped to a mossy ledge. Cautiously he felt about. To one side was empty space. At his back was solid rock, and upwind—a waiting puma.

He heard the click of its teeth as the jaws snapped shut, pictured it in his mind as it lay crouching there. The bulge of muscle on the massive forearm, cruel curved claws flexing in and out of their sheaths, polished fangs gleaming with hunger-drip. He could feel the round fiery moons of its eyes fastened on his, and sense the liquid quiver of a myriad muscles as the strong haunches edged up to power the killing spring.

As well this way as another, if die he must, thought Kioga. Braced to take the charge, he waited.... Came the sound of air hissing on something soft as a great long body sprang to full stretch, the padding thud of forepaws, and then—

And then an immense purring creature crushing against his thighs, its flat silken sides sleeking against him. At his hand gaping jaws that seized but did not bite. A huge long agile cylinder of furry tail clubbing against him. Only after another moment did Kioga recognize this ally of a better day.

"Mika!" he muttered. "The gods have sent you!"

As he roughed the huge soft head, Kioga's thoughts were in the past. A youth, lithe and muscular as the panther at his side, coursed the forest depths on the trail of a great stag. Together, acting in perfect concert, beast and man laid the quarry low in an open clearing by the light of a yellow moon. He had been that youth, and this his wild companion, unchanged today save that now Mika had grown to be bodied like an Indian lion, heavier and stronger by far than when Kioga had seen him last.

If beasts have tongue, Kioga must have spoken to Mika in that soothing purring tone. Some understanding surely passed by thought-transference or otherwise, for the great cat twitched and quivered nervously, its silver coat rippling to the play of sliding muscles beneath it.

And when Kioga walked forward again, the lithe beast was at his side, half a length to the rear, not more nor less. When an hour had gone, they still strode thus, but now it was the wild thing which led, and the human thing who followed, one hand ever at Mika's shoulder. The panther, a hunter by sight, the man, whose nostrils were the keener—thus they slipped silently through the mesh of tangled leaf and bough. Emerging at a shadowed forest pool, each slaked his thirst.

But of a sudden, at a short signal from Kioga, the lithe

puma stiffened, only its tail-tip slowly oscillating. Again intelligence passed between them. An electric quiver flickered along Mika's satin sides. Then in one noiseless bound both melted into the shades nearby. The shadowed glade was empty of life and sound.

Long moments passed; a drop of dew condensing on a mossy bed dropped into the pool with a clear bell-like sound. The underbrush trembled, parted. A tall buck stood there, listening before emerging to lower muzzle to water. The soft throat swelled with every swallow, each gurgle amplified by stillness.

Then lightning struck. A silver bolt of doom crushed down the buck before it could so much as lift its head. A thickset paw curved round, drove its sickles home behind the horns and wrenched. A snort, a crack of breaking bone, a breath outblown—as soon as that the warm young prey was dead.

From the thicket came Kioga now, to his first feed of fresh-killed meat in many a long day. As Mika ripped open the belly to get at the inner organs, the Snow Hawk attacked the quarter with his knife, severing a thick slice of juicy deer-ham and eating it on the instant.

Having devoured their fill, man and beast denned up close by to sleep.

Even in Kioga's dark world there were mitigating joys, which reached him now through the ears.

From down the valley the bugling of two wapiti pealed out, rhythmic, pure and clear across the distance, echoing and reechoing. Outside the cave, a small dark bird fluted a prelude to its evensong, then hurled six top notes up to where the stars were coming out. This was a woodland thrush, a mocker-bird peculiar to Nato'wa. Its song, the Indians say, is the first the spirit hears on approaching the Happy Hunting Ground. Kioga listened for the second bars.

They came suddenly, chiming forth in leisured golden swell. All through the purple glades the liquid stanzas floated one by one, no two alike, purling forth like water from a magic spring, each drop a different one. Theme after theme, ardor and triumph and rapture expelling one the other from that tiny silver throat, whose wondrous mechanism mixed plain air with sound, and brought forth Eden's music.

So for an hour this ounce of feathers held a stricken warrior thrall before its muted clarionet grew still. In that one hour a mocker-bird was king. But when sound's own incarnation nodded on its nest, the nighttime jungle slowly came to life.

A snow-leopard's hoarse grating from a ravine nearby. Aloft the *honka-honk* of wild geese wedging homeward for the night. From some far watchtower the long-drawn mournful howling of wolves assembling, sinister and grim, boding ill to all who eat not meat, and many more that do. Everywhere, near and far, the startling hoot of hunting owls. Then, jarring out in frightful volume, the chest cough of a hungry tiger, whereat every other voice paid tribute of utter silence, until his black-barred highness had passed. . . .

Kioga slept. For no good reason he dreamed of hotel beds and gleaming table silver and linen white as snow—and was awakened from his dream by the rumble of a tiger's roar and the dying bellow of a stricken buffalo bull. An hour later morning dawned.

Eating again of the previous day's kill, the hunters rested a while after the manner of wild things. Then, after rising to stretch, the great cat played about, leaping, bounding, rolling soundlessly over before the Snow Hawk, and striking mock blows with heavy forepaws. But Kioga did not retaliate as of old, and the puma soon desisted, for this was only one of many signs that Kioga was not himself.

Probably the white-toothed creature never did come to understand the nature of the Snow Hawk's affliction. Such abstract things are not within the compass of the animal mind. But a sense of uneasiness grew out of its own fierce nature. Ever and again the yellow glare of its eyes fell upon the man. The gaze which never hitherto could sustain Kioga's, now saw only open gray-green eyes with no expression behind them.

Frequently Kioga sensed the beast in this act of glaring. Ere now, a glance had been enough to bring Mika to instant terms. What the creature might do to him in the absence of that dominating glance, Kioga knew not. Jungle beast, caged or free, is inherently deadly, once beyond control.

And so when Mika's gaze burned on him, the Snow Hawk sought to soothe him in deep purring tones. Thus matters went for several days, and man and beast remained together until the kill was quite devoured. On the fifth day while moving through a tangled thicket well up the mountainside, the twain surprised a monster moose lying upon a ledge some ten feet below their level. Mika, detecting it first by sight, shrank down quivering. Kioga, warned thus of prey, almost instantly caught its scent, and knew where it lay when he heard the occasional grinding of its teeth on tender twigs.

Now a meeting with Muswa in full autumn antlers is not a

thing to be undertaken carelessly, even by such a hunter as Kioga. In this season, however, Muswa lay stripped of his horny armament, awaiting the hardening of the tender velvet-covered branches just beginning to form upon his head. Although at a later season Kioga might have foregone the risk in his present blind state, now—he lifted his hand from Mika's twitching shoulders.

This was the signal of consent. The long cat slunk crouching forward, gathering, readied—and sprang powerfully down. Simultaneously the Snow Hawk also dropped, thinking to strike before the prey might fairly gain its legs.

But in his eagerness he oversprang, and either way it would have been no use; for another, upon whom the hunters had not reckoned, betrayed their presence. A moose-bird rose screaming in the branches from its vigil over the lazy moose. Warned just in time, the great deer reared and swerved.

Mika, who had sprung for the shoulder, fell instead upon the haunch, taking hold with but one clutching paw. Kioga, who at best had not aimed at all but dropped blindly down, received a side-blow from the great deer's antler. Full grown and hardened, the horn would have slashed him through, but soft and tender as it now was, it only clubbed him aside.

As the moose crashed away, the puma was scraped off upon a branch and fell full upon Kioga, who lay stunned where his head had struck the ground.

The Snow Hawk was only dimly conscious of the moose's loud escape; but he was sharply aware of long keen hooks driving into his chest as a heavy weight bore down on him. When he stirred, two great paws applied traction through their claws. Swiftly he realized the truth.

Mika was upon him, the lust to kill multiplied for having lost the moose. Blood ran from Kioga's ear, warm fresh and salt—a madness in Mika's nostrils. A hideous bubbling snarl issued from the puma's throat, like nothing Kioga had ever heard it utter before. And in an instant he understood—unhappy creature, Mika was struggling between instinct and intelligence. The uncompromising beast within cried to clutch, tear, eviscerate; while the brute mind, its function blurred by the smell of blood, delayed.

But mind was being overpowered by instinct. The claws drove deeper. The long incisors drew apart. The blue-black lips gleamed as they approached the Snow Hawk's pulsing throat, fanning him with a damp hot panting breath. Eyes fixed on the Snow Hawk's, Mika was crossing that jungle borderline which separates the ordinary forest killer from the man-eater, undeterred by the only light which might have stopped him now—the arresting gleam of human eye.

Suddenly Mika checked, as if a lash had exploded before his face; for in that selfsame instant expression had returned to the eyes of the Snow Hawk, and few wild things can long sustain human gaze.

To Kioga, straining his sightless eyes upon the grinning jaws before him, it seemed as if from darkness two great golden disks came suddenly into focus. Within them he saw sulfur fires burning brightly. As he lay silent, thinking this some illusion of the senses, the rest of Mika's snarling face became sharply outlined. And at the same instant he saw the cat shrink sharply back, as one caught in some guilty act might do. He heard its uncertain snarl, and saw the struggle the animal still waged against the thirst for blood, the long tail lashing furiously, the dog-teeth dripping.

And then, thrilling to the wonderful truth, Kioga was on his feet in one mighty bound. Loud, commanding, full of the power to enforce, his voice caught the seething panther away from the intent to spring upon him.

"Down, Mika! Back, wild brother! Down, and be still!"

More than the words, it was the piercing gaze of the seeing eyes which brought the beast to submission. With head low, slowly it came forward, still snarling, to take the touch of the Snow Hawk's hand. Presently the snarl subsided, and Mika lay panting as one spent by some consuming passion.

But beside him the Snow Hawk, though stunned just a moment before, stood quivering to the miracle of sight returned. Not since that hour at the stake when a war-club had numbed him, had he looked upon a living moving thing. As in the moment of his blinding, his neck again felt numb where spine meets skull.

Touching the spot, he found it wet with blood, but the stiffness was gone. Apparently some small nerve there, some vital link in the wiring between eye and spinal cord, had been depressed the winter through, and now suddenly freed of pressure. Or else—

But if your sight, long gone, had just returned, you would not long pause to wonder why. Nor did Kioga.

The myriad things his eye had long forgot now crowded in: The slow light, rising up to pearl the southern sky and melt into the flaming wonder of northern dawn. The sun, a goblet brimming fire, whose face Kioga had not seen for many a month. Nearer by, an immense spider web, each strand in its geometrical pattern gemmed with a pure and sparkling drop of morning dew. And everywhere the stately forest gilded by sunrise.

On a neighboring mountain lake the mists moved like regal gray swans before taking silent wing to vanish in the sunlight. The stony cliffs were red as fire, the lake deeps bluer than vitriol, the forest emerald green and filled with dusky shadows. On a distant peak an endless turban of spotless snow was being unwound by the upper winds.

Dazed by this view of all he had so long been denied the sight of, and still uncertain of the permanency of his cure, Kioga moved through the forest. At his side Mika slouched, a different Mika, now that the disconcerting empty look had gone from the master's eyes.

Slowly they moved at first, for during the term of his blindness, slowness had been thrust upon Kioga. Uncertain were his first few leaps from place to place in following where the sinuous puma led. But after a little time growing confidence quickened the Snow Hawk's movements again. A ravine here yawned before him, across which Mika had sprung easily, waiting on its other side. Before the jump Kioga hesitated, poising as the eaglet stands before making its first flight from crag to crag. Then, leaping the gap, in one long bound Kioga pursued his wild companion, like an animal long caged, now free.

Up to a narrow ledge he sprang, and raced its length, and leaped again to another higher still, surefooted as the beast he trailed. Fast though Mika went, Kioga followed now as swiftly, abandoning himself to the intoxication of leaping and climbing recklessly after all these months of sightless hesitation. Swift along a slanting tree he sped, to bound catlike through twenty feet of space and land on another bole, as light almost as the air through which he lithely flew. A short quick dash, the flash of muscled limbs, and the Hawk took wing again in soaring flight, before alighting in perfect control of balance, with motion utterly arrested.

Upon a lofty watching-place he paused then, exultant. None of his matchless vital strength was lost! Before he went farther, he paused to give thanks to his Maker, in whose own mold his fine physique might have been cast.

Wheeling then, he found Mika's eyes upon him again, two white-hot probes blazing up, as they had been blazing when his sight returned. Well he knew the nature of this tameless animal. For his safety, he must make sure of Mika.

One hand closed about his knife. He drew the other across a stone to cut the skin, and thrust it bleeding under Mika's nose. The silken ears screwed back. Blue fires flickered in the puma's eyes. A hoarse snarl rose muttering in its throat. But from the bleeding wrist the beast drew back. Again Kioga tempted, and again Mika refrained, though twitching nervously in every cell.

Should Kioga risk its treachery, or drive home his knife while yet he could? Might not those white fangs again be at his throat in some critical moment?

Slowly the Snow Hawk raised the gleaming blade, drew back his arm for one hard thrust into the warm side. And then his resolution weakened, for beneath his hand the soft hide vibrated to an inner purr. He could not bring himself to strike.

"I am a man, and you are a beast," he thought aloud, sheathing the knife. "Yours it is to lust at the smell of blood, for nature made you so." Then, on another note: "Up, wild brother!"

At the familiar command the puma rolled erect, quivering and eager. And thus the man with beast at heel turned valleyward again.

But now Kioga led where even Mika could not follow. Dropping sheer thirty feet down a rugged cliff, he alighted in the domelike crown of a tree below, vanishing within it. Then through the forest midway, agile as quicksilver, trapezing from branch to limb in long arching swings, pausing only to rob a nest of an egg. On again in easy bounding career, balancing along the high catwalks of the topmost canopy at a pace resembling flight. Here two great suspended vines linked cliff with tree and hung in huge skeins like the braids of a giantess. Across these Kioga swung, and so to earth again after that swift arboreal passage, to await Mika on a sun-bathed ledge....

Storm caught the pair roving toward the valley, and in the lee of an overhanging scarp man and animal crouched back, waiting for it to end. Rain curtained them in, and dashed them with its spray. Lightning threw its molten links from cloud to cloud. Thunder rocked the mountains in rumbling bombardment.

When the storm had lifted, they continued on down, sprinkled with liquid moonstones when passing through each ferny glade and inhaling the rich piny air, freshened by the rainfall. On their way they glimpsed an eagle, striking down a flying wildfowl. A fox appeared, a fat hare drooping from its jaws. And from the sequestered shade of a devil's-club thicket a rare beast came prowling forth, and again they paused to watch.

It was a snow-leopard melanoid, dark as lampblack, with coaly reflections shimmering on its glistening coat. On a ledge, two hundred feet away, it sprang upon and carried low a deer.

And seeing these things, Kioga felt the hunting urge, half forgotten, flame hotly into being. His cup was not yet full, because he had not killed. Too long had he subsisted on a scavenger's fare and dined upon the kills of others. He craved to test his strength anew, to satisfy himself that he was completely whole.

To this end he hunted alone, following the nearest stream with eyes alert to catch the spoor of game. But the recent rains had washed away all footprints. In his search he found the prey before he found its signs.

Close beside a waterfall, in a still pool off from the rushing stream, a huge black rock appeared to move. Fixing it with his eyes, the Snow Hawk watched intently. Then slowly, rising full of might, and streaming water, a buffalo bull heaved up on all fours. Kioga knew this species well, a woodland variant of the prairie bison, perhaps master of some small band adapted to this forest habitat. And of such a size that nothing less than a tiger would dare molest it, wallowing here in the open.

But now a hunter more to be feared than Guna crept upon the bull until its small red eyes were visible. Not twenty feet separated the bison from the man in concealment when Kioga bared his knife. Waiting until the bull turned its head aside, with one mighty spring he hurled himself through space.

Hard and true he struck upon the bull's high hump, his weight and impetus throwing it to its side in the stream. Then seizing hold by the long neck wool, ten times Kioga plunged in the metal knife, goading the bull each time into a prodigious splashing jump along the stream.

Up on the bank the shaggy beast then rushed, but there its wonderful vitality gave way. The forelegs buckled under. The short black horn plowed up the sand, and the buffalo lay dead.

For a few seconds Kioga savored the moment of triumph. And then again, as in the happy days of other years, the Snow Hawk's call to meat rang loudly through the glades, summoning Mika to a favorite kill.

Deftly Kioga removed the animal's skin and laid it aside.

The horns, too, he kept for uses known to him. Laying open the back with his sharp knife, he exposed the long dorsal tendons and cut it all away, along with many another cord whose location only a jungle anatomist could know. Severing the hooves, these too he threw aside. Then with a great blow of a stone he split the skull, and removed the brain. This and the beast's own liver, mixed to an emulsion, he spread upon the raw hide, wrapped all up together and sank it with stones in a river pool.

When he and Mika had satisfied their hunger, it was nightfall. The following morning he woke, again to know that surge of joy at being sound in every sense.

Climbing several thousand feet, he sought one of those cedar treelets whose toughness comes of long slow growth on the heights. Cutting one down laboriously with his knife, he split out a stout stave, heated it over fire, straightened it, then charred it carefully and scraped away the char. Across the forming bow he later stretched a length of gut to give it added strength, and fixed this on with buffalo-hoof glue. Of strong back-sinew he twisted a good cord, and then strung up his hunting-bow.

From the willows growing near a stream he made a dozen long straight shafts. With one of them he shot down a sleeping owl, and from its long wing-feathers trimmed vanes for his arrows, gluing and binding them on with sinew. Buffalo-bone yielded arrowheads, which he fitted to the willow shafts.

Having fleshed and tanned the bull's hide, he whetted his knife and cut eight long tapering strips, whereof he plaited another stout whip, bound to a leg-bone handle. Thus armed, he strode without hesitation along the hidden paths of the greater forest carnivora.

When he returned to the vicinity of the bull's carcass, he heard strident sounds of protest, and discerned Mika sprawling angrily on a lofty limb, while a prime young tiger lay athwart their kill, devouring it.

A hard-hurled stone brought savage protest from the feasting robber. Another, striking its chest, brought Guna charging forward upon the insolent man-whelp flourishing a long black snakelike thing in one hand. But leaping upon a ledge nearby, Kioga plied the lash, driving the tiger whence it came, and aiding its retreat with a bark of the stinging bullhide lash. . . .

And far away on another mountain's side, in the Ghost Country, two white men, aided by several Shoni tribesmen, were erecting a monument of stones to the memory of the

Snow Hawk. They fixed upon the monument a wooden slab, bearing a simple legend burned theron.

A while the whitemen stood silent, with bared heads, then turned away, followed by their red-skinned companions.

A little later one of the Indians returned alone. Upon the rocky pile he laid each weapon on his person, a tomahawk, knife, bow, and ten good arrows. Beside these he placed a haunch of venison—and by it a woman's small skinning-knife. Then he too slowly turned away.

In such manner James Munro and Dan La Salle abandoned all hope for Kioga. So too the faithful Kias, in his way, bade farewell to a lifelong friend, on behalf of himself and of Heladi.

And in the hidden cave, deep in the Tsus-Gina-i, a bit of bark, thrust through a finger-ring, was Beth La Salle's last tribute to one who had gone away.

XXII

That night, from some far ravine, came a weird wild cry that brought Mika uncertainly to his four padded feet—the wail of a she-puma. Listening, Kioga's comrade prowled into the forest.

With Mika gone to answer the mating call, Kioga set out to reach the Hiwasi River, on which he had last seen his American Indians paddling northward the previous autumn, after he had freed them from their Shoni captors. But his blind wanderings had taken him far, and the spring rains had washed out his trail.

Reasoning that in his blind wanderings he must have come far north of the Shoni realm, he plunged into the forest due westward. And thus after several days of travel he came to the uppermost tributary of the Hiwasi, known as the River of Lost Canoes.

On this stream, assuming them to have come so far in safety, he should find some traces of his missing protégés. Scouting either shore for several days, he came at last upon signs of an old camp. Encouraged by this indubitable evidence of their passage, Kioga paused in his search. A tree lay prone beside the river; finding the trunk free from cracks or decay, he went to work, and by burning, and hollowing it carefully, he shaped forth a rough dugout canoe.

Of other materials near to hand he carved a paddle. A long sapling shod on either end with buffalo horn would serve as either canoeing pole or spear. Well armed and with a sound craft beneath him, he now pushed off, and turned his face upstream, scanning either bank for signs of the band's nightly camps.

In one day he found old traces of two more camps, almost obliterated by time, but discernible nevertheless to the Snow Hawk's practiced eye. Frequently along the shore he glimpsed a branch, broken off long ago by human agency, the direction of its pendant end showing the direction of the band's progress. At a fork in the stream another trail-mark had been erected: Upon one large stone a smaller rested, and to its left side another lay, indicating that they had taken the left fork.

So, by continuing watchfulness, Kioga ran down these old signs of passage, coming at last upon a camp which evidenced a longer pause by the band. A tree had been bared of bark for several feet; and burned upon the wood was a large wading bird, upside down. In some manner Big Crane had died, and the band had paused to leave this memorial.

At the next camping-place Kioga found the remains of an old canoe below a rapid, and not far away another monument—this time recording death of Sitting Coyote. Disaster had overtaken the band and wrecked their canoe, but only one had perished. Charred ashes and a stone scraper ashore spoke of another canoe built, in which to carry on.

Then one night, just at dusk, the old signs gave way to clearer prints, hardly more than a week old. Swiftly tracing these into the forest, Kioga came to a cave, back from the river. All signs pointed to an occupancy of many months.

The Snow Hawk rekindled the dead fire and looked about him. There were heaps of bones in here, a supply of firewood, several bark eating-dishes and utensils. Here was the discard of weapons manufactured on the spot, there a little pile of obsidian chips where someone had spent many hours making arrow- and spearheads. But in the rising flames he saw something on the flat wall which explained much that had befallen the band since its liberation from Hopeka village. The stone bore this strange legend, done in charcoal and Indian pictographs:

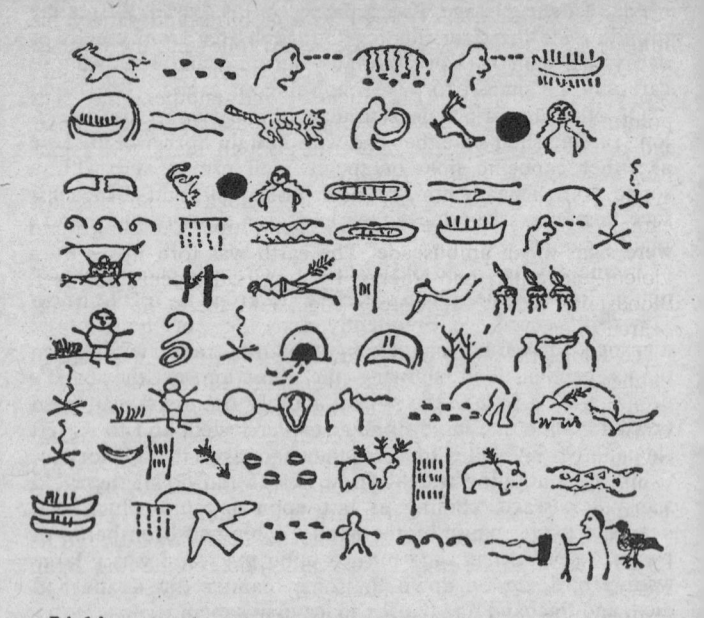

Linking together the ideas suggested by the drawings, Kioga translated the message thus:

Tokala the Fox deserted the band. We looked for him, but rain washed out his trail. We saw ten canoes filled with enemies. We hid under a riverbank. A tiger seized Big Crane. We stopped to mourn. Our canoe overturned and Sitting Coyote was drowned. We built another canoe and went on. At sundown we camped. Stayed here three days. It snowed. Ice formed in river. We broke camp, took to river, but ice was too thick. Enemy scouts found our camp and overtook us. We fought a battle. We killed three men and took scalps. Could go no farther. Grass Girl was ill. We found a good cave. Hid canoes in forest. Held another council and decided to stay here. Grass Girl's second child was born. We named him Gets-Away. Kills Bull took Pretty Eagle to wife. Remained here six moons. Killed fifteen dear and a bear. Ice finally broke up. Took to canoes again. Snow Hawk follow. We will wait three days where river ends.

(Signed) Old Crow Man.

Lingering only to arrow a few wild birds and satisfy his hunger, Kioga took up the chase again, following the river to its last navigable point. Here he found concealed the band's two canoes hidden in the thickets, and another trail sign pointing up the mountainside to a high pass across the divide, and down into the western foothills which mark the beginning of the Great Plains of Nato'wa.

Upon a stream flowing westward Kioga found the last camp, and a new and almost finished canoe. On the ground were signs of an ambuscade. The earth was torn up as by a violent encounter, and tracked by a myriad moccasined feet. Bloodstains led to the water's edge, and there the trail appeared to end.

To Kioga the story was clear, almost, as if he had seen it happen. Preparing to embark again, the American band had been fallen upon by the Wa-Kanek, on their way into the rich mountain strongholds of the Shoni to avenge their defeat of the previous autumn and plunder the villages anew. There would be no more signs from the band, he thought sadly, as he completed the canoe which they had begun.

But in this Kioga erred. As he paddled downstream he found one more message. In a still pool beside the main channel an arrow floated, attached to a thong weighted to the bottom by a stone. Someone had contrived to let him know that they had been carried off downstream. Of itself this was a tribute. The simple faith of the band in Kioga's promise to follow had endured throughout all these months.

In contrast to the brawling mountain rivers of the forest lands, the stream on which he now floated was but a languid serpent twisting sluggishly through its wooded banks, finally split into several channels by willow-choked islands swarming with wildfowl. Here, one would say, there could be no further trail; but to eyes trained like Kioga's:

On the still waters near the shore floats a thin dusting of petals and pollen from the spring blossoms of trees and plants. Close to shore on the silent surface he passes, observing the willow stems at waterline. For perhaps an inch above the present water-level each stalk is coated with the yellowish powdery drift—raised by the wash of forging canoes. A wavy line of drying drift on a sandy bar confirms the first signs. Where the still water is clear of pollen, he next observes the shallow bottom for traces of mud-roil raised by newly passing paddles. In the underwater grasses he looks for—and sees—a darker line where the round of a canoe has forced the spears to either side. A freshly bruised willow near shore, a broken water-plant—these and twenty other marks guide him in this seemingly uncanny deciphering of the undecipherable. And at every bend he watches for shore-marks where canoes may have been drawn upon the bank. Scarce a swimming duck could pass in these revealing shallows without leaving a trace which those keen eyes would note.

Following the trail with growing caution, Kioga came now to where a spider, mounted on a reed, floated from its spinnerets a silver thread across the trail, repairing damage done its web within this present hour. The fresh break in the strands showed at the height of Kioga's own head. Bending low, he passed beneath the web and shortly came upon the place where the Indians had disembarked. All vigilance now, he observed how the stream lost itself in a swampy savanna inhabited by snakes and birds and prowling beasts of the plains. And it was here, in the last of tree-cover, that he found hidden many dugout canoes. These are often used by the Wa-Kanek in transporting captives and plunder from Shoni territory when their horses are otherwise employed.

Before proceeding any farther, Kioga towed these craft to a different hiding place far in the mazes of the swamp and concealed them carefully, the better to hamper future raids upon his own tribes. For though they had denied him, the Shoni were still his people, and their well-being was important to him.

Tying up his own canoe, he then took his weapons, and slipping through the edge of the swamplands, came at last to the end of leafy concealment. Parting the branches, he looked out over open rolling plains stretching endlessly before him. Somewhere in those billowing grass-grown hills the Wa—Kanek camped. And among them, captives again, were the members of his missing band of American Indians.

As he would have stepped forward, some instinct murmured—he drew back instead. And well for him he did! For a flashing arrow whisked past his face, struck a limb, and glanced into the ground close by. Facing whence it came, he slipped behind a fallen tree, watching, listening, and trying to scent his hidden enemy. Picking up the shaft, he gave it a quick glance. Shorter than a Shoni arrow, and pointed with chalcedony where theirs is of obsidian, he recognized it for a plainsman's bolt. A Wa-Kanek rear scout lay in wait, dangerously close.

Ensued then a long half hour of silence, the wonderful patient waiting of Indian foes, each watching for the other's first false move to drive in a killing shaft. Nor could Kioga allow his adversary more than three such moves. He had but two remaining arrows of his own, one a faulty shaft, and that with which he had been so suddenly saluted—three in all. Whereas the unseen doubtless carried a full quiver.

Fixing his eyes on no one point, and thus commanding a view of all, Kioga watched, well knowing the foe waxed as anxious as himself to end the meeting with a true heart-shot. And presently, to test the mettle of the enemy, he exposed himself. A quick shaft flickered through the intervening leafage. A close shot, but hastily loosed, for it went high—yet even so, flying only a hand's breadth from his head. The enemy was no mean marksman.

Then came that for which Kioga had waited, a tremor of a bush as the other changed position, that a quick return might not find him sleeping there. Aiming a little ahead Kioga drew and let fly. A sudden commotion evidenced the foe's astonishment, though the shaft had glanced too low to do damage. But in that moment's discomposure Kioga retrieved the other's second arrow, an equally light straight slender shaft of exquisite workmanship and balance.

Selecting then the worst of his arrows, which still numbered three, Kioga nocked it to the cord and looked forth again. This time he descried the upright plume of a warrior's headdress, a trifle too readily shown to disguise that old trick of drawing an enemy's shots. But again Kioga loosed, allowing something for the faulty arrow. The feathers of the wabbling reed, but not its point, knocked down the plume.

Instantly the hideous painted features of a Wa-Kanek warrior showed in mockery above a fallen log, and as quickly vanished on the echo of a derisive yell.

A moment Kioga waited, silent. Then, chancing all on a sudden thought, he observed the direction of the cross-breeze, and allowed for his stronger bow and the lighter arrows which the foe had sent him. One of these he then set against his string, holding the other with the bow hand in a position favoring rapid nocking. Drawing back the cord, he held lightly and steadily for an instant, before loosing the arrow. Swiftly as the one shaft flew, the second—Kioga's last—fled after, as if drawn along by the first, which whisked within an inch of the hidden Wa-Kanek.

Instantly the warrior rose to jeer anew—and jeering, stood smitten through the skull by that hard-driven second shaft.

Well served by the arrows of the foe, Kioga was halfway across the field of shooting before the man fell upon the log which had sheltered him. Swiftly the Snow Hawk appropriated all those perfect arrows, a small arm-shield of purported "medicine" value, the belt containing knife-sheath, pouch of colored face-paints, and sundry other small articles. The warrior's bow he struck into the ground erect beside the body; the knife he placed upon the breast.

Then swiftly, lest further loss of time cost his migrant band dearly, he struck out alone among the foothills in search of the dead man's mount, which should be picketed somewhere hereabout.

A snorting sound, the clatter of hooves, and a medley of growls issuing from a coulée led him swiftly thither. He beheld first a ring of prairie wolves, lesser cousins of the great mountain breed. These circled in narrowing snarling periphery about a fallen horse, around whose legs a twisted picket rope was tangled. Nearby, telling eloquently of a gallant defense, three wolves lay crushed and broken by the pounding hooves of the fallen animal. But exhaustion was heavy now upon the struggling horse.

Quick singing cuts with the snaking whip brought yelps of pain from the wolves, which scattered and fled like wisps of yellow mist at the voice of man so near and loud and suddenly at hand.

At Kioga's approach the fallen horse heaved erect and stood a moment quivering in every muscle, foam flying from its champing jaws to fleck the deep broad chest. Slowly Kioga came nearer, drinking in the beauty of that perfect stallion. Full sixteen hands tall it stood, garbed in winter coat of smoky gray, a sight to kindle an Arab's heart. Legs slim as a wapiti's, long and straight as rods of tempered steel, whereon for all its heavy coat the tendons showed forth cable-clear. Eyes large and brilliant in a small, fine-chiseled head; muzzle short and smooth, its flaring nostrils sucking in the prairie air. Body short, compact, close-coupled; flanks sleek—here surely was the mount of a powerful chief.

Down again it fell, in rope entangled. Instantly Kioga was at its head, pressing it to earth, stroking, caressing, speaking not in words but only in sound—for thus the heart of beasts is reached. Soon its struggles ceased, its breathing eased, the eye-whites no longer showed. Holding to its rope, Kioga moved aside. Unaided the stallion rose on nimble feet to yield presently and nibble at a proffered handful of grass. Then to cool water Kioga led it, rubbed its sweating limbs with grass, and washed clean the wounds of recent battle.

Then mounting, he tried its paces, felt out its gait, watched its responses, working it in a small circle, as he had learned to do in civilization from men who never dreamed of such a horse as this. After a little he knew that seldom before had man bestrode the very wind.

Of the Nato'wan horses little is known. The land itself is still a wilderness, with few of its fauna classified. But science says that long before the white man came, there roamed through North America a horse as large or larger than the steeds we ride today. Such is the testimony of the asphalt pits and fossils found from Texas to Alaska.

Perhaps in some forgotten time, when the continents of earth were linked together in the North, a set of common ancestors gave life to all the wild breeds. As to this, even experts disagree. This much, however, is certain:

The horse of far Nato'wa is not the animal known to civilized man. Perhaps it is related to the extinct true-American horse, for that too was tall and swift; perhaps descended from the wandering herds still roaming northern Asia, and bred to greater stature by man, or influenced by milder habitat....

On the broad trail of the Wa-Kanek horse-band Kioga now followed through the swelling hills, keeping ever to the valleys until twilight overtook him. Dismounting and picketing his horse, he climbed to the top of a ridge, scanning the hills ahead. Though he saw no signs of human presence, somewhere in that billowing waste the nomad Wa-Kanek dwelt. The horse would know where. Remounting, he gave the stallion its head, and after a moment of hesitation the animal swung into an easy gallop bespeaking vast reserves of power. With the motion of that fine beast's barrel between his thighs, Kioga came back to the plains, unvisited since his boyhood.

Just once, upon an open stretch, he asked for speed, and felt that surging animal all but leap from under him as it fled through the falling darkness. When the moon had risen high, they paused for another reconnoiter and more cautiously then went forward, for Kioga had caught the smell of woodsmoke.

Leaving his mount in a coulée, Kioga scouted forward. From a ridge he saw the red core of a watch-fire burning; five men lay about it, feet to blaze. A sixth sat erect and alert; and as Kioga waited, he woke another. Among the Wa-Kanek no camp is ever left unguarded. The watch was changing. Peering about, Kioga saw no tents, nothing but this small fire and a string of horses in the near shadows. A mere scouting-party, perhaps, waiting the return of the warrior Kioga had killed, ere continuing on in the track of the main band.

Beyond view of the camp Kioga sprang to horse again; and two hours before dawn, on topping a rise, came into view of the Wa-Kanek camp, already astir and preparing for the travel of the coming day. Speculating, it seemed to Kioga that he might unite himself with the captive American Indians in one of several ways: Either by attempting a nighttime liberation; by slipping in the next night and leading the band to fall upon their sleeping captors; or by approaching openly on foot, and when received among the Wa-Kanek, seeking other means. The second plan involved hazards of discovery, but delay was most undesirable, for in another day or two they would unite with the main Wa-Kanek tribes, and torture or death would swiftly follow for the captives.

Deciding on the third method, Kioga hobbled his horse and neared the camp on foot without attempting concealment. A sudden outcry announced that he was seen, and several warriors rushed to their arms. Advancing with the sign of peace, the Snow Hawk suffered them to come near, hoping that none save his own band would recognize him as the former war-chief of the Shoni.

While others covered him with their ready arrows, two Wa-Kanek braves met him fifty yards from camp. When they spoke in their own tongue, he shook his head. Thereafter they resorted to the universal sign-talk, demanding to know his identity and business.

"I will answer to your chief alone," signed Kioga, adopting the haughty air best used in dealing with these suspicious and headstrong savages. "Take me before him. I bring big news."

The two exchanged glances. Realizing they were many and he but one, they permitted his approach, surrounded him, and thus entered the watching camp.

Among others whose eyes were on him, Kioga saw at last the members of his own band. After a single meaningful glance their way, he knew by their startled expressions that he was recognized, and he turned away. To the single tent in the encampment the guards led him, pausing before the closed flap to cough as notice of their presence. And soon a strange hoarse testy voice from within, giving some brief command in Wa-Kanek. By the paintings on the tepee Kioga judged that here slept a prominent personage, by the tone of harsh command, one of unquestioned authority.

Ensued a wait of half an hour. Then with a rustle of garments someone was approaching the flap from within, when suddenly there came an interruption from beyond the camp: A wild shrill yell of triumph, followed by the pound of several galloping horses, hard-driven. Wheeling with the others, Kioga saw a bombshell thrown amid his plans.

Too late he regretted his oversight in failing to run off the horses of the rear-guard scouts. For down the nearest hill a band of five horsemen came rushing, leading the fine gray stallion by its rope behind them. In another moment they would be in the camp, adding to the rising uproar—during which it was all too probable that Kioga would be cut down without a hearing.

In this moment of crisis there remained but one slim hope. Without a second's hesitation Kioga seized this. Hurling his guards aside, from one he snatched a war-club. Swinging it freely, he bounded toward the band's horses, picketed in one string. A moment to drag up the picket-rope, a spring upon the nearest mount, the kick of heels dug deep—and then away to the thundering roar of one hundred and twenty racing hooves, straight into the path of the oncoming horsemen.

In utter consternation the yelling Wa-Kanek could loose no arrows without cutting down their own scouts, bewildered like themselves by this amazing turn of events. Of the scouts, three wheeled their mounts aside. Two others, grasping the situation, bore down upon Kioga.

He met the first headlong, hurling him aside with the shoulder of his horse. But the second, who led the gray stallion still, swung wickedly with his club. Though it merely grazed Kioga, it broke the back of his plunging mount, and the beast sank beneath him. Leaping clear, Kioga laid low the warrior with his own hurled club, and drawing his knife cut the rope which held the gray stallion.

Springing them upon its back, he performed a lightning pivot and leaned to the wondrous mechanics of the gray bolt's gallop, urging it on with lips at its ear. Like lightning from a cloud that swift horse responded, and in another twenty seconds he would have left pursuit hopelessly behind; but unhappily the other scouts had turned, and though dropping swiftly back, had swung and thrown their leather lariats. One missed, but two others settled about his body, snatching him from his seat.

With screams of triumph ringing in his ears he struck the ground and felt his bonds go slack—but only for an instant. Then he glimpsed what lay in store for him. Speeding past, not twenty feet between them, his captors swerved apart in unison. Caught between both ropes, he would be torn in two.

Slashing with his knife, he successfully severed one rope. Then running as swiftly as he might with the other to lessen the shock when the dragging rope drew taut, he sawed at it with the dulling knife. But this strand did not part, and its ensuing jerk compressed his vitals, snapped him from his feet, and dragged him swiftly campward at its end.

On rocky ground, he had surely been broken and crushed by this ordeal. But the heavy grass somewhat cushioned the shocks; and thus, still clutching his knife, he was drawn conscious through the camp, and men struck at him as he slithered swiftly past. Snagging at last and breaking, the rope released him. His course was checked almost before the door of the painted lodge. His knife flew from his grasp and fell before someone standing there. Rising dazed but still undaunted, Kioga stood disarmed, waiting for the end, but determined to sell his life dearly. Like hounds upon the cornered quarry, the braves rushed in for the kill.

Then, shrill as the voice of a screaming eagle, a cry slashed through the bedlam. The great authority before the lodge was calling off the dogs of war. And despite the white heat of flaming passion, the warriors stopped in their tracks—a thing which Kioga noted with subconscious wonderment. The reaction of relief was such that his strength now ran from him, and he pitched forward at the feet of the figure at the lodge.

A little time he lay deaf to all that happened near him. Soon sounds came through again—quick voices, the snort of horses. Sensations also came—cold wet upon his hurts, rough horny hands feeling of his brow and pushing back his hair. At last he looked up, through narrowed lids, to see an old woman's shadowed face bending above him.

A small woman she was, dressed in buckskin richly studded with elk's teeth and worked with twisted horsehair. The early sun fell on a seamed but characterful face. Thin pursing lips, long hooked nose, black and glittering eyes, wide-spaced above prominent cheekbones, and sunk deep in a mesh of wrinkles—these, and a proud, fearless carriage of the head, marked her as one of keen mental vigor and great determination.

As she looked down upon him, crooning with a strange and touching tenderness, the Snow Hawk saw that her cheeks were wet with tears. Opening wide his eyes, he looked straight into hers.

Then, oddly, she drew in a breath of quick surprise and shrank back, the old eyes narrowing as she scanned Kioga's face anew. The quick staccato of her words beat down on him in questioning tones. He shook his head, and made the hand-signs for "I do not understand." Reverting to signs, she tried again.

"Whence came you?"

"From the forest-land to the east."

"How do you ride the gray stallion?"

"The prize of war, Mother."

The old woman's breath caught suddenly in her throat at that word. "You remember me, then?" she asked with an enigmatic expression on her face which the Snow Hawk was to remember later.

"How could I forget?" he answered, anxious to fathom the reason for her peculiar actions, and pitying her too, he knew not why.

"Last night I dreamed you would return," she said in a low voice. "The Great Ones are kind. But do you remember no word of your own tongue, my son?"

"I speak only Shoni and the hand-talk," answered Kioga. "I have dwelt long among the forest people."

"*Ai-ho*," she said heavily. "Yes, you have been gone long. But no matter. You are returned." Again her horny hand smoothed back his hair. "Returned a mighty warrior—you who were such a fearful child! But tell us"—including with a sweep of the arm the chiefs and warriors nearby—"what of Twenty Man, who owned the gray stallion?"

Held by those penetrating eyes, it seemed to Kioga that nothing could long deceive the keen brain behind them. And so, though he had lent himself to deception in this matter of identity, he spoke the truth of Twenty Man.

"I killed him, Mother, who would have killed me first."

"Ah!" Quick and sharp her exclamation came, as she looked about her and said something in Wa-Kanek; whereat the men nodded, eyeing the newcomer with intent interest.

"Do you know who Twenty Man was?" she then asked with the hands. "But no—you would not remember. He was the greatest warrior in all our tenscore bands. You will gain fame of this, and hatred too, for his family is strong among our people."

"He died with honor—I will swear that by the knife."

"May his spirit rest!" signed the old beldame. Then, to the others: "Give him food and drink. Clean his wounds and let him rest. You, Me-kon-agi, instruct him in our tongue. What he has forgotten will soon return. Now, go." Looking straight before her, with folded arms, the old woman took their instant obedience with the air of one long accustomed to it;

211

and again Kioga marveled at her control over these fierce-eyed warriors.

Spurning their aid, he stood erect unaided, looked long into the mystery of those sharp black eyes of hers, then turned without another sign and allowed them to lead him whither they would.

As he went the old woman was chanting softly in a hoarse voice what later he learned was the Song of Thanksgiving.

XXIII

In the village of Hopeka among the Shoni people, Beth La Salle and the others now shared the lodge of Menewa, father of the Indian maid Heladi. The whites were not long learning the Shoni tongue, and many a tale was poured into their ears about the Snow Hawk. Some were fact, some hearsay, some purest fiction; but all arose out of the strange mystery surrounding his early life.

Beth heard from the lips of half-grown children tales of many a rescue from the jaws of wild beasts in the days of Kioga's outlawry; of food mysteriously thrown to the starving in midwinter; of succor to those wounded, benighted, or lost in the tangles of the farthest wildernesses. Men spoke that name with awe and respect, women with a sign of regret that he was gone.

This was the man Beth had thought a savage creature of passion and might alone—to whose gift of everything she had made no return! For a time she was near prostrate with grief.

But the bravery of Heladi braced her spirit; the tragedy of Kioga's passing had drawn Beth and Heladi together in bonds known sometimes to those who have shared a mutual sorrow and danger. Along with Tokala the Fox, they now occupied one lodge-section in Menewa's great dwelling.

Flashpan was installed in another part with his chest of trade articles—and his monkey. He conducted a brisk business in trinkets and was amassing a considerable store of animal peltry, the first white trader to pursue this calling among the red men of far Nato'wa. Flashpan was looked on with some awe, partly because of his association with Placer the monk, and partly because he did things which were, to the Indians, inexplicable.

Each day, rain or shine, he went forth in a canoe with whatever Indians he could persuade to go along, and explored all the shallow creeks nearby. He carried a little pan; and at various places along the streams he would step knee-deep into the water, scoop up a panful of sand and slosh it gently around. Occasionally he would extract a few yellow grains from among the sands, and examine them closely, muttering the while; until at last, in a certain stream, his panning showed quantities of gold.

Beasts of the forest and the forces of the elements meant nothing to Flashpan now. He was one in spirit with Croesus of Smyrna, Darius of Persia, and the naked black slaves who worked Egypt's sweltering gold-mine tunnels under the whips of the Pharaohs. . . .

The hand of one of his Indian friends fell upon his shoulder.

"Guna!" whispered the other, and in broken English, pointing downstream alongshore: "Man-eater. Hungry. He come fast!"

"Shet up, blast ye!" answered Flashpan testily. "Shoo 'im away, Redskin. I hev found a gold crick, an' I aim to find the mother-lode, spite o' tigers and devils and hell's-fire! I—"

But the Indians waited to hear no more. As the black-barred tiger came into view on one shore, they retreated to another, shouting to Flashpan to follow.

The tiger crouched quivering among the reeds. Not to be dissuaded from his pursuit, Flashpan suddenly paused, gazing intently into the waters at his feet. At that precise instant the tiger's tail snapped erect; simultaneously Flashpan dropped to his knees in the stream. And the long heavy body of the springing cat soared over him, impaling itself upon the dozen spears in the hands of the Indians.

Utterly oblivious, Flashpan knelt there in a glittering riffle, white-faced and with bulging eyes, sifting through his hands a continuous stream of wet sand thickly powdered with pure gold. He scarcely heard the shouts of the Indians nor the roars of the tiger.

For he, who "liked the lookin', not the findin', sir," had at last struck treasure!

"Lordy! Oh, Lordy. . . . I've struck it rich—rich! An' this is only dust. Somewheres up that crick is the mother-lode, the pocket it comes out of!"

And thus, muttering already of the riches around the next bend, Flashpan filled his pockets until they would hold no more, and dazedly waved his Indians back to Hopeka.

Among the Indians friendly to the whites were Brave Elk, loyal to Kioga until that final moment on the stake; Walks-Laughing, simple-minded medicine man; old Menewa himself, and the warriors he controlled; in addition to the allies of Kias, lifelong friend of the Snow Hawk. To the trusted members of this little group the secret of the *Narwhal*'s hiding-place had been revealed. Messages were exchanged between James Munro and his men aboard the ship, apprising them of circumstances in the village. . . .

Munro himself, along with Dan Kias, and a handful of others, now absented themselves in the northern wilderness on a canoe-voyage of exploration. The journey ended in a council among the headwaters of the Hiwasi. Curious as to what lay in the great mountains beyond, Munro prevailed upon the Indians to accompany him in a further search. The expedition came to an end far up a mountainside. Close to exhaustion, and handicapped by the rarefied air, the little band paused.

While they rested at this highest camp, Kias shot down with an arrow a large hawk, which fell into their midst, pierced through by the lucky shaft. The Indian brought it before Munro, calling his attention to its beak: Upon the horny upper mandible were a series of Indian heads, graved into the surface with exquisite skill, in the manner of intaglio work, and supplemented by minute characters which baffled interpretation. And about the dead hawk's leg was a small band of beaten copper, also engraved.

"Man's handicraft," said Munro in answer to Dan's query. "But who they are—shall we know? We've come as high as we can go."

On returning to Hopeka, Munro set about to locate a certain ivory tusk, reputed to be in the possession of a northern tribe, and mentioned conspicuously in Lincoln Rand's old logbook. Long search brought it to light among the Tugari, who dwell among the headwaters of the Hiwasi; and after some bargaining, Munro traded for it ten packets of steel needles, six hatchets, and a dozen small hand-mirrors, and bore it home to Hopeka for study.

Two weeks later a hunting trip on the coast, far north of where the *Narwhal* lay concealed, brought him yet another scientific find, more valuable by far than the quantities of walrus meat which the hunt provided. Among the kills was one old bull, the largest of the lot, with enormous tusks. But their great length thrilled the scientist less than the remarkable carvings, worn but still discernible from roots to points.

The technique of these carvings was startlingly like those on the elephant tusk; and some of the mnemonic signs resembled those upon the beak of the hawk. To find creatures thus adorned while still living, by unknown artisans, gave rise to liveliest speculations in Munro's mind. Laborious efforts at translation indicated some strange, unknown Indian culture, with an economy as closely dependent upon some living form of the elephant, as was that of the American red man upon the buffalo. What a strange race they must be, whose glory is borne into the high heavens on the wings of a hawk, and carried even to the depths of the sea on the tusks of a walrus!

But Munro's eagerness to delve further into the mystery of that lost race was halted by developments at Hopeka.

Day by day, the machinations of that red Machiavelli, Half-mouth, were adding fuel to the fires of unrest among the Shoni tribes. A second and more vicious skirmish was fought between the two factions almost within sight of Hopeka; and the corpses floated past in view of the uneasy inhabitants. The village was become an armed camp, with neighbors arming against one another.

It was bad enough to have become detested by those medicine men from whose superstitious mumbo-jumbo Munro had delivered the snake-bitten child of old Seskawa. But the scientist now incurred the active enmity of Half-mouth as well.

Half-mouth's fame rested upon foundations of fear, and his skill as a magician. In this art he was without peer among all the Shoni. To the observant scientist, the workings of his craft were clear and simple, yet a source of admiration, for Shingas was indeed a past master in the deceptive arts.

Munro would have done nothing to betray a fellow magician had not Shinga himself provoked him. But one night when the Indian had performed several feats of magic for the gathered tribesmen, he ended his exhibition with a feat which invariably evoked gasps of astonishment from his audiences; and thereafter trouble came fast.

To the uninitiated, it was indeed a farsome sight: With a sharp knife Shingas allowed a confederate to slash him across the bared abdomen, whereafter he seemed to bleed profusely—from a gaping wound.

To the great Half-mouth this was apparently a mere

scratch, for with a gesture he drew about him his robe, performed another trick, turned his robe over to his confederate and—behold!—Shingas stood before them unscratched!

Turning then to Munro, Shingas spoke for the benefit of all those about him. "The paleskin is all-powerful, it is said. Let him do this thing, or confess the weakness of his magic."

Laughing tolerantly, Munro would have allowed the shaman to pass his spectacular trick off as true magic. But the Indians had long desired to see the works of him who had raised a child from the dead, and they now clamored for a public demonstration of the occult.

Challenged thus, Munro must perform or else suffer loss of the prestige which his previous acts had gained him. Accordingly he began a demonstration which lasted for an hour. Simple devices came first; gradually he progressed to more difficult illusions, until at last he held the entire assemblage spellbound at the wonders wrought by his skilled fingers and hands. Munro then suddenly flashed back to the shaman's own feat, addressing the Indians thus:

"You saw Shingas cut himself open and cure himself in the time it took to remove his blanket. That is great magic. But mine is greater still, for I will make the blanket tell you how the deed was done." And before the shaman could forestall him, Munro seized and flung the blanket open, holding one end.

A great slab of animal fat, deeply slashed, flopped to the ground, followed by a pierced skin bladder, still oozing the red berry-juices with which the shaman had simulated blood. The people gasped with astonishment. Then someone laughed, and in another moment gales of merriment swept the villagers.

In that moment was born Half-mouth's undying hatred of the white man who thus exposed him to one of the strongest forces in red men's society, the light of public scorn. And he began to plot secretly to destroy Munro and his associates.

That night there came to the lodge of the pale skins the gift of a side of venison and a basket of small fruits. Accompanying the gift were the compliments of Half-mouth himself. Evidently the animus of the recent past was to be considered forgotten.

Munro set the meat to roast and invited the generous donor to be present at the Feast. But Shingas lay in apparent pain resulting from overindulgence at the previous night's feast. . . .

Passing out some of the fruit from Half-mouth's basket,

Munro found the eager monkey at his elbow, and gave him a liberal helping. Before he could turn away, Placer bit into a wild plum—then suddenly screeched, while an extraordinary expression overspread his simian features.

Ejecting his first bite with force, the monkey thereupon flung the remainder of his fruit piecemeal in every direction. And when Flashpan would have eaten, he protested with such excitement that the little man desisted, to humor his pet.

Two of the Shoni, however, swallowed their fruit before Munro sprang up abruptly to his feet, fear clutching at his heart, and struck the remaining fruit from the hands of Beth and Heladi and Tokala.

"Don't touch it!" he ordered sharply. "I believe that devil put something deadly in it."

Scarcely had the words left his lips when the two Indians fell to the ground doubled up in agony. And not all Munro's knowledge aided them one iota, for the poison was one for which he did not know an antidote. Before the horrified eyes of the party, the Indians expired.

Dark-faced and terrible, Kias turned vengefully toward Shingas's lodge, but Munro's hand on his wrist held him back. "Wait, Kias! We have others than ourselves to think of."

For a moment he thought Kias would fling off his hand. Then conquering his all-powerful hatred, Kias agreed, and said with an expression impossible to convey: "I will wait. But when it comes time for him to die—leave him to these hands. One of these who now lies dead is my clan-brother."

All night Shingas waited patiently in his lodge for the white men to finish what he had intended to be their last feast. But not a mouthful more of his donation was eaten save by a flock of crows, found dead beside the venison on the following day. And while Shingas waited, the prey—far from being dead—was making plans to quit the village.

Munro had assembled his friends and allies about him in Menewa's lodge and stated their position in this way:

"We are only a handful compared to the numbers of the enemy. We can't take sides without exposing ourselves to treachery from either side. It's time we chose a middle road and made plans to safeguard ourselves."

Old Menewa answered to that. "Swift-Hand, we look to you for counsel. Since the Snow Hawk has gone away, the Long Knives increase in numbers and boldness. We older chiefs are powerless. If you wish to escape to your great canoe-with-wings, we will give what help we can. But what then will we do, our numbers lessened by your departure?"

Before replying, Munro considered several facts: The damage to his ship would not yet have been repaired sufficiently to permit an immediate sailing. In a few months winter would be here again, discouraging departure until the following spring. His first responsibility was the safety of his white friends; but the Indian people who had come to trust in him could not be forsaken in their present position.

"We are not ready to desert our good friends," he answered at last. "There is another way, I think. A league up the Hiwasi there is an island called by you the Isle Where Ravens Talk, which splits the river. If we could secretly fortify and occupy that island, we could laugh at danger. Those who wished could join us there in safety."

This, after further discussion, was the plan decided upon.

Accompanied by the ship's carpenter, Hansen, Dan, Kias and several of his braves, Munro went forth the next day ostensibly on one of his ordinary journeys—to the astonishment of no one but Shingas, who learned with amazement mixed with fear that the whites had survived his poisons.

Landing upon the Isle Where Ravens Talk, they quickly scaled its heights and surveyed the terrain for its possibilities of defense. A spot was chosen a little back from a lofty cliff where some ancient slide had deposited rubble. With the materials at hand, a beginning was made upon a wall.

Water from a tumbling spring nearby was diverted by means of a hollowed half-log, and a kind of mortar mixed of clay and stones wherewith to bind the double wall into a homogeneous whole, and the space between was further strengthened with branches and vines to retain the mortar. When Munro departed, leaving further construction to Hansen, the work of fort-building was well advanced. Thereafter each day a few Indians were directed thither with arms and as much food as they could carry without arousing suspicion.

So little by little the fort-to-be was provisioned; at the end of a week, though by no means completed, it was in a condition suitable for occupancy whenever the hour of need should arise.

But Munro meanwhile was far from idle. Digging along the riverbank in a stratum of red earth he had noticed, he uncovered at last a streak of rust-colored sand which indicated a considerable iron content. And of this many back loads were transported aloft to the fort.

He confided his plans to Flashpan, and the miner turned his cunning fingers and clasp-knife to certain mysterious tasks; he also gathered up a supply of wild turkey leg-bones, which he split and laminated together with glue and bits of wire. One by one he carved pieces of wood into peculiar shapes.

From the walls of certain caves, which Munro located after a long search, he then scraped quantities of a whitish salt-like substance; and from an old inactive volcanic crater upriver he removed baskets of encrusted stuff with a sulfurous smell. All these objects and ingredients found their way ultimately into the building fort.

And the whites were not a day too advanced in the execution of their plans. Each day told a grimmer tale than the preceding one. Indians went out of Hopeka in their canoes, never to return. Frightful tales of massacre and internecine warfare were brought in by those who made the river passages in safety under force of arms.

The rivers were full of painted specters, their movements sudden and mysterious, who waylaid travelers and killed stragglers. Savage men roamed about like lynxes and wolves, ravaging everywhere. Being always in motion, they were gone when pursuit arrived. Thus the blind warfare of the forest continued without cessation.

Those terrible indicators of violent killing, the scalp-racks, daily sagged lower under the weight of drying trophies. The wilderness uprising, born of discontent in a few savage breasts, was now well under way. The union of the Seven Tribes, accomplished at such great labor by the Snow Hawk, was crumbling back into the old bloody enmities. Where peace had endured a while, red barbarity was returning, the more terrible since no man knew the secret affiliations of his brother.

One night a spy in the employ of Kias came to Munro with warning that all the whites had been singled out for slaughter an hour before dawn. At this point in the Indian uprisings, Munro, aided by Kias, quietly managed the transfer of his entire party from the palisaded village to the little fort on the island. Twenty-odd of Kias's men covered their silent retreat from the side gate of Hopeka, and, in a slashing downpour of rain, followed. Numbers of other villagers came later, fearing to remain in Hopeka.

An hour behind them, the raging Half-mouth pursued swiftly; but the fury of the elements aided the whites and their party. To the accompaniment of mighty crashes of thunder and blazing flashes of lightning, the fort was occupied.

XXIV

Now it came about that, returning through the gathering storm from the vain pursuit of Munro and his party, Half-mouth and his warriors fell in with another band of canoe-men occupying a cove in which they were seeking shelter. As the parties approached one another hostilely, Shingas observed that there were white men in the other canoes. Thus he first encountered Mad Crow, the renegade white, in company with the mutineers from the *Narwhal*.

The sign of peace was made between the nearing canoes, and in a little while the parties were holding a council under the concealing overhang at the cove's edge. Half-mouth discovered new and strange allies in the persons of these white rascals. An astute savage, nothing could have pleased him more than to set one group of the hated whiteskins against another. And presently he saw a way to accomplish this.

Betraying the facts of Munro's departure from the village of Hopeka, he watched the faces of Slemp and his cohorts, seeing only mild interest. But at talk of rich skins to be obtained, the white men pricked up their ears. And when Shingas produced a skin pouch containing a little gold Flashpan had forgotten to carry to the fort, the gleam of cupidity came into his hearers' eyes.

Quick to play upon this cupidity, Shingas reasoned that so long as he could hold forth hope of more gold, these men would be his eager slaves. And so, to their queries as to quantity, he said:

"The whiteskin had twenty times as much as this, hidden away. Destroy him and his friends, and I will lead you to its hiding-place."

"Done, ye red rascal!" ejaculated Slemp exultantly. "We'll be rich, my lads—rich as kings!"

"An' what good'll it do us here?" answered Branner pessimistically.

"We'll not tarry long," swore the other. "Just let us get our paws on Flashpan's dust, an' the rest is easy."

"What about the ship? Who's to tell us where she lies?" demanded the doubter.

"There's ways o' makin' deaf-mutes talk," cut in Mad Crow, the renegade, with a meaning grin. "Leave them details to men as ain't afraid to use 'em." And turning again to Shingas, he engaged the shaman in a long harrangue in Shoni dialect. The result of the talk was that Shingas agreed to lead the white men to Munro's hiding-place—which still remained to be found—and aid in their destruction.

Little could they foresee, however, the preparations at the island fort, where Munro and his men were hewing timbers and squaring them with the adz. These they laid horizontally, overlapping at the ends, strengthened by crosspieces and stayed with iron spikes.

On the inner side of the double wall more mud mortar was poured, while on the outer side great squared stones were cemented into place. Towers, five in all, were next erected, access up into which was by wooden ladders. Appropriate loopholes were provided, so arranged as to expose every approach to the fort's front to both cross- and lunging fire. And two embrasures were left, as for cannon.

Within, close against the walls, were sleeping and living quarters of wood and stone, upon the connecting roofs of which sentries might patrol while their relief slept below, available at call. These rooms took up three inner sides of the fort, and joined one another by heavy doors, boltable from either side. At the rear of the enclosure was a large roofed-over space. This roof could be lifted or lowered by means of ropes.

Within these strong walls a small army might be housed free from possible attack from any quarter save the cliffs across the river one hundred yards away. Loopholes were constructed on that side, and log head-covers as well. Munro was convinced that in the event of hostilities, the marksmanship of the Indians would be sufficiently balked by these precautions.

The fort within was now a veritable beehive of activity. Tokala the Fox watched with excited eyes these preparations for hostilities. At one point Hansen had set up a crude lathe, operated by foot-power transmitted to a cord which rotated a heavy stone. After each pressure the cord was drawn up by a supple branch cemented into the vertical wall.

Carrying out Munro's instructions, the women worked on deer-skins, sewing them into the shape of large fool's-caps, to which were attached pipelike appendages of hollowed reeds.

The scientist himself, aided by young La Salle, worked well apart from the others in a room off the main enclosure. Beth cast many an anxious glance their way. Even Tokala was forbidden entrance to that room, which presented a strange appearance—like some alchemist's den of ancient times. And indeed a strange chemistry was proceeding within it.

Great clay vessels of simmering liquid stood above a charcoal fire. Into these the men threw measured quantities of the pale saltlike stuff Munro had collected from the cave walls. As this dissolved, cool water was added to promote the rise of a scum, which was skimmed off. The operation was repeated until the solution was clear and bright. They then filtered it, setting aside the deposited crystals to dry, ere beating them gently into a powder. These, among other operations, refined their crude saltpeter.

Crude sulfur had been heated in condensing apparatus brought from the *Narwhal*'s engine room. The vapors, led through pipes, chilled and condensed, finally, into a clear yellow liquid which was drawn off and cooled.

Instructing Dan in further methods of filtering, cooling, and stirring, Munro left the cubicle to tend his stone furnace. The pipes of the deer-skin bellows he directed into its lower part, which was filled with charcoal. Into the upper part, in a crucible designed to tilt, he placed quantities of the washed iron-sand. Closing the furnace, he then ignited the charcoal and called for Tokala. The boy came running, eager to serve in these exciting preparations.

Munro showed him how the hands must be held upon the deer-skin cones, kneading the air within them forward, to direct a steady blow upon the charcoal. Alternating with others, Tokala never ceased his operations for a moment. The smelter was faithfully tended.

Now Munro made molds in a bed of sand. Some were flat and open for casting ingots. Beside these, with a tireless patience that surmounted all discouragements, Munro next built hollow molds of several sizes, with cores of baked clay.

When at last the iron was molten and skimmed free of slag, the crucible was brought out, and the hot metal run into the molds. The flat pigs resulting were used as anvils whereon to beat out other necessary tools. Of the successful hollow castings, Munro handed six, long and pipelike, over to Flashpan. After scraping out the central cores of hard clay, the miner squinted through them critically and carried them away.

Another of the successful castings was in the form of a small gun of the falconet type, some four feet long, with a two-inch bore. With infinite labor this was pierced for a touch-hole at the breech, and mounted behind the wall-embrasure, with its muzzle pointing downstream.

So under the amazed eyes of the Indians the strange work went forward, amid showers of hot sparks, the crackle and hiss of pouring metal, and the acrid chemical smells issuing from the little blast furnace. But they were beginning to understand something of its meaning at last. For never had they owned such tomahawks as those made of this new iron, nor knives so hard and keen as those forged out of the fresh ingots.

But of the operations in the cubicle they were to remain ignorant a little longer. Within it Munro and Dan worked continually now, pulverizing the saltpeter and sulfur and fresh charcoal. This done, the ingredients were mixed—according to the classical formula, seventy-nine parts saltpeter, three parts sulfur, eighteen parts charcoal. The mixture was spread out, moistened, and allowed to cake dry. Some was powdered fine, for use in small arms. The remainder was carefully broken down with wooden mallets and sifted into sizes through barken mesh of various widths.

A little of the fine gunpowder was then sent to Flashpan, who sat polishing his first experimental muzzle-loader.

This was a strange but ingenious weapon: The barrel, a cast-iron tube, was mounted on the carved wooden stock with copper bands. The trigger, of bone, actuated a spring made of thin layers of turkey leg-bone. This, in turn, snapped down the hammer, whose jaw bore a piece of flint.

Because the working parts were naturally fragile, Flashpan had contrived a movable plate of bone which gave easy access to spring and trigger mechanism. Now for the first time, with gleaming eyes, he took of the powder sent by Munro, poured a charge down the barrel, tamped in a cloth patch, and dropped upon the patch a close-fitting leaden pellet. Ramming charge and missile carefully home, he rose and carried his weapon out among the Indians in the fort.

Taking a small stone, he poised it upon the new-built wall and moved back fifty paces to the inner wall, the savages watching absorbedly the while. Raising his smooth-bore,

Flashpan sighted along the slender barrel, held upon the stone, and pressed the trigger. There was a flash of sparks and a quick report. The small round stone took flight, whizzed across the cañon, and shattered against the cliff beyond. And Flashpan smiled a superior smile.

Compared to the rifles they had lost to the mutineers, his creation was a fragile and uncertain thing. It needed a loading-rod, a ramrod, powder-horn and cloth patches below the bullets. It demanded time for reloading after each shot, wasted much powder, and would be hard to clean. And yet it shot straight, and hit far on a light charge of powder. Its recoil was light, its report flat; there were no cartridges to stick in the breech. Indeed, it had no breech, and therefore no likelihood of a treacherous burst. Its trigger-pull was clean and crisp; its peep-sights of bone reasonably accurate. Above all, it was light in the hand; and to Flashpan, at least, a thing of pride, with its polished stock and gleaming bone and copper fittings; while to the savages it was a thing of great magic, provocative of awe as well as curiosity.

But the high treble of Tokala now directed attention to a canoe-load of Indian warriors on the Hiwasi, far downstream. Foremost in the craft sat Half-mouth, seeking trace of Munro's party which had eluded him in the storm in retreating to the fort.

With a shout of triumph Flashpan handed his smooth-bore to Dan, and leaped to the falconet pointing through the embrasure.

"They's pizen *an'* pizen," he muttered, measuring out five double handfuls of coarse powder and ramming it lightly back into the breech. "See how friend Shingas likes *our* brand!"

Against the powder he pressed a circle of tree-bark cut to size; finally a solid round-shot of three pounds, weight was pushed in against the crude patch. While the Indians crowded about, watching in complete fascination, Flashpan aimed this larger gun, primed the touch-hole with loose powder, and applied a light to it.

There was a fizz, a spurt of flame, and with a jarring blast the falconet belched out its missile. The frightened Indians fell back in dismay; but rallied by Dan's encouraging words, turned their eyes downstream.

A long moment elapsed. The Indians in the distant canoe were seen to cease paddling at the strange sound of the approaching shot. Suddenly the canoe rose in air, lifted by the mighty splash of the round-shot. Then it overturned, hurling its occupants sprawling into the stream, to swim ashore and vanish yelling into the forest, while the echoes rolled back from the cliffs near and far. The first cannon had been fired in Nato'wa. Flashpan's face dropped in dejection.

"A *leetle* short," he muttered disappointedly, "but I 'low 'twas a fair beginnin', an' better luck the next time."

Munro and Dan laughed. But in the village of Hopeka, to which the frightened warriors repaired, it was believed that lightning had struck the canoe out of a clear sky; and the medicine men were hard-pressed for some interpretation of this strange happening....

Ponderous and crude though their early guns were, those that followed improved over the first few. Flashpan even sought to rifle his barrels, and in some measure succeeded, gaining greater accuracy and striking power. But time was of the essence. They required many guns for defense, which at this stage meant firing down into the faces of possible foes at point-blank range. Therefore accuracy was in some measure sacrificed to speed of manufacture, that all might be better armed. And in the inner enclosure Flashpan drilled Kias and several of the Indians in the handling of their new firearms.

Thereafter the little miner cut down the long castings into pistol-size, and with Dan's aid fashioned several handguns on the same principle as his first rifle. Two of his flintlock guns were dispatched to the *Narwhal* by Indian runner, along with a quantity of powder, iron ball, and a letter explaining their present situation. These all reached the *Narwhal* safely; and Munro received a reply from Barry Edwards, stating that all was well on board, repairs proceeding briskly, and no sign as yet that the ship's whereabouts was known to their enemies. In return for the guns, he sent back a package of fine Ceylon tea and some tobacco. Welcome as both were to the white men in the fort, the reassuring news was best of all.

Leaning back for a moment's rest Munro looked about his fort and faced the future with greater confidence.

XXV

The Snow Hawk was given to eat of dried buffalo tongue and a meat dish called by Me-kon-agi, *pumakin*. While eating, Kioga glanced about, observing where the prisoners were kept under guard.

"What will become of them?" he signed.

"They fought a valiant fight. Torture, perhaps. A pity, though. Our tribes have need of warriors. But Magpie is sometimes cruel."

"Magpie?" queried Kioga. Me-kon-agi glanced up quickly, to rectify a statement which he thought the stranger might resent.

"Magpie, your mother, greatest of our chiefs," he signed. Thus, for the first time, Kioga learned the power of the old matron-chief.

Later he contrived to pass the prisoners again, and counted heads. Old Crow Man was there, Grass Girl with her two babes, Kills Bull, Scalps Three, and Pretty Eagle, now the pregnant wife of Kills Bull—all, excepting Tokala, who now remained of the band which had left civilization behind to realize the promise of the old Indian life.

In passing, he dropped near one of them a bit of leather with the encouraging "brave-heart" sign drawn in charcoal. He observed with approval that they concealed all interest in him.

Turning then to Me-kon-agi, "Teach me to speak the Wa-Kanek tongue," he bade; and thus by first translating simple hand-signs, he began to learn the language of the plainsmen. . . .

Among the Magpie's braves, Kioga already stood in high repute. And now to those he had wounded, Kioga made prompt amends before the entire camp. Pausing before High Bear, he splintered the club on a great stone, making these signs:

"Unworthy weapon to have struck down one so brave as High Bear."

Then to the other, proffering a tomahawk: "Yellow Hand's arm is broken. Wash out the offense. Strike off this offending hand."

The savage looked up suspiciously for any sign of mockery. The face above showed only grave regret. Accepting the tomahawk, he raised it high. Expressions of protest showed on the faces of others nearby, but none spoke; for by Wa-Kanek custom, the injured party may claim redress. Impassively Kioga placed his hand upon the ground. Down came the tomahawk—but not upon the Snow Hawk's hand. In twenty bits the weapon flew, shivered on the heavy stone. Yellow Hand spoke a few words to Me-kon-agi, who grunted in approval and translated in sign for Kioga and all the observers thus:

"My hands speak for Yellow Hand. When this tomahawk joins together of itself, he will ask redress."

A great shout arose, for next to a deed of heroic daring the Wa-Kanek horsemen love nothing so much as the generous gesture by an injured party.

That night the camp again was on the move. Two scouts rode on ahead. In the forefront of the main band old Magpie bestrode a befeathered mare. Thus mounted, she was a different person. Gone was the halting hesitating walk and bent carriage; in its place the graceful poise of one born beside a horse-travois, and schooled from childhood in equestrian skill.

Beside her, and a little back, rode the honor men. On her right side rode Gro-Gan', a famous shaman; of whom it was said that he snored louder than any ten other men in all the nation. On her left, in place of equal honor, rode Kioga on the tall gray stallion, now his to do with as he would. Then came the mounted prisoners under watchful guard, and finally the riders on the flanks and rear—High Bear, Yellow Hand with his broken arm in a sling, Six Coup and Chases Them. And in all that band, who a few days earlier would have cut his throat, not one man could Kioga now call enemy.

Near evening the forerunners drew in to report contact with Magpie's own home scouts. Just before sunset, topping another rise, the tents of a great village came suddenly into view—a sight to stir the blood of any man.

Six and fifty cow-skin lodges crouching in a mighty circle on the plain, with sunset's gold encarnadined; from each great cone a bluish plume of smoke uprising to spread a haze above the scene; before each tent a tripod, hung with medicine-bundle and shield, catching the last lights of the setting sun; in the open spaces flat bison-hides pegged out to stretch and dry; meat-racks groaning under strips of curing buffalo; before the lodges splendid horses, caparisoned and gaily decked with colored feathers. To one side along a winding stream, the main herd cropping grass and drinking from the river.

Feeding their eyes upon a scene each loved, the homing band stood etched against the sunset. And now from below, horsemen galloped to meet them.

Between the tents naked children ran about among the squaws. Warriors and old people swarmed forth to greet the well-loved Magpie and to learn of Black Shield's return— Black Shield, her youngest son, long captive to the Shoni. Of this great thing the village talk buzzed mightily. Men and women crowded near Kioga, to look upon his face, marveling that his eyes were not dark like theirs, but glowing blue-green in the firelight.

For this publicity Kioga paid the price of constant supervision. He could not again communicate with the prisoners, who were led to an inner lodge, still guarded against the hazard of seizure by the eager villagers.

Soon to Kioga came a message from the Magpie's painted tent. As all had been told to do in Kioga's presence, the messenger addressed Me-kon-agi in sign-talk. "The Magpie speaks. The camp moves tomorrow. Come now to her tepee to hear her words."

The tent-flap was open. Entering, the two men waited upon her.

"Sit," said Magpie, without looking up.

Observing her, Kioga glimpsed signs of an inner uneasiness. At her left squatted the imposing figure of Gro-Gan', who watched the Snow Hawk fixedly. For several minutes the old woman did not speak. Then holding in her lap the knife Kioga had carried into camp:

"By this knife, I knew you for my son," she signed slowly. "But one wise in many things"—indicating the medicine man at her side—"would question you, that there may be no error. Answer with straight tongue, for he reads minds and hearts."

The shaman then addressed Kioga, not unkindly:

"At morning the sun rises red. By day it grows yellow and sets red. Spring grass is pale, then green then brown. A fox or an owl changes color with the season. These things are as the Great One made them. But"—and here the shaman's watchful eyes stabbed Kioga's—"when first Black Shield was carried away by the forest people, his eyes were brown. Now they are pale as new leaves. We have talked of this among us. How may it be explained?"

Magpie glanced up and as quickly down again, but Kioga saw fear in those deep-sunk eyes. Unless some acceptable explanation were forthcoming, quick violence might end his life. Slowly he answered:

"I would wait until all the great men are assembled and speak of this strange thing before them."

The shaman grunted, but found no fault with this, for he loved a good assembly. That night, before a great council, he put his question once again. Considering the character and office of Gro-Gan' more than the plausibility of his explanation, Kioga now answered in hand-talk:

"Oh respected wise ones, to whom all things mysterious are clear: Once, when still a boy, I fasted from food and drink for three days. I climbed upon a mountain to seek my *Manito*, who would remedy my poor vision. I had a dream. A white hawk came and spoke to me in the language of men.

" 'Give me your eyes,' he said, 'and I will fly with them to where Those Above dwell, beyond the sky, that they may make them whole.'

"So saying, he plucked out both my eyes and carried them away. In the morning he returned while I slept. When I woke, behold, as I leaned above a pool to drink, I saw my eyes were blue. 'How, then, Spirit Hawk?' I said. 'You have brought back the wrong eyes, for mine were brown.'

" 'True,' he answered; 'but henceforward these are yours. The Great Ones were angry that the eyes of mortal man had looked upon their mysteries. So they gave me a different pair and kept the others. Are not they keener than your own?'

"And when I looked, indeed this was true. My sight was cured.

" 'But how will my people know me?' I asked. And Spirit Hawk spoke thus: 'Fear not. Someday you will meet one who will recognize you and explain this mystery. He who does so will be the wisest of all living men.' Then thunder roared and lightning flashed. Spirit Hawk flew into the sky, and I saw him no more."

During this recital there was silence in the crowded medicine-tent. "Since then," concluded Kioga, "I have sought in vain for one who could explain this mystery. And now again, oh shamans, do I hope. What is the answer to this miracle?"

Amazed, but no whit doubting this curious tale—for anything may happen in a fevered dream induced by hunger and thirst—all those in the lodge turned to the rows of silent medicine men. One after another shook his head. When none remained but Gro-Gan', all eyes fell upon that far-famed mystic. Like silent children, they waited for his interpretation of the medicine-dream.

Uneasily Gro-Gan' looked around him in this illustrious company. Swiftly he cast about for some good answer. He sensed the growing popularity of the Magpie's protégé, and felt the people's hope for a reply favorable to Kioga.

Tensely watching the workings of that crafty mind to see if his subtly sown seed would flower into rose or poison-weed, Kioga caught a sidelong glance from Magpie. It startled him by its mixture of admiration and understanding. Here was one, he feared, who was not hoodwinked by his strange tale.

A restless stir among the assemblage. Utter silence followed as Gro-Gan' stood up to make his revelations.

"This is the answer to the mystery," he said solemnly. "Spirit Hawk was a messenger from the Great Ones. The taking away of the eyes was a sign of their anger with all our wars. The return of the sight was a sign of favor, a good omen for our people." A deep-toned murmur ran through the council circle. "The Wa-Kanek will thrive from this day forward." Throwing wide his arms, powering his speech with fervent oratory, Gro-Gan' concluded: "Our bands will be reunited, the feuds of clan and family wiped out. Good hunting will be the rule. Many buffalo will fall. Our men will steal many horses. Our women will bear many children. The Wa-Kanek nation will increase, and our foes will stand in awe of us. I am Gro-Gan'. I have spoken!"

That night Magpie again summoned Kioga to sit in upon a meeting which was to decide the fate of the prisoners. One chief favored outright slaughter. Another argued that to separate them among the various bands were preferable. A third wished them put to torture as a test of mettle, and if they survived with honor, adoption into the tribe. Kioga offered no speech until Magpie turned to him with a question.

"What thinks Black Shield in this matter?"

The chiefs heard in wonder this unprecedented asking of a young man's counsel. Noting their feeling, "Wiser heads than mine should decide this, Mother," said Kioga. "But have I leave to speak my mind, oh councillors?"

Mollified by this deferential speech, and eager as always to please the old woman, two of the chiefs gestured assent. But not until each had nodded agreement did Kioga respond.

"Are not these able-bodied men?" he asked. "Did they not fight well before capture? Do they not conduct themselves as brave prisoners, ignoring the gibes of our people? Are not their women well-formed and fertile—one with two future warriors at the breast, another quick with child?" He glanced about the council and won a general chorus of guttural approval. "What shall we gain, then, by slaughter? Feed them, rest them, take them on the hunt or to war. Thus you make them useful to you. Dead, they are no good to you. That is my mind. But it is for older heads to decide their fate."

After further talk, all but one agreed. In concession to the single dissenter, it was required of the captives that they submit to ordeal, the women alone excepted. Before the entire village a shaman pierced each captive through the flesh of the breast with bone skewers, drawing through the wounds a length of lariat rope, thus joining them all together. Then to the beat of the medicine-drums they were required to dance themselves free. Having done, so they were stripped and whipped with leather quirts to the river. The rite ended in purification ceremonies. That night, with song and ceremony the members of the migrant band came to the end of their long trek from one continent to another. Their goal was attained; their heritage of a wild free life renewed.

XXVI

Accepted thus among the Wa-Kanek, Kioga spent a day or two in company with Me-kon-agi. In language he progressed rapidly. But more than that, he learned that by the custom of the Wa-Kanek a man was a nobody until he had performed the several grand exploits which are required of all who would speak in council.

Of these the first was setting forth unarmed to capture horses from the enemy. By the reasoning of the tribesmen, to run off an enemy's horses is not on a level with common theft, but rather is in the nature of knightly enterprise.

That night, saying nothing to any man, but slipping out alone and unnoticed after the Indian manner, Kioga found the gray stallion among the other mounts, roped him and mounted.

Riding the tireless animal at a swift pace westward, an hour before dawn of the second day Kioga first glimpsed the glowing tents of a village, perhaps a mile away. The silence of midnight lay upon the plain. Somewhere a wolf's howl rose quavering. But the village was asleep.

Downwind came the scent of grazing horses moving about in the inky blackness. Hobbling his own horse, Kioga stole toward the village on foot. Within calling distance he flattened against the grassy plain, with head alone upraised, seeking amid the prevailing scent of horses, the scent of him who doubtless guarded them.

Presently he could discern the form of an Indian sentry lying upon his back amid the herd, counting the stars of heaven and chanting a hunting-song. Ever closer crept Kioga, silent as the very genius of the night. The hunting-song ended abruptly in a gurgle—the sentry threshed the grass with kicking feet, but silently, for about his head a light robe had been thrown, stifling all outcry. When his struggles ended, strong fingers bound a strip of the robe across his mouth, which was stuffed with grasses to prevent his giving warning.

Recovering his senses, the astonished Indian saw a dark form moving among the herd, speaking in soothing tones and gathering up all the lead ropes as he went. In bunches of five Kioga tied these to his own long rope. Rounding up the last of the animals, he urged them gently away at a walk to where the gray was concealed. Running them a mile farther, he secured them and returned to within a hundred yards of the village.

Selecting from among his arrows one with a round and hollow head, perforated with two small holes, he placed it against his bowstring and winged it away between the foremost great skin lodge and the others round about.

The arrow flew true, wailing its piercing song among the tepees of the village. It ended its career striking with a hollow sound against a war-shield hanging on a tripod.

Roused by the startling noise, braves were already darting forth from the lodges, weapons in hand. When the village was thoroughly roused, Kioga made known his presence. From the ridge whereon he stood blacked against the graying sky of dawn, the Snow Hawk sent pealing forth the sharp high war-yell of the Wa-Kanek.

Pausing only to note that he was seen, and to savor the clamor with which the Indians realized the loss of their horses, Kioga wheeled away, touched heel to mount, and fled back to where he had left his booty.

The day was fading before he paused to rest the animals; another dawn found the village of Magpie gazing with amazement upon the approach of a lone horseman, dull-eyed from lack of sleep, but convoying a band of forty fine horses. Straight before the lodge of the old matron, Kioga brought them.

Handing the rope to Me-kon-agi, he left the Indian staring, slipped from the gray, and retired to his lodge. Dropping upon a buffalo robe, he slept the moment his head touched the bison-wool cushion.

Emerging from her tent, Magpie looked from Me-kon-agi to the herd and back again. "The mounts of Wolf Jaw!" she muttered with startled eyes. Then: "*Ahi*, but he lost no time! How Wolf Jaw did rave on learning of this! A lesson in horse-taking to the chief of the Fox Warriors. No good will come of this. But let us laugh while we may, warriors, for Wolf Jaw will soon be visiting us!"

And suiting the action to the word, Magpie laughed loud and long. . . .

And the visit Magpie anticipated was not long in materializing. Several days after Kioga's return with the horses, a scout brought in word that twenty men were approaching on foot across the plains. Later in the day, weary and footsore, an angry band of Wa-Kanek tribesmen entered the village, pausing sullenly before the Magpie's tent.

At their head stood Wolf Jaw himself, a savage more than six feet tall and burlier than most of his race, hiding his fury beneath a mask of frigid calm.

Presently Magpie emerged, looked upon her silent eldest son, and said by way of greeting: "*Hau*, warrior, you have come far. Your moccasins are worn through until we can see your toes. Since when do horsemen of my tribes go afoot?"

Black as midnight grew the face of Wolf Jaw. From his great height he looked down upon the aged woman, conscious of the mockery running through her words. Little of respect appeared in his answering voice: "Since the men of Magpie's village steal horses from their own kin, old woman!" Then, unable longer to contain his fury: "Where are the sneaking women? Be they five or ten, I'll cut off their ears."

"They are not ten, nor five, oh Talker-With-the-Big-Mouth," answered Magpie calmly. "And mayhap 'twill be thine own ears that come off, *ehu!*"

"Show me who did this thing!" demanded Wolf Jaw, carried away by his rage, and seizing Magpie roughly by the arm, he threatened her with upraised hand.

But an instant later, by what strange violent twist of magic he never knew, Wolf Jaw crashed flat upon his back to count the strange constellations appearing before his eyes.

The infuriated chief awoke to the realization that he had erred on the side of foolhardiness in daring to raise a hand against Magpie. Still writhing in that unbreakable grip, he was drawn to his feet. His band stood surly and disarmed by the warriors in old Magpie's village.

Pinioned then by Me-kon-agi and several other village braves, Wolf Jaw was held in check, while Magpie, furious at this outrage, opened the bursting vials of her wrath upon his head. Finally, "Bind him to a stake," she ordered grimly. "Fetch my quirt."

Both orders were swiftly carried out. With her own hand Magpie then dealt twenty lashes, sparing neither vituperation nor energy in the process.

When she had done, Wolf Jaw lay striped and humiliated as never before in his life of uselessness to the tribe. Finally, breathing hard, Magpie gave her last orders:

"Give back their horses. But mount them, one and all, backward, and drive them thus from my village." And with that, she stormed into her tent, to sit rocking back and forth before the fire for many an hour.

Wolf Jaw's answer to the reverses suffered in Magpie's village was aimed directly at the Snow Hawk.

Delivered through the mouth of Red Horse, a mounted messenger, and enunciated loudly before all the village, it was a long and acrimonious harangue. The substance of it was that Wolf Jaw defied the Black Shield to come forth mounted and armed for close combat, and that he, Wolf Jaw, would gladly repay him for the affronts of the previous day.

Since Wolf Jaw was renowned as the foremost exponent of mounted fighting among the Wa-Kanek, this was a challenge which even Me-kon-agi would have thought twice before accepting. Indeed, in taunting Kioga, comparatively untrained in the management of a horse, the bitter Indian anticipated a refusal, which would repair his prestige so that he might hold his head high again. Little did he expect this insolent reply, carried home to him by his messenger:

"Meet me on the Flat-Where-the-Rivers-Fork. Bring along as many of your men as wish to witness your downfall; arm yourself with whatever weapon you choose. But be sure to bring your strongest medicine-charms—and an extra horse to bear home your shield when you lie dead."

At the appointed place and time, two Indian horse bands converged upon the junction of the two rivers. Flanked by twenty of his men, Wolf Jaw stalked up and down on a big-boned roan with ornaments tied in mane and tail. He rode in a deep, high-pommeled saddle from which little less than a lightning bolt might be expected to hurl him. At its horn hung rope and club. In his hand the great chief bore his feathered lance, bladed with copper; and above his crown was a splendid war-cap whose many feathers fluttered in the breeze. As he strutted back and forth, the vainglorious savage boasted of his previous victories.

"He is afraid to come forth from his burrow, lest the wolf snap him up. Coward once, coward always! Like boy, like man. And who denies that Black Shield was a cowardly child?"

"It may be so," said one of his warriors. "But here he comes."

Wheeling in surprise, Wolf Jaw saw his enemy approaching.

The Snow Hawk rode a smaller but active horse in lieu of the gray stallion, which he did not wish to risk in this encounter. In contrast with Wolf Jaw, he was naked to the light cincture about his waist. That single plume, painted now in recognition of his earlier exploit, still hung from his hair. His limbs were bare to the high moccasins. He rode lightly upon a plain bull-hide saddle, which was equipped with the usual coil of rope and a war-hammer.

Scarce had he appeared, when Wolf Jaw drew apart from his followers and stood waiting on the field, toward which Kioga presently rode, followed by the good wishes and advice of his friends. Where Kioga's men stood, many more of the villagers had appeared; and people from Wolf Jaw's distant village likewise increased the crowd.

Voicing a derisive yell, Wolf Jaw heeled his big-boned mount, and with headdress flying and lance couched in the crook of his arm, bore down upon Kioga, quirting his horse incessantly.

In turn the Snow Hawk came streaking up the grassy stretch, riding as if welded to his seat. Like his foeman, he carried his lance as if to ride it to the mark. But before they came together, the Black Shield was seen to poise the slender weapon and launch it forth. A yell of excitement greeted the cast.

Luck was with the enemy, whose mount, stumbling, threw him momentarily sidewise in his seat; and the long lance, grazing his head, merely carried away the ornate headdress, which it pinned to earth behind him. And then a sigh went up from Kioga's friends; for as he neared the other, Wolf Jaw's couched spear leveled at his breast must in another instant have transpierced him. The sigh was followed by a shout of admiration and wonder. For almost at the instant of being hit, him they knew as Black Shield dropped behind his mount's body on the off side; the spear passed harmlessly through empty air, as he clung with left hand and heel only, and the echo of his laugh reached those who watched.

Pivoting, Wolf Jaw returned to the attack, intent upon skewering this unexpectedly wily prey upon the lance. But it was not to be, for with his war-hammer, Kioga dashed the splintered spear to earth. Seizing his own club, the Indian then met Kioga head-on. The crack of stone on stone sounded sharply as the Indian sought to beat down the Snow Hawk's guard. But none knew better than Kioga this art of cut and parry, and the other's club was first to fly from his numbed hand. For the fraction of an instant Wolf Jaw rode at his opponent's mercy. But Kioga appeared to ignore this opportunity, and permitted him to pass on unbludgeoned.

At once Wolf Jaw reached for his rope. But even with the thought he heard the hiss of thrown lariat, and the Black Shield's hard noose snapped down about his waist, pinning one arm to his side. Desperately he slashed himself free, and riding swiftly near his fallen warbonnet, snatched up Kioga's abandoned spear, and poising this, returned to strike anew.

A jeer from either side greeted Wolf Jaw's act. For in retrieving the spear he broke a rule of combat forbidding the use of any arm abandoned. And almost at once the desperate Wolf Jaw again violated a canon of horseback combat—the rule which calls it unethical to kill a mount in order to destroy its rider. With one mighty cast the Indian drove the spear through the lungs of Kioga's animal, and the luckless beast sank to earth, blood pouring from its nostrils.

A lightning twist, and Kioga avoided being pinned as the thunder of Wolf Jaw's coming drummed loudly in his ears. But the Indian leaned far over, dropped his coil neatly about the Snow Hawk, and snapped it tight. Yelling in triumph, Wolf Jaw spurred cruelly, and in another instant would have jerked Kioga into the deadly drag which seldom ends in anything but death.

Silenced in anticipation of the approaching end, the onlookers waited tensely, scarce breathing. Only one among them sent up a shout of understanding. Me-kon-agi alone had seen the meaning of the leap which carried Kioga across the fallen horse, taking secure purchase about its round barrel with the Indian's rope.

Wolf Jaw had overreached and was spurring his own downfall. As the rope's slack leaped taut, those watching saw the Indian fly bodily from his horse and come crashing to earth, still in the saddle, which had been jerked completely from his mount. Unluckily for Wolf Jaw, the saddle was uppermost, and in falling struck him senseless, while his horse pounded away across the plain.

His friends carried him away unconscious, later to think over the bitterness of defeat at the hands of this despised upstart, and to awake among braves who had lost every stitch of clothing they owned, in bad bets upon their fallen champion.

But in Magpie's village there was great rejoicing, for the old beldame's men, inherent gamblers like most of their race, had also wagered their all upon the outcome—and won.

During this time among the Wa-Kanek, the Snow Hawk had sought to forget what was past. The white woman he had known and loved, the period of his life spent in civilization, his friend James Munro the scientist—all these he put from mind.

But one day a Wa-Kanek warrior returned from a lone raid into forest territory dominated by the Shoni. Among the man's trophies stripped from a fallen foe were objects at which the wild horsemen stared in wonderment: a neck-lace of empty cartridge shells first caught Kioga's eye. Then from a captured pouch the warrior produced several circles of copper and silver. They were coins—American coins of small denomination. The pouch contained a tiny red-painted magnet, to whose horns clung the familiar bit of iron, and also a small strip of translucent stuff, evenly perforated at either side—a discarded bit of exposed motion-picture film.

All of these trifling items had been scrupulously wrapped in deer-skin, after the manner of medicine-charms. Clearly their dead owner had considered them possessed of magical properties.

So too did the Wa-Kanek. Me-kon-agi bid fifty horses for the magnet only. Gro-Gan' raised it to a hundred. But the owner would not part with his jealously guarded trophies. Of all who examined them, Kioga alone knew them for what they were.

Another surprise awaited him:

In a captured scalp which the returned warrior next showed, woven into three strands of hair, was a length of cheap gold-plated chain—one of the small trinkets from the *Narwhal*'s trade-chests.

With narrowed, puzzled eyes and speculative gaze, Kioga scrutinized these things intently; then, leaning back, he laughed inwardly at a momentary uneasiness. Doubtless they were but a few survivals of the American yacht's enforced visit to Nato'wa many moons ago. In that belief he strove to dismiss the matter from his mind. And yet—he could not.... Perhaps it was for this very reason that he decided upon a raid into the domains of the P'Kuni, and persuaded a little group of the most adventurous to go with him.

With ceremony and dance the little band prepared themselves for their journey, and set forth well armed and mounted at dusk on the long trip into the hunting-grounds of the hostile tribe.

At dusk of the fourth day they came upon the bloody work of the fierce scalp-hunting foe. Three Wa-Kanek tents of an outpost clan stood silent and forlorn upon the grass. On one a raven perched.

Dismounting, Kioga and Me-kon-agi read a grim tale of surprise and merciless slaughter. In one tent the inhabitants lay in recumbent attitudes, slain in their sleep. The other tents told of an alarm too late to save the scalps of the inmates. Each person, including the three children, had been hacked and mutilated in frightful manner, and among them the Indians recognized relatives and friends.

With zeal to meet the foe and avenge their dead multiplied, they then rode on, sleeping by day, riding in darkness as much as possible; the night being short, however, much of their travel must be done in the light.

On the afternoon of the fifth day, swollen black thunderheads loomed upon the horizon, and the fresh damp wind of impending storm fanned them briskly. Thunder grumbled into the distance, and soon the prairie grass that swept the horses' bellies bent in obeisance to the winds.

Casting frequent anxious glances into the sky, Me-kon-agi counseled seeking shelter and was seconded by Gro-Gan', who accompanied the party as invoker of good fortune. Kioga agreed, and they paused in a deep hollow beneath an overhanging bluff—and none too soon. Like charging battalions the swollen clouds rolled near in awesome shapes, swinging close above the hills and looming in mighty masses like strange monstrous creatures of the sky seeking prey upon the earth.

Then came a whisper, as if some mighty giant drew breath between his distant mumblings. Mud-brown clouds thronged the vault, shot with ominous green and copper hues. Chained golden lightnings throbbed intermittently amid the looming vapors.... The whisper rose to a deep disquieting drone. A gleaming curtain advanced out of the distance, preceded by a strange and terrifying quiver of the ground.

Suddenly a prairie fox went floating past, as if blown by the breeze. Close behind him came a pair of wolves, and twenty more in as many seconds. Then a little band of antelope bounded along, as if giving chase to their natural enemies who fled before them. Close above them, with driving pinions, came ten white majestic birds, immense in size, voicing a strange, low-keyed trumpetlike cry, resounding deep and resonant. They were another species of vanishing American to which Nato'wa is the final sanctuary. Common to these savage plainsmen, they would have proved a rare sight to a continental bird-lover—*Cygnus buccinator*, to an ornithologist; trumpeter swan is their better name—pursuing as it were a band of eagles winging in their van.

A band of young wild horses raced near the waiting Indians. After them came beasts less fleet of foot: A small herd of bison, with tongues hanging a foot from their mouths, a crippled elk, an aging grizzly bear—none too slow to flee what came behind. All the plain was filled with birds and beasts of each degree.

The antelope herd wheeled, milling, pawing the earth, darting out and back, bleating in piteous uncertainty, then whisked away, padded heavily along unnoticed in their very midst. Twenty yards away a tiger of the tawny plains variety clawed frantically at a bank and took snarling cover there. For in this moment the emperor of all living beasts was one with the timid hare, disdaining not to hide from the onrushing terror.

Even the Indians drew their horses closer back within their shelter, and they were pale beneath their bronze; and Mekon-agi shouted above the nearing roar: "The storm-gods do their worst this day. Draw in and wait. You'll see—"

The tempest swept closer still. A mighty terrifying sound was heard, as of countless hooves beating the earth. Before their shelter the grass was lashed flat by a sudden storm of milky pellets. And a female of the most timid of Nato'wan prairie game, the star-gazelle, crept shivering into the hollow under the bluff, leading a little fawn. Both crouched quivering among the Indians, driven in this extremity to seek haven among men, the worst foes of all.

The full violence of the hailstorm now raged. The ground was as one great resounding drum bombarded by a myriad gelid spheres. A mighty bison bull fell suddenly not far away, struck down by hailstones large as apples.

The storm was over as quickly as it had begun. In its swath the plain was littered with dead and dying things, and covered with a sheet of glittering pearl as the hailstones jellied together, melting slowly into the warm earth. Everywhere the caribou-birds were busy. None others, save a band of Indians and a star-gazelle with young, moved upon this field of desolation. . . .

Nearing at last the border of the P'Kuni domain next day, Kioga and his band proceeded with greater caution, keeping to the deep ravines. When they must expose themselves, they rode close against their horses' necks with blankets updrawn, in simulation of the shaggy buffalo who were their daily companions on the plains. And so riding ever in the gullies and scouting the country ahead before crossing any prominent ridge, they finally glimpsed the bluish smoke of a camp-fire rising from behind a hill.

Secreting themselves and their mounts in a gully, fringed with prairie grasses, they waited for dusk, and while waiting planned the raid to come. And that success be assured, Kioga argued against the folly of lingering to take scalps.

"We have come for horses," he said. "Let us leave revenge to the near-clansmen of the slain. We shall double our prestige by returning, every man alive, to give away his plunder."

The Indians agreed, though with reluctance. Remembrance of the newly killed dead of their own tribe was still fresh in mind.

Leaving their horses in the ravine and stripping to the barest essentials of weapons and apparel, the little war party left its hiding-place at dusk. Nearing the village, the raiders divided, each going his separate way according to an agreed-upon plan. Kioga was to concentrate upon lifting as many horses and as much equipment as he could make away with. The others were to prowl among the shadows near the tents and take care of any likely to give the alarm, liberate Wa-Kanek captives, if any, and carry off all possible plunder. All were to meet at the ravine an hour before dawn, unless an alarm was given before that time, in which case it was to be every man for himself. . . .

The P'Kuni village slept deep and unsuspectingly, slumbering off the victory-feast which had celebrated the return of the scalp-laden warriors. And ten stealthy shadows stole ever nearer, blending at last with the shadows of the tall dark lodges. Nine separate shields vanished from beside nine separate lodges. One by one Kioga's band slipped forth to deposit the booty in the ravine. The take amounted in all to six fine bows, four otter-skin quivers stuffed with arrows, many spears, war-shields, articles of medicine-value, and a long string of fresh scalps ripped from Wa-Kanek skulls only two days before.

Kioga, meanwhile, had done his swift work among the enemy horse herds, and came out of the darkness leading sixty of the finest, many equipped with their war-paraphernalia. Unhappily, several of his company had arrived before him, and not content with the fruits of their raid, they must return to raid anew. Kioga, hastening to dissuade them, heard and saw a sudden stir in one tepee.

Six Bear, busy killing and scalping in defiance of orders, had knocked something inflammable into the coals of the lodge-fire. A squaw's scream of terror rose shrill and strident. Several dark figures sped forth, dropping further booty as they came. In a moment uproar rose among the clustered tents.

Two of Kioga's braves, caught in the middle of the village, were seen making a wild dash for liberty, the P'Kuni in close pursuit with tomahawks brandishing. Equipped with wings of fear, the marauders outraced the villagers and reached the plain amid a shower of following arrows. There for the first time Six Bear faltered and stumbled down.

Aided by two companions, he rose again; but by now the P'Kuni, strung out loosely behind, were gaining on them. The Snow Hawk's voice checked their demoralization:

"Back to the horses! Carry him between you. I will follow in a little while. Haste, or we are all dead men!"

The Indians melted into the night. Kioga waited, hidden in a small hollow. The P'Kuni, pursuing in long open formation came on, one by one. Several were grappled by an indistinct shadow with the agility and strength of a tiger, before the remainder took warning that danger lurked in the hollow. And before they could rally united, a fleet figure sped away at an angle from the direction taken by the pursued.

The hounds were turned. Arrows and tomahawks flew

thick about the Snow Hawk's head, piercing the ground about him as the Indians followed yelling. But not their swiftest runner could hope to match strides with the Snow Hawk, and soon he left them behind, circled, and came back to where his anxious band awaited him.

"To horse!" he ordered. "Spare not the quirt! Pursuit will follow." And springing upon the gray stallion he set an example which the others imitated, leading the P'Kuni war-mounts behind them.

And with most of their horses gone, the P'Kuni could only count their dead and wounded, and their losses in plunder.

Thus, to the tune of victory Kioga led forth his first Wa-Kanek exploit band; and of those who returned, none save Six Bear and Kioga himself, who had suffered and ignored an arrow wound, bore more than the scratches of travel.

XXVII

Soon came an event which sent Magpie into a frenzy of fury. A band of P'Kuni hostiles attacked another of her villages. The toll of that midnight visit was forty dead. Of these more than half were children, the remainder old men and squaws.

Worst of all the P'Kuni, victorious and drunk with success, were reported on their way to attack Magpie's own village in the absence of the hunters. Striding up and down within her tepee, she vented her wrath upon Wolf Jaw and his subordinate warriors.

"How shall our handful of braves repulse two hundred P'Kuni scalp-hunters?" she demanded at length.

Wolf Jaw shifted uncomfortably; then indicating the Snow Hawk with a hand: "Ask the mighty Black Shield," he answered sullenly. "He knows all things, or so you'd have us think."

"Our ways are still strange to him," defended Magpie swiftly.

"Strange or not," ventured Kioga, "it is plain to me that we need to fear the P'Kuni."

"How," questioned Wolf Jaw sarcastically, "would you meet them with our little force?"

"Small or great would be the same," returned Kioga quietly, "since we shall not face them. We will abandon our village; we will give the P'Kuni our lodges as a gift with all their contents."

Magpie wheeled upon him almost fiercely. "Flee? Like cowards, without a fight? What words are these? Your wounds have let your blood out. Your mind is still weak."

Such counsel from Black Shield the fearless sounded strange in Magpie's ears.

"My knees may be weak," answered Kioga, "but my head and heart are strong. And they tell me there is a way whereby if we give all, we give nothing. Listen."

The old woman gave careful ear. The fire crackled lower as Kioga talked. A silence ensued, broken by Magpie at last, who spoke with narrowed eyes glittering excitedly. "*Ehu-ah*! But you have a good head, my son! A moment, while I think.... It is good! We'll do it!"

Five minutes later the heralds were calling Magpie's message through the camp. "Move! *Move*! Collect your horses and weapons. Leave everything else behind. The P'Kuni are coming!"

Seeing that Magpie and Kioga were already leaving, surrounded by their warriors, the others followed suit. The village emptied. On its outskirts Kioga assembled his men and gave instructions.

All who could be spared returned, and entering the tepees, spent some time therein, at an occupation invisible from without. Then all followed on the track of the main band, vanishing in a long black line among the eastern hills. As they disappeared from out the west came two painted P'Kuni horsemen, to pause upon a hilltop and sweep the plain and its deserted village with their eyes.

On another watching-place, flattened against the crest of a ridge like serpents, three silent figures watched the foreign scouts, behind whom black storm clouds were swelling up. Not the breath of a breeze stirred on the prairie. But the distant thunder whispered threatfully behind the scowling clouds as the silent watchers vanished in a ravine.

Thus the P'Kuni warriors, keyed to the highest pitch of ferocity in anticipation of strong resistance, came upon a deserted village which they took in its entirety without the loosing of a single arrow. The silent ring of tepees contained not a single occupant. The exodus had been not long before.

That it had been hasty and inspired by fear the P'Kuni did not doubt, for upon the flat were many fresh-killed buffalo, abandoned. And in the tents the pipes were freshly filled, waiting only to be smoked.

Upon the waiting meat the P'Kuni warriors fell, to glut themselves with the eagerness of famished men. In the abandoned tepees they made their bivouac for the night, accounting themselves favored by their lucky spirits. Here they would sleep out the storm, already raging. Pipes were lit. The usurpers cast themselves upon the comfortable buffalo-robes.

"They must have been expecting us," remarked one warrior facetiously, puffing with satisfaction upon a well-filled pipe, and little knowing what truth his words had uttered....

Those were no lucky spirits who crept upon the gorged enemy, but specters of vengeance. Down their naked backs the warm rains flowed. Their dripping horses trod fetlock deep in mud. When the riders slipped from their backs, it was to crawl forward upon the P'Kuni in a mixture of mud and muck whose sole virtue was that it helped camouflage them from their foes.

With all the tepees tightly closed against the storm, their task was made the simpler. Only a handful had been left on guard by the P'Kuni. Not by the wildest stretch of imagination could have any foe have been expected to assail them on such a night as this.

Creeping up under cover of robes and darkness, Kioga's men arranged for the quick disposal of the sentries. Whipping nooses deftly about the necks of the sleepy guards and stifling all outcry, one by one the sentries were hauled through the muck, to where other Wa-Kanek waited, knives in hand.

Large and well occupied were the tents. Men smoked and joked who did not sleep; meanwhile the rain pelted heavily against the thick sides of the comfortable leathern lodges, and the wind sang among the closed vent-holes above.

Now silent rain-wet shadows slipped from tent to tent, knotting the laces of the door-skins. When all was in readiness, at a given signal a shadow host of Indians on foot poured rushing into the village. Suddenly the strongest men tore up the lodge-poles, precipitating the tepees down upon the earth.

The village fire suddenly rose higher with a gust of wind. In its light a fearful scene of carnage was enacted. The tents lay fallen, like immense bags covering struggling, squirming forms. Unable to see their assailants and terribly handicapped by the stifling covering of buffalo-hide, which closed them in amid the smoke and flames of the lodge-fires, the P'Kuni suffered awful execution.

Soon fell a silence more terrible than the clamor preceding it. Such had been the fury of the attack that only one man within survived.

And that one owed his life solely to Kioga's intervention.

Aghast at the extent of bloodshed, the Snow Hawk glimpsed a lean young warrior snaking forth stealthily from a hole slashed in an outer lodge. With yells his men would have fallen upon this last of the survivors, but Kioga intervened.

"Killing is at an end," declared the Black Shield. And to the P'Kuni: "Take this horse and return to your people. Tell them to think twice before again they attack the Wa-Kanek. Tell them day and night are all alike to us. We never rest; we never sleep. Tell them that, you who are the last of two hundred warriors."

With that he brought his quirt down upon the P'Kuni's mount. Horse and rider vanished into the darkness.

The white man's war is dark and ugly, cold-blooded as the intertwinings of two serpents. The red man's warpath glitters with excitement. Deeds of daring rank above bloodletting. Following this second victory over the P'Kuni, the Snow Hawk faced an embarrassment of applicants eager to accompany him on raids or forays of any kind.

As Kioga rose in the estimation of the Wa-Kanek, Wolf Jaw lost proportionately, until one night there came to the Snow Hawk a deputation of warriors bearing a pipe which they offered to him on behalf of the Fox Warriors, the same warrior society that Wolf Jaw long had headed.

Having smoked, Kioga was escorted to the towering ceremonial lodge of the Foxes, and its ritualistic secrets revealed to him. And that night a question he had long pondered resolved itself into a solution. These competing societies, for all that they trained men in the arts of war, also sundered the nation as a whole, introducing rivalries often bitter and hostile. The cohesion of Magpie's scattered tribes would be impossible so long as such a condition existed.

Inquiry had informed him that the next largest society was that called the men of Flint, headed by White Bear, a famous chief long estranged from the Magpie, to the detriment of both.... Wolf Jaw was superseded. Kioga turned toward the enlistment of White Bear.

245

XXVIII

Master now of as many men as he cared to command, Kioga and a small band set forth at sundown to visit the village of White Bear, chief of the so-called Flint Warriors. Arrived at Mitoka, or the Smoky Village, to the advancing heralds he spoke thus:

"Black Shield, son of Magpie, would smoke a pipe with White Bear and cement his friendship with these gifts." Whereupon he produced a pipe ornamented with intricate carvings and plumes, and in addition a pair of prize piebald mares.

The herald accepted the gifts and passed into the village, crying the news of Black Shield's coming. In a little while he returned to conduct the visitors into the presence of Magpie's long-estranged son. The meeting was in silence according to Indian practice. Kioga and his band were conducted to a half-open tent, beneath which each took his place in the proper order of precedence. The pipe was lighted and passed from hand to hand. No sound interrupted the age-old decorum of the council.

When all had smoked, White Bear stood up. Kioga beheld a man in the prime of life, six feet six inches tall, and the very antithesis of Wolf Jaw in the simplicity of his attire. He wore a plain blanket, unadorned. Three long feathers, tipped with fur, and notched, were all his headdress. He spoke disdainfully and straight before him, looking neither to right nor left.

"White Bear has counted many *coups*, and leads the Flint Warriors. You have humiliated one of his own blood. His heart is therefore bad toward you.

"White Bear is no enemy of Magpie. Though his brother chiefs would make a league against her, he will not join it. The Magpie is proud and jealous. White Bear was ambitious for honors. She cast him forth, and would share no power with him. His heart is bad about this, and he came away to ride at the head of the Flint Warriors.

"I know not why I tell Black Shield this. Why should a seasoned warrior counsel with a nobody? When your deeds qualify you to speak, do so then, and I will hear you. When this council is over, leave my village before my men slit your throats. Take back your pipe and gifts. I am White Bear. My tongue is straight. I have spoken!"

A curt and arrogant reply to Kioga's conciliatory approach. But reasoning that there was probably some justice in White Bear's grievance, Kioga withheld any open resentment of the contemptuous terms. Not so his companions, whose eyes reflected the anger in their hearts. In the heat of passion hot words would have threatened battle, had not an interruption come.

From the edge of the village two herd-boys came running in with news that the P'Kuni were riding hard upon them from the west. White Bear jerked out orders to his own men:

"We talk, and the enemy comes to catch us asleep and half our warriors out hunting. Up, braves! To horse and follow me!"

The council came to a sudden end. Kioga's men rose uncertain as to what they should do. But not Kioga! Pointing after White Bear, "We will follow him," he said quickly.

Me-kon-agi interrupted: "He has refused our offer of friendship; why should we aid him, after his insults?"

"Because we are all Wa-Kanek and there is enough enmity within the tribes," snapped Kioga in reply. "We'll show him deeds that will prove our right to say yes and no in council. What say you to that, Gro-Gan'?"

Thus appealed to, the medicine man threw up a hand, his tomahawk washing in it. As one man the others followed him, rushing to their horses.

There was confusion in the village as the mounted warriors swept through. The P'Kuni scouts, finding their surprise nipped in the bud by the vigilance of the herd-boys, withdrew to lure the warriors farther onto the plains. Nothing could better have pleased White Bear in the absence of his hunters.

But dismay followed when from the ravines on either side of a cut there poured three times his own strength of riders. The warriors of White Bear were swiftly surrounded by a mobile ring of mounted P'Kuni, discharging their arrows in swift succession from behind the necks of their mounts.

Thus far had the fighting progressed when Kioga and his thirty warriors joined the fray, appearing as from nowhere to fall savagely upon the P'Kuni rear, hacking them down with their war-hammers and tomahawks. White Bear, to his amazement, found himself reinforced by those whose friendship he had refused with such contempt. The one he had so recently labeled an unseasoned stripling was hewing a valiant way through the P'Kuni.

Suddenly Black Shield's horse sank, struck through by a spear. A P'Kuni chieftain, yelling in wild triumph, leaned far out in his saddle above Kioga with war-ax upraised. But as it came whistling down, Black Shield sidestepped. White Bear saw something snakelike coil from his hand, writhe forth and lap about the passing warrior's throat, as Kioga wielded the lash. An instant later the P'Kuni came out of the saddle heels over head; and one of Kioga's followers ended his fighting with a slash of the tomahawk.

Not ten feet apart, Kioga and White Bear crouched behind their dead mounts. A sleet of arrows fell hissing thick about them. But seeing the accuracy with which Black Shield was bringing the enemy from their saddles, White Bear was moved to laugh outright in sheer joy of battle. Glancing at him in astonishment, Kioga met the older man's eye and heard him yell: "Two horses that you cannot bring down their chief on the painted mare!"

Kioga glanced across the waving grass-tops, tore an arrow from the body of his horse, and laid it on the string.

"It is worth a higher bet," he called. "For five horses I'll put my arrow in his medicine-shield."

"Ten you cannot even hit him!" retorted White Bear. The distant chief paused, dismounted to cut and rip the scalp from one of White Bear's dead.

"I'll gamble!" returned Kioga, taking careful aim. The limbs of his bow bent slowly back. The flint point pricked his bow-hand knuckle. Carefully he allowed for distance and the little breeze—and let the arrow fly. Close along the waves of grass it sped, a neutral streak.

"You lose!" cried White Bear, confident the arrow would not carry home.

"I win!" cried Kioga in answer. To the amazement of White Bear, the shield leaped from the saddle and rolled, transfixed by the arrow. "And now the rider," called the marksman, aiming above the distant empty saddle. Swift as thought, another arrow spun away. Before it was half sped, the P'Kuni warrior swung up to his seat, then threw up both hands—in one the scalp—and fell to earth as if lightning had struck him.

A loud cry of admiration came from White Bear.

"I'd rather call you friend than foe, if the Great Ones spare us," he shouted.

Kioga laughed.

"Was that not what we came for?" he called, between arrows.

The P'Kuni had little war left in them now. The deadly shooting from behind the fallen horses had taken the heart out of them. They were in retreat, pausing not even to drag off their dead. . . .

White Bear selected ten good mounts to make good his wager with Kioga, laughing the while. The Snow Hawk presented him with the arrowed shield. They drank from a common horn cup. Again Kioga broached the subject of his visit.

The brows of White Bear knit; then he smilingly said: "It is long since I looked upon Magpie's face. I'll go with you, warrior, and tell her of that shot."

And so, with twenty warriors accompanying them from his village, he returned with Kioga to Magpie's tents. The meeting took place before the painted lodge. The tall warrior looked down upon the aged woman with apparent coldness. She returned his gaze fiercely, unrelentingly. The man was first to yield, and held forth a pleading hand.

"Mother forgive. I was in the wrong. I hungered for honors. I could not wait. Admit me to your tent again."

The Magpie swallowed with working throat. She made a wry face and spat, angry that tears should be in her eyes. "Pah! I love you too well. Come home and be welcome. There is work to do, and I am getting old."

One morning, sleeping soundly in his tepee, with his feet to the fire and his head against the painted draft-screen pictured with his exploits, Kioga was awakened by the cries of the heralds. From a far bluff a smoke signal rose into the sky, announcing the finding of game. The cry "Buffalo! *Buffalo!*" ran through the camp like wildfire.

Two parties left the village to take part in the hunt. One was under Me-kon-agi and numbered Kioga among its group. The other was organized by Wolf Jaw.

Leading spare ponies, each band stole through the cuts and ravines until they came upon signs of buffalo.

Shortly thereafter, topping a ridge, the herds were viewed. As far as the eye could see the shaggy bison thronged the plain, their enormous humps looming everywhere. Wolves hung on the outer fringes of the herd, eager to drag down the sick or weak. Vultures and buzzards circled overhead, and far aloft eagles gyrated with motionless wings.

At a signal from Me-kon-agi his Indians began the circling movement of the "surround," streaming off to either side. When they had ringed a part of the herd, they hurled their mounts in among the shaggy legion.

The buffalo horse Kioga rode was well trained in its work, quick-footed as a cat. Ranging up beside a plunging hump, he drove his arrows deep, and in the first few minutes he brought down many buffalo, until his arrow supply was exhausted. Returning for another quiver, he paused a moment to watch the scene. The men were doing well, milling the herd with practiced skill. A cloud of choking dust overhung the plain.

An Indian's horse stepped into a badger-hole and went down. Before the man could rise, a lean old bull swerved and gored him fiercely. A rush of black forms passed over the spot, and Kioga could not see who it was had fallen. . . .

When the kills were finally counted, again Wolf Jaw's party stood at a loss. The rival party had slaughtered eighty-seven bison, identified by their red-marked arrows. Wolf Jaw's band had killed but fifty-three.

The humps, tongues, and boss-ribs were highest prized, and the best of each of these was set aside to regale the hunters. And of all who later feasted on the juicy roast hump and the succulent marrow of the leg-bones, the eyes of none gleamed brighter than the members of the migrant band Kioga had brought all the way from another continent.

But one face was missing from that familiar roster this night. For Old Crow Man, who had gone forth rejuvenated by the hunting prospect, who knew the bison herds of America before the white robe-hunters left them rotting on the prairie, was no more. It was Old Crow Man whom Kioga had seen tossed and trampled by the buffalo.

The hunt was over, but not its sequel. On the skirts of the herd a grizzly bear had been roped down by a dozen warriors and goaded almost to madness with lance-points. In an enclosure of ropes and tepee-poles a huge bison bull was being tormented, preparatory to pitting one against the other.

When both animals were deemed fierce enough, the bear's bonds were cut, liberating him into the bull's enclosure, round which the Indians had gathered to witness the baiting. Almost instantly the animals came together. Bellowing with head down, the bull pounded in full charge upon the grizzly. Evading lightly for all its mighty bulk, the bear reared and scored bloody furrows along the bison's flanks. Hooking the horny foe with one paw, the grizzly swung suddenly upon the bull's back and reached forward to seize the muzzle and crack the spine.

Unable to shake him loose, the bull charged the pole fence, with all the power which comes of insane rage and pain. At once the flimsy structure collapsed.

Crowding near the enclosure, the Indians had sat their horses, Magpie and Kioga among them. Now bison and grizzly rolled struggling on the ground under the very forefeet of Magpie's horse, dust rising above them in a cloud.

Amid the bellowing of the locked beasts rose the startled shouts of the Indians. The nearest warrior, in an excess of bravado, dropped from his horse and sank an arrow in the bear. He had not time to rue his foolhardy act.

With a swiftness past all comprehension, the grizzly whirled, and its jaws chopped shut upon the savage's face. A muffled cry was all he uttered as the bear flung him aside. And the bison, charging through the scattering Indians, trampled him in gaining the freedom of the open plain.

In all the wild excitement, the Indians fell over one another in avoiding the fierce rushes of the angry bear. Old Magpie, not so quick as her younger companions, allowed her mount to step in reach of the bear's claws. One mighty slash of the hooked paw, and her horse was crushed to its knees. Lacking other intervention, that had surely been the end of the old matron-chief.

But as the bear turned to attack the fallen Magpie, there came a sharp pound of hooves. Sensing a new menace, the animal pivoted to face a grim-eyed warrior, looming suddenly behind a feathered lance, its bronze point gleaming.

The bear struck at the oncoming weapon. The copper point, slightly deflected, but with Kioga's weight and all the force of his racing mount behind it, drove through flesh and bone, and buried itself in the sod.

For a short space the impaled grizzly lay quivering, then heaved upon its feet. But almost too quickly for eye to register, the rider had dismounted and leaped forward to attack.

The bear lunged, its curving claws slashing empty air, for Kioga was under the blow. Seizing the deep-sunk blade, he writhed round behind the animal. With knees clamped upon the bear's barrel he twisted his fingers in the shaggy mane, sank his horn spurs deep, clung, beyond range of jaws or claws.

Now the mighty beast reared. Kioga, however, only made

good his hold, seeking firmer grip upon the knife, to plunge it yet again with greater effect.

Down came the bear, rolling over and over to dislodge its unseen assailant, but vainly. Still Kioga hung on, waiting. Then suddenly the knife came forth halfway, then stabbed plunging in again. Gouts of blood sprang from the bear's nostrils as in its death throe it twisted facing the human enemy.

A long-drawn gasp sounded from the onlookers. It was seen that the brute had seized Black Shield against its hairy breast. Together they went down for the last time, the long black claws cutting deep, the snapping jaws seeking a death-hold.

Then the monster form went lax, and the claws fell limp and loose. An instant later a dozen spears were plunged into the dead beast as the Indians cast off their lethargy.

With a low cry Magpie bent at the Snow Hawk's side, raising his head upon her arm. The dying animal had done dread work. Kioga's throat was torn and streaming blood. The pulsing jugular lay exposed, and claw-wounds in chest and shoulder yawned red and terrible.

Of all who stood silently about the fallen warrior, only Wolf Jaw gloated. For it seemed to him that Black Shield's medicine had failed him now and forever.

XXIX

Some miles north of Hopeka village, and on the River Hawasi, there is a cave called by the Indians Place-Where-We-Hide.

Slemp, chief of the *Narwhal's* mutineers, and the white renegade Mad Crow, had here assembled their followers, red-skinned and white. With Shingas, their newest ally, they were busy mapping out a plan of action to attack the island which James Munro, unknown to them, had fortified.

To this riverbank lair came one of Half-mouth's scouts with the tidings that the hiding-place of the enemy was atop the cliffs on Isle Where Ravens Talk. More than that they could not tell, for they had retreated under a hail of arrows which cost them two braves.

Well the white conspirators knew that the *Narwhal* had carried no arms heavier than these rifles they had stolen from aboard her. Possibly they had overlooked some small arms, but that the enemy could be equipped with cannon was inconceivable, if they thought of it at all. News of the wrecking of the Indian canoe had reached them, but the whites dismissed that incident as the work of a boulder dislodged from the cliffs above.

Confident, then, in the superiority of their arms over those of Munro and his companions, the mutineers prepared an immediate offensive on the enemy's position, in hope of forcing them to give over Flashpan's golden hoard and the secret of the mother-lode.

Failure had thus far followed all their attempts to locate the well-hidden *Narwhal*. They had therefore a double reason for wishing to capture someone who might be forced to tell them where the vessel was berthed. Without means of escape to a land where it might be spent, gold would be useless to them.

Setting forth in canoes and disembarking on the island, they hid their craft under the dense overhang near shore, and began the climb upward toward the enemy's reported position.

Within the fort the garrison of whites and Indians had not slackened their efforts to make the place defensible. The walls had been strengthened. The habitable interior was also enlarged to accomodate the Indians who from day to day joined Swift-Hand in his stronghold.

In the arms room the *clang-clang-clang* of the forging hammers told of knives and swords being turned out as fast as primitive methods would permit. One falconet was kept trained upon the approach to the spring from which their water supply was diverted. Meanwhile they sank a shaft in hopes of tapping a more certain supply within the walls themselves. Communication with the *Narwhal* was being maintained steadily once a week. As fast as new guns could be turned out, a number were taken to the ship, which was by now well stocked with smooth-bore small arms, powder, and bullets.

Long since, the white occupants of Fort Talking Raven had lost any outward resemblance to modern civilized folk. The men were garbed in fresh buckskin and soft-soled moccasins, with coats of elk-hide, fringed and embroidered. Gone too were the mannish things that Beth had outworn. The dress of an Indian maiden had replaced them, save that Beth wore rather more above the waist than did Heladi. Even Placer had his headfeather, of which he appeared inordinately proud as he danced about on his devious errands.

So the white men changed their dress and certain of their ways. Not so their wild companions. Savage before their union with the whites, Munro saw them savage still—and never more cruel than tonight when two of Kias's scouts brought in a prisoner.

No common foeman he who entered fettered through the gates between his gloating captors, but one at sight of whom the Shoni bristled like wolves that bay a panther. Here was no fellow Shoni, an adversary only since yesterday, but a bitter racial enemy—a Wa-Kanek warrior.

Three tarnished metal buttons from a seaman's coat—reckoned a high price by the purchasers—had bought the captive from his previous captors—river-men of the upper tribes. Fresh marks of torture were livid on him. Yet in the fierce eyes beneath the scowling brows there was no fear. Only defiance lighted them—and amazement as he looked upon the white-skinned men.

With the interest of a scientist Munro gazed upon this fierce and haughty captive. And putting to good use his exhaustive knowledge of Indian dialects, he questioned the hapless man.

"You have never seen white men before?" Munro asked, not without a note of sympathy.

"I knew one other white man," the captive replied after a moment. "White of skin and blue of eye. A great chief newly come among my people—and braver far than any ten of these ignoble Shoni."

Munro's eyes widened, for these few words painted an unmistakable picture in his mind. Could it be possible?

"Your life as gift if you tell us more of him," Munro replied eagerly. He turned to the assembled warriors for confirmation of his offer; and they, after some hesitation, made the signal of agreement. For the same thought was now in every mind. Could it be—Kioga?

Munro glimpsed Beth and Heladi, newly arrived; close behind them came Dan, and Tokala. All waited for him to confirm by a further description that the Snow Hawk still lived. But—they waited vainly.

Conscious of the intense interest his words had aroused, the Wa-Kanek, perhaps believing that he could exchange his knowledge for freedom, folded his arms and with a jeering smile refused to utter another word. Threats, cajolery, entreaties—to each in turn he showed stony indifference. And in a blaze of anger at the man's stubbornness, a Shoni brave named Tecoma suddenly plunged a knife into the defiant captive's heart.

That night Dan heard Beth sobbing in the darkness of her tent. . . .

Yet even this time of desperate anxiety within the beleaguered fort had its light moments.

Upon the wall near the open cooking room ravens were wont to sit, observing Flashpan's cooking, and occasionally daring to swoop and thieve in his absence. Here also Tokala often lingered to watch and wonder at Flashpan's dexterity in pancake-juggling, and listen to the miner's wild tales.

"You're a funny man," said Tokala one evening, slipping an affectionate little arm about Flashpan's shoulders.

Flashpan grinned and rolled his cud.

"That's account the good Lord made me out of his leftovers—after he finished with the rest o' mankind. Satan was a-pullin' His laig, which 'counts for a few mistakes hyar an' thar."

At this moment a raven, bolder than most, dropped down and speared a deer kidney from under Flashpan's nose.

Quick as a wink the irate cook hurled his knife at the robber. As luck would have it, he struck the raven to earth with a crippled wing. Instantly remorseful, he would have picked it up; but a wounded ravens friendship is not thus easily won. A few quick jabs of those iron mandibles, and Flashpan withdrew.

Tokala was more successful. In a few days the injured bird was eating from his hand and performing the function of kitchen scavenger.

"What'll we name him?" wondered Tokala, stroking his newest pet.

"Name him Bonus," suggested Flashpan, "on account of he ain't no extra dividend." And as Bonus the raven was thereafter known. Not the least of his accomplishments was a remarkable gift for mimicry. Unfortunately that power was accurate but not discriminating. Rumor soon had it that Flashpan was cultivating its vocabulary, for presently the bird learned to repeat words better left unsaid. Thus another and highly vocal member was added to the fort's varied roster. . . .

Never a moment passed but what keen eyes were watching all the approaches to the fort. To this duty, Munro had assigned Kias and his savage warriors. Tokala attached himself to whichever group offered the greatest promise of excitement. At this moment he was a dark blot upon the south wall. With bow and short arrows in hand, the Fox lay bemused by the darkness, the huge stars aloft and the forest sounds rising up from the wilderness below the fort. The moon veiled by gathering clouds, illumined a patch of the river, which gleamed through a space between two trees. Upon this space Tokala's eager eyes were focused.

Quick to adapt himself to the life his ancestors had lived, Tokala listened to the stirrings of forest life. The sounds of daytime beasts were still, but nearby he heard the brittle rustling of a porcupine's quills as it foraged in the gloom.

Two wolves slunk past, hunting. Presently, where the wolves had passed, another shape took form against the patch of moonlight. It was entirely black, save for the phosphorescent eyes burning like candles in a dungeon. A panther prowled on past, the long tail twitching.

Ever deeper grew the stillness. Then slowly and with infinite stealth another something rose into view—a trimmed exploit-feather; in a moment more, a knot of hair, and then a human head. Stiff and rigid now, Tokala waited. A second head rose up beside the first. Tokala tossed a pebble toward the nearest sentry in the fort—who happened to be Kias. The boy directed his attention to the moonlit spot.

A moment Kias watched those silent heads. Then, "Go down," he whispered to Tokala. "Tell Swift-Hand. I will keep watch."

Climbing down the nearest ladder leading from the wall, Tokala burst round-eyed into the room which munro made his headquarters. Dan was there, and several red men too. Flashpan dozed on a robe in one corner. "Kias sent me!" said Tokala excitedly. "Indians—"

Munro waited for no more. To Tokala, "Wake the warriors!" he ordered quickly. "Warn them not to make a sound."

Flashpan came awake, still sleepy-eyed, to grasp the situation in a moment.

Munro uttered a few words of instructions to the Indians filing in at the door: "We will be attacked. Keep them off with arrows, if possible, and save your powder. If they get too close, open fire. Don't rouse the fort unnecessarily."

A moment later ten men mounted to the wall, scanning the ravines below and waiting for the moon to break through the clouds. Then at last the silver circle gave intermittent light.

Here and there a human form moved from place to place down on the slope, vague shadows skulking among other shadows, and visible only to the practiced eye. Just below him, Kias heard the rattle of a stone disturbed by human foot. Instant silence followed. Then came the hiss of a breath indrawn. A lean and sinewy figure paused below, almost within spear's length, to peer intently at the wall.

Slowly the savage raised himself. Lean, wiry fingers appeared atop the wall, testing each handhold as he came. His plume preceded his dark head above the topmost stone.

Then came a crushing impact. The wiry fingers loosened and slipped away. Without an uttered sound, the warrior fell, a tomahawk wedged deep in skull.

With a leap Kias was back at Tokala's side. There was a vibration of a bow-cord in the boy's ear. A shaft from Kias's string leaped out across the darkness. Of those two motionless heads first seen, one suddenly jerked up and back. A shadow-hand clutched wildly at the air. The head was gone, and the second vanished suddenly to one side. And then the hush was split by that fiercest of all fierce utterances from human throat—the Shoni war-cry.

No answer from the fort. With arrows waiting at the cords, the defenders bided their time. As that hideous sound died away, swift shadows appeared from where none had been seen. From every glade the warriors sprang upward.

As if to favor the defenders, the moon's floodlight came out, throwing the attackers into bolder relief. Down whizzed the waiting shafts. At the first barrage six warriors fell. Two others dragged themselves to cover in the shadows. Like wolves, the remainder came on, taking shelter wherever they found it.

Silence still from above, but the eyes of the fort watched them, and it was Flashpan who first descried a familiar form lurking in the background.

"Bucky Slemp, or I'm a Chinyman!"

"You're right," returned the scientist. "A devilish alliance *that* is!"

"Aye, sir—askin' Satan's pardon. Now how d'ye s'pose them sons o' sin all got together? There's Branner too, by gum—an' who's that other one?"

"A one-armed man," answered Dan, intently peering.

"Let me wing him in the other," begged Flashpan, advancing the barrel of his gun. "He's like a snake a-lurkin' thar and urgin' on the redskins!"

"Not yet, Flashpan!" admonished Munro sharply. "There's

more here than I understand. How did they get together with the Indians, and what are they after? If they learn we're armed, they'll stand off beyond our range, and pick us off from across the river. If they intend to attack again, let them come in close before firing. I don't relish bloodshed. But we're here, and here we stay. If they want to put us out, let them come and try!"

"Aye, by thunder!" answered Flashpan gleefully, "an' every mother's son as comes, we'll make him welcome!"

As he spoke, the bowstrings twanged again, two by two. But now the enemy, from shelter on the slope, were returning the shafts with interest. A number fell among the Indian women and children in the enclosure. Someone cried out in pain—a random shaft had hit home.

Other arrows played a *rat-a-tat* upon the wooden walls, quivering where they struck. Once again the Indians broke cover and came rushing up. But their rush was stopped in full swing by the keen swift flights of arrows from Kias and his warriors. A moment more saw the Indians retreating before the unexpected resistance from above. Arrows from within the fort whined after them.

One among the fort's warriors could not forbear an Indian's taunt, exposing himself the while in mockery upon the towering wall, a fair target for any waiting arrow from below. A sharp warning came from Munro—but too late.

There was a crisp and ringing report—a rifle shot. The taunting warrior jerked suddenly erect, his words snapped off half uttered. Then sprawling flat upon his face he fell, half on, half off the wall.

Kias and Dan were first to seize him, preventing his falling down among the Indian dead who strewed the slope. The warrior, limp and still, was carried from the wall. By the light of torches within the arms room Munro examined him while the roused fort-dwellers looked silently on. There was no pulse—the man was dead, shot through the body.

The first casualty in the fort, Sacowa was buried deep beneath the eastern wall. Less fortunate those Indian dead, lying along the slope! At dawn, with a rush of beating wings a great king-vulture came planing down. After it, one by one, the flock came following, darkening over the bodies, uttering hideous noises. Flock after flock of ravens fluttered heavily nearby, muttering raucously.

Isle Where Ravens Talk was well named for its carrion-birds. . . .

Day was well advanced before a sentry on the east wall

came to report scouts active in the forested cliffs across the river gorge a hundred yards away. Then a form appeared—a white man.

It was Slemp, gun in hand, who stood forth upon the cliff, eyeing with astonishment the outer walls of the fort, whose every feature he could see from that position. A hail came across the distance:

"Ahoy! You in the fort."

"What d'ye want, ye son of snake and swine?" came Flashpan's unmistakable cracked voice, defiantly.

"Every ounce of gold you've got, or we'll starve you all out!"

"I been thinkin' as much," muttered Flashpan to Munro who stood close by. "Shall we give it up, sir? Mebbe it'd do some good."

"I don't see how," returned the scientist. "I can't imagine Slemp honoring any kind of treaty. Tell him to go to the devil."

Flashpan smiled happily and conveyed the message, interlarded with a few sparkling additions of his own, concluding: "If ye want it, ye cross-bred penny-wit, come an' take it from us!"

"That we'll do!" roared the other, sending a bullet whining against the log head-cover from behind which Flashpan had answered. "You haven't heard the last of Bucky Slemp!"

"Nor you the last o' us," grumbled Flashpan, looking carefully to his guns.

Of smooth-bores they now had a round dozen, and some skill in the use thereof. In each embrasure a crude but serviceable cast-iron demi-cannon squatted in wooden trunnions, replacing the earlier falconets. Between each gun were piled a score of balls. Behind the walls, the falconets had been equipped with wheels made of round sections of logs, pierced for a wooden axle, and each of these could be trundled wherever most needed. And each was loaded with iron scraps and bits of slag, ready to greet the new attack—which swiftly came.

This time the advance of the enemy was better managed. The whites had so contrived that their red allies should bear the brunt of the fighting. Once more the Indians advanced in irregular order under cover of the ravines and undergrowth.

Crisply Munro passed the word among his waiting archers and riflemen: "When they break cover, give them the arrows.

Wait for my order to fire your guns. Don't waste a single shot."

With a rallying yell, the Indians swarmed from the thicketed glades and rushed the fort, pausing only to discharge their arrows upward. For a moment it must have seemed that the fort was abandoned, for no sound or answering yell issued from it. The attackers were almost at the walls before the fort's reply came—a singing feathered storm of well-aimed shafts.

Thinned but unchecked, Half-mouth's warriors came howling on, under the very walls of the fort, and into range of plunging fire from above. From the overhanging base of the parapet, through loopholes cut for that purpose, a dozen round-mouthed muzzles were suddenly protruded. Loudly from above came the echo of Munro's order:

"Fire!"

A withering blast of gunfire took the savages full in their faces, working deadly havoc. In the bedlam which ensued, the figure of Mad Crow, the renegade, was glimpsed darting to one side. The occupants could hear him cursing.

The savages were in retreat, striving to drag off their dead and wounded.

It was a fatal delay.

Upon the wall Flashpan was manning his gun, training it down upon them. He applied a light to the touch-hole. Came the flare of priming powder and then a blast that shook the fort. Six pounds of iron scrap slashed among the enemy, of whom scarce one escaped the hail of heated iron. None, indeed, were left to drag away the fallen.

There would be no further assaults upon the south wall. Instead there came a different kind of warfare. Hidden among the trees on the lip of the gorge opposite the fort, Slemp and his confederates began a sniping fire. All day long this continued at irregular intervals. But the log head-covers performed their function well. And no damage resulted to the defenders until a sentry standing somewhat back from the wall went limp and sank with a bullet through the head. A cry of triumph came from across the river.

No chance shot, that; for an hour later an ounce slug ripped into the breast of an Indian mother playing with her children in the central enclosure; she died within the hour. Yet again, near sundown, the unseen enemy scored. This time a ricocheting bullet lodged in the leg of an aged Indian. Attending the wounded man, Munro sent Tokala to fetch Flashpan. Probing for the bullet in the old man's limb, he spoke:

"Flashpan, that sniper must come down. It's up to you. Can you reach him with your smooth-bore?"

"If he's in sight, mebbe," answered the miner. "Leave it to me."

From a position at the east wall, Flashpan looked long and vainly for the hidden sniper. Finally he placed a small folded robe upon his head, and atop this his seaman's cap, fairly simulating a human head. Thus laden he strode quickly along the parapet.

His hope was realized. A sharp report rang out. The log head-cover rained splinters, and the cliff behind the fort threw back a flattened bullet. Lining up chip in cliff and notch in log, Flashpan peered long and intently across the chasm in the direction thus indicated. At last, on a line with notch and chip, he saw slight movement on a tree limb, and caught a glint of metal.

From his powder horn Flashpan poured an extra large charge, and pushed down a patch with particular care, before ramming down the copper bullet.

Resting the long barrel lightly upon the parapet he drew a careful bead upon the patch of deeper darkness in the tree across the gorge. Slowly he elevated the muzzle for the distance, aiming a little to the left, allowing for a light breeze that blew. Gently his crooked forefinger pressed against the bone trigger. Then:

Boom!

The smooth-bore's heavy report had not died when from the tree came a scream of pain and a clatter as the sniper's rifle fell. Followed a heavy noise of breaking branches as the sharpshooter too went crashing down. Sounds of excitement and human voices could be heard. Laying aside his gun, Flashpan jumped to the demi-cannon commanding the river. The larger piece roared.

The heavy ball hurtled nearly true, smashing through brush and undergrowth into the midst of the invisible enemy. As they scattered, the banging of the smooth-bores began, though to little effect at that range.

Thus, though they had lost three killed, the fort was still in strength, and all but impregnable to the assaults of the enemy. But counting on discouragement to dampen their ardor for further battle, Munro reckoned without Slemp's foxlike cunning.

XXX

Far to the west of Fort Talking Raven, before the tall painted tent of old Magpie, a great bear-skin hung stretched to dry upon a rack. Blanketed feathered figures stood wonderingly before this evidence of Black Shield's victory over the beast.

But near the lodge stood a silver-coated stallion, unridden for many a day; and the Indians before the lodge spoke in softened tones.

Kioga would have preferred to endure his hurts in solitude. But the penalty of fame is publicity, even among the people of the Tall Tents. Twenty medicine men, at one time or another, had come at the anxious Magpie's bidding, to exhort the evil spirits from her favorite.

Sudden silence greeted the appearance of the old matron-chief, who emerged from the lodge lean and gaunt after her long vigil over the wounded Black Shield. A small brown naked boy plucked at her deer-skin skirt, with a childish query that spoke the thought of all the older folk gathered nearby: "When will Black Shield ride again?"

"Tonight, perhaps, or on the morrow," answered Magpie with a tired but happy smile; and the faces of men and women lighted up.

But in the lodge of Wolf Jaw the news was received with ominous silence, for among the twenty who had sought to aid Kioga's cure was Many Hunts, whose piercing eye had fathomed Black Shield's true identity.

"You heard?" demanded Wolf Jaw fiercely of his assembled friends. "These many weeks I've called Black Shield impostor. Now Many Hunts confirms me—and was he not with our warriors at the battle of the Painted Cliffs, where the Shoni chief Kioga turned us back? Did he not look upon their blue-eyed chieftain? Who would better know than he that Kioga and Black Shield are one and the same?"

Meanwhile to Kioga came Me-kon-agi, ostensibly to smoke a friendly pipe, but in fact to warn his friend.

"Wolf Jaw and his fellows," he said hurriedly, "hold secret councils. Men come and go at every hour. They mean no good."

"Watch carefully," replied the Snow Hawk in an undertone. "And fear not: I am stronger than they think. I but pretend a weakness.... Magpie approaches. Go now, and be alert."

As the warrior took his leave, Magpie drew nearer, well pleased by Kioga's advanced recovery, to speak to him in softened mood. "The night is warm. Let us ride," said she; and willingly Kioga accompanied her out a way upon a high ridge commanding a view of the village.

It was dusk on the prairie, the hour of rest and ease. Close above the tents a hazy scarf of blue was hanging—smoke from within the lodges. As darkness fell, the skin tents glowed redly with the supper fires. The air was crystalline and wonderfully transparent. Arcturus shone down in blazing splendor. Sirius soon joined the watchfires of the immortals, green-white. Then out came Vega, diamond-blue and cold as ice, and Betelgeuse, orange with age and slow decline; then Capella—a liquid yellow pearl, and Aldebaran, glowing steadily like a blot of phosphor in the sky.

To their ears came the sad chanting of the Old Warriors Society, and the musical notes of heralds' voices rose and fell in regular rhythm as they moved among the lodges. At Kioga's side the gray stallion nuzzled his arm and sent forth a neigh, long-drawn and silver-noted, across the swelling prairie.

Magpie's talk was of matters closest to her heart, the welfare of her scattered tribes.

"I am the Magpie," she said in a hoarse and quivering tones; "I have gone to war, counted *coups*, taken scalps. But I am old. My bones grow heavy. My voice weakens, since some no longer listen, as of old. 'Tis time I named a chief to fill my place."

Foreseeing the trend her thoughts were taking, Kioga made as if to speak. She gestured him to silence, and continued:

"Among our people the woman owns the lodge and all within it. She owns the children, the tribal lands. Blood kinship is traced through her line, and she selects candidates for chiefs of clan and tribe."

Pausing a moment, she sat staring into the distance. Then again the hoarse monotone of her voice continued: "You are my only son. You are young, but you are wise, cunning as the wolf. You have been back with us but a few moons. Yet already your name is like a torch borne in the dark.... Respect to the aged—wait until I finish! I have named your name before the council. We shall see tomorrow night what comes of that! *Ehu*—now speak, for I have done!"

But Kioga was past speaking. Intending daily to clear himself, daily he had found himself deeper involved in his role of Black Shield. Because he had come to love and respect old Magpie that role had seemed all the more blameworthy. Yet he, who shrank from no pain inflicted on himself, drew back from giving pain to this lonely old matron who walked so proudly through life.

Constantly assuring himself that today would be the last of the imposture, each day had found him postponing revelation, until at last he had decided to carry it out to the end. He would perform such deeds as would wipe out what slight wrong existed in permitting this bereaved old mother to think him her son. But now—

The voice of Magpie recalled him:

"Say you nothing to this honor?"

"Mother Magpie," he answered solemnly, "this I say: Tomorrow morning you will do me honor. Tomorrow night you will stone me from your village."

In amazement she looked at him. Then her hearty laughter at what she took to be a joke carried back to the village.

For Kioga wielded, by tacit consent, a power second only to that of Magpie herself. Admitted to blood brotherhood in the war fraternities, he knew all their secrets. Never before had the fortunes of the Wa-Kanek run so high, nor the herds swelled to their present dimensions.

Where war and individual valor were the only sources of social standing, he had in a few moons risen to high place. And on the morrow, said Magpie, he would be nominated to succeed her. And yet he was not a happy man, for reasons which deprive many another of contentment; he could not foresee the future, nor forget the past.

How were the Shoni doing? What of Kias, the noble-hearted friend of other days? What of Heladi the beautiful, and Tokala, whom he had left in her care? What of James Munro, that guide and mentor of his days in civilization? But above all, what of Beth La Salle, memory of whom linked him to another way of life altogether? These were thoughts which had crowded one another during the long hours of his recovery, as now.

"*Ehu!*" said Magpie at long last. "A warrior thinks of someone far away."

Kioga started, as before when this keen old woman had seemed to read his very mind.

"Farther than the stars, oh Mother," he answered gravely.

"Go, then, and bring her here. I'll give my tent, my herds, and all I own to make her welcome."

"It cannot be," said Kioga quietly.

"Cannot? That from you, who slew Twenty Man and brought all our victories to the Wa-Kanek! Do I hear aright?"

"Some things may not be done, Mother. Man cannot shoot down the stars with his arrows, nor cast his noose about the sun."

"Is she then so out of reach?" wondered Magpie. Then, violently: "Bah! Take a hundred horsemen—take five hundred!—and go for her. If any stand in your way, strike them down. If even then she will not come, drag her by the hair, *ehu*! That's how I was won!"

Kioga could not forbear smiling at her vehemence, but—

"How bright the stars this night!" he answered evasively.

Magpie snorted, and grumbling, left him. A man must be a fool who dreamed of only one, when ten willing wives might be had to keep his lodge!

Kioga did not immediately follow, but rode farther out to water his horse along a wooded stream bank. Dismounting, he bent to cup a handful of liquid to his own lips. As he did so the image of a human head—not his own—appeared on the still moonlit pool below him.

Giving no sign that he observed, Kioga calculated the angles of reflection while drinking, and rose to remount. Directing his horse casually past the thicket which concealed a lurker, when near the spot he released the reins and dropped unexpectedly upon a hidden warrior.

Grunting in surprise, the Indian sought to strike with his knife. But in an instant Kioga's hand was at his throat, one knee at his breast, while he disarmed the stranger.

Recognizing him by headdress and face markings as a Shoni of the Tugari tribe, Kioga spoke in the man's own tongue.

"What seek you on Wa-Kanek hunting-grounds, Tugari?"

"Who are you who know my tribe and tongue?" gasped the other.

"Whom seek you?" repeated Kioga.

"I seek the Snow Hawk, rumored to be alive among the Wa-Kanek," answered the Shoni brave.

Kioga permitted him to glimpse his features in a better light. "Whose face is mine?"

The Indian started. "I would know you anywhere! Have you never heard men speak of Wehoka?"

"I recall you not, warrior," said Kioga slowly; "but no matter. How go things among the Shoni?"

"Ill—very ill," said Wehoka heavily. "The Long Knives have risen up again. White-skinned men have come among them."

It was Kioga's turn to start. "*White* men! Speak carefully, Wehoka. What manner of men be these?"

"White of skin and pale of eye—not unlike the Snow Hawk," answered Wehoka. "They dwell in a mighty place which they call 'fort'—and fight with weapons that blaze and thunder."

"By what names are they called?" demanded Kioga swiftly.

"One known as Swift-Hand leads them," said Wehoka. "And he sends the Snow Hawk this!"—drawing from his pouch a roll of birch-bark, with this note scrawled thereon:

To Kioga—(Lincoln Rand)

Dear Friend:
Rumor has it that you are still alive. This comes to you by Wehoka. There is no time to tell you all that has happened since you left America. We are among the Shoni. Dan and Beth La Salle are here. We are in desperate straits.

If this reaches you too late, you will find our last messages and keepsakes to you buried seventeen paces from the corner of the south wall. A notched log marks the place.

If you live and can aid us, use utmost caution in approaching. We are surrounded, cut off from our ship, and threatened momentarily by capture.

Wehoka has instructions to seek aid among the northern tribes, who are less influenced by the Long Knives. He can best tell you of his success or failure. We pray for the impossible in hoping this will reach you. Meanwhile we place our faith in God and the resources He has given us.

James Munro.

Momentarily staggered by this astounding news, Kioga swiftly gathered his wits. These tidings were almost unbelievable, and yet the note was undeniably authentic. Turning to Wehoka:

"What of the upper tribesmen—did you meet with them?"

"Yes. Two canoes wait my return at the three forks of the Hiwasi."

"It is good, Wehoka. I know the place well. Go as you came. Await me there and recruit others if more warriors may be found."

"*Ahi*!" said Wehoka eagerly. "Delay not. Time is short."

Parting without another word, the two went their opposite ways, Kioga mounting and spurring toward Magpie's village. To aid those in the fort, quick action was needed.

When still some distance from the village, he glimpsed a small fire in a hollow on the plain. An unusual number of shadows were grouped around it, but whether friends or foes, he could not tell.

Approaching stealthily, by the dim light he first descried the face of Wolf Jaw. Instantly suspicious, Kioga circled the hollow in search of the means to approach within hearing, which he found in the narrow ridge behind which the group were hidden from the village.

Writhing nearer, the Snow Hawk heard the harsh voice of Wolf Jaw. "Hitherto," Wolf Jaw was saying, "he has deceived us. But his hour is come. Who this Black Shield is you all now know. He is an impostor. Doubtless he slew Magpie's true son. And therefore I say he must die, and with him those who are close to him. And if it comes to that—if even old Magpie stands against us—" He left the sentence unfinished.

A hubbub of mingled protest and agreement rose; for Magpie was both loved and feared. At last, however, a young and fiery warrior, whose name was Falling Star, rose and spoke: "I too weary of the Magpie's counsel. What Wolf Jaw says is good for all the tribe, I think. If need be, I will take her life."

Listening, Kioga bethought himself of what he had so recently learned from Wehoka. Time was of the essence, no matter what he did. But to leave his friends unarmed against the secret plottings of Wolf Jaw was not to be considered.

Might not the fort already have fallen? Might not its inhabitants even now all be dead? The answers to these things were in doubt. But there was no doubt as to the fate of Magpie and Kioga's friends. At any moment Wolf Jaw might bare his tomahawks.... At once Kioga crawled back to his horse and rode straight to the village.

What immediate action Wolf Jaw may have intended was interrupted unwittingly by Magpie herself, who this night gave a great feast in honor of Kioga's recovery. Following the feast came a parade on horseback. The fires were fed with buffalo chips until they roared hotly. Prancing horses moved in and out among the tapering lodges, to the tune of singing and the heavy beat of thumping drums.

The eyes of old Magpie were on Kioga proudly. Bareheaded, astride the finest horse on all the Nato'wan plain, he rode as if sprung from his mount's own spine. Its tail and mane were hung with painted plumes; beneath its saddle of fine buffalo-hide trimmed with elk-skin was a back-protector of antelope, worked in multicolored horsehair designs; the rings and cinches were of polished copper; the stirrup leathers were draped with gleaming weasel-tails; even the breast-straps worked with rare silver proclaimed the high station of the rider.

Enviously, and with eyes gleaming in anticipation of Black Shield's downfall, Wolf Jaw looked on. By prearrangement he and his band but awaited the moment of Kioga's elevation to high chieftainship to strike the blow which would fell this upstart and all who supported him. . . .

When the parade had ended, came presentation of the symbol of high chieftainship—a certain medicine-shield noted as an heirloom, handed down from one generation to the next.

Forth from the lips of Gro-Gan' rolled the sonorous syllables of ancient Wa-Kanek, impressive as the Latin of the Roman Church.

"Oh Black Shield, I speak to your heart. Behold this shield of your forefathers. It hung before the lodge when you were born. It shaded your eyes when you grew in the cradle-board. And so with many chiefs before you. By the power of this shield you become the Keeper of the Herds, the First Hunter, Chief Over All Chiefs. So long as you hold to it, no harm will befall you. It is *wakan*—sacred, possessed of great power. Take it in your hands. Bring only honor to this ancient shield."

With affection and pride in his voice at being able thus to honor this friend of many battles and adventures, Gro-Gan' held forth the priceless heirloom. No slightest sound disturbed the council, save the rustle of rich robes and the click of bone ornaments.

Kioga turned to face the council. His face seemed oddly white beneath its summer bronze. He did not touch the extended shield, but answered Gro-Gan' thus:

"Not many moons ago I came among you, oh councillors. You accepted me as Black Shield, the son of Magpie. I shrank from telling Magpie that Black Shield was dead. I thought to replace him in her heart, and by my deeds rise to high place among you. But the office of hereditary chief is too great. I cannot take the sacred shield, for I have no Wa-Kanek blood. Nor am I Shoni, though I held high place among them. I am of another race, of white-skinned men, dwelling where the sun sleeps."

Completely dazed, the council stared at him. Not a muscle in the faces of all that circle moved, but amazement looked from every eye. In a deathly silence Kioga concluded:

"All that I possess belongs to Black Shield. My horses I give to Mother Magpie—long may she rule! My tent and all my robes and weapons I give to my loyal friends." One by one he removed his ceremonial ornaments, stripping down to waist-cloth, and piling all his vestments before him. "Thus I amend my offense to you who honored me. Black Shield is dead. He died a brave man, laughing at his pain. I who used his name was once your greatest enemy, known to the Shoni as Kioga the Snow Hawk, a chieftain. Now I reduce myself to nothing. I ask your forgiveness—and tonight I bid you farewell."

Pausing an instant before Magpie, Kioga searched her face. It remained expressionless, but haggard beyond words, the eyes tightly closed.

Disarmed by this unexpected stroke, Wolf Jaw and his cohorts sat gaping with the rest. But Kioga had not yet done with them.

"If my deeds be adjudged wrong," he continued, "what of those dozen men who came with hidden tomahawks to do murder at this council?"

At these words Wolf Jaw went white to the lips, and all his confederates with him, for well they knew themselves but a minority in this assemblage. Relentlessly Kioga went on:

"Rise, Wolf Jaw—and those twelve to either side of you. Rise and throw aside your robes, that all may see how you prepared to slay not only Black Shield, but Mother Magpie too. Rise up and show your teeth, wolves!"

A moment the accused chief sat stripped of poise and self-command, returning the Snow Hawk's gaze as a viper might return an eagle's. Already White Bear and other ranking chiefs were getting up, suspicious of treachery at what was to have been a peaceful celebration.

Even now the furor might have died, reparations been made, and the incident overlooked. But Falling Star, the firebrand among Wolf Jaw's followers, rose from where he sat near old Magpie and sprang toward her with brandishing tomahawk. In a moment the council was in an uproar, during which Wolf Jaw and his little band were swiftly overwhelmed and stripped of their arms. A hundred chiefs of every rank rallied round the sacred person of Magpie.

With satisfaction Kioga saw the enemy exposed beyond all further hope of injuring those attached to him. And amid the general confusion he disappeared.

XXXI

Immediately on quitting the council, Kioga turned his steps toward his own tent. The gray stallion, saddled and in full caparison, he led away by the rein, tying it before Magpie's lodge. Returning for his rope and weapons, he approached the village herd, roped out a horse and mounted. Uproar, he expected, must follow his revelation; he would depart before it had time to begin. Without a word to those who followed wherever he went, he rode off in an easterly direction, leaving the village behind.

For several hours he traveled at a rapid gait. A Wa-Kanek party passed him going in the opposite direction, but he carefully circled to avoid the meeting. Echoes of the Brave Heart Song came to him from the traveling band. He listened for the familiar words:

>Moon-Woman shuts her sleepy eyes....
>>*Hai-yeh' ho! Hai-yeh-ho!*
>
>We'll take the foeman by surprise....
>>*Hai-yeh' ho! Hai-yeh-ho!*
>
>The time is come; we steal away....
>>*Hai-yeh' ho! Hai-yeh-ho!*
>
>To raid their tents at break of day....
>>*Hai-yeh' ho! Hai-yeh-ho!*
>
>And carry many shields away....
>>*Hoh! Hoh! Hoh! Hai-yeh-eho!*

The sound of the chanting died away far back upon the plains. How things had changed since these warriors had gone forth at his bidding! Swiftly Kioga continued on his way, and finally after many hours he arrived where begin the mountains which gird the Shoni realm.

Removing the fine saddle, he gave the horse its liberty. He hid the saddle in a deep unoccupied cavern, rolled a great stone across the entrance, and began the climb which would carry him across the mountain divide separating the domains of plainsmen and forest-dwellers.

Topping this divide at last, he found himself looking down upon that vast mountainous area north of the Shoni strongholds. Below him was home, the forest, the mountains he loved. He drew in an exultant breath.

But behind him, far out across the plains, old Magpie stood before her tent. The silver stallion was tied to the door-flap. All its caparison gleamed in the firelight. Across its back the leathern stirrups were tied, and at the saddle-horn hung three broken arrows in token of Kioga's farewell. Nearby stood Me-kon-agi, Gro-Gan', and all the chiefs and great warriors of the tribe the Magpie ruled.

And as she stood quivering, unable to speak, men turned away. For such a thing had only once been seen before—when she thought her son had returned from captivity: Two great tears rolled silently down her wrinkled cheeks....

High in a rocky aerie Kioga slept an hour; and in the morning he knew again the touch of cool leaves parting to admit him into the green chambers of the damp pine-scented forest. Traveling almost continuously, snatching only a little sleep now and then, the Snow Hawk came at last to a familiar scene—the torn area marking the landslide which had so nearly carried him to his death. And skirting the rubble at its lower end, he came unexpectedly upon a curious structure made of stones, the work of human hands. At its top two hawks had built a nest, and defied him to draw nearer.

Wondering what had inspired the erection of such a monument, he scanned it intently, and came to a wooden slab bearing this inscription burned into it:

> RAISED TO THE MEMORY OF KIOGA
> CHIEF OF ALL THE SHONI TRIBES
> WHO PERISHED IN THE LANDSLIDE
> FROM WHICH THESE STONES ARE TAKEN
> ERECTED BY THOSE WHO SOUGHT HIM
> LONG AND FAITHFULLY
> *Rest in Peace*

Recent lightning had struck the rock-pile, obliterating the names of all who had subscribed to the memorial save that of James Munro, which appeared in a lower corner of the slab. . . .

Far up the mountainside a storm gathered. Lightning licked from cloud to earth. Weary with long and restless travel, and conscious of the drafts the morrow would make upon his strength, Kioga turned westward toward his old cave. There he would sleep out the storm.

Climbing the steep trail, he pushed in the door, entered, and kindling a blaze with his fire-bow, made a light. Glancing about him, something lying on the little shelf caught his attention—a finger-ring of gold, through which was thrust a little cylinder of birchbark. With narrowing eyes he drew forth the curl of bark, smoothed it, held it to the light, and read:

> *I came all the way from America, with Dan and James Munro, to tell you what I should have said before, had you not left us so suddenly. Since fate willed I should never see you again alive, I take this means of telling you, instead. I have loved you from the first, and will to the end. I leave this note and this ring. Though you will never read the one nor wear the other, it will always comfort me to know that you would find them here if you could only return. —Beth*

Dazzled by the message contained in that note, Kioga's weariness vanished. From that moment rest and shelter ceased to exist for him. Rushing quickly but methodically from place to place, he took up a short but deadly bow, a quiver of arrows, and belted on a knife. Then he plunged forth into the storm.

Where every other living thing had denned up for the duration of the downpour, the Snow Hawk fled through the forest with the speed and directness of the bird for which he was named. His way was often illumined by the lightning, but at other times he threaded the trackless mazes of the forest by instinct alone, speeding toward the river rendezvous with Wehoka and his canoe-men. . . . Morning and storm's end found him still traveling, tireless as a steel automaton.

It was now that season of the polar year when the daylight wanes, giving way to the enduring gloom of Arctic winter. The forest depths were hung with velvet robes of darkness, yet along the river on whose banks Kioga moved there was light enough to see by for a few hours daily. Pausing at dusk to sate his hunger with late juicy berries growing along the stream, he suddenly caught the telltale purl of water at the prow of a moving canoe. Lying silent beneath the thorny foliage, he heard voices and sought to identify one of several as that of Wehoka, Munro's messenger.

And as he crouched listening, something long and coiling came to life beside his arm. A gleaming triangular head reared slowly up, forked tongue darting in and out. Glistening lights reflected from the scaly geometric markings on a snake's lean back. Not ten inches from Kioga's eyes the cowled reptile fixed them with its own lidless terrible stare. The flicker of an eyelash, an exhaled breath, would draw an instant poison-stroke.

But Kioga neither blinked nor breathed. Like a creature without nerves he lay utterly still, both watching the snake and listening for the Indians' voices. Presently the reptile lowered its hideous head and gliding slowly across Kioga's outstretched arm, flowed off into the thickets. And in another moment he heard the unmistakable voice of Wehoka. Rising quietly to his full stature, with upraised hands, he said:

"Peace to you warriors!"

Unluckily, he had not counted upon the alarm into which his sudden appearance would throw men so keyed up with excitement. Hardly had the words left his lips, when two spears and a heavy club flew at him.

Nothing could better have conveyed the sanguinary spirit of those times. Men struck first and parleyed later—if possible. And when the Indians realized their mistake, the damage was done. Their spears had passed harmlessly into the bank. But the club had struck more nearly true. As they came upon him Kioga lay felled by the flying missile.

"We have killed him!" declared Wehoka, looking upon the fallen Snow Hawk.

"Not so easily," came a voice as Kioga slowly sat up to look around him. Quick hands would have raised him, but the Snow Hawk rose unaided, scorning assistance.

"I have been long coming. It may be that we are too late. But dip blades, warriors! Let us be on our way!"

In an instant, propelled by sinewy hands, the longboat leaped downstream.

XXXII

At Fort Talking Raven, matters had reached a critical stage. Ever closer shrank the ring of Half-mouth's warriors. Ever more fraught with peril were the hunters' forays into the surrounding wilderness in search of game to feed those hungry mouths within the overcrowded fort. The hidden canoes, which Munro's warriors had been wont to use in obtaining fresh supplies of iron sand, crude sulfur, and saltpeter, had been discovered and captured by the enemy.

Yet the fort still managed to maintain the appearance that all was well.

In the arms room a strange array of weapons had taken form. There were short thrusting spears, and long lances for manning the walls, and loose-coupled military flails hastily designed for use in the event the enemy again attempted to storm the fort. But as yet the defenses remained impregnable to all assault from without.

No small part of Munro's time was taken up in caring for his wounded. In came Eccowa, having successfully run the gauntlet of lurking savages in his trip from the *Narwhal* to the fort with messages. Half his scalp hanging down upon one shoulder evidenced his close passage with the knives of the foe. A dexterous flip, a score of stitches using deer-gut to close the wound—and Eccowa was pleading to be sent with further communications.

Kias himself, hunting in the forest nearby, came fainting into the fort, mauled by a snow-leopard before its den of young. The wounds were gashed, given a liberal sprinkle of permanganate in the incisions and fang punctures. An hour later Kias was standing guard again at the north wall.

And this entry from Munro's diary of those dark days:

> *Brave fellows, these savage stoics! Yesterday Cimita came in, his hand a mass of lacerated tissue. Wolf-bite. Beast killed by companions. Would gangrenous overnight. Amputated above wrist, stump cauterized in*

boiling deer-fat. Healing satisfactorily. Cimita went unconscious with pain. First question on regaining senses: "How will I shoot my bow?" Hansen our carpenter is making him a wooden hand.

Thus Munro's heroic surgery, aided by the unflinching stoicism of his patients, saved many who otherwise must have joined those buried beside the east wall, each with a terse epitaph burned into a peeled wall-log above his grave.

Meanwhile came word from Barry Edwards that on board the *Narwhal* repairs had been effected. Unfortunately, fire had broken out in the galley and eaten through a sail-locker, destroying most of their spare canvas. But fresh sails had been made by Kamotok of the dried intestines of whatever deer or sea lions they killed in the ship's vicinity.

The falconet sent from the fort had been mounted near the forecastle hatch; and a cradle was already constructed aft to receive the larger cannon Munro had promised to send later in the week. All powder and ball previously sent was safely stored on board.

Everything, indeed, was well on board the *Narwhal*; but at Fort Talking Raven, several odd happenings gave Munro cause for troubled thought. The first was the interception of several additional new-made smooth-bores intended for the *Narwhal*. These, along with a large supply of gunpowder, were seized by Half-mouth's warriors almost within view of the fort walls. Half of Munro's men bearing these supplies for the ship did not return.

An hour or two later fire broke out in the east tower, and was extinguished at a price of almost their entire water supply. And thus far none of their borings had tapped another source of supply.

Dozing on his rifle one night, Flashpan was suddenly awakened by a jerk upon his moustache, and a nervous little simian hand tugging persistently at one ear.

"*Dang* ye, monk—that whisker ain't no bell-rope!" he muttered irritably; but on feeling the tremble of the little body on his shoulder, peered squinting intently out into the dark. "Hist—what was that? Oh, bah! Ye've got me nervous, Placer. Owls, ye little coward, owls—hootin' like goblins, back an' forth. A fine sojer y'are, Placer—a fine soj—"

Once again Flashpan went silent, listening. From the darkness came a sound, faint but unmistakable, of several rolling pebbles. "A better sojer than me," amended the miner very softly. "Suthin's a-prowlin' out thar—bigger'n an owl.

But whut—er who?" Flashpan fastened his gaze upon the blackness. Then urgently: "Oho! Injins, b'gum. An' I cain't leave me post. But you can. Go git that leetle Injin pal of yours, Tokola—git Tokala, monk! Bring 'im here quick!"

A moment Placer hovered hesitant; next he turned a doubtful cartwheel in the darkness; then suddenly he vanished like a dark flash, swinging down the inner wall and galloping back to where Tokala slept beside his leather water bucket. A moment later the boy, wide-awake and led by the monkey, appeared stealthily at Flashpan's side.

"Son," whispered the miner swiftly, "bad bizness is in the wind. Injins—sneakin' up toward the spring. I had it covered with the falconet. But the powder's soaked. Somebody poured water into it—an' she won't shoot. Go wake Doc Munro an' Kias an' Dan; tell 'em—*quick*—whiles I git this gun in workin' order."

Without a word Tokala vanished.... Flashpan heard the sound of guarded movements back within the fort. A few moments later three dusky shadows slipped out in the shelter of the inner wall. They were Dan La Salle, Kias the Shoni, and Tengma, his foremost warrior. Armed with pistols, tomahawks, and a smooth-bore apiece, they crept toward the spring, concealed by the log sluice. Unnoticed, behind these three came another slower shadow—old Menewa, gripping a tomahawk and eager to aid in the defense of the fort which sheltered his daughter Heladi and others of his friends and loved ones.

Flashpan, meanwhile, worked frantically to empty and reload his falconet.

Menewa had not yet reached the spring when the first of the invaders climbed up the opposite side of the ridge, closely followed by seven others. Straight into their faces Dan and his two Indians fired their pieces, flinging aside the smooth-bores to blaze away with their several single-shot pistols, before using their clubs and tomahawks. Surprised in their attempt to divert the spring, the savages faltered, but only momentarily. Though five had fallen at the volleys of the defenders, as many now replaced them. There in the moonlight, in full view of all those in the fort, a fierce fight raged, hand-to-hand.

From above Beth and Heladi were watching the struggle with dilated eyes. Suddenly the Indian girl uttered a sharp cry. Brave old Menewa had appeared suddenly to reinforce Dan and his men, swinging right forcefully with his long spiked club. But in his eagerness the old man overreached, stumbled on the precarious footing, and went down. Simultaneously a hostile warrior rose beside him, aiming a smashing blow at his skull.

Using his gun as a club, Dan threw himself upon the enemy—struck, missed, and went down before the blow intended for Menewa. But in falling he bore the savage also to his knees, and as his last conscious act drove his fist wrist-deep into the Indian's stomach. That, curiously, was the blow which ended the battle of the spring. The hostiles, having failed in their surprise, gave over the attack and retreated. And as Kias and his warriors retired, bearing Dan between them and with Menewa following, Flashpan let go with his reloaded falconet, throwing a shot among the raiders. There after the guns were booming again, hastening the departure of the enemy.

Sick with fear, Beth saw Dan brought in, covered with blood. Kneeling at his side, Munro examined the great swelling where the club had struck, touched pulse and heart, and reassured her.

"Hard hit, and no mistake. But with care he'll be all right. Keep cold packs on that swelling."

And so it happened that, groping his way out of the unconscious state, Dan La Salle found slim brown fingers moving gently over the bandage round his head, which was pillowed in Heladi's lap. With wonder he saw that her cheeks were wet as she bent above him, and at that his heart gave a mighty bound. For never until now had she given any sign of returning his love.

Feeling him stir, she raised his head against her breast, with some little murmur of endearment. Observing them, Menewa and Beth exchanged smiles. Beth's was crooked and quickly gone. Heladi and Dan had each other; but who was there who could ever occupy the place left vacant in her own heart and life?

Until now the perils of their situation had forced other matters into the background of her mind, and better so; for in some measure she had reconciled herself to Kioga's passing. But the growing attachment between Dan and Heladi opened the old wound. Heavy of heart she turned away and went toward where the fort's injured were sheltered, that she might forget her grief in allaying the pain of others....

Although the spring was preserved, a question still remained: How were the enemy learning of their plans, and of conditions at the fort? Surely not from outside. More probably from within.

Just after dawn the following morning, the boom of a cannon came from the cliff across the river. Almost simultaneously a ball screamed into the fort, struck the wall, rebounded—fortunately injuring no one.

How had the enemy obtained that weapon? The question was soon answered, in part; for a hurried checkup showed that one of the falconets and a quantity of powder and balls were missing.

All that day Flashpan estimated ranges and gave shot for shot in an attempt to destroy the enemy battery. His efforts were useless. Slemp altered his position after each shot. The quarters for women and children had thereafter to be kept closed, lest some wanderer be struck by this new menace.

More of the traitor's work was now discovered. When Flashpan went to the powder room that night, the door was ajar. Instantly alert, the miner drew his pistol, entered cautiously, and discovered that of all their powder supply, scarce enough remained for twenty demi-cannon rounds. And several smooth-bores had also vanished from the gun room.

Running upon the rampart to inform Munro of this misfortune, he found the scientist and Kias intent upon something near the west wall.

"Your eyes are sharp, Flashpan," said Munro. "What do you make of that spark up at the spring?"

The miner turned his eyes upon it. For a moment he too was puzzled by a tiny speck of light, moving like a firefly toward the source of their water. In an instant realization flashed upon them.

"A fuse!" cried Munro.

"Aye!" roared Flashpan. "And half our powder's been sneaked out!"

Munro face paled at information which gave that spark a suddenly terrible meaning.

"Flashpan, they've planted a charge at the spring! If it explodes, we're without water."

"Leave it to me, sir," began Flashpan with his customary readiness to assume any responsibility. His voice was drowned in a terrific detonation at the spring. A great ledge of rock slipped into the fort, showering earth and stones down on the enclosures. The primitive sluiceways which conveyed water into the main storage vessels did not fall. But the flow of fluid through them ceased; the spring was destroyed, the fort waterless, save for what rain-water might be caught.

A desperate council was in discussion of plans to ferret out the traitor, when there came a muffled explosion. The heavy door of the arms room burst out, torn from its hinges. A billow of smoke rolled over a dead body blackened by powder burns. Flashpan's search was ended before it had well begun. Eccowa lay dead, a coil of barken fuse still clutched tightly in one hand. The traitor was exposed at last; and the eye of the enemy, within the fort, was shut. . . .

Across the gorge, however, separating fort from riverbank, a gnawing fire had long burned against the bole of a certain immense tree rooted near the cliff's edge and slanting precariously outward over the river.

Hour by hour the burn, fed and tended faithfully by Branner, Slemp's confederate, cut deeper through the mighty trunk. At last Slemp ordered the fire extinguished, waiting on a coming storm. Glancing across the river he rubbed his hands gleefully.

"Let 'em guard the front door," he muttered. "We'll enter by the servants' entrance, and serve up somethin' they ain't expectin'."

The storm struck swiftly, a typical sudden uprising of the elements, accompanied by great resounding thunder-bursts and knives of gleaming lightning stabbing through the darkness. A wall of wind advanced toward the fort, bending the mighty forest trees like weed-stalks.

Clutching an out-jutting ledge with both hands, Slemp watched the weakened tree trunk intently, wiping rain from his eyes. As the wind pushed, it leaned far out across the stream. Then with a snapping, splintering sound the trunk and roots gave way; a second later the distant crown crashed down on a ledge of rock across the stream on the island. The moat about the fort was bridged.

Within Fort Talking Raven all were busy, filling skins with rain-water; and amid the uproar of the elements the rash of the tree bridging the river passed almost unnoticed. Somewhere near another forest giant had fallen—that was all.

But that was not all. Halfway across the fallen bole, sixty warriors were coming cautiously, armed to the teeth. Nearing the fort, they were covered by heavy foliage of the great tree's crown. Thus a large force of the enemy had made the crossing before a yell from Kias warned the fort. Discovered, the Long Knives raised their fearful war-whoop, throwing the fort into a confusion of women and children running for shelter in the rooms below the walls, and warriors rushing to their arms.

Emerging startled from the hospital room, Munro looked on a sight that chilled his heart. Swarming into the fort from that seemingly unscalable river-side wall, came Half-mouth's savages.

Dismay—that terrible heart-sinking of one who knows not how he has been outmaneuvered—clutched at Munro momentarily. Massacre was within his walls.

But at sight of what transpired Munro's old self-command returned. They were surprised, but far from beaten. From the south parapet his sentries poured in a galling fire upon the storming savages, dropping the entire front rank in their tracks. An instant later Kias and his warriors suddenly appeared, charging down upon the intruders and meeting them with their own kind of weapons. Fierce and sudden as was the attack, the resistance was even more fierce and more savage. From the towers the smooth-bores spat smoke flame, and hot lead, doing dreadful execution at that range. On the south wall Flashpan trundled around his falconet. Aiming just above the opposite wall, he touched off a blast, and cleared it of every enemy with one rattling slash of iron slugs.

Otowa, one of Kias's warriors, leaped for another falconet, swung it round and trained it on the Long Knives and pulled the cord. Probably, however, the ball had rolled toward the muzzle, owing to the pitch of the slanting barrel; at any rate, the gun burst with a terrible crash, killing Otowa with its flying fragments. This was their last casualty of the fight. For the ferocity and desperation of the defenders, coupled with the power of their smooth-bores, proved too much for the invaders, who scattered and quit the fort as they had entered, leaving behind their dead.

In the growing light of morning the bridge was clearly seen spanning the river; and at its far end Slemp had thrown up a breastwork of rubble and earth, commanding a view of the fort from the shelter of the immense stump.

Dan and Hansen, equipped with iron axes, slipped forth under cover of the trunk and fell to chopping, in an attempt to loosen the bridge and cause it to fall. But it was a futile effort, productive of small result. The iron-hard wood of the tree dulled their inferior tools. And a charge of precious gunpowder, touched off during the following night, did little more than settle the crown of the tree more securely upon the wall, while decreasing the already scanty supply of powder.

Flashpan next attempted to cut through the great trunk by bombarding it with his demi-cannon, but since the balls must be hurled aslant the fallen trunk, the damage was negligible, nor could the missiles do more than graze the enemy earthwork hidden behind it. After several further attempts-Flashpan desisted.

Long since, Munro had shipped his accumulated treasure of robes and skins and scientific finds to the *Narwhal*. Last to go were his camera and carefully preserved films, and one cannon, their smallest.

The night after the latest skirmish with the enemy brought final word from the *Narwhal*. Three of Kias's most trusted Indians returned from the ship by trail and canoe, bringing with them one whose coming brought especial joy to Flashpan and his monkey. Placer was first to detect the presence of Nugget, the miner's faithful dog, and he rode his old friend madly about the walls while all the fort laughed at their antics.

Though the forest runners had pierced the warrior-cordon in the short period of laxity following the repulse of the red raiders, the Long Knives quickly renewed their vigilance. Open to momentary attack, it was now clear that lacking ammunition and water, and unable to procure food, the fort could not much longer hold out against the besiegers.

And at this desperate eleventh hour, Munro sent out his last messenger to the ship. Unwilling to risk losing Kias, he chose instead Chacma, a lean and taciturn Wacipi warrior, true as steel, and penciled this note for the little crew on his hidden ship:

My dear Barry:

Your messages arrived and glad to learn that all is well with you. With us things are critical. The fort is now cut off. If this message reaches you, it will be a miracle. We can't hold out much longer. I tremble for Miss La Salle and our women and children if the savages attack us again in this condition.

If you do not hear from us within ten days, this will be your authority to set sail, and return, if possible, to America. A chart of the shoals and reefs is in my cabin. It would be useless for you to attempt to come to our aid. A few days will see our finish, barring aid from the Almighty Himself. We are saving our last bullets for each other.

We all send our best wishes.

Munro.

Bearing this message, Chacma departed secretly from the fort. But just before he had left, as it happened, scouts brought to Slemp and his white renegades information they had long awaited: The berth of the *Narwhal* had at last been discovered.

Knowing that the ship might change her location, but that the fort must remain until they returned, the renegade whites set off for the coast, leaving the Indians under Half-mouth to maintain the siege. It was their intention to take possession of the *Narwhal* against the nearing hour when the fort must fall; having obtained Flashpan's treasure for themselves, they would then leave the fort and its gallant defenders to the tender mercies of their Indian allies.

So it came about that just as Chacma was drawing forth a dugout from its place of concealment in an under-shore cavern, the longboat bearing Slemp and his men swept suddenly into view, propelled by several muscular paint-streaked savages—Long Knives, by the paint markings on faces and breasts.

Slemp leveled his gun and spoke:

"Halt, you! Stand where you are!"

Wheeling, Chacma found several guns trained upon his heart. Recent experience had taught him their killing power. In no doubt as to what would reward disobedience, and knowing how much depended upon his arrival at the *Narwhal* with that message in his pouch, brave Chacma nevertheless sought to escape into the shore brush.

Slemp's gun cracked; Chacma fell face forward into the underbrush as the canoe came upon him, bleeding from the head and by every evidence already a corpse. From his waist Slemp plundered the pouch. And presently he turned triumphantly to his companions, flourishing Munro's message.

"We've got 'em smartin' in the fort," he declared with gleaming eyes. "An' here's our passport onto the *Narwhal*. We'll take the ship first thing we do, and then come back and take the fort. Our luck is changed, boys!"

Attracted by sound of the shot, and flattened close against a cliff a hundred feet above, a narrow-eyed witness to the death of Chacma looked down upon the scene and sought vainly to overhear what the white men were saying. Now as the swift canoe forged downstream out of sight, that lurking shadow dropped to the river beside the fallen Indian and sought for signs of life.

Irked by the comparatively slow progress of the Shoni canoes, Kioga had hours since taken to the river overhang for several miles; whereafter by a short route which avoided the longer windings of the river, he came upon the scene of

Chacma's downfall. Despite the appearance of death, the Indian still lived. Cold water at lips and temples revived him enough haltingly to answer the few questions Kioga put to him. Presently he could speak no more, and in a few minutes expired. And though Kioga had learned much, there were certain facts he had not uncovered. Chacma had not told whither he had been going when attacked; nor did the Indian live long enough to realize that he had been robbed of his message to the *Narwhal*. Had Kioga learned the contents of that note and the intentions of the renegade whites, matters would have gone altogether differently.

As it was, Kioga put aside all thought of pursuing the canoe bearing the whites, and turned back to intercept his Shoni warriors.

Slemp's canoe proceeded swiftly in the opposite direction as far as river travel permitted. The mixed party then set forth overland through the forest, and came finally to the sea-cliffs. Down the narrow paths they filed, guided by their scout who had located the *Narwhal*; soon they found themselves above the well-camouflaged cove in which, until a few days ago, the ship had remained successfully hidden. And dispatching a Long Knife warrior in place of Chacma to the ship with Munro's written message, Slemp concealed himself with his band a short distance along the shore.

On board the *Narwhal* young Edwards, assistant to Dr. Munro on many previous scientific enterprises, saw the arrival of a messenger, with mixed pleasure and apprehension. Insufficiently versed in the marks of clan and tribe to be able to pierce the impostor's identity, he received the silent savage with a show of welcome and the gift of a trinket.

After having read Munro's tragic message, he could think of little else, in his preoccupation with ways and means of aiding those in the fort. Besides himself, only Edson the mate and Kamotok the Eskimo were on board the *Narwhal*. Indeed, it was Kamotok who unwittingly had betrayed the ship to the enemy, for the barking of one of the dogs, brought on deck for exercise, had attracted attention in the forest.

Rereading the note, Edwards laid its contents before the others. "We can follow orders, or we can go to their aid," he said tersely. "Which will it be?"

For answer Kamotok took down from the cabin wall his favorite harpoon, and tried its edge on his thumb suggestively.

"You're my superior, Mr. Edwards," said Edson quietly, "and I'm here to take your orders. But not if you order me to sail and leave them starving in the fort."

"If the three of us go," said Edwards, as though to himself, "it will mean leaving the ship alone."

"Ship or no ship," returned Edson, "I'd rather pass out trying to help 'em than tell the world we don't know how they died. This fellow"—indicating the watchful savage—"can take us to the fort. And to make sure of him, Kamotok can keep his harpoon handy. But I'm speaking out of turn, sir. You didn't ask me."

"Edson," said Barry Edwards softly but fervently, "you're a brick."

In sign-talk Munro's young scientific collaborator then made clear to the Indian their desire to be conducted back to the fort. The savage nodded understanding. Arming themselves and taking along as large a supply of food as they could carry, the three men quitted the ship to carry aid to the unfortunate occupants of Fort Talking Raven—led by Slemp's own warrior!

They had scarcely vanished inland before Slemp and his men drew near the ship and stealthily boarded her by way of her rope ladders stretched from rocks to deck. At high tide they cast off her lines and warped her slowly out of the cove which had been her station for many months. By means of her engine they turned north a little distance and dropped anchor. Assuring themselves that the ship was well provisioned and equipped with small arms, powder, and shot for the little homemade cannon mounted fore and aft, they left her under guard and set out toward the fort. Its inevitable downfall accomplished, its gold once seized and brought hither, they need worry no longer about an avenue of escape out to sea and back to civilization.

XXXIII

A sudden attack upon Fort Talking Raven by Half-mouth's savages, persisted in to the bitter end, might this day have carried the stronghold. But long impatient with a method of warfare which had cost him many warriors and his white confederates nothing, in the absence of his pale-face allies, Shingas played a waiting game for a time.

Hourly the savory smells of meat, roasting in the hidden bivouacs of the enemy, drifted up to the fort, multiplying the hunger of its inmates. The last of the collected water was exhausted, with little prospect of rain to replenish it. Their rations had reached the vanishing point. Yet no one complained. All went about their duties silently.

Of those who had gone forth to pierce the enemy line, none had yet come back. Finally Kias, twice scouting out alone, returned. "In numbers they are like the pine needles. They watch night and day," was his report before the tense little circle of the defenders. "No man may pass through."

The words fell like sentence of death upon the ears of all within those battered walls—all save one, small and unnoticed, intently listening on the fringe of the council circle.

With quickening heart Tokala repeated the words through silent lips. From face to face his sharp eyes flew. The confident smiles of yesterday were gone. On each was graved the lines of care and of near-despair. Even Flashpan worried fiercely at his straggly moustache; and at his side, as if to set the final seal of calamity upon the fort, crouched Placer the irrepressible—now the picture of simian dejection.

Day by day Tokala had listened at the councils of his elders. The rumor that Kioga still lived had set his heart on fire. The leaving of Wehoka on his search had thrilled him to the core. What if his elders now discredited the report—Tokala had a faith that knew no obstacles! To him the Snow Hawk was immortal.

"*No man may pass.*" Again the words echoed in his ears. And then Tokala's eyes came suddenly alight, like windfanned coals. In an instant the great idea sprang full-born into being. "If not a man, mayhap a fox might pass!"

On the very verge of blurting out his thoughts, Tokala bit his tongue to stop the words. These about him were full-grown men; and he, the Fox, was nothing but a boy—good enough to swab the muzzle of a gun, perhaps, but in times of danger cooped up in the redoubt with the women. If they divined what he contemplated, it would surely be forbidden.

He stole to the wall and climbed rapidly the ladder near the south tower. Peering over the inner rail, he took a last look. As before, the circle of men sat grim-faced about the fire. Tokala turned away.

Near the tower was kept a length of rope from the *Nar-*

whal. Groping in the dark, he found an end, made it fast to the nearest cannon, and tossed the strand over the wall. Quietly he slid down to the outer ground, paused to listen for any sound to indicate discovery from within or without the walls. There was none. With every nerve keyed to highest tension, he slipped into the nearest thicket.

Not a hundred feet from the walls he came upon the first evidences of the enemy—the glow of small camp-fires, hooded from view of the fort and closely spaced. One by one of these he crept past in the gloom, seeking an avenue through which he might slip. In circling he came at last to the river Hiwasi. Here too the Long Knives were waiting in numbers. But cunning and sly deceit might yet prevail. Not for nothing was Tokala named the Fox! Boldly he stepped forward into the fire's light, tomahawk in hand.

As one man, the squatting warriors sprang quickly to their feet, ere relaxing on perceiving that a mere boy stood there. One of their number seized him roughly by the arm, demanding fiercely: "What do you here?"

"I am from Hopeka," quoth Tokala defiantly, writhing in the warrior's grasp. "I would fight the enemy." A general laugh arose as Tokala brandished his weapon.

The brave who held him turned grinning to the others. "Shall we admit him to our band—what think you, warriors?"

"*Ahau!*" came an answer. "Let him stay. We may grow hungry. Little boys are sweet and tender."

"How will you be eaten," asked the first warrior sternly of Tokala, "—roasted or boiled?"

"Raw—if first I take an enemy scalp," answered Tokala swiftly; whereat another laugh rewarded his daring.

"He is too small to take a life," said a third savage. "What use will he be to us—if we do not eat him?"

"I will sharpen your knives and clean your guns," said Tokala, gaining confidence momentarily. "I will watch while you sleep."

"*Ho!*" answered the first speaker. "Wisdom from the lips of childhood! Better in the camp than in the belly." Laughing at this crude sally, the warrior gave Tokala a fat deer leg-bone to gnaw on. "When you have done with that, act as you talk. And see to our knives as well. White men's scalps are tough."

Tokala did as he was bidden, assiduously whetting away at arrow-points and knife-blades with a flat stone. Presently a warrior lay back and dozed. Others followed suit until but two sat up, awake.

"I weary of this kind of fighting," said one at last. "I too will sleep. Keep watch, oh Crooked Nose!" And with that he too lay back.

Minutes passed, the silence broken only by the monotonous scraping of Tokala's stone. For a time Crooked Nose watched, gaping and stretching to keep awake. Glancing at the other sleepers, he took from the fire a lighted stick six inches long. Removing a moccasin, he placed the stick between great and second toe. Closing his eyes, he nodded the little time it took for the stick to burn short and wake him. A glance around showed Tokala still at work. No one could take them by surprise. Taking up a longer stick, the sentry repeated the trick and composed himself again.

This time Tokala's eyes were on him keenly. Softly he crept near and gently moved the fire-stick. Crooked Nose stirred. Tokala drew back, not again to touch the stick. Instead he threw a handful of damp earth upon it, quenching the little flame.

Watching the man a moment, Tokala crept back to his little heap of weapons. Glancing round, he saw that none were awake. Now from the guns he shook the priming powder, replacing it with earth; and from each arrow quickly stripped the guiding feathers. A last pistol remained of the few firearms the little band had acquired from the fort itself. Looking to flint and steel as Flashpan had taught him, Tokala thrust it through his belt. The fire flickered and dimmed as the warriors slept. When it brightened again, Tokala's place was vacant.

Along the banks of the Hiwasi, Tokala crept north away from the immediate area of hostilities. The forest animals, which had quitted that noisome vicinity, became more abundant. He almost trod upon a sleeping water snake—he heard it strike as he jumped away; and he startled a deer, which fled in turn. Some prowling creature which he could not see sneezed almost at his elbow; and across the river a tiger's eyes burned redly at the drinking level.

But the Fox kept the stream in hearing, and clutched his pistol the more tightly. Hour on hour he trudged the trail, more wearily as time progressed. At last, in exhaustion, he paused in a gorge through which the river ran. Upon an elevated ledge he lay down to steal a moment's rest. He had no chance to fight off sleep. It assailed him the moment he stretched out. . . .

But sleep and fate were this night brothers. When Tokala

awoke, it was to glimpse two canoes forging down the river. And in the foremost, alive and in the flesh, sat—Kioga!

In his haste to greet the Snow Hawk, Tokala almost slipped from the ledge with excitement. But eager hands hauled him safely into the canoe, and anxious ears heard his swift account.

"Two hours yet to sunrise," said the Snow Hawk when he had done. "The Long Knives will be guarding only against the escape of those inside the fort. If we be quick, we'll pierce their line in safety."

His words proved true. Tokala had slept but a little while, and as the two canoes raced toward where but recently he had sat amid the enemy, the camp was just awakening to find that their youthful guest had disappeared. Indeed, hardly had Crooked Nose announced the fact, when Kioga's longboats shot into their view. The surprise was complete. The speeding craft were broadside on before the enemy seized their weapons and leveled them at the paddling warriors.

Then uprose furious yells of quick dismay. For Tokala had worked cunningly. Not a gun discharged its bullet. Loosing forth their arrows, the Long Knives saw them darting every way but the right way; for nothing is more erratic than an unfeathered shaft—and the Fox had stripped them all of vanes.

Infuriated, one of the Indians raced along the bank, thinking to dislodge a great stone upon the passing canoes.

Tokala, holding the heavy pistol in both hands, steadied the muzzle on a gunwale, leveled and fired. The ball flew wide, but checked the Indians' enthusiasm nonetheless. In another instant the danger zone was well behind.

When the savages delivered their final attack against Fort Talking Raven, it was with the one weapon against which the fort would be helpless. At a little past midnight the first arrows, tipped with flaming pitch, arched crackling into the fort. Such as could be immediately reached by the besieged were instantly stamped out. But there were others which pierced the tower, well dried by the previous fire, and swiftly set it to blazing.

With axes Dan and a number of others attacked the blaze, chopping away burning timbers in the tower. They checked the fire finally with buckets of earth, taken in this hour of extremity from atop the new graves at the east wall. But in the overhanging pall of smoke the Indian attack came with terrifying suddenness. From the north rampart, via the great fallen tree, and up over the south walls, Shingas poured his strength of men in two fierce waves of stout, well-fed warriors, each bearing a torch in one hand and a tomahawk in the other.

The half-starved men within the walls met them hand to hand. Already the women and children had been herded into the redoubt formed by the living quarters at the north wall. From every corner the falconets spoke loudly, scattering death among the invaders. On the south wall Dan and ten warriors coped as best they could with the storming party, driving their lances home before many of the Indians could grasp the parapet in the upward climb.

But soon the falconets were silent for lack of ball. Still the enemy poured into the fort. Beside himself with battle fury, Flashpan went berserk. Uttering a blood-curdling whoop, he vanished in the furnace room and reappeared bent under the weight of several deer-skin bags.

During a momentary lull Munro could hear him shouting down upon the enemy, as from the sacks he drew forth nuggets of gold by the double-handfuls and shoved them back into the falconets in lieu of other shot. He worked swiftly, with a mad glare in his eyes and a wild twist to his moustaches.

"Gold ye wanted, was it?" he shrilled out above the enemy warriors' heads to where Mad Crow the renegade could be seen urging on his red-skinned warriors. "Then gold y'll git!" cried Flashpan.

Aiming his guns, he waited until the Indians drew closer. Then with a crash he loosed the first barrel, mowing down the attackers with richer slugs than ever came from cannon's mouth before. Now the second muzzle spewed forth its deadly treasure. Crash after crash, yell after frenzied yell from Flashpan, bespoke the swift exhaustion of the little miner's gleaming hoard. When all was gone save a small quantity, he threw the empty bags upon their heads, then rolled forward the falconets themselves, and hurled his seaman's cap, his empty pistol, and whatever else came to hand, down full upon the enemy heads.

A moment later, wrapped in wisps of smoke like the very genius of battle, the miner, crouching gnomelike, vanished actively down the stair and ran toward the redoubt, where presently all the defenders assembled and knelt to fire, backs to wall.

Here and there among the gallant little company a figure toppled forward and lay still. Hansen was of these, grievously wounded through the chest by a Long Knife arrow. Kias, twice wounded by bullets from guns which Flashpan had fashioned, fought on. Munro loaded and fired continually, though suffering from an immense swelling over one eye raised by a flying missile.

One by one the others followed Flashpan, slowly backing, in this final retreat, toward the last stronghold—the living quarters, whose slitted loopholed walls formed the fort's redoubt. Sixty Long Knives held the fort at last—all save that redoubt bristling with the muzzles of Munro's guns.

Three times the invaders charged those staring slits and loopholes, thrice withering before the blast that scorched them from within. But when for the last time the Long Knives came forward, the guns were all but still. Ammunition almost exhausted, their poor strength strained to the final limits of human endurance, the emaciated defenders but waited for the end, determined to save their last bullets for each other.

Pale but calm, Beth and Heladi sat side by side, speechless amid the uproar. Equally calm, but grim with the expectation of death, Munro and Dan knelt at their posts, grimy with sweat and powder-smoke. The occasional twang of a bow sounded within the redoubt, but the arrows were almost all gone. Within the redoubt children clutched at their mothers' skirts; an occasional bullet found its way in at the loopholes and struck viciously into the stone wall at their backs.

Suffocating smoke from the smudges lighted by the enemy began to penetrate the redoubt, adding tenfold to the miseries of the occupants. Amid the eddying whorls, a savage painted visage appeared suddenly at one loophole, and reaching in, pointed a pistol at Dan's head.

Snatching up a musket from the ground beside her, Beth thrust its muzzle against the paint-streaked temple and pulled the trigger. She saw the painted face disappear, and herself leaned against the wall, suddenly sick and faint. Recovering, she returned to continue loading the muskets until Munro and the men still on their feet subjected the enemy to a final murderous crossfire.

It was, however, but a futile gallant gesture by that indomitable little band with their backs to the wall. As the attack continued unabated, despair invaded the redoubt. Alone, the white men and their Indian friends could have fought to the bitter end without flinching. But realization of the fate awaiting their women and children embittered these final moments. Complete dejection had at last overwhelmed the wonderful resistance which had withstood all assaults but those of hunger and thirst.

Grim and white-faced, the besieged charged their weapons for the last time. While some guarded the loopholes, with heavy hearts their companions turned toward those who could not be permitted to fall into the cruel hands of the Indians for torture.

Knowing that death by pistol-shot was a mercy compared to capture by the Long Knives, the aged and the women and their few children quietly bade one another farewell and stood forward. With a last murmur to Beth, Heladi came over to Dan. Without a word she went into his arms, gave him her lips, then drawing swiftly back, stood erect and ready. As he grasped his pistol, beads of sweat mingled and rolled down Dan's blackened brow, streaking it white. The weapon in his hand shook and fell as if his arm were paralyzed.

"Quick, Dan!" Heladi urged.

"God forgive me—I can't do it!" cried Dan, his voice choking.

Beth stood suddenly forth, cool as ice.

"Let me," she said quietly. Yielding up the pistol, Dan turned aside. There was a moment's pause. He wondered dully if Beth could bring herself to perform the heroic mercy for Heladi, at which he had weakened. But he reckoned without her pioneer ancestry. He heard a click and the puff of priming powder close behind him—and simultaneously a cry from some near place without the walls; as deep and sinister a yell as ever broke from human throat.

Dan's blood ran cold. For all his manhood, Munro himself felt a little shiver run up and down his spine. Kias leaped as if snake-bitten, and twenty warriors with him.

Wheeling, Dan turned toward Heladi, expecting to find her crumpled. He saw instead a strange glad light in her eyes, while Beth stood staring at the pistol which had missed fire.

Again came that singular yell, closer now, every syllable clear and distinct. Amid all the uproar Munro could make nothing of the excitement among his Indians. But the meaning of the cry had affected the Long Knives as well. Checked in full rush, a babel of tongues arose, questioning, answering, denying—but what, no white man could have told.

Then, of a sudden, clear and shrill above the din of battle, came a lesser piercing cry. A small active figure appeared above the wall, where the fallen tree had overtopped its height. Two rifles instantly swung upon it. But Flashpan shouted:

"The cowards have sent a boy to do their dirty work—don't fire!" Then menacingly to the figure on the wall, obscured by smoke and semidarkness: "Who be ye? Quick!—afore I drop ye!"

"Tokala!" came the treble answer, and then in shrill notes of boyish triumph: "Kioga the Snow Hawk comes, with Wehoka and twenty warriors!"

"Hooray!" howled Flashpan, then suddenly realizing Tokala's peril; "Git off the wall! Jump—I'll catch ye!"

Obeying, Tokala fell through space, his impact carrying both to the ground, but without injury. Together they were pulled by eager hands into the redoubt.

Quick commands brought order out of chaos. Munro led his little band from the fortified redoubt, through the chain of rooms, to where they commanded a view of the northern wall.

As they watched, a face appeared above the log headcover. At sight of it Heladi caught a sudden breath. Beth's heart stopped as if she looked upon a ghost. Munro and La Salle stood rooted and speechless, doubting the evidence of their own eyes.

But on glimpsing that familiar and unmistakable face, Kias the Shoni gave the single welcoming call "Kioga! *K'gonami!*—*Kioga!*"

The words were like some magic formula poured into the arteries of the Indians of the fort. Back to the wall they had stood—defeated, all but defenseless. But Kias's answer to the battle-yell, which had so often led them on to victory, ran like an electric shock through all their frames.

They flung wide the heavy doors and hurled themselves upon the startled Long Knives. From above, one by one and two by two, Kioga's warriors were coming into the fort. From twenty feet above the wall, amid the branches of the fallen tree crown, Kioga was seen to drop, alighting upon a ledge like a bundle of loose-coiled springs, to bound along it toward the south wall where the fighting now raged hottest.

In among the combatants he darted, dealing those lightning blows whose every fall laid low a warrior. Two savages sprang upon him, and were themselves hurled senseless to the base of the parapet. Aim and fire before, it was cut and thrust now. Roused by the advent of assistance Dan and his men fought with new fury, plying their clubbed pistols and reversed rifles with terrible effect, driving the Long Knives back into the fires they themselves had kindled.

In less time than it takes to tell of it the wall was cleared.

Just below the wall the gates sagged to the assaults from outside where a group of Half-mouth's Indians, unaware of what was transpiring within, sought to batter down the barrier. Presently the doors gave way before the ram. Snatching up a military flail, Kioga dropped to the gates below, carrying down a Long Knife in his spring.

With tremendous swings of the deadly loose-coupled weapon he drove back the invaders almost single-handed, while several warriors tried to shut the ponderous barrier. But one of the huge iron hinges had parted and their efforts proved of no avail. Waving them aside, Kioga set back and, shoulder against the gate, locked loins and thighs, and turned on the mighty generators of his strength.

The massive gate lifted, creaking. Exerting every ounce of his power, the Snow Hawk crashed it home, and Munro jammed a log against it. The fort was closed against the enemy outside.

Within, the battle raged with doubled fury, the Long Knives determined to sell their lives dearly, the defenders striving that not one man should leave alive.

Like wolves and leopards in a common pit, the entire court was filled with fighting warriors, red and white. No quarter asked, no quarter given; knife to club, tomahawk to spear.

Here stands a Long Knife, striving to wrest a club from his foe. Then—stone meets skull, and the victor seeks another foe. There struggle two warriors, locked like twining, twisting serpents, each with a broken knife, carving his opponent's back to ribbons. Upon the wall two combatants at throat-grips wrestle. One falls to knees and drags his foeman down; both topple to the court and lie inert and motionless, still locked....

A little rain begins to fall. No one notices in the heat of battle, smoke, and blazing logs. From above a voice calls out. As one man the defenders leap from the court and man the walls. Forty bows strain at full tension; forty gut-strings twang with a single aeolian chord. The barbs slash down and pierce and kill. It is the end. The fort is held. In the court nothing moves, nothing twitches. All is death below the swirls of heavy smoke.

A door opens in the arms room. A girl comes forth—Heladi, savage woman, inured to sights of blood and sudden death. One look, and she turns back, to faint into Beth La Salle's open arms.

On the walls men speak in bated tones. Rain falls with a mounting roar. Thirsty men drink from little pools and slosh water on their heated brows. All look away from that central court.

Suddenly a small figure, wandering in search of a long-tailed monkey, darts out among the dead. Shrinking from one to another, like one entranced by goblin horrors, he stands quite still at last amid the dead.

Thus Kioga found Tokala as he returned from a last glance over the sound wall to see the enemy in full retreat. Placer the monkey had sprung from nowhere to Tokala's shoulder, gibbering there like the very soul of fear. Snatching both into his arms, the Snow Hawk bore them from the reeking court into the arms room.

He spoke no word as yet to Beth, but hurried out again and, mounting the north wall, paused to watch a savage bit of drama being enacted on the tree which spanned the river.

The battle was not quite over. Seeking only escape, out upon the great bole Shingas stumbled. With a deep whoop of triumph, Kias the Shoni closed upon the shaman from behind. Then above the river the full ferocity of primitive men was given grim play.

They were at each other's throats, Shingas armed with a knife, Kias bucklered only by his vow to avenge his fellow clansman, victim of Half-mouth's gift of poisoned meat. The shaman, turning, brought his knife upward in a curving stroke aimed at Kias's vitals, but Kias's fingers linked about his wrist, turning the blow and twisting until Half-mouth dropped the knife flashing into the river below. For an instant the shaman fought with teeth and nails, seeking to maim or gouge.

With deadly purpose Kias waited his chance, and struck suddenly with his clenched hand, knocking breath from the witch doctor's body, and flinging him prone across a limb. Reaching swiftly for the shaman's braids, he worked them into a knot, reinforced with a strip of rawhide. With the remainder of the rawhide thong he tied Half-mouth's hands behind his back.

In an instant the grim work was done, and Shingas hung swinging from a limb by his hair, only space and the river far below him. From the fort the occupants could see his eyes roll upward as a dark shadow winged slowly by, and a great raven paused; then alighted on a branch that sagged under its weight.... Then came others. Slowly the ring of black drew near. In a moment more the hanging figure was blotted from view by black wings and feathers.

The Indians in the fort watched steadily; the whites turned aside, revolted. But they were spared any outcry from Shingas. Fear did swiftly what the carrion-birds would have prolonged.... Shingas had died of utter terror. Darkness shut out the sight. The night passed; in the morning only a few strings of hair still blew in the breeze. Ravens, the Indians say, do not devour hair.

Inside the arms room Beth La Salle, with swiftly beating heart, saw the door swing wide to admit one for whom she had crossed a continent and two seas. Panic seized her when she glimpsed Kioga's strange arresting eyes, the strong lines of his features softened as never before. Rigid and trembling, she felt strong arms encompass her swiftly.

But presently her civilized woman's restraint returned. Sensing this, Kioga held her less fiercely.

"Why do you draw back?" he asked her softly. "Did you come all this way to Nato'wa to do that?"

Some of her deserting wits returned.

"How can you be so sure of that?" she asked.

For answer he removed a little scroll of birch-bark from his belt-pouch and held it where she might read the despairing note she had left in the mountain cave, in the belief that he was dead. This time she did not draw back....

Deep dark eyes upon Kioga, Heladi stood with Dan watching the reunion of the white girl and the Snow Hawk, with an emotion not even the uneasy La Salle could fathom. He knew Heladi had given him her love, believing Kioga dead. Would the Snow Hawk's revival raise that old barrier between them?

As Kioga and Beth came into the court, Dan La Salle withdrew to one side. Beth drew back a little also that Kioga and Heladi might meet alone. And she too knew a twinge of fear, for Heladi seemed more beautiful now than ever.

But Kioga and Heladi remained apart, still looking upon each other in silence, the man with simple pleasure, the girl with thoughts that will ever be a mystery. When they spoke it was in softest Wacipi—Heladi's dialect—that no one in the fort could hear. But presently the Indian girl's eyes lowered. Quietly she moved away and came to stand beside Dan. Removing an ornament from about her neck, Heladi placed it round Dan La Salle's. Thus, by the custom of her tribe, she made known her pledge to him.

Repulsed, the Long Knives licked their wounds in the forests surrounding Fort Talking Raven. Though discouraged and decimated by their final defeat, in the return of the Snow Hawk they had perhaps the one spur that could have induced them again to attempt the storming of the walls. For of all men Kioga, former warrior-chieftain of the Seven Shoni Tribes, was one who could swiftest wreck their plans and organize opposition to the Long Knife rebellion.

Already the Indians had retaken possession of their work opposite the north wall, which Kioga and his warriors had found abandoned on their arrival at the bridge. Commanding this with a falconet, ready to blast down whosoever set foot upon it, the Long Knives also thronged the forest on the island itself; while up and down the riverways word had passed that the Snow Hawk was still alive, bringing consternation or wild rejoicing wherever the news became known.

In Fort Talking Raven, affairs had improved. One of Kioga's warriors had brought in a load of dried meat from the canoe supply. Rain had replenished their water store. Others of the newcomers shared their personal belt supplies of acorn meal with the hungry occupants of the fort. And as if sent from heaven itself, the night brought a flock of migrating geese to the walls. Twenty were shot down, cooked, and eaten. And that night, by the firelight, amid stillness broken only by a far wolf's howl, Kioga told his listeners all that had befallen him since the time he had left civilization to return to Nato'wa.

Later, in council, it was determined to quit the fort. From the warriors he had encountered on the river Kioga had learned that a friendly welcome would await the Indians at the upper river villages. Without an adequate water supply and with food scarce and hard to bring into the fort, it seemed wiser for the whites to strike seaward to the well-provisioned *Narwhal*, before it had time to act upon Munro's earlier instructions to sail away.

Under cover of dark and fog, in the silence of the night, the plan was executed. Using ropes and a block from the ship, one after another of the occupants were lowered to the riverbank. Kioga's warriors brought up their sturdy dugouts. And an hour before dawn the enemy besieged an empty fort.

XXXIV

Having made their farewells within the fort, in utter silence Kioga embarked his own party in the waiting dugouts and gave the signal to push off. The Indians paddled off northward toward the distant friendly villages. The whites, accompanied by Kioga and his red-skinned friends, turned southward.

The paddles dipped as one; the shore faded behind; the mists enwrapped them.

In silent procession, roped together to forestall separation, the three craft moved slowly downstream with their human freight. Thus they passed the junctions of streams, and Hopeka village itself, well covered by the friendly vapors. Then suddenly, intensified by the mists, a questioning call rang out, close by.

Instantly the paddlers ceased laboring. Watching from amidships in the central canoe, Beth observed all the warriors' eyes fixed upon a single point. Seated at the bow, eyes riveted upon the water close below, crouched the Snow Hawk. On his signaling hand the eyes of all were fastened. What he saw to be guided by on that ever-changing surface only Kioga knew. Among the myriad ripples only his eye could have detected the little whirls of recent paddles, at sight of which he signaled for a sharp left turn. The turn was made. A moment later the voices of Indians, close behind them on their quarter, could be distinctly heard.

Their present movements were a blind groping in a world of nacreous half-tones. The mists hung down like muslin veils, visibly rising a few feet, then lowering inexplicably. Sometimes they had a glimpse of open space for fifty feet, through wisps of smoky cloud hanging in tenuous passages, then merging into obscurity again.

Skirting close to shore, they heard a snow-leopard grate harshly. Dog and monkey showed teeth and fangs; but as if comprehending the need for silence, they made no sound. An instant later they glided upon a cowering fawn, so silently that it started only after they had passed. The analogy was clear: Both the deer and they were now among the hunted. . . .

Not until this moment had Beth realized how completely the outcome of their daring break from the fort hung upon Kioga's instantaneous decisions. Yet with the enemy longboats fairly surrounding them, she experienced not the slightest fear, but only a fierce exhilaration. A wave of pride and gladness surged over her as he returned, saying; "We're almost through them now."

He spoke too soon. Others had played the silent waiting game. Across their quarter, distant some ten yards, two longboats rushed upon them under full way. It was close and fight this time, accomplished by the war-dugouts with astonishing quickness. The canoe bearing the white party dropped back, facing the foe to present a narrow mark.

The remaining two darted forward. The four combatant craft came together with a rush. Sheer weight told. The dugouts, hard-driven, crashed into the lighter birch-barks, glanced off and drove onward. And as they passed, with their hooklike river spears, Kioga's men slashed the bottoms of the enemy, which filled rapidly.

Another moment found them well past the point of danger. Behind them the canoe-pack was in full cry now. But the mists still hid one foe from the other. The gauntlet was run.

Bristling with random shafts and river-men's slim spears, the dugouts made swift headway toward their destination. The fleeing band camped that night on shore having left their canoes behind on their journey to the coast. . . .

By the light of the cooking-fires Munro made his last entries in his diary, confiding it and his store of sketches and drawings to a runner, who went ahead of the main party with a note informing the *Narwhal* of their coming.

(*I pause perforce at this point in my narrative, faced by a difficult dilemma. Until now I have drawn upon the record kept by James Munro—a record whose latter passages are writ in ink made from gunpowder mixed with water. But Munro made his final entries before dispatching the diary to the* Narwhal. *The diary, consequently, tells nothing of what transpired thereafter. Happily, I possess two other sources enabling me to continue—the written confession of one of the renegades; and an astonishing motion-picture film which, taken by the aid of the new infrared photography, is truly extraordinary.*

It will be remembered that the Narwhal *actually returned to the ken of civilized men. Her sails were torn as by grapeshot; the arrows and spears of a strange race protruded from her sides. She bore a peculiar equipment of primitive guns, and a priceless treasure of aboriginal relics and artifacts. And there were none but dead men aboard her.*

Yet through the medium of pencil and paper, in obedience to the scourging of conscience and the fear of death, one of those dead has spoken. What immediately follows is taken from his written confession.—Author.)

Reduced to plain essentials from the poorly written, illiterate, and badly sequenced notes of an ignorant seaman, I adduce the following facts, found under the icy hand of one who was dead aboard the *Narwhal* for many months before the winds and currents cast her out of unknown seas with her strange and absorbing riddle.

Under sail and engine power the *Narwhal* made good her escape to the open sea, following the chart Munro had drawn on his course inland. Branner, shot dead at the wheel, was carried below and laid in the main cabin. Mad Crow also died of gunshot wounds, sustained in the cabin when a shot came through the open porthole. Only Peters, the writer of the confession—one of those succored from the ice by the *Narwhal*—and the wounded Mitchell, Slemp's right-hand man, remained alive to pilot the ship.

After their ordeal of passage through the reefs, neither had the strength to carry the dead on deck for burial overside. Fortunately, it turned freezing cold. The dead were speedily refrigerated.

The engine soon failed. The *Narwhal* proceeded under a few square yards of sail—the gut-sail of Kamotok's manufacture. Mitchell, suffering from his wound, grew steadily worse and threatened to do Peters violence. One day, as the sick man stood on deck, he suddenly drew a pistol. Peters fired first, and at a roll of the ship Mitchell pitched over into the sea to sink and vanish.

With food in plenty, Peters could not eat. His teeth had been shot away in one of the raids on the fort. Hoarfrost sealed up the door leading to where water was kept. Peters's diminished strength was unequal to bettering the door down.

Perceiving his end near at hand, belatedly he sought to make peace with his Creator by writing a full confession, ending with the following entry:

December 26, 19—

Today ... *(indecipherable)* ... last day. All dead ... but me. Last day. God forgive ... *(remainder indecipherable)*

So ends that illiterate note found under the cold hand of the last man to give up his ghost on the death-ship *Narwhal*. With food and drink on board, and every possibility of surviving for several years, the icy finger of the frigid North found a way into the vessel and robbed all on board of life; then as if in grim jest preserved one man in the semblance of life and cast the ship before the eyes of living men.

Thus from the hand of an actor in the drama comes knowledge of what befell the *Narwhal* after she sailed from Nato'wa on her last voyage which was destined to end in fire, explosion, and shipwreck in northern waters. Thus ends the saga of the *Narwhal*—a science-ship, discovery-ship, warship, and at last, funeral-ship.

But of the Kioga the Snow Hawk, of James Munro, Beth, Dan, and all the others of that gallant little company which held a wilderness at bay, there remains a little more to be told.

Delivered to me this day was a small round tin containing a long strip of newly developed motion-picture film—the contents of the little camera found among other treasures on board the returned *Narwhal*. The expert who developed it apologized for the imperfection of the work—as if he could be held to blame for the conditions under which it was exposed four thousand miles away in a savage wilderness, known only to a little handful of civilized men.

How that camera came to be actuated—who trained it upon the scenes it so faithfully recorded upon sensitized film—and why—may never be known. Perhaps in a spirit of derision, by one of the renegades making away with the ship. Perhaps—but no matter.

I took the little tin into a darkroom in the private museum which bears James Munro's name. I ran it into a projection machine, flipped a switch, and awaited the result with tense excitement.

The square of linen became suddenly illumined. Into its blank whiteness drama stalked with a suddenness that took my breath away. I was no longer in a small museum in the heart of the largest city in the world. I was thousands of moles away on a ship near the shore of the last, most savage wilderness left unexplored on this earth—Nato'wa.

The whir of the projection machine might have been the wind vibrating through the crags on the sea-cliffs. What I saw the camera had seen, and those renegades on the ship as well. I even imagined the sounds were reproduced, so startlingly realistic was my illusion of being at the scene. . . .

I heard the creak of blocks and the roar of waters inshore. Across my vision slipped a vertical face of wet rock, against which a great swell broke, tossing up whitest foam. The wall ended. Into view came a party of whites and Indians who for a moment stood gazing in amazement. Among them could be recognized not only Dr. Munro and Dan, Beth and Heladi, and Kioga, but also Barry Edwards, the mate Edson, and Kamotok. Apparently the latter group had discovered their guide was an enemy, had made way with him, and had somehow found and joined forces with the others.

Bows were bent. Arrows whisked across the waters toward the ship, striking sharply and vibrating where they pierced wood or sail. Several spears hurtled through the air and struck here and there on the ship.

Suddenly the *Narwhal* quivered, as from the bow the saker spoke crisply. Behind the party on the shore a ball struck sparks from a great rock. But there was no further firing of that forward gun. A copper knife, hard-thrown, struck the ship's side before she sheered away from shore—taking the outgoing channel leading to the open sea.

Now several savages, trundling a demi-cannon, appeared along the shore. Another followed with a leather bag, and behind him came a moustached figure—unmistakably Flashpan. The gun was turned and aimed. Flashpan rammed home a powder charge taken from the leather bag, rolled in a heavy ball, and leaped to the breech.

Chips flew from a great boulder behind Flashpan's head as a bullet from the ship struck it. In nowise troubled by his peril, Flashpan inspected flint and lock, made ready to fire, drew back, and jerked the cord. The crude cannon leaped. A gigantic mushroom of smoke burst from its muzzle. Its ball, intended to hull the *Narwhal* amidships, flew high, lodging in the mainmast with an impact that rocked the craft from truck to keelson. But the shore continued to recede, while Flashpan labored at his gun. Another burst flashed out from the demi-cannon. A shower of granite stones slashed through sails and rigging like grape-shot. By now the *Narwhal* had almost run past the danger zone. But there were still keen eyes to reckon with.

From a pointed crag a pair of eyes squinted down a

smooth-bore barrel and put a bullet into the after cabin an inch from where Branner stood crouching at the wheel. Instantly the slim shadow that was Tokala passed the marksman another loaded gun. Again the crack of the weapon. This time the helmsman went down, limp as a thong of leather.

Slemp, dragging himself toward the shelter of a cabin, rose to his knees. Again another of Flashpan's smooth-bores flamed, but the bullet went two inches wild. All the loaded pieces had now been fired. Flashpan danced about, beside himself with impotent fury.

Behind him knelt Dan La Salle, reloading hastily. Slightly to his right stood Beth, gazing out upon the vanishing *Narwhal* with an indescribable expression. Beside her, Heladi watched Dan load the guns. Close behind them Munro saw his *Narwhal* making an escape, with what emotions I can only guess.

All of this, you will realize, was as I glimpsed it, thrown upon a screen at the Munro Museum, in the heart of New York City. Yet so swift and realistic was the action that I seemed to hear the echo of the guns resounding among the cliffs where a myriad pinions beat the air—ivory-gulls frightened aloft by the heavy detonations.

Then suddenly, as if from nowhere, a tall, wonderfully proportioned figure stood forth in the garb of a Shoni Indian. With a few words to Flashpan he fitted an arrow to his bow, drew back the string, and aimed as if to shoot about the ship. But his intention was plain when the arrow leaped from the cord, spinning rapidly as it came.

I saw the shaft in flight, followed its beautiful parabola in full soaring arc.

Slemp, struggling to drag himself within the cabin, had been for that instant within the focus of the lens. He, too, must have seen the arrow coming, by the expression of fear on his features. But if he saw it, he was powerless to evade it. Its impetus drove it deep, piercing him and emerging from his other side.

Ashore there must have been a hush following that wonderful shot. Kioga had not changed stance from the moment of loosing, but poised watched his arrow's arc, the personification of the hunter-warrior depicted on some ancient frieze. And then—

Then came a growing obscurity. A fog-bank was closing down upon the *Narwhal*, aiding in her escape; and finally blankness—utter-blankness.

I was back magically from an unknown land, standing in a house in the heart of a great city, yet trembling in every fiber at what I had seen. The film was ended, and with it—for the present—my story of that land of mists and mystery, Nato'wa.

Munro's gallant band failed to hold that little outpost of civilization, Fort Talking Raven. But it was a glorious failure, in the best tradition of their race.

James Munro, scientist, who left behind the world and its prizes to probe the rumor of an unknown land and race; his loyal little indomitable band, tempered in fire and steeled by common adversity—these few souls are a symbol, as were the Pilgrims, of destiny. Their home is the last unconquered land in this modern world. Their neighbors are the savage vagabond hordes of the warlike Shoni. The roars of wild beasts disturb their slumbers. Their waking hours are filled with alarms.

But they have pioneered the way, hewn out the early routes to this unknown land. Their quiet tread foretells the tramp of many feet. In this twentieth-century world of crowded boundaries, the march of empire is unending. Other men will strive to reach Nato'wa—men who lust for adventure, free air to breathe, gold; good men who follow the lure of distant drums, and men of fiercer temper who ever seek new frontiers whereon to fatten by their lawlessness.

But will aid to Kioga and his little handful of friends come in time? Has all the heroism of these modern pioneers been in vain? Shall there be no men of iron will and brazen courage to succor them before it is too late?

I do not know, nor they, nor any mortal man. The answer is written in the tight-wrapped scroll of things to come.

DAW BOOKS

Lin Carter's bestselling series!

- [ ] **UNDER THE GREEN STAR.** A marvel adventure in the grand tradition of Burroughs and Merritt. Book I.
(#UY1185—$1.25)

- [ ] **WHEN THE GREEN STAR CALLS.** Beyond Mars shines the beacon of exotic adventure. Book II. (#UY1267—$1.25)

- [ ] **BY THE LIGHT OF THE GREEN STAR.** Lost amid the giant trees, nothing daunted his search for his princess and her crown. Book III. (#UY1268—$1.25)

- [ ] **AS THE GREEN STAR RISES.** Adrift on the uncharted sea of a nameless world, hope still burned bright. Book IV.
(#UY1156—$1.25)

- [ ] **IN THE GREEN STAR'S GLOW.** The grand climax of an adventure amid monsters and marvels of a far-off world. Book V. (#UY1216—$1.25)

DAW BOOKS are represented by the publishers of Signet and Mentor Books, THE NEW AMERICAN LIBRARY, INC.

THE NEW AMERICAN LIBRARY, INC.,
P.O. Box 999, Bergenfield, New Jersey 07621

Please send me the DAW BOOKS I have checked above. I am enclosing $_____(check or money order—no currency or C.O.D.'s). Please include the list price plus 35¢ a copy to cover mailing costs.

Name_____

Address_____

City_____State_____Zip Code_____

Please allow at least 4 weeks for delivery